# WHEN YOU WEAR ´

## (Book 4 of 7 in the No

Author: Jonatha

First published Dec 2017

Publisher: JJ Cox Publishing Limited

All intellectual rights belong to the author.

2

## The Nostrils Series

# Prologue

In January 1995, a twenty-two-year-old Libyan born man, by the name of Hassan Achachi, was bludgeoned to death in a McDonalds in Shepherds Bush, by a group of white youths, after he'd accidentally knocked into one of them, at a nearby ice skating rink. The postmortem examination recorded that the victim's skull had been smashed into seventeen pieces.

Hassan's best friend, Tareq, who had been with Hassan that evening, had managed to get away unhurt. He escaped through an emergency exit, when he saw the gang enter the restaurant and start to issue a series of threats, which included the words, 'Paki cunts'. Hassan had been bolder. He had bravely, but as it transpired, tragically, held his ground, and even according to eyewitnesses, told them to 'fuck off'.

It is a moot point that the victims were of North African descent and not Pakistani.

The gang consisted of six local teenagers, the youngest was fourteen and the oldest sixteen. I always suspected that, because of their youth, Hassan underestimated the danger he was in. He was, after all, a fit and strong adult, who boxed successfully on the amateur circuit. Hassan probably thought he could hold his own but was wrong.

One of the gangs circled behind him and, before he knew what was happening, Hassan had been struck on the head with a blunt, heavy instrument. He fell to his knees, semi-conscious, and was hit at least a dozen more times. He crawled under the protection of a nearby table and, instinctively, curled into the fetal position, but died a few moments later and, well before, medical aid arrived.

The weapon was later identified as two snooker balls wrapped up in a sock. The gang had taken the idea from the seventy's cult film Scum, with which, according to sources, the young lads were absolutely obsessed.

The police had botched the murder investigation and allegations flew that the reason the case hadn't been taken seriously was because the victim was Libyan.

That the investigation was sub-standard was entirely accurate, but this was nothing to do with the race of the victim. It was just an incompetent piece of police work. In 1994 the Job was desperately short of decent Detective Inspectors because, a few years earlier, the Metropolitan Police had stopped paying overtime to that rank. Consequently, experienced Detective Sergeants weren't taking promotion.

The shortage had to be filled, so the Job offered the role of Detective Inspectors to uniform officers who had no investigative experience or qualifications. A few of them signed up because the job of a DI was quite glamorous.

One of the uniform Inspectors to come across to the C.I.D. was Darryl Overton, who led the Hassan Achachi murder investigation. In fact, it was his first case. To make matters even worse, he'd spent the last two years running the property store at Belgravia Police Station, so he didn't even have any recent policing experience.

Talk about being thrown in at the deep end. Darryl had to deal with a Cat 'A' murder, with multiple scenes and half a dozen suspects, without a day's preparation. As a result, the investigation was a disaster from the start and absolutely nothing was done properly.

Two years later, an Irish High Court judge, led a public enquiry into the whole affair. The findings of the enquiry were that the investigative failings were a result of racism and corruption, although the latter allegation was never clearly made out. The judge decreed all white Metropolitan Police officers were 'unconsciously racist'. A phrase that became synonymous with policing in that era. The reputation of the Metropolitan Police was severely damaged and morale amongst all ranks hit rock bottom.

Those of us that knew we weren't racist, were really insulted to be labelled as such; even most of our black colleagues thought the findings were simply wrong. With that said, a few of the latter, not many, but enough, seized the circumstances and rode their careers forward great distances on a wave of racial indignation.

I thought it was very interesting, how certain key facts about the murder never came out because, I suspected, they didn't fit in with the indisputable theory that it was a racist murder. For example, the gang that killed poor Hassan had, in the previous three months, attacked several other victims, all of them white. One victim, who was only twelve, had been hit so hard that he was in a coma for a week; the others were less seriously injured, with missing teeth, smashed jaws, and broken limbs.

The gang members were out of control and if a white kid had bumped into them on the ice rink and then gone to McDonalds, he would have been murdered, in just the same way that Hassan Achachi had been. But no one was ever allowed to say that in the distorted world that became the Metropolitan Police after the Achachi Enquiry.

There was one other matter that really hindered the investigation. Hassan's friend Tareq, said he had witnessed the murder and gave a statement that he didn't leave Hassan's side, until the police arrived, at which point, he left because he was, he said, scared he would be arrested because his leave to remain in the country had expired.

Several eyewitnesses, however, had seen Tareq running away much earlier and, more evidentially significant, there was no trace of Hassan's blood anywhere on his clothing, which would have been impossible if, as he claimed, he'd stayed with him, rendering first aid, until he saw flashing blue lights.

This lie caused the police investigation untold problems because, subsequently, Tareq was unable to pick out the suspects, during identity parades. The reason he couldn't pick them out, was because he wasn't there, but of course, if you believed that he was there, then the obvious reason he couldn't pick them out was because the police had the wrong suspects, which they didn't.

The whole affair played heavily on Tareq and, three years later, he was found hanging in his garage, having taken his own life. At the time, he was on bail for fraud, having allegedly stolen funds from the Hassan Achachi charity that had been set up to assist aspiring boxers from ethnic communities and, for which, he had been a trustee. I always felt great sympathy for Tareq and, personally, viewed him as another of the gang's victims.

By every account I heard, Hassan Achachi was a thoroughly decent, honest, and law-abiding young man, who had his whole life ahead of him.

As well as a capable boxer, Hassan was an aspiring poet and several of his works were published after his death. I hated poetry but Hassan Achachi's was good, and he might even have made it, one day, in that most difficult of careers. That Hassan had achieved so much in his short life, was even more amazing, when one considered, he'd been orphaned as a baby and had made his way on his own to the U.K. when he was in his early teens.

No, poor Hassan didn't deserve to die but nor did any of London's other eighty murder victims, that year.

This incident, however, was to have a profound and lasting impact upon British policing and to create an unforgiving and toxic atmosphere for the average white officer.

# Chapter 1

Wednesday 9<sup>th</sup> April 1997

We were the spare team that day and should have been catching up on case papers and correspondence. Then we had a meal booked at Skorpios, a fantastic Greek restaurant, in Phillip Lane N15.

We were having breakfast when the DI called and asked me to come to his office. I wolfed down my full English and dropped three quid on the table, as I put my coat on.

"Whatever he wants, tell him to go and have carnal knowledge, elsewhere." Colin suggested, unhelpfully.

"Let me make a note of that, is that C A R N A L?" I asked.

"Do you want me to come with you?" Bob asked, more helpfully.

"No, you're all right, mate. I'll call you if it's anything important."

"Don't forget to put your tie on." Dot reminded me.

I often wore my tie undone around my neck, particularly first thing in the morning, but the DI, a nice guy called Phil Flower, absolutely hated it, and always berated me, if he caught me so attired.

"Thanks, mum." I said, to Dot.

Fifteen minutes after I'd left my team in a café in Tottenham High Street, I exited the DI's office holding a copy of a search warrant to an address on the Plymouth Rock Estate.

The scenario was common enough. Yesterday, a suspect had been stopped driving his car, by late turn, in Brixton and when they searched the vehicle, the officers found a handgun under the front seat. Of course, the driver denied it was his. I mean, he would, wouldn't he? He'd be highly unlikely to say, 'Oh officer, if you're referring to a black 9mm beretta, that'll be mine'.

We had been asked by our Brixton colleagues to turn his home address over, to see if there were any other firearms, or indeed, any evidence linking him to the gun, like ammunition or a holster. The search warrant had been issued under the Firearms Act.

I wandered over to the B.I.U., the Borough Intelligence Unit, to ascertain whether there was anything known about the suspect and/or the address. When I'd first joined the Job, the B.I.U. was called the Collator, and an experienced PC, assisted by an elderly female civvy, performed the role. Now, the B.I.U. was led by a Sergeant, who had a team of, perhaps, eight officers and civvies to assist him; a few of whom were usually WPCs, who were on light duties, because they were pregnant. Others were officers who had returned from sick to non-operational roles.

I came away from the B.I.U. with a map showing the layout of the address, a list of the suspect's impressive previous convictions, considering he was only twenty-two, and the information that he lived in the flat with his mother.

I didn't realise it at the time, but by the time I left the B.I.U., I had made my first critical error that day, because I hadn't asked for any research to be undertaken on the suspect's mother. Had I done so, I would have learned that she had twice been deemed, under the provisions of the Mental Health Act, for conduct constituting a serious risk of harm to others.

As the suspect was already in custody, we didn't have to make an unannounced forced entry, which made life much easier because, for once, we didn't have to arrange the repair of the front door before we left. What's more, we weren't searching for drugs, so there were no concerns that the occupier would flush anything down the toilet, before letting us in.

A large black lady answered the door, wearing an old grey dressing gown; she was in her mid-forties and completely bald. She seemed fine and, I assumed, she was probably quite used to having officers search her home, whenever her son got arrested.

We were polite, respectful and on our best behaviour, after all, the suspect's mother hadn't done anything wrong. I felt a little sorry that she should have to suffer this indignity. I did, briefly, consider whether we should restrict the search to only the suspect's bedroom but that would have been pretty meaningless. The last place he was going to hide any contraband was in his own room.

The suspect's room was interesting because the wardrobes were full of expensive clothing and he even had a brand new flat-screen computer, something I'd never seen before. Next to the computer was a receipt from an electrical shop in Tottenham Court Road for the top of the range Packard Bell – it cost £1600, more money than I made in a month. The screen was only an inch thick! Clearly, whatever the suspect did, he made a good deal of money.

After an hour, we were nearly done and had found nothing. There was only the kitchen left to search and I sent Colin, who had spent most of the search chatting to the mother and keeping her sweet, back to the office, to get on with his day. That was my second mistake.

The three of us who were left, Dot, Bob, and I, looked through a few drawers and cupboards and then I opened the one under the sink. I saw a brown cardboard shoebox, and had to smile, because I kept a very similar one under my own sink at home. It contained everything I needed to clean my shoes, polish, dusters, dubbin, shade cleaner and an old toothbrush. I opened this one, expecting to find it used for the same purpose but what I saw made me utter the most unprofessional phrase, which I repeated several times.

"What is it?" Dot asked, who was standing to my left.

I stood up and put the box on the drainer, holding it only by the corners, to avoid leaving any prints. I should have been wearing gloves, but I'd taken them off, about ten minutes, previously, when I'd unconsciously decided that we weren't going to find anything.

"What's in it?" She asked.

"About three kilos of cocaine." I replied.

"We need to get the Photog, here, so I'll put it back, but take a look."

Dot reached across, tentatively lifted the lid and placed it to one side. Simultaneously, and in a kind of slow motion, we both leaned forward to take a closer look.

I heard footsteps behind me and assumed it was Bob coming to see what I'd found, but that was my third, and almost fatal, mistake. It wasn't Bob, it was the suspect's mum, and she was wielding a razor-sharp carving knife, which she was about to plunge into my back, with all the force she could muster.

Bob reacted, immediately. He dived across the kitchen, like David James and, instinctively, grabbed at the weapon, but all he could get hold of was the blade itself, which was only inches from my back. Of course, in doing so, the edge cut deeply into his palm, but he fought back every natural instinct and didn't let go.

They fell to the floor, both were screaming, Bob in agony, and the suspect's mother in distress. It took several minutes to get the mother under control and, all the time, she was trying to pull the knife out of Bob's hand, but he held on, tightly, until the struggle was over. As soon as he let go, the overwhelming pain caused Bob to pass and out and he didn't regain consciousness, until he was in the ambulance and the paramedics had filled him full of morphine.

In contrast, I didn't have so much as a scratch on me.

Bob Clark saved my life that day, and I owed him one.

# Chapter 2

Friday 3rd July 1998 – over a year later.

Tottenham Police Station, London

I sat at my desk, drinking an instant black coffee, from the least disgusting mug I could find, and contemplating the mountain of paperwork before me. There were buff-coloured registered dockets, orange unregistered dockets, case files, C.P.S. memos, printed emails, statement forms (otherwise known as MG11s) and an assortment of other correspondence, the latest of which was a letter from a woman in India, who alleged her husband had bigamously remarried in the UK and was now living on our ground. As evidence, she had included photographs from two weddings, one of which, I assumed, was hers and the other from the second unlawful marriage.

It was nine o'clock and the paperwork would have to wait because I was going home. I had been on duty since seven that morning and had just bailed my last prisoner. I was knackered but the overtime was always welcome.

I phoned Jackie, my wife, but her mobile was switched off and went straight to voicemail, which meant she was still at work. She was a nurse at St Margaret's, in Epping. As she was on a late, I hoped she'd be getting home at about the same time as me, which would be nice, as we could sit up chatting and drinking wine, one of my favourite pastimes, after a long day.

A pretty, female, uniformed officer wandered into the office.

"Can I help you?" I asked.

"Sorry, I'm a bit lost. Is this the C.J.U.?" She asked.

"No, this is the C.I.D. office, the C.J.U. is upstairs, immediately above this one."

I pointed, unnecessarily, upwards.

"Thanks." She replied and turned abruptly on her heel.

"Just arrived?" I asked.

She turned back, somewhat flustered by my unexpected question.

"Yesterday. I left training school last Friday, Sir. I err ..." She stammered.

"I am not a Sir; my name is Chris Pritchard and I'm a DS here. Welcome to Tottenham, you'll love it." I said, with the broadest smile I could muster, after fourteen hours on duty.

"Thanks, Sergeant." She replied.

As she walked off, it was hard not to recall my own first tentative steps in the Metropolitan Police. Back in 1983, I'd been a very young PC at Stoke Newington. Why the Job had wanted an eighteen-year-old boy, with absolutely no experience of life, was still quite beyond my explanation. They were a difficult, few years, but I got through them and now, fifteen years later, I was a pretty ordinary Detective Sergeant, who was halfway through his service, and working at one of London's busiest police stations.

I went to stand up when a letter on the adjacent desk caught my eye. It was addressed to me, but someone had put it on the wrong desk. I sighed, knowing that my curiosity would demand I open it. It was from the C.P.S. and related to a file I'd submitted seeking their authority to charge a local councilor with corruption in a public office and false accounting. The C.P.S. case worker wanted a few more actions undertaken, before they'd decide, and the letter set out exactly what was required, and by when. I thought they were being over cautious, there was already plenty of evidence, but I wasn't insensitive to the fact that one of the suspects was a high-profile member of the local Labour party, called Anna Abolla, so I understood their guarded approach.

I reached into my in-tray to retrieve my copy of the C.P.S. Advice File, but, instead, I pulled out an unfamiliar plain buff cardboard folder. Anticipating that I'd forgotten all about whatever it contained, I opened the folder to glance at the contents.

At first, I wasn't quite sure what I was looking at; then, but only for the slightest ticks of a clock, I thought it was some kind of joke. When I realised what was going on, I felt physically sick.

I was staring at an assortment of words, cut from various newspapers, and several old National Geographic style pictures of monkeys and other apes. These were resting on pages of plain A4 paper, on to which, various other words and photographs had been glued. I pulled one of these from the back and placed it away from the assorted mess. The different words across the top of the page read 'BLACK officers not WANTED. Go back to the JUNGLE', and underneath was a picture of a family of chimpanzees in a rain forest.

I instinctively glanced around to see whether anyone else was in the C.I.D. office, they weren't. I gathered the various pieces of paper, placed them back in the folder, and considered my options.

I knew my fingerprints were now all over the papers and I was tempted to dispose of the whole lot via the nearby shredder, but something told me to be smart, not instinctive. Then the thought hit me that there might be other incriminating evidence somewhere about my desk, so I conducted the most thorough of searches. I was glad that I did. I found a pair of scissors, I never knew I had, in my second drawer and several more cut out racist words had been carefully placed, right at the bottom of my third drawer. I concluded that, whoever was trying to fit me up, had made a careful and thorough attempt. I made a mental note to check my own car, just in case, whoever it was, had 'borrowed' my keys, while I'd been out and about on enquiries.

Should I formally report the incident? That seemed like a sensible thing to do but the Job was absolutely paralyzed by the issue of race, and I wasn't quite sure how they'd react. If I did report the matter, I could certainly see the focus of any subsequent enquiry being completely misplaced and I would, forever, be branded and remembered as, 'the Detective Sergeant with the racist letters'. In 1998 such a label would be career ending.

On the other hand, if I didn't say anything, I could subsequently be accused of trying to cover up racist behaviour, so, quite frankly, either way, I was in trouble.

I took a decision.

I put on a pair of exhibit gloves and with a duster, which I always kept, to polish my shoes, I painstakingly wiped down both sides of every single piece of paper and picture. I was very thorough because I wanted to make sure there wasn't a chance that anyone would be able to connect me forensically to the buff folder and its contents. It did, momentarily, cross my mind that I might also be eliminating the real suspect's prints, but upon more careful consideration, I realised that, whoever had gone to such lengths to incriminate me, wasn't going to be so stupid as to drop themselves in the mire.

Having completed the task, I placed the folder in an evidence bag that I then sealed, jotting down the seal number. Standing on a far desk, I removed a polystyrene ceiling tile and cellotaped the evidence bag against the back, before replacing the square. And all the time, I wore my plastic gloves.

With my work complete, I undertook another comprehensive sweep of my desk, just to make sure, I hadn't missed anything. Then I sat and wondered who, in god's name, would want to do this to me. I excluded my own team; Colin, Bob, and Dot, as we all got on so very well. In fact, I'd go further than that because this was, quite simply, the best team I'd ever worked on. We were all so very different but, somehow, the sum of the whole was greater than the sum of the parts. And there was a bond between us, an unspoken promise that we would support one another. We were a little family within a family, or a band of brothers, as the Bard of Avon, had so aptly described such camaraderie, half a millennium ago.

I'd been at Tottenham for the last three years and I'd had the odd run in with one or two people but nothing that would merit such an attack. I was, genuinely, flabbergasted. I tried to work out whether anyone would prosper from my downfall, but I couldn't think that anyone would. Nor had I misbehaved, in the, 'shagging someone else's wife', sense, since way back in the Stoke Newington days of the mid-eighties.

For many years I had led a very uneventful life. I didn't piss people off, tried hard to get on with everyone, and was neither flash nor brash. My wife was a nurse, so we had enough money, without being rich, and I drove an old VW Golf. We had a small house in Staples Road in Loughton, and a big mortgage in Halifax, or rather, the Halifax. In my younger and more vulnerable days, I had taken some risks and misbehaved a bit, but for the last ten years, I'd just got on with a regular life.

I was a good detective, not as good as I thought I was, but then, who is?

It was a complete mystery to me, as to who would want to fit me up for sending racist material. I couldn't think of anyone who would want to do such a thing. I genuinely couldn't.

I decided to take a bit of a risk but a necessary one. We had just started using email to communicate with one another and, I had discovered by chance, that you could email yourself. So, I sent myself an email in which I set out what had happened, very much in the same way I would have written a statement, and in it I included exactly where I'd hidden the item. I told the account precisely as it had happened. I included the fact that I'd wiped off my prints, explained why I was too afraid to report the matter, and even said that I had no idea why anyone would want to do this to me. The email was automatically timed and dated and would act as a permanent record. I reviewed the draft studiously and pressed send.

I wondered how long it would be before the first racist letter arrived and who would be the recipient? I was curious to discover how the protagonist would point the finger at me. I knew I'd have to be on my guard and check my desk regularly to make sure nothing else suddenly appeared.

It is difficult for anyone to understand just how toxic the subject of racism was in the Metropolitan Police in 1998.

If a member of the public, or for that matter, a disgruntled colleague really wanted to damage a police officer's reputation, all they had to do was suggest he or she was racist. The officer would be suspended for months, possibly years, and their career would be in ruins. There'd been the case of a poor guy over in Croydon, who'd been accused by a black colleague of using the word 'nigger' to refer to a robbery suspect, who punched an old lady in the face, before stealing her handbag. He insisted that he used the word 'shitter', but the Police Complaint's Authority had taken the case on, and they suspended the PC and two Sergeants who, they alleged, had heard the comment but failed to act. The case dragged on and on until the black PC was covertly taped by a friend, who was nothing to do with the police, admitting that he'd lied in anticipation of receiving a large payout in compensation. The friend sold the tape recording to a national newspaper and the case was thrown out, but the PC and the two Sergeants ended up being suspended for nearly two years! They all left the Job, too hurt and offended to ever again want to police the streets of London.

The bottom line was, the Met in the 90s was in a real mess and someone, although I didn't know who, was trying to drop me right into the middle of the mire. Whoever it was, I thought, must really hate me.

## Chapter 3

I was old school and believed that there were only three people allowed to use the Custody Suite entrance: an arresting officer with a prisoner, the Chief Superintendent, and the early turn Detective Sergeant. That Saturday morning, I fell into the latter category.

As I walked through the heavy one-way door, at the rear of Tottenham police station, my eyes immediately glanced to the white board, behind the Custody Officer's desk, where the names of the prisoners were recorded against their respective cell numbers, alongside details of the offence for which they were in custody and key detention times. This board dictated the morning's work for my team.

The C.I.D. 'day' was split into two basic divides. The morning shift, the early turn, deals with any prisoners who have been arrested overnight and the afternoon shift, the late turn, investigate any crimes which have been reported either overnight or during the morning. Of course, this wasn't a hard and fast rule, a crime might come in overnight that early turn had to investigate, immediately, or, a prisoner might be arrested during the afternoon, which late turn might have to interview and charge.

That morning, the white board was practically clear which was a rare, but very welcome, occurrence. The few prisoners showing had already been charged and were awaiting their appearance at court, in a few hours' time. It was a good start to the day and meant we would be able to catch up with outstanding case papers and related enquiries.

My optimism was short lived. When I entered the C.I.D. office the sight of the night duty DC, a chap called Jeremy, still there and typing up the Night Duty O.B. was enough for me to know that something had happened because, at ten past seven, the night duty shift should be tucked up in their beds.

"You still here?" I asked, stating the obvious.

"Hi, Nostrils; not for much longer, now that you're in." He replied.

He stopped typing and turned around; a few yards away the printer sprung to life, in response to Jeremy's last keyboard instruction.

"I've typed it all up, but I wanted to see you in person before I went. We've had a very nasty stranger rape. The victim's a twenty-three-year-old, who works at the Spurs; she's single and lives alone in a rented, ground floor flat, in Trinity Road."

"What an actual, proper rape? Not an ex-boyfriend, or a partner whose been caught out being unfaithful, or a 'consent withdrawn', or a victim suffering harmless delusions, or something that happened twenty years ago?"

"No, a genuine, pucker, stranger rape and a proper victim, too." Jeremy said.

"Gosh, they're rarer than rocking horse shit. What happened then?"

"At about 10pm, the victim was at home, when the suspect climbed in through her bedroom window. Over the next six hours, he subjected her to a series of indecent assaults, including rape, buggery, and forced oral. Originally, he said he was going to kill her because he didn't want to go back to prison but, somehow, over the next few hours, she managed to persuade him that she really fancied him and wanted to have a relationship. When he left, she even gave him her mobile phone number so that he could call and arrange to meet up, later today. She's proper lovely, Nostrils. Poor fucking cow has been through hell."

It was rare to hear another detective speak so candidly about the impact of a crime upon a victim, and that Jeremy had done so, in fact, said a great deal about the crime, itself. Like police officers of both genders, I had become somewhat cynical about the offence of rape. The pressure groups would have you believe that because 'no means no', it must necessarily follow that all rapes are as serious as one another, which was complete rubbish. A victim who is 'raped' on a Monday but has consenting sex the following day with the suspect cannot be the victim, in the same sense of the word, as the victim of a stranger rape. But like many things these days, that was a position no one was allowed, officially, to take.

"Who's doing what, and where?" I asked.

"There was a S.O.I.T. on night duty, Elodie, you know, the gorgeous little French girl."

I did indeed know Elodie; Jeremy's description was quite apt. S.O.I.T. meant she was specifically trained in sexual offences investigatory techniques.

"This is, actually, her first case; she only finished the course a couple of weeks ago. She's with the victim, at the rape suite in Hornsey. The F.M.E., Aronovitch, the old Jewish lady doctor, she's doing the examination, as we speak. The suspect reached orgasm several times, and in every orifice, he didn't use a durex so there should be excellent forensic evidence. When the examination is complete, Elodie will do first recall. The victim's mother is with her. Tomorrow, they'll take her to the clap clinic and get her the morning after pill."

"And the scene?" I asked.

"Preserved. Uniform are maintaining a log but we'll need to get S.O.C.O. there, first thing, and a dedicated Exhibits Officer to seize the bedding and other evidence. She deliberately poured him a glass of wine, so that she got his fingerprints. Can you believe that?"

"Jesus. That's one cool customer." I replied.

Jeremy shook his head.

"Not when I got to the scene; the poor thing was going absolutely hysterical. It was hard to watch, Nostrils, it really was. It could have been my own daughter. The first unit on scene did an excellent job and had to, quite literally, pull her out of the shower before she turned it on and washed away our forensics. We were out and about in West Green Road when the shout came out and were the second unit there."

"Any idea who the suspect is?" I asked.

"Any idea who the suspect is? We know who it is, where he lives, even his shoe size." Jeremy replied.

"You're kidding, right?" I asked, in astonishment.

"He told the victim his name, Mitchell Manson, the night duty Station Officer, Nellie, did the C.R.O. and CRIMINT checks which revealed two previous for rape, both very elderly victims. He's forty-four and has spent sixteen of the last seventeen years in prison. He was released on Thursday, on licence, from a prison on the Isle of Wight."

"Hip, hip, hooray for the Parole Board. What address was he bailed to?" I asked.

"His sister's address in Finsbury Park, but we went there, and there's no reply. We spoke to a neighbour, who said the female occupier was in the Whittington Hospital and had been for weeks; they didn't believe the male had been there, although they couldn't swear to it. I am pretty certain the place was deserted but it might be worth considering an O.P., if the suspect fails to appear, later this morning."

"Fails to appear. Where?" I asked.

"Mitchell Manson is due at Highbury Vale police station, at midday, today." Jeremy explained.

"To do what?" I asked.

"Sign the Sex Offenders' Register. If he fails to do so, it's an immediate recall to prison."

"Who's dealing with that?" I asked.

"CRIMINT shows a DC Dick Anderson; apparently, he spoke to the suspect just before he left prison and made the appointment. I've left a message for him to contact the control room downstairs, as soon as he gets in."

"He's not going to appear, is he?" I said.

Jeremy shrugged his shoulders.

"I think he will..." He replied.

"... but if he doesn't, and he's not at his sister's, there's not going to be a lot to go on. I mean, this guy has spent his whole adult life in prison; he's got no footprint anywhere. I suspect, he'll end up sleeping rough somewhere."

"Where was home, originally?" I asked.

"According to CRIMINT, he grew up in local authority care in Sussex, Brighton. Maybe, he'll gravitate to the south coast?" Jeremy suggested.

At that moment, a mobile phone started ringing on Jeremy's desk and he got up, made his way quickly over to it, and picked it up. As he did so he said:

"That's the victim's phone; I wonder if that's our suspect calling to arrange his date?"

"Don't answer it, will you. If it is him, let him think his new girlfriend's still asleep and that everything else is in order."

Jeremy looked at the screen and scribbled down the incoming number.

"It's a Holloway number, could be our man I suppose?" He said.

"Does the DI know? Have you informed him?" I asked.

"The DI's gone, Nostrils. Fuck me, you were at his leaving do on Wednesday, remember?"

I did know that the DI had moved on, I was just having one of those moments.

"Do we know who we're getting? Or is the appointment still shrouded in mystery?" I asked.

"I think she officially started last Monday but she's been tied up with the S.M.T. and meeting the local community. She's been spotted a couple of times. She's a carrot cruncher." Jeremy replied.

"What? A transfer in, at Detective Inspector rank? From where, do we know?" I asked.

"Hampshire, Surrey? Something like that." Jeremy replied.

"At least it's not a rural force; is that all we know, nothing else?" I asked.

"We'll soon find out." He replied.

## Chapter 4

I had two DCs and one TDC on my C.I.P.P. team; these were, respectively, Colin Harte, Bob Clark, and Dorothy McDonald. On paper I had a fourth member, a DC, called Rik Patel, but he was on long-term sick leave.

Colin was an enormous black fellow; he must have been 6'5" tall and over twenty stone. He had been the World Aikido Champion, for two years running, in the late eighties, and there'd been numerous articles in police publications detailing his exploits. Many people, myself included, thought Colin was the hardest police officer the Metropolitan Police had ever employed. For a couple of years, he dated a PC I'd worked with at Stokey, a woman called Thompson, who was a Judo instructor. They'd had a child together, but had broken up shortly after the birth, and Colin never saw his son or her mother, again.

Colin also had a habit of replacing common words and expressions with off beat terms. So, he might call the Superintendent, 'the crown' because of her badge of rank, or he might describe a house as, 'a residential square shaped collection of bricks'. It was amazing how quickly he could come up with these. And he never used the same term twice!

Colin wasn't everybody's cup of tea. He was flash, possessed, perhaps, a little too much confidence; oozed charm and, genuinely, didn't give a damn what anyone else thought about him, but as soon as I got to know him, we struck up a friendship. I think, in so many ways, he reminded me of my old friend Andy Welling. I decided to keep him by my side, as long as circumstances would allow. Consequently, initially I arranged for his transfer to Burglary Squad, when I took over that team, and made sure he followed me, when I moved into the main office.

In complete contrast to his colleague, Bob Clark was a white DC, about my age, and annoyingly fit and healthy. In his day, he had been a keen M.P.A.A. boxer, representing the Met, at various events. As far as I knew, as far as anyone knew, because Bob was a private person, he lived alone and spent his spare time running 10Ks. The only other thing I knew about Bob was that last year, he'd won the Metropolitan Police's photography competition with a picture of a Kingfisher. I'm sure it was great, but it wasn't my thing. I thought Bob was probably gay; not that I cared, in the slightest. I suffered from many phobias, but homophobia, wasn't one of them. When he did mention his private life, it was usually about his parents; his dad had died, quite recently.

As a detective, Bob was excellent. Methodical, logical and with an eye for detail. I found him an invaluable member of my team.

I owed Bob a massive favour. Last year, we were searching a suspect's house on a warrant when, completely out of the blue, the suspect's mother, a woman in her mid-forties, who up until that point, had been as good as gold, attacked me from behind, with a kitchen knife. The woman had a history of mental illness and was never charged. Bob received a Chief Superintendent's Commendation for what he did to protect me, but he deserved more. I knew, I would never forget what he'd done.

The final member of our team was Trainee Detective Constable Dorothy McDonald, or rather, 'Dot', as everyone called her.

Dot was, well, normal. She lived in South Woodford with a DC from the murder squad, at Edmonton. She was in her mid-thirties, had dogs and cats instead of children, and talked about, one day, leaving the job and buying a kennels and cattery out in the sticks. She was an interesting character, having grown up in India, where her father, a Presbyterian Reverend, ran a Mission caring for and educating orphaned children. As a result, Dot often looked at things a little differently, and possessed a sound moral compass.

I liked Dot, but more importantly, I trusted her judgment, even though, in terms of service, she was, by far, my most junior officer. I don't think Dot was bothered about promotion, which was a shame, because, one day, she'd have made a great Superintendent.

By nine o'clock, my team were all in, and we sat in silence as Elodie, the S.O.I.T., briefed us. As she did so, she constantly referred to her notes.

"The thing the victim feared most wasn't dying. The unbearable thought that kept running through her terrified mind, was that her mum, who was coming round in only a few hours, to go shopping with her, would be the one to find her.

She knew that her mum would ring the doorbell and, when she didn't answer, would use her own key to let herself in. She would call out jovially, imagining that her precious daughter had overslept having had a glass too much red wine, the previous evening. She would take her coat off, hang the garment on the hook in the hall, and put the kettle on, before going into the bedroom, where she would discover her daughter's lifeless corpse, soaking in a pool of fresh blood.

So, while the victim says she would rather have died, she decided, for her mum's sake, that she had to survive, no matter what it took.

Only a few hours earlier, at about 10pm yesterday evening, the victim, who was an administrative assistant at Tottenham Football Club, had opened the sash window in the bedroom of her ground floor flat, which was only a few hundred yards from the main entrance at White Hart Lane.

She was about to dry her hair but feared the combination of the oppressively hot summer evening and the heat of the hairdryer, would melt her. She turned over her favourite tape, to listen to side two of the Lighthouse Family's Ocean Drive and gave her hair a final patting down with her small hand towel.

The victim stood before the full-length mirror, which was immediately adjacent to the window, and switched the hairdryer on. The blast of hot air, however, was overpowering, so she flicked the device off, turned away from the mirror, slipped out of her white bathrobe and into a pair of her boyfriend's freshly laundered boxer shorts, which she gathered from underneath her pillow.

When she turned back around, standing in her bedroom, was an unknown white male, about forty years old.

She says the shock nearly stopped her heart; her knees weakened, and her vision started to tunnel. She lurched to her left and, putting her hand out, collapsed onto the bed. She was, quite simply, more terrified than she had ever been in her life.

'It's all right, it's all right...' The suspect said, trying to be reassuring.

'... I won't hurt you. I just need some money.'

She says his voice was rough and deep, almost gravelly, and his accent, uneducated, hard, and firmly rooted in the East End.

'I'm really scared'. The victim said.

'Don't be frightened, I won't hurt you honey. I just need some money, that's all. I've just got out of prison, and I need you to lend me some cash. I'll pay you back.'

The victim says the suspect used the term 'honey' all the time.

The suspect was now sitting next to the victim on the bed, and he put his right arm around her back. This act made the victim suddenly realise that she was, apart from the boxer shorts, naked. She went to stand up, while simultaneously reaching for her, recently discarded, dressing gown. The man's arm however encircled her back and his hand squeezed into the side of her right hip, and, before she had raised herself more than a few inches, he pulled her back down."

As she spoke, Elodie demonstrated the suspect's actions, with her own right arm.

"The victim says she was shaking now, uncontrollably.

'What do you want?' She asked.

'How much money have you got, honey?' He asked.

'Let me go and I'll get my purse, it's in the kitchen'. The victim replied.

She tried to speak with a degree of authority, but her attempt failed.

The suspect insisted on going with her.

The victim went to stand but her knees were too shaky, so she was forced to sit back down, on the edge of the bed.

'Let me help you up, never let it be said that I'm not a gentleman.' He said.

The victim thought this was a strange thing for him to say, about being a gentleman.

The suspect stood up, positioned himself immediately in front of her, and took her by the elbows. As he leaned forward his chest touched her breasts and she felt physically sick. From somewhere, she found the strength to stand and stumble towards the kitchen. The suspect walked immediately beside her, putting his hand on her shoulder, and gripping tightly, in a gesture demonstrating complete control. On route, she reached again for her dressing gown, but the man firmly nudged her forward and away from the garment.

In the kitchen, the victim retrieved her purse, while, simultaneously, trying desperately to conceal her breasts. She found only eight pounds; she knew it wasn't much but desperately hoped, it would be enough.

'I can give you my bankcard if you like. I can tell you the number and you can withdraw up to two hundred.'

The victim held both the cash and the card forward like a beggar proffering a bowl.

The suspect took her offering, which he immediately discarded on the worktop surface.

'I've changed my mind. I don't want the money anymore. I want you instead.'

The victim's last sensation was that she was wetting herself, and then, there was nothing.

When she regained consciousness, a few moments later, the victim was laying on her bed. Her boxer shorts had been removed and the suspect was undressing, with his back to her, as if he was shy.

She watched him with a surreal aloofness. She describes the suspect as about forty, quite short, perhaps five foot six, and slim, with cropped dark hair and indeterminable tattoos, sporadically placed, all over his body. When he had removed his disgustingly grey Y-front underpants, he turned around. The victim knew what her fate was going to be. She was aware that she should fight but knew she would lose. She says she wondered how her life could possibly have changed so radically, in such a terribly and tragically short time.

The suspect sat on the bed, his naked hip touching her waist, and started to stroke her cheek. She shivered uncontrollably, with absolute revulsion.

'I am really, sorry.' He said, his voice little more than a whisper.

The suspect had leaned towards her and was breathing on her face, now. She could smell alcohol. He gently kissed her forehead, like a parent would to a child. She noticed the disgusting state of his teeth, which were stained yellow, and clearly rotting. She says she was crying, uncontrollably.

The suspect kept saying he was sorry.

'Please don't.' The victim kept pleading.

But the suspect said that he had to do it and, repeated again, that he was sorry.

He then said, he wasn't going back to prison and that, when he was finished, he was going to have to kill the victim. He said it wasn't his fault, it was 'the system' and then he said, 'you can't beat the system.'

So, we know the suspect has just got out of prison.

'Please don't hurt me. I won't say anything to anyone, I promise.' The victim said, her sheer desperation evident in every syllable.

'You're so beautiful. You really are. I've never seen anyone as pretty as you.' The suspect said.
The suspect stroked the victim's face, with the forefinger of his right hand. The victim says she could smell tobacco on his yellow stained fingers.

The suspect asked if he could kiss her and she nodded, what else could she do? But her nightmare had only just begun.

Like a scratched record playing the same few seconds of music, again and again, the terrified victim says she kept turning the same seven words, over and over, in her mind, 'I'm going to have to kill you, I'm going to have to kill you, I'm going to have to kill you …'.

Over the next six hours, the victim was digitally penetrated, raped countless times, both per vagina and per anus, and forced to give and receive oral sex. The suspect reached orgasm countless times; he didn't use a Durex. During these assaults, she retreated into herself, to the deepest darkest depths of her mind, where she sought solace, in memories of her family and close friends.

In between assaults, however, the victim ruthlessly exploited every opportunity to befriend the man. She cuddled him, she caressed him, she whispered sweet nothings, she nibbled his ear, she kissed his hands and, at one point, even cut his toe and finger nails.

The victim learned that only last week the man, whose name was Mitchell Manson, had been released from somewhere called Camp Hill. That he claimed back in 1990 to have been wrongly convicted of assaulting a lady; it was, he said, a case of withdrawn consent, whatever that meant. Now he was free, he was, he said, going to get his conviction overturned. In the meantime, he was temporarily living with his sister in Finsbury Park.

The victim pretended to share intimate details of her own life; she said she worked hard to craft a story designed, with the sole intention, of saving her life. She told the suspect that she was single, but desperately wanted to find someone and settle down. She said she was always attracted to the wrong sort of men, to rogues and players, who just wanted to sleep with her. She said that she had been terrified when he had climbed into her bedroom through the open window, but that she had really enjoyed the sex and then berated him because she knew that he was going to be like all the others and never contact her again. As the hours passed, the victim repeated this complaint until, eventually, it drew a response.

The suspect protested, he wasn't like all the others, and he would contact her again. She asked for his mobile phone number, but the suspect didn't seem to understand the question. When she realised that he'd been in prison from a time before the existence of mobile phones, she asked for his sister's phone number, but when he didn't know it, she wrote down her own mobile number on a piece of paper and got him to promise to call her tomorrow, when, she said, they could start 'a proper and meaningful relationship'.

At first, the suspect seemed skeptical, but the victim got him to ring her mobile number from the house phone and, when it rang, and he realised, with genuine surprise, she'd given him the right number, the victim said he was convinced.

When the suspect kissed the victim goodbye and climbed back out of the sash window, he had forgotten that he had promised to kill her. Instead, by the victim's bravery, guile and sheer will to survive, the monster now genuinely believed he had a date for Saturday evening."

As Elodie recounted the victim's evidence, the four of us sat in complete silence. No one uttered so much as one word.

The victim had been both incredibly brave and unbelievably smart and it was quite difficult not to get upset, when we heard details of the terrible and terrifying ordeal he'd put her through. That might have been unprofessional, as detectives we were meant to remain detached, objective, and aloof but we were also human beings and, in my fifteen years as a police officer, I hadn't heard a more harrowing victim's experience.

## Chapter 5

I asked Bob to do the scene and Dot to make sure that Elodie handed everything over.

Colin and I drove over to Highbury Vale police station, which was a short journey across north London.

I did, briefly, flirt with the idea of telling Colin about what I'd found in my desk the previous evening but decided it was probably wiser to keep everything to myself, for the time being. I was, however, interested in picking his brains on the subject.

"Can I ask you a race related question?" I asked.

"Of course, mate." He replied.

"Is the Met racist? I mean, you've been in it for like, eighteen years, haven't you?"

"Yeah, a bit." He replied.

I was shocked. It wasn't the answer I was expecting, and it certainly wasn't the reply I wanted to hear.

"Really?" I replied, a little too incredulously.

"Listen, Nostrils. It's not as bad as they say but it is there. You probably wouldn't even notice, but I do."

"Go on, give me some examples."

"Ok, last week, Dot was in the office, discussing a burglary she'd been to, and she described the victim as, 'a really nice black lady'. She would never had said that if the victim had been white, I mean she would never have mentioned her colour, she'd have just said the victim was, 'a really nice lady', wouldn't she?"

"But Dot's not racist, is she?" I asked.

"No, she's not, but why did she say that? On some level, Dot was surprised the victim was so nice because she was black. Or at least, that's how it came across to me."

I didn't know what to say. Although I hated to admit it, Colin's logic was unchallengeable.

"Have I ever said something like that?" I asked.

"Good god, no." He replied and I breathed a sigh of relief.

"You're much worse!" Colin said.

I laughed out loud.

"I'm serious." He replied.

"What the fuck are you talking about?" I asked, a little nervously.

"Oh, I know you're alright, Nostrils. You're a nice fella, and I know your best mate was black and he died of the old, arse hole injected death sentence, and all that, but fuck me, what about what you said last week?" Colin said.

"Mate, I have absolutely no idea what you're talking about." I replied.

"Seriously?"

"Yes, seriously." I replied, definitively.

"You've got a short fucking memory, Nostrils. How did you ever pass the Sergeant's exam?"

"Go on then, what did I say?" I asked, absolutely convinced that either, he'd got me mixed up with someone else, or he'd misheard something, I'd said.

"We were going to Edmonton to nick that guy for flying kites, do you remember?"

"Yes." I replied.

"We were stuck in traffic, in the High Street, by Lordship Lane, and a blonde bit of crumpet crossed the road in front of us …"

Oh my god, I suddenly knew where this conversation was going, and I was mortified.

"… I commented that she was very attractive …"

"I think your exact words were that you, "could do that some serious gynecological damage'." I interjected, hoping to score, just a few, damage limitation points, before he completed the sentence.

"… but you didn't share my view because you said she was 'black man's meat'." Colin said.

His recollection was absolutely right. I had said that, and what's more, I hadn't given the comment a moment's thought, so comfortable, did I feel in Colin's company.

"Oh, fuck me, I'm mortified." I said.

Colin laughed.

"I am so sorry, mate; I really am. I didn't mean …"

But I didn't bother finishing my explanation because nothing I could say would make the situation better.

"You did ask the question. You see, Nostrils, it's the little things, and the little things count, too. I mean the Job's probably better than a lot of institutions, you know, like the armed services, or the House of Lords, or the Church of England, but it's way behind the N.H.S. or the teaching profession."

"I am profoundly sorry, Colin. I never even realised what I'd said." I explained, feebly.

"Just like Dot didn't. It's all right, mate, honestly. Just remember, the little things are just as important as the big things. Now stop looking so devastated, you are forgiven, just don't ever describe my white whoring bitches as, 'black man's meat', again."

"Deal." I replied, meekly.

That was an interesting exchange, but it unsettled me. Was the Met racist, after all? If it was, then my entire belief system was wrong. I was genuinely offended by the findings of the Achachi Enquiry and dismissed them as politically generated to placate the growing ethnic community of London. If, however, someone I trusted and respected, thought we were racist then, well, I didn't know quite what to think. I needed to know more.

"Do you think the Met's racist in its interactions with the public?" I asked.

Colin chewed that one over for a few seconds.

"Probably not, particularly these days; in fact, everyone's so bloody scared, a black youth can get away with a great deal more than their white counterpart. I've got a cousin who's a cop in LA. From the stories he tells me, I think we're years ahead of them, in terms of race, but we're not there yet, mate."

"That's really surprising." I replied.

"Why, did you honestly think the Job was perfect?" Colin asked.

"No, of course not. But I've never arrested, charged, or stopped and searched someone, just because they were black, ever."

"I believe you, Nostrils; but we are the new generation. What about the old sticks, the ones that joined in the late sixties and the seventies? They're still in the Job and don't tell me that racism not ingrained into that generation. I mean, they can't help it because it's how they were bought up. Remember, Love thy Neighbour?"

Love thy Neighbour was an early 1970s ITV comedy about a white family and a black family living next to each other. It was extremely racist, with the two main characters trading insults such as 'sambo' and 'honkey'.

"I do, actually." I replied.

"That was acceptable in the seventies because the culture was so different, back then. But the people who were brought up in that culture are still policing London, today."

"What would you do to fix it?" I asked.

"Time is the only thing that'll do that. And, obviously, we need many, many more black officers." He replied.

"But they won't join, it's a chicken and egg situation." I said.

"Perhaps. If the Met wanted to recruit them, they could. Pay them five thousand pounds more than their white colleagues and watch them flood in. Pay it at the end of every completed years' service, for the first five years." He suggested.

"That would be illegal, wouldn't it?

"Not if they pass legislation, they can make anything legal by an Act of Parliament."

"I don't think the Federation would like it." I said.

"Fuck the Federation, they're half the problem. Have you ever seen a black Federation rep?" He asked.

"So, you support the A.E.M.O. then?" I asked.

A.E.M.O. stood for the Association of Ethnic Minority Officers and it was pronounced, 'emu'.

"A.E.M.O. shouldn't be needed, not if the Federation was different, but they are needed. Someone must stand up and be counted for the few of us."

"Are you a member?" I asked.

"I am Nostrils, of course. It's a great support group. I've got a lot of time for them." He replied.

"I'm not sure, myself." I replied, skeptically.
"Listen Nostrils, do you know how often I'm the only black officer or black person in a room?"

"What do you mean?" I asked.

"If we do an early turn spin, at the briefing there might be twenty officers, I will be the only black person there. If I'm in a busy canteen, often the only black person there. If you were the only white person amongst a whole group of black people, would you notice? Be honest."

"Yes, of course I would." I replied.

"Well, that's been my life for the last eighteen years. Not only, was I the only black recruit in my intake at Hendon, I was the only black recruit in the entire Training School for the whole sixteen weeks I was there! No wonder I'm a tiny bit sensitive about it." He said.

We pulled into the back yard and our conversation came to a natural close. I was slightly surprised by Colin's views, but I left the car a wiser man, because of this conversation. For a start, he'd probably changed forever the way I viewed the A.E.M.O. More importantly, he'd really made me challenge some of my traditional thinking.

At Highbury Vale we met Dick Anderson, the DC who was running the Sex Offenders' Register for Islington. We explained what had happened and I shared my view that we were only going through the motions, because there was no way, Mitchell Manson was going to appear, at the allotted time. Before I'd even finished expressing my opinion, Dick took a short call on his mobile phone.

"Your man's here. He's at the front counter…" He said.

Dick checked his watch.

"… in fact, he's twenty minutes early."

I didn't mind being wrong.

"Where are you going to put him?" I asked.

"There's a small interview room next to the front counter. One door enters from the public side, the other from the station office side. I'll sit him in there and then you can come in and do your bit."

"Do you want to register him first?" I asked.

"No point, mate, he'll be going straight back to prison for breach of licence, whether you charge him today or not." He replied.

I sent Colin around the front of the nick, so he could cover the exit via the public door, just in case the suspect tried to escape, when he realised what was going on. I kept out of sight, while Dick met Mitchell at the counter; not that my presence would have meant anything to him, but it just seemed the sensible thing to do.

"Use the door on the right and go into the interview room, Mitchell. I'll meet you there, in a second." Dick said.

I heard the door open and close and then saw Colin enter the front counter area and take up position just outside the door.

Dick went into the interview room, and I followed him. Already seated, at the other side of a small table, was a white male, in his early forties, who appeared agitated. Even before I'd sat down, I noticed the smell emanating from the man; it was a stale, dank, unpleasant odor, so characteristic of the great unwashed, so many of whom, I had had the displeasure to work with, so closely, over the last fifteen years.

I also noticed that the man fitted the description given by the victim; he was the right colour, height and build.

"Can I confirm your full name and date of birth please, Mitchell?" Dick asked.

"Mitchell Charles Manson; fourteenth, January, nineteen fifty-five." He replied.

"Thank you, Mitchell. Before we deal with your registration as a sex offender, I would like to introduce DS Pritchard. DS Pritchard is from Tottenham police station, and he'd like to discuss something with you."

"What?" He replied, cautiously.

"Mitchell, I'm investigating a serious assault that took place, last night, in Trinity Road, Tottenham. A white male broke into a house by climbing through an open sash window and indecently assaulted the occupier. You fit the description of that man and the victim says, he told her his name was Mitchell. That was you, wasn't it?"

"No" He replied, sheepishly.

I went to speak but noticed his eyes had darted quickly to the handle of the door, and I knew, he was going to make a bolt for it. I don't know which one of us went first, but not two seconds later, I was in a full-scale fight. This was no push and shove; this was a nasty vicious battle. Within seconds, the table and chairs had overturned, and I grappled to get a decent grip on Mitchell and bring him to the floor. I could see Colin trying to join the affray, but the angle of the upturned table was lodged, in such a way, that prevented the door from opening, more than a few inches. While this was good news, as it meant Mitchell's escape was impossible, it was very bad news for my safety, as the violent suspect now turned all his efforts towards inflicting damage to me.

From behind, I was aware that Dick was trying to help but there simply wasn't sufficient room, in this tiny space, for him to make a meaningful contribution.

"I'm going to bite your cunting nose off." Mitchell said, repeatedly.

I found myself lying on my back, lodged awkwardly into the leg of the upturned table, pushing Mitchell's face away from my own, with every ounce of strength I had in me. I had hold of the collar of his tracksuit top with both hands but, no matter how far I lifted this away from me, he was still able to close the gap because of the stretch, in the fabric. If I tried to move my grip, and get a better hold, perhaps around his neck, in the second of readjustment, he would be on me.

I could feel his every pant on my cheek and had turned my face to the right, in the hope that, should my arms fail to keep him away, he would sink his teeth into anywhere on my head that wasn't my eyes, which I closed as tightly as I could, for additional protection.

He was getting nearer, now, and I felt his tongue on my right ear, which triggered a renewed burst of energy, and I growled, while lifting his face up slightly and away, but, at this second, his top ripped and his head suddenly fell, with real force, against my own.

Our heads clashed with a dull, sickening thud, which caught us both by surprise. I opened my eyes. The impact had been on the top of my head, but Mitchell had been less fortunate because the contact had split open a huge gash just above his right eye, which immediately started to bleed; drops of thick, disgusting blood fell on my face.

Then suddenly, Mitchell was gone.

# Chapter 6

When he realised that entry from the public side to the interview room was blocked, Colin had cleared the front counter in one leap and forced his way into the interview room, by ejecting poor Dick, with little grace but considerable force. This action provided Colin with a clear path to my aid. And what did he do? Colin, literally, lifted Mitchell off me and held him, horizontally above his head, and up against the wall. It was a show of sheer strength that I had never witnessed previously or since. Circumstances had combined to assist my rescuer, who was just reaching for Mitchell, when our heads clashed, and, therefore, the suspect had at that precise moment. been somewhat dazed. Nonetheless, he must have needed super-human strength to lift, at least eleven stone, straight up and above his head.

For the second time, in a little over a year, I owed my well-being to one of my band of brothers.

Thirty minutes later, we were in the Custody Suite at Holloway police station, where the Sergeant had to put four officers around a handcuffed Mitchell, to stop him attacking me; against whom, he seemed, to have taken a particular dislike.

While he was being booked in, he continued to spout hatred in my direction, threatening to, 'bite my cunting nose off' and 'eat my fucking liver'.

I must admit, the aggression was so undiluted and so forceful that, even I, a police officer of fifteen years' service, was somewhat taken aback, but I put on the bravest of faces and, at one stage, even managed to rouse a round of laughter from those present, when I asked him, 'Mitchell, we're not married are we?'. The fact that everyone laughed really made him angry and made me feel, just a little, better.

We were all examined by the F.M.E.

I had a large and impressive bump on the top of my head and applied a bag of frozen peas, generously donated, free of charge, by the canteen ladies. I was given a note to take to a local hospital to undergo a series of tests because Mitchell had bled over my face, but I was quietly confident that none would have been able to enter my bloodstream.

Mitchell needed stitches, but his violent disposition made a transfer to hospital impractical, and the F.M.E. authorised his continued detention and a review in four hours. His bleeding had stopped so he wasn't going to get any worse. I managed to persuade the F.M.E. to sign him off as 'fit for interview' just in case we got a chance to speak to him, formally; though, I doubted that would occur with his current attitude. The F.M.E. asked whether we had the authority to take intimate samples, but I told him we were waiting for the Superintendent.

We wrote our arrest notes up in the canteen, over breakfast. All in all, it felt like a good morning's work. I spoke to Elodie, the S.O.I.T., who had finished for the day and was on her way home. She was on night duty, so she needed to get to bed. She told me the victim was going to move in with her mother, who lived in Wood Green, but that she would really appreciate a visit from the officer in the case, before the end of the day. I said that we'd need to have finished with the suspect first, to avoid any suggestion of cross contamination.

By the sounds of it, Elodie had done an excellent job and, after she'd hung up, I called Dot, who'd been with her for the last hour. Dot immediately focused on an issue I'd spotted from the beginning and, which if we weren't careful, was going to cause real problems for the successful prosecution of Mitchell Manson.

"Chris, we could be stuffed here?"

"Go on." I said.

"The victim was with the suspect for at least five hours, during which time, she told him, repeatedly, that she found him sexually attractive, that he was, 'just her type' and, 'exactly what she was looking for'. She even told him that she loved him, on at least three occasions. To cap it all, she told him that he was fulfilling one of her rape fantasies. Now, I know, and you know, that she was only saying that because she didn't want him to kill her, but it could really muddy the waters as far as the issue of consent is concerned."

Dot was spot on.

"I agree. I mean, he's got two previous convictions for rape, both elderly victims, octogenarians in fact ..."

"What?" Dot said.

"Octogenarians, people who are in their eighties. I only learnt that the other day because it was an anagram in the Telegraph crossword." I replied.

"Chris, what are you talking about?" Dot asked.

"Ignore me. Anyway, even though our suspect has got previous for rape, because of our wonderful legal system, the jury won't be allowed to know about these convictions." I said.

"And if he plays the consent defence, all the forensic evidence in the world will mean diddly squat." Dot pointed out.

"I agree, I know. The interview will be crucial. We've got to get him to say that he knew she wasn't giving genuine consent." I said.

"Remember, one of the first things he said to her was that he was going to kill her, after he'd raped her, because he didn't want to get caught and go back to prison. Even if he admits just that, the jury will probably understand why she pretended to be enjoying the whole thing."

"Jury? Listen to me, Dot. I am going to do everything I can to make sure our victim doesn't have to go through the ordeal of giving evidence and reliving last night. Fuck me, can you imagine if she has to be cross examined about her own sex life?"

"How are you going to make sure of that?" Dot asked.

"I'm going to get Mitchell Charles Manson to plead guilty."

"Good luck with that one; you won't get him to plead. This is his third rape offence, whether he pleads guilty or not, he's got to get a mandatory life sentence, under the new legislation." She said.

"Fuck, I hadn't realised." I replied.

"If you can get him to put his hands up and plead guilty, I'll buy you dinner, at the Ritz. I mean it."

"And if I can't, what do you want in return? What's your side of the bet? I asked.

"Nothing, Christopher. I don't want anything in return; just prove me wrong and send this evil bastard down for the rest of his life, without the poor victim having to give evidence; that will be enough."

"Deal." I replied.

## Chapter 7

Like all good C.I.D. officers, I liked an informal chat with my prisoners before I interviewed them. While not strictly allowed, the practice is, essentially, harmless because nothing either of us said would be admissible in evidence. I have to admit, I had some reticence about going into Mitchell's cell, but I thought, I'd at least have a chat with him, through the wicket.

I asked the Custody Sergeant if he had a problem with me speaking to Mitchell.

"Be my guest, mate; but don't blame me if he tries to scratch your eyes out. I don't think he's your number one fan."

I thanked the Sergeant, walked down the cell passage, and looked through the spy hole. Mitchell was curled up in the fetal position, on the bunk, and crying his heart out. I watched him for about thirty seconds, slid the catch across on the wicket and let it drop open, with a metal clunk. Mitchell's eyes opened and he looked up, a defeated and desperate human being.

"Hello, mate..." I said, in my gentlest voice.

"... can I get you a cigarette?"

He nodded.

"If I get you a cigarette, I'll come in for a quick chat. You're not going to bite my nose off, are you?" I asked.

He shook his head.

I returned a few minutes later with a borrowed cigarette, a lighter and the jailer, who had to unlock the cell door, and let me in.

"Are you sure you want to go into his cell?" The jailer asked.

I nodded.

As I walked in, Mitchell sat up. He was holding a blood-stained bandage against his right eye.

I lit the cigarette and handed it to him.

"Thanks, boss"

"Look at the bump on my fucking head!" I said, with a smile.

I tilted my head forward and pointed. I was very conscious that, in so doing, I was leaving myself completely vulnerable to an attack, but the gesture was also a show of trust.

"Sorry, boss." He replied.

Even if I hadn't already known, I could have guessed immediately that he'd spent his life in prison, because only ex-cons and C.I.D. officers use the expression, 'boss', in that way.

"It's fucking huge." I said, laughing.

Mitchell shrugged his shoulders and looked awkward.

"How's your eye?" I asked, with such affection that a third party might think I was talking to my favourite child.

"It'll be fine, boss. My own fault, I know."

"Now you've calmed down a bit, we can get you across to the hospital to get it stitched." I suggested.

"No thanks; I don't like needles, boss. I'd rather just let it fix on its own. Can I say thank you?" He said.

"Thank you?" I replied, interested to learn why he was grateful, and, hopeful, that I could turn it to my advantage.

"I thought I'd get a right hiding, boss, you know, when I was put in here." He replied.

"When were you last arrested?" I asked.

"Eighty-nine, I think." He replied.

"I stopped them; they wanted to kill you, what with, you know, what you did last night. The woman, her name was Clare Maddison, her boyfriend's a police officer. Honestly, Mitchell, he'd given orders for you to be beaten to within an inch of your life and he wanted them to concentrate on your balls. You're lucky I was here to stop them."

It was complete bullshit. Clare's boyfriend wasn't a police officer, and the simple truth was that this was 1998 and prisoners no longer got a hiding.

"I owe you one, boss." He said.

"Okay, I'll tell you what you can do."

I waited for him to respond but, instead, he took a deep draw on his cigarette. I realised he wasn't going to bite.

"Do you want a brief?" I asked.

He shook his head.

This was very good news because a brief would advise him to go, 'no comment'. I was, however, conscious that he could change his mind at any time.

"Let's get the interview sorted, then, Mitchell. Let's get this over and done with."

He nodded.

I couldn't leave him alone in the cell, while he was still smoking, so we sat there in silence.

"You know that whatever happens today, you'll be recalled to prison, don't you?" I asked.

I didn't want him to think that, under any circumstances, he was going to talk his way to freedom.

"I know, boss." He replied.

Mitchell stubbed the cigarette out on the floor, my cue to stand up.

"I'll set the interview up …" I said.

"… can I get you anything else?"

"I get a phone call, right. The Sergeant said I could have one, when I came in. Can I have my phone call please, boss?"

"Who do you want to phone? Your sister?"

"God no, boss, she doesn't give a fuck about me. I want to speak to my girlfriend." He replied.

"Who's that?" I asked.

"Clare. The Sergeant took a bit of paper off me, when I was searched; it's got her telephone number on it. I'll need that, boss."

"Mitchell, Clare is the woman who you raped last night."

"I didn't rape her, she wanted me. I must admit, I'm a bit fucked off to discover she's got a boyfriend who's a copper, but I'm sure she'll tell him to fuck off now we're a couple." He replied.

I wasn't quite sure whether he was being serious.

"Mitchell, you've been arrested for raping Clare. She's saying you forced her to have sex with you last night." I explained.

"What a bitch." He replied.

# Chapter 8

I wanted to seize the opportunity and get Mitchell interviewed before he changed his mind and decided he wanted a brief. When I told the Custody Sergeant, I could tell he was skeptical, but he didn't have the strength of character to challenge me.

I got hold of Colin, who was chatting up a couple of young WPCs in the back yard, and within fifteen minutes, we had started the interview. After the statutory introduction and having got his confirmation on tape that he didn't require a solicitor, I asked the first question.

"Mitchell, please take your time and tell us what happened last night in Trinity Road, Tottenham?"

"I met the woman of my dreams, boss." He replied, as if that was all that needed to be said.

Colin and I exchanged glances.

"We're going to need a little bit more detail. Can you start by telling us what you were doing, just before ten o'clock, yesterday evening?"

"I'd had a few drinks in a pub in the High Street, I don't remember what it was called. Anyway, I'd run out of money, so I thought I'd go and do some earns. I went up a couple of side roads, to see if anyone had left a door or window open. It was really hot, so I thought I might be in luck. I was in a road, not far from the pub, when I saw a window open, down the side of a house. I wanted to get in and get out, you know, perhaps have a handbag off, so I could carry on drinking."

"Okay, so you were looking for somewhere to burgle?" I asked.

"Not burgle, rob. I wouldn't have broken in." He replied.

I       suspected he didn't know the legal difference, and it wasn't important anyway, so I simply said:

"Go on."

"Anyway, I had a butchers and made sure the place was empty, I mean, I didn't want to scare anyone, and then I climbed in through the window. It was a bedroom, and I had a quick look around for any money, but I'd only been in there a few seconds, when this woman came in. She was wearing a white dressing gown and was quite young. I was really scared; I mean proper frightened. She asked me who I was, and what I was doing. I said I was sorry to disturb her, but could I lend some money. She said, 'I'm not giving you any money, but I'll give you something else', and then she took her dressing gown off, really slowly and sexily, and dropped it on the bed. She said she wanted me to fuck her, that it was her fantasy to be raped, and that she found me really good looking."

I       t was difficult to listen to such bollocks but in some ways, it could have been worse. His account was too unbelievable; if he'd been smarter, he would have told a gentler, more credible version of events. I was quite content to let him tell this ridiculous tale, but the downside was that it did make the chance of a guilty plea less likely and I really wanted that more than anything else.

"We kissed, I mean, we proper kissed. No one has ever kissed me before, ever. She nibbled my ear; she actually nibbled my ear with her teeth. It made my neck, and the side of my face, go all funny. She told me she loved me, proper loved, not just once, but proper loads of times. Then she asked me out on a date, tonight."

He glanced up at the clock in the interview room, as if he was calculating whether he'd be out in time to meet her.

"She even gave me her telephone number. I mean, I've never had a proper girlfriend before I was ..."

Mitchell stopped talking and suddenly started to cry.

"Mitchell, you are clearly upset. Would you like to take a short break?"

He nodded.

"The time is one-thirty, and I am turning the tape off because Mitchell has requested a short break."
The beep beeped and the tape stopped.

Colin nodded towards the door, and we stepped outside, but not away from, the interview room.

"Mitchell's putting on quite a performance, isn't he?" Colin said.

I nodded.

"Do you want me to have a word in his listening orifice, you know, while the tapes are off?" Colin suggested.

I smiled; sometimes it was great working with a good old-fashioned detective.

"No, it's all right. It's such complete bollocks that he's never going to convince a jury." I replied.

"Yeah, but we want him to plead, don't we? The more he tells this tale, the more he'll start to believe it." Colin replied.

Colin was right. I'd seen it, time and time again. The more a suspect repeated the same story, the more convinced they became that that was what had actually happened. It was one of the reasons I wasn't a huge supporter of lie detectors. It wasn't just with suspects; I think it was a very human trait. On my first day out of training school, I'd been shot at by a blagger, on his way out of the Abbey National, in Stoke Newington High Street. I'd told the story many times; it was my 'go to' story, so to speak. The shotgun had probably been discharged from about twenty-five or even thirty yards, but, every time I'd recounted the event, the blagger had got, just slightly, nearer to me. If I took a lie detector, I reckon I could pass, even if I claimed he'd been only five yards from me.

When we re-started the interview, I decided it was time to probe Mitchell's account.

"Mitchell, did you tell the victim that you'd been in prison?"

"Victim? Do you mean Clare?" He asked.

"Yes." I replied, curtly.

"I might have mentioned it." He replied.

"In what context?" I asked.

"What does that mean?" He asked.

"Why did you tell her that you'd been in prison?"

"She asked me if I had a girlfriend, I said I hadn't because I'd been inside."

"Mitchell, that's not what Clare has told us. She says, that you told her, you'd just got out of prison and didn't want to go back, and that to avoid being caught, you were going to murder her, after you'd indecently assaulted her. That's in fact what happened, isn't it?"

Hearing the truth seemed to knock Mitchell's confidence and he responded with an almost silent 'no'. I decided to push home the advantage.

"Mitchell, when you forced her to have anal sex, you split her anus, you literally, split her anus by 18 millimeters. Why did you do that? Don't insult me, or her, by claiming she wanted you to have anal sex with her."

My voice was firm, my intonation unforgiving.

"She didn't want anal sex." He replied.

Colin kicked me under the desk. We had the answer we wanted. We could prove the rape.

"So why, why did you force her?" I asked.

"I was being nice." He replied, incredulously.

"Please explain?"

"She said her pussy was sore, we'd done it so many times. I was doing her a favour." He said and I could have sworn that I detected, just the hint of a smile.

There was a time, when I'd first joined the job, a time before tape recorded interviews, when Mitchell's reply would have merited a severe beating but, and I mean this sincerely, by the late nineties, the Metropolitan Police was a much better place. Nonetheless, and once in a blue moon, an event would have me remembering the good old, bad old, days and Mitchell's shameless response was just such an occasion.

"But you knew she didn't want to have anal sex?" I said.

"She didn't seem to mind once it was up there, boss. In fact, she said she liked it."

Oh, how I wished it was 1983!

# Chapter 9

We kept the interview going for another hour but didn't get any further, in terms of evidence. As we suspected, he started to believe what he was saying. We had an admission to anal rape, but I wanted more.

Besides, the authority had come through to take the suspect's intimate samples, so we needed to get that done before the evidence started to wane away and, by good chance, the F.M.E. had just arrived to examine another prisoner. Colin had completed the Advanced Exhibits Course, so I let him crack on. It would only take thirty minutes.

The Custody Officer told me that he'd had several phone calls from a DI at Tottenham who was trying to get hold of me and who was becoming increasingly frustrated by the fact that my mobile phone was switched off.

"I did tell the DI you were in an interview ..." He assured me.

"... oh, and there's someone at the front counter to see you." He added.

The person at the front counter was from the Probation Service and the wonderful name, by which he introduced himself was, 'Dan, Dan the Probation Man'. I took him to the canteen to fill in several forms, which were the Home Office papers required to be completed, in order to revoke Mitchell's licence.

I learnt that Mitchell Charles Manson wasn't born with that name. He had changed his name, by statutory declaration when he was eighteen, from Mitchell Donnelly. Dan spent nearly an hour filling me in on Mitchell's antecedents, which were really interesting to learn.

We faxed the completed forms over to the Home Office and had to wait for signed ones to be faxed back to us. Dan thought it might take an hour, so I asked him to wait in the canteen.

I'd completely forgotten to turn my mobile phone back on after the interviews and picked up a somewhat stroppy message from a woman who introduced herself as, and I quote, 'your new Detective Inspector'. I picked up a more important message from a woman called Sandra, who was the victim's mother, who asked me to call her, urgently. I did.

"Hi, is that Sandra? It's Chris Pritchard, here. I'm the officer in charge of your daughter's case."

"Oh Christopher, thank you so much for calling me back. We were just wondering whether you can confirm that he won't be released, will he?"

"No, Sandra, I promise you he won't. As we speak, we're revoking his licence."

"What does that mean?" She asked, before I'd had a chance to explain.

"The man, his name is Mitchell Manson, is currently on parole. What he's done, means we can cancel his parole and take him straight back to prison. We're completing that process now and he'll be back in prison, very shortly. I can confirm that, without any question or doubt, Mitchell Manson will be back in prison by, the very latest, tomorrow night. Tonight, he will be in a police cell again because before I finish here, I will charge him."

I thought Sandra might, quite understandably, question me about what he'd been in prison for, and why someone, somewhere, had decided to release such a dangerous man, but she didn't.

"Thank you, Christopher. I'm going to ask you a favour?" She said.

"Anything, ask me anything. If I can, I will." I replied, reassuringly.

"Please come and see Clare. Please tell her, to her face, what you've just told me."

"Are you sure she'll be happy to meet me. I find that sometimes, victims of ..."

I hesitated because I realised, I was about to use the word 'rape' but, after the tiniest moment of doubt, I decided not to fuck about.

"... rape, are very nervous around males, they don't know."

This was entirely true.

"Don't be silly, Christopher; although, I appreciate your consideration. Elodie said she'd come round, later. I think she starts at ten, if you could come with her, that would be perfect."

"Of course, Sandra. I'll see you at ten."

I phoned the DI back, but her phone went to answerphone, so I left a message explaining that I was tied up with a prisoner at Holloway but that I'd be back later.

Colin took me out into the yard where it was a gorgeous sunny afternoon.

"I can't leave the Probation guy, for long, Colin, what do you want? Oh, did you get the intimate samples? Is that what this is about?" I asked.

"Yes, no, I mean; yes, we got the intimate samples. Our suspect hasn't washed for a week, so I'm confident we'll find plenty of traces of the victim on him. How the poor victim managed to do it without throwing up on him is a mystery to me."

"Thanks for that, well done." I said.

"Listen Sarge, I've got a proposal." Colin said, in a slightly conspiratorial voice.

"Go on."

"Joanne Cunningham works here, now, in the C.S.U."

I vaguely knew Joanne; she had been a trainee DC on another C.I.P.P. team but she'd been transferred to Holloway when she was promoted to the substantive grade. I really didn't know her well and couldn't think why Colin was telling me this information.

"What about her?" I asked.

"Joanne is wearing a skimpy summer dress and high heeled white sandals. She looks stunning." Colin said.

"Oh, for fuck's sake, Colin, we're busy. You're a …"

"No listen, Chris…" He interrupted me.

"… I think you should take Joanne into the next interview with you. Just mix it up a bit, put him off his stride; get her to cross and uncross her legs, a few times; let her dress ride up."

I hated the idea, and I loved the proposal, in equal measure. I hated it, because the action amounted to an admission of failure, on my part. I thought, I was a great interviewer, every detective did, but deep down inside, I knew I was good, but probably no more. I loved the idea because I thought the proposal was genuinely innovative.

"What would Joanne think?" I asked.

"She's up for it. I filled her in about the allegation and why I wanted her in there." Colin replied.

Clearly, he hadn't waited to get my approval first, but in some way that was, politically, safer for me.

"Go on, then." I said.

"Well done, Sarge. I like your style." Colin replied, cheekily.

"I need a quick word with her DS to make sure he's happy with us using her." I said.

"She's up for it, too. It's Debbie Barclay. I used to work with her at East Ham, known her for years. She's as sound as fourteen ounces and as sweet as a nut; actually, she's probably the best Sergeant I've ever worked for." Colin replied.

"Great" I replied meekly, avoiding the obvious inference.

Colin had clearly not only had the idea to use Joanne but also made all the necessary arrangements, as well. I really don't know why he was asking me at all, but I wasn't bothered, he just wanted to get the right result for the victim.

"I'll tell you what; I'll sort out the licence issue with Dan Dan the Probation Man and you and Joanne do the interview. There's a drink in it for you both, if you get a hands up. It'll be a piece of cake, with Super Joanne." I said, extending my right arm upwards in a Superman pose.

Colin laughed out loud.

## Chapter 10

Within two hours, not only had we served the Home Office Licence Recall Notice on Mitchell, Colin and Joanne had obtained a complete confession. I was agog when they told me. I took a copy of the interview tape to our car in the back yard and pressed 'play', on the stereo; this, I had to hear.

The first ten minutes had involved Colin asking lots of questions such as, 'are you seriously expecting me to believe that this clean cut twenty-three year old, attractive young woman, was physically attracted to a forty year old, dirty, smelly, ex-con, who'd just got out of prison and had entered her flat, as a burglar, to steal?' and Mitchell replied with the same responses he had used with me, 'she told me she fancied me, she told me she loved me, what was I going to think?'. Then there was a short break in questioning, and you could hear a rustle of papers; a chair slide across the floor and a sweet female voice said:

"When you had sexual intercourse with Clare, you knew, didn't you Mitchell, that she wasn't truly consenting?"

"Yes, miss." He replied, quietly.

"Clare was only pretending to agree because you'd just threatened to kill her, hadn't you?"

"I had, that's right, miss. I'm sorry, miss." He replied, louder this time.

And then Joanne dropped her own voice, almost to a whisper.

"Mitch ..." She used his name in a way which would suggest they had been the best of friends for years.

" ... why did you do this to her? Clare's a really nice, normal, young lady; just trying to make her way in the world. Why, Mitch, why?"

"I'm evil. I need to be locked away, forever; please make sure they never let me out, again; if they do, I will do this again, I can't help myself ..."

He was crying now; you could clearly hear his sobs.

"...they shouldn't have given me parole, this isn't my fault, it's theirs. Please tell Clare, I'm sorry, please, tell her that I'm begging for her forgiveness. Please tell her, I know what it's like ..."

I'd heard enough and flicked the stop button on the tape player.

This was quite brilliant news and, while it wasn't a certainty, it was highly likely that poor Clare wouldn't have to give evidence.

I popped into the CSU to find Joanne and to thank her Sergeant, Debbie, who I'd never met before. Joanne was a white DC in her early forties, typical of her breed, attractive, short, trim, and very grown up. Debbie wasn't as typical, because Debbie was the first police officer who I'd ever met who was in a wheelchair. I had a chat with them both, thanked them several times over, and said I'd put something in writing to the DCI to formally record my appreciation.

As I was about to leave, Debbie asked me if she could have a word, in private. I wondered what this woman, whom I had never met before, could possibly have to say to me that couldn't be said in front of others.

"You're the guy that had that run in all those years ago with Kitty Young?"

I was, it was a long story but, in brief, Kitty Young was a young WPC who joined my relief at Stoke Newington, in about 1985. We had a several spats, she lasted three days and resigned. Then she sued the Job for racial discrimination and despite the fact I knew she'd forged evidence against me, won her case and was awarded £80,000. Oh, and she got a personal apology from the Commissioner. She rejoined Kent Constabulary the next year and took promotion. Within a few weeks of her joining Kent, and I'd been at C.I.B. at the time, we received information that Kitty was socialising with some serious criminals. If I recall correctly, she was sleeping with some big London villain, which came as a surprise to me because, for some reason, I thought she was a lesbian. When the information came in, we passed it straight to our counterparts in Kent, but they were in a right pickle because they were too afraid of the race thing to do anything meaningful, and they just filed the report.

"How do you know about Kitty?" I asked Debbie.

"Because Kitty told me. She once described you as, 'a chauvinistic pig, the likes of whom should be removed from the police in the same way that a surgeon would cut out a cancerous tumor'."

I can honestly say that the force, and the completely unexpected nature of her sentence, made me physically reel and, for once in my life, I didn't know what to say.

"Sit down, Chris; sit down." Debbie said, gently.

"Are you, her friend?" I said, as I tried to regain my composure.

"Good god, no. I can't stand her. Though, I confess, were you to hear us talk, you might be mistaken for thinking otherwise." Debbie replied.

"How do you know her?" I asked.

"Because Kitty Young is the Chairperson of the National Association of Disabled Police Officers, and I am the Secretary."

"Kitty Young's disabled now? What happened to her?"

"Disabled? No, she has dyslexia, apparently that counts as a disability, these days."

"I'd have thought the Association of Ethnic Minority Officers was more up her street."

"She was a member of Emu but left complaining that it was too dominated by men."

"You know, Debbie, I really don't know the girl. We spent three, or maybe four, shifts together and then we exchanged blows across an Employment Tribunal, and it was a long time ago. They used to call her, 'eggshells' because working with her was like walking on them. I only worked with her for a few days but, if you ask me, working with her was more like walking on broken glass. I do remember one amusing occasion, though. We went to a sudden death, and she found the victim, a male who had strangled himself with a long scarf; any way, she was so soft, she fainted and fell right into the lap of the corpse. I'd been searching another room and, when I went into the lounge, it looked, to all intents and purposes, like she was kneeling down giving him a blow job."

Debbie laughed.

"I like that story; anymore I could use at our next meeting?"

"You can't ..."

"... I won't, I'm only kidding you." Debbie replied.

"When did you last see her?" Debbie asked.

"Eighty-eight, ten years ago, but I think we actually worked together in eighty-five or six." I replied.

"Well, I've got some bad news for you, my friend. Kitty Young is your new Detective Inspector. She was posted to Tottenham this week."

"You've gotta be fucking kidding me?" I said.

"I'm afraid not, Chris. Nostrils, she referred to you as 'Nostrils'." Debbie replied, as if she had suddenly remembered.

"Yeah, Nostrils is my nickname."

"Where did that come from?" Debbie asked.

I really wasn't in the mood.

"It was a long time ago and is a very boring story." I replied.

Debbie sensed my attitude and asked the right question.

"How are you going to cope with Detective Inspector Kitty Young?"

"I don't know, any suggestions? I mean, has she got any redeeming features? Has she perhaps, grown mellower in her middle age?"

"You'd hope, wouldn't you? No, if anything, since the Hassan Achachi Enquiry, her power has grown, irrevocably."

## Chapter 11

I took great delight in informing the Custody Officer that we had sufficient grounds to charge the suspect and that we could do so, whenever he was ready. He had two prisoners to book in, so he informed the prisoner that he was about to be charged, which allowed us to get on with doing his fingerprints and photograph, and the rest of the case papers.

I had a guilty secret; I absolutely loved taking fingerprints and prided myself on taking perfect sets, every time, and always at the first attempt. It was a messy business, black ink would get everywhere, but I found the whole process strangely cathartic. When, years later, they replaced the old-fashioned ink and roller, with a new system, based on computer imaging, as a matter of principled objection, I refused to ever fingerprint anyone, again.

All things considered, we got Mitchell done in almost record time. Within twelve hours of arrest, he was charged and awaiting court, the next day. I would take the case myself, although I'd probably not be required, as the C.P.S. would do everything.

When we all regrouped at Tottenham, it was ten to nine. Dot was full of praise for Elodie, who she said, had done an outstanding job with the victim. Bob had completed the forensic examination of the scene and recovered piles of exhibits, which were stacked high in their brown paper bags, on and around his desk.

Colin amused and fascinated everyone with his recount of the interview with Mitchell who crumbled the moment he handed the questioning over to Joanne.

"She coughed, moved her chair back about two feet and turned it at an angle. Then slowly, almost seductively, with both her hands Joanne gently pulled at the sides of her dress and the hemline rose three inches to well above her knee. Then she crossed her legs, and it rose even further. She smiled at Mitchell, like she would smile across a room at a stranger to send a clear and unambiguous message that she really wanted to get to know him better. Mitchell was captivated and I was tempted to lean across the desk, and with my forefinger, gently lift his bottom jaw up from its gaping position. Then, with a velvet voice that smelt of sexual promise, she started to question him. He was like putty in her hands and responded with every conceivable right answer. There wasn't anything he didn't admit to; it was a complete and utter master class in interviewing." Colin explained.

While Colin had been talking, I'd been putting the kettle on, and Dot had walked over to one end of the C.I.D. office to pick up the big blue binder that contained everybody's duty states. A duty state was a large A3 pre-printed piece of paper, which split the week into days and, on which, you recorded the hours you had worked, as well as, your general movements and assignments during the day. It was an important document and, if someone needed to know where you were and what you were doing, all they should have to do would be to check your duty state.

Dot opened the binder, clicked open the metal bracket and removed her own duty sheet, which she placed on her desk to top and tail for the day.

"What the devil?" She said.

"What's happened?" I asked.

"Someone's shown me off duty at 1800 hours." She replied.

She went back to the blue binder and flicked through several others.

"We've all been shown off duty at 1800 hours and by DIKY." Dot said.

"That'll be our new guvnor, Detective Inspector Kitty Young. Don't worry, chaps, I'll put a line through the entry, and I'll show you all off, myself. Leave it with me." I said.

I can't say that I greeted the arrival of my erstwhile protagonist with unrivalled joy. I hadn't seen the woman for ten years but the last time I had, she'd been prepared to commit perjury and forgery to win her battle with the Metropolitan Police and she didn't give a flying fuck, that by doing so, she was going to do me irreparable damage.

But I had to be careful here, and very shrewd.

Since the public inquiry into the Hassan Achachi investigation and their declaration that all police officers were, 'unconsciously racist', the Job seemed incapable of objectively dealing with anything possessing, even the hint of, a racist slant.

There was the well-covered case of a poor Chief Inspector who, during a public order briefing, innocently used the expression, 'calling a spade a spade'. It was only a few months before his retirement, but he was disciplined and sacked. No one provided any evidence to suggest he meant it in a derogatory way, and he called black witness after witness who testified that the guy had been their faithful friend and/or colleague for decades and never exhibited a racist trait, in his life. But the Chief Inspector had to go, not because anyone believed he'd done anything wrong, but because the prevailing toxic political environment demanded it.

Now that fate had put me in a head-to-head with Kitty Young. I thought there had to be only one winner; if it was going to be me, I'd have to be smarter than smart.

No matter what, I wasn't going to let anything spoil what had been quite an excellent day. We'd caught and sent back to prison a dangerous criminal who would never be released from jail, again. In fairness, it wasn't the most complicated case, and all credit to the night duty station officer, a civilian called Nellie, who'd done all the CRIMINT searches and identified the suspect. My team had, however, dealt with the matter effectively and achieved the right result for everyone concerned; even, in a strange way, for Mitchell Manson who'd be much happier when he was inside again.

Everyone made their way home, except me. I was waiting for Elodie, who was due in at ten, and when she arrived, we would go and see the victim, Clare, and her mum, Sandra.

The C.I.D. office was a right mess; the C.I.D. office was always a right mess. It was on the first floor of the nick and, as you entered, there were four pods of desks along the right-hand wall. Each pod was the base of one C.I.P.P. team; usually comprising of a DS and three to five DCs and trainee DCs. And, just so you know, the DS always had the desk next to the wall that was facing the entrance to the room. Furthermore, as a DC, the nearer your desk was to the DS, the higher your status. It necessarily followed, the trainee DCs, like Dot, were at the other end from the wall.

Along the opposite wall, the left wall as you entered, were a thin line of desks upon which were the O.T.I.S. terminals, the computers through which you got access to your emails, CRIS (the crime recording system), CRIMINT and the electronic case papers programme.

Detectives were therefore invariably in one of three places, the Custody Suite dealing with prisoners, sitting at an O.T.I.S. terminal, or out on enquiries. Ten years previously, there would have been a fourth, the pub; but the days of drinking on duty were rapidly fading and, by and large, the job was a better place because of this trend towards sobriety.

I was at one of the O.T.I.S. terminals typing up some of the paperwork for the Manson case, when a young uniform officer came in, whose face was vaguely familiar to me, but whose name was long forgotten.

"Sarge, do you know where the new DI is, Kitty Young?" He asked.

"No idea, mate. Is it anything I can help you with?" I replied.

"Her car's parked in the back yard and it's blocking in one of our units. It's been there, all evening. I had to do a car check, as it's locked, and there's nothing on the dashboard, you know, like people sometimes leave a note and a mobile number."

"What is it?" I asked.

"It's a black BMW, three series, brand new and very nice." He replied.

"     Leave it with me. I'll give her a ring and check her office just in case the keys are on her desk." I replied.

"Thanks, Skip."

The back yard at Tottenham was the smallest backyard in the world. We couldn't park all the police vehicles in there, so there was certainly no room for officers to park their own cars.

I carried on with the case papers but, not two minutes later, an email popped up in the bottom right-hand corner which required my immediate attention. It was from DI Young and read as follows:

Report to my office tomorrow, as soon as you come on duty. Please treat this direction above all other responsibilities. I look forward to seeing you.

I read the communication twice and really didn't know what to make of it. I also wondered where she was, because she had to be sitting at an O.T.I.S. terminal somewhere. I got up and had a gander around a few of the now empty offices, but there was no sign of her. I thought about emailing her back and asking her to move her car, but something inside told me not to.

At about quarter to ten, I went downstairs and spoke to the night duty Inspector. He agreed to allow Elodie to skip parade and come straight out with me to see the victim. I filled him in on how the day had played out and he seemed genuinely thrilled that we'd arrested and charged the suspect.

## Chapter 12

I sat in the parade room waiting for Elodie to appear; it seemed less pervy than loitering around outside the female changing room. I chatted easily with the night duty guys as they came on duty, most of whom I knew well, having been at Tottenham since leaving C.I.B., three years previously. They were a great bunch, and several had spent a month working on attachment to my C.I.P.P. team during their probation.

Elodie arrived just before ten and we slipped out before parade kicked off.

I had my own car parked in the back streets which I suggested taking. No sooner had we got in the car, than we realised, neither of us had details of the address we were going to, so I drove round to the front of the nick, and parked in the middle of the carriageway, where there were a few dedicated police bays. I entered the nick via the front office, jumped over the counter, in one deft movement, and took the stairs, two at a time.

As I entered, I saw the back of a small black woman, who I guessed was the DI. She was standing at my desk and appeared to be searching amongst my trays and papers. I stopped in my tracks and reversed slightly, so that I was almost out of sight. She was ferociously rooting around and then I heard her say:

"I'm not exactly sure what I'm looking for?"

I had no idea who she was talking to, as the office was completely empty, and then I realised when a metallic voice said:

"Well, I don't know."

"I can't find anything, but his desk is stacked high with case papers." The DI replied.

I decided to walk slowly and quietly away. I thought it was better that the DI didn't know, I knew she was riffling through my desk. I went back to the car and lied to Elodie. I said that one of my team had locked the case papers in their desk overnight and asked her whether she could find the address by another means. She said she'd scribbled it down somewhere, that it was probably in her tray in the parade room and scuttled off to retrieve it.

Not two minutes after she'd gone, I saw a black BMW pull out of the back yard, wheel spin hard and speed off towards the one-way system.

There was an obvious reason for the DI's actions, she was making sure that the racist material was still planted on my desk but that didn't quite fit. For one thing, she had only just started at the nick, and I had to question whether she would be so brazen, and so revengeful, she would get involved in such a dreadful act, almost before started. It also unsettled me, she was obviously on the phone talking to someone else, who was also involved, and that didn't make any sense, either. Maybe when I met her, she would explain what she was doing.

\*\*\*

It was a fifteen-minute drive over to Dunbar Road in Wood Green, but all the way Elodie and I chatted about the victim so that I could get a feel for how to best conduct the meeting.

Elodie spoke with such a strong French accent, it was like having a conversation with one of the female waitress characters from the BBC programme, 'Allo 'Allo. Despite the slightly comedic edge this leant to the conversation, her respect and admiration for the victim shone brightly.

The house in Dunbar Road was a typical London suburb terrace, built between the wars, and the door was answered by Sandra, the victim's mum, who greeted Elodie like a long lost relative, before inviting us in, and shaking my hand. We walked through the small hallway and turned left into the lounge, which at some stage, had been knocked through into the dining room, at the rear. Sitting at the far end of the settee was Clare, a slight woman, who looked desperately frightened and extremely pensive. She was wearing an old tracksuit and had her legs drawn up to her chest, in a very defensive position. Elodie walked over and touched her knee before sitting down on the carpet next to her. It was a simple move but just the right thing to do; it was a way of saying, 'I'm here with you'. I sat diagonally across the room, in a single chair.

Elodie introduced me as the officer in the case and the person who had arrested and charged her attacker.

I smiled weakly.

"I am not going to ask you how you're doing, because I can't even begin to imagine, but I will promise you this. I will do everything, within my power, to make sure that the person who did that to you, will never get out of prison. I also promise, I will do everything I can, to make sure that you don't have to give evidence. But I can only promise you that I'll try, I can't force the suspect to plead guilty and, if he doesn't, I can't force the jury to convict him."

As I'd been talking, I saw Elodie reach up and hold Clare's left hand; her mother, who was sitting immediately on her right-hand side, was holding her right hand.

"I understand that. Elodie explained." Clare replied.

"I charged him, late this afternoon. He'll go, in custody, to Highgate Magistrates Court, tomorrow, and they will remand him in custody for trial; so tonight, he is in Holloway police station and tomorrow night, he'll probably be in Pentonville prison."

"Can I go to court tomorrow? I want to see the monster that did this to my daughter." Sandra asked.

"You can; and, if you want to go, I'll take you, but don't, please. No good will come of it. You won't see anything meaningful, and you might make the suspect feel more important because you've made all the effort to be there."

Sandra huffed and then nodded her agreement.

"Come and see him sentenced to life, instead. You'll just have to wait a little bit longer." I suggested.

Sandra nodded.

I talked the pair gently through what had happened that day. How we knew he'd be coming in to sign on the Sex Offenders Register, the fight in the interview room, his confession during interview, and, finally, the charging process.

It was obvious from the conversation, that Elodie had already explained to them, the suspect was out 'on licence' and what that meant. I was therefore a little surprised, but grateful, they didn't ask me any awkward questions which would have been better directed at the Parole Board like, 'why on earth did you give him parole?'.

Suddenly, Sandra jumped up off the sofa.

"Where are my manners? Where are my manners? Officers, please what would you like to drink? Tea, coffee, beer?"

I had to smile inside; who gave a fuck about such trivial things? Yet, here was this woman, so impeccably mannered, that she felt disappointed to have, momentarily, forgotten to offer us a drink.

I joined Sandra in the kitchen and helped her make the hot drinks; that is to say, I watched her, while she did the rest, and we chatted about anything and everything, except the real reason we were there. We returned a few minutes later with trays, pots of tea, cafetieres and an assortment of biscuits. The activities were a welcome charade that allowed us, momentarily, to forget what had happened. When the moment was just right, I asked the line I'd turned over in my mind several times.

"Clare, if there is anything you ever want to know about what is going on, you just ask. No matter what time, no matter what day, I will, if I physically can, be there for you. I may sometimes have to tell you something which you don't want to hear, but I will never, ever, lie to you; nor will I hold anything back."

She nodded.

"And the same goes for you." I said, to Sandra, but I made a joke of saying it, as if it was a bit of an afterthought.

"Thank you, Christopher." She said.

We spent the next ten minutes making small talk about several of the Spurs players. Clare was a full-time employee at the club and did something in marketing. She tried to explain but I wasn't really listening. When the hot drinks were no more, I said that it was about time Elodie and I left them to their evening, and I stood up.

"Before you go, Chris ..." Clare said, and I realised this was the first time she'd spoken directly to me.

"... I need to know, why. Why he did this to me?"

"I can tell you, if you want to know, I can tell you exactly why this happened, but I can't explain why it happened to you." I replied.

"Go on then." She said, a steely determination suddenly detectable in her voice.

**Chapter 13**

"Mitchell was born in 1953 in Winson Green, Birmingham, to a sixteen-year-old woman called Edith Stacey – there was no dad. His first few years seems to have been quite happy until, when he was six, his mother moved in a new and much older boyfriend, who's elderly father was a paedophile, with a particular taste for very young boys. Mitchell's mum and her new boyfriend often left the 'step-grandfather' babysitting. This was when the abuse started. The step-grandfather threatened Mitchell that, if he said a word to anyone about what was happening, then he would kill the boy's mother.

This abuse went on sporadically for about a year and then tragically, when he was seven, Mitchell's mother died of ulcerated intestines, which was probably undiagnosed stomach cancer, and, at about the same time, Mitchell's stepfather was sent to prison. This combination of circumstances meant Mitchell suddenly found himself living with his step-grandfather, the paedophile.

For the next four years, Mitchell was kept in the cellar of his step-grandfather's house; quite literally, chained to the wall, with a mattress and unchanged bedding on the floor, and a bucket in the corner, to use as a toilet. He was fed on scraps and, the report I've seen, estimates he didn't see the light of day for four years."

I glanced up. Clare was now sitting in the middle of the settee, with Elodie on her left, and her mum, on her right; all three were holding hands. They were captivated by the life story of the monster.

"Anyway, it will come as no surprise to you, the step-grandfather was the linchpin of a paedophile ring and he sold, 'half hour slots' to his friends and associates. Poor, Mitchell."

I suddenly realised that my use of the word adjective 'poor' to describe Mitchell was probably insensitive, and I glanced at the three sat opposite me but, as none of them seemed to have noticed, I decided not to break my tale to apologise.

"There is no doubt that Mitchell suffered the most horrendous abuse. He was buggered every day and forced into having oral sex with countless men.

When he was about ten, the step-grandfather met, and moved in, a woman called Mary, who was a fiercely devote Roman Catholic. Mitchell thought that his life might improve but it didn't. Yes, every Sunday morning, Mitchell was given a wash, in a big tin bath in the kitchen, with hot water heated from the kettle, and then changed into clean, new clothes and was taken to church: and yes, every Sunday, he shared some of the roast dinner, but by teatime, Mitchell was back in the cellar, chained to the wall.

Oh, his life changed in another way too, but only slightly. Some of his new visitors, he recognised from Church, as priests and their entourage.

His ordeal finally came to an end, in 1964, when the step-grandfather died of a heart attack. That day, Mary came down to the cellar, took the padlock off the chain, and was never seen again. Mitchell, who was now eleven, spent several weeks living in the house, on his own, before he set light to the curtains in every room, and burnt it to the ground. He was arrested by the police who attended the scene of the fire, standing there in the street, still holding a box of matches and a can of paraffin.

When Social Services researched his records, they identified, he'd only ever attended school for four terms, back in 1958 and 1959, and that thereafter, he'd completely disappeared off their radar. He was unable to read or write and had no social skills, whatsoever. Alarmingly, but perhaps not surprisingly, Mitchell had a pathological hatred of old people and, within three weeks, had been arrested for beating up the elderly woman who cleaned the Children's Home, where he now lived. Later, he was moved to more secure accommodation.

In the wreckage of his former home, the authorities found the remains of thousands of black and white photographs, which captured the most horrendous abuse upon the young child. Some of the details are simply too graphic for me to tell you.

For the rest of his childhood years, Mitchell was moved around the country, in and out of Homes. His attendance record at various schools was practically non-existent and his literacy levels never rose above that of the average ten-year-old.

In 1971 he joined the army, and for a few months, his life looked like it might get onto the straight and narrow. He was sent to Northern Ireland but got into a pub fight, during which, he bit the nose off a Military Policeman. He was court martialed, sent to military prison in Aldershot, and then, disgracefully discharged, when he'd completed his three-year sentence.

This was in 1974 and Mitchell was just twenty-one. The next year, he broke into the house of an elderly couple in Vauxhall, severely beat them, and raped the female occupier. He was caught, convicted, and sentenced to fifteen years.

He was released in 1984 but offended again, that year. He broke into an Old People's home in Streatham and raped an eighty-six-year-old woman. He was arrested and convicted, and this time, sentenced to life, with a minimum tariff of fifteen years. He was released after serving thirteen years; in fact, he was released last week.

Mitchell has a pathological hatred of old people; is a degenerate sex offender, and completely incapable of living in society. Why the Parole Board saw fit to release him, is beyond me, and on behalf of the criminal justice system, I offer you, what are probably meaningless but genuine, heartfelt sympathies."

I had been staring at the carpet, as I told Clare and her mum Mitchell's life story. I wanted sensitively to relay the story but also, honestly and dispassionately. I thought, they had a right to know.

Dan Dan the Probation Man had given me all the details, earlier in the day. He'd brought with him Mitchell's record, which ran to two full box files. It included numerous paper cuttings of the various trials, he'd been the subject of; one of which, I could have sworn, I remembered seeing; although, it had been published fifteen years ago. It was from the front page of the Daily Mirror and, underneath the headline, which read, 'The Streatham Monster,' was a picture of the face of a very old, white lady, with grey hair. Even though the photograph was black and white, the woman's face was obviously hideously swollen and terribly bruised.

We sat in silence for a few seconds. I looked up to see their reaction. Tears were rolling down both of Clare's cheeks and she made no attempt to wipe them away.

"Are you all right? Would you rather have not known?" I said, quietly.

"Oh, the poor man …" Clare said.

"… I only had to go through a few hours, he suffered for years."

Clare was crying for her attacker. I had never witnessed such a show of compassion, and for a few seconds, I held her gaze; then, I felt a tear rolling down my own cheek. In that moment, I respected Clare Maddison more that I have ever respected another human being, before or since.

\*\*\*

I dropped Elodie off back at the nick and made my way home, exhausted but happy. When I got in, I was delighted to discover that Jackie too, had just got in from work, so we sat up and chatted, over a bottle of red wine.

Jackie was a nurse at a hospital in Epping and, after a couple of years in geriatrics, she was back working in her favourite job, Accident & Emergency. In fact, that was the reason we'd met, years ago when I'd set fire to myself. A battery and some coins in my pocket created a circuit and my trousers went up in flames. I was taken to Bart's and Jackie was the nurse who looked after me. We started going out, a few days later, and were married in 1988.

We were close too; well, for a couple who had been married, so long. I'd never forget how, at the beginning of our relationship, she helped me through a few difficult times. It's a long story, better told elsewhere but for a few years, I was addicted to heroin. It really wasn't my fault, someone else had injected me, while I was unconscious, but once you've experienced the sensation of the most powerful drug in the world, it's very difficult to imagine a life without it.

I was on the drug for about three years but managed to break the habit, through a combination of sheer bloody willpower and Valium. It was probably the hardest thing I'd ever done; it was certainly the best thing. My wife, Jackie, had been brilliant throughout and I owe my life to her support, dedication, and love.

Just occasionally, I still dreamed about taking it; those were the best dreams ever.

I really struggled to give it up. The Job was very supportive, and I went to lots of counselling sessions and self-help groups. I even spent several weeks in the Police Convalescent Home. Eventually, I stopped injecting; instead, I smoked or snorted the odd bag and when I say, 'occasionally', I really mean, 'every day'.

There were times, through those dark years, when Jackie really should have left me, but she didn't. As a result, I owed her more than it was possible to express but when I was pissed, I still tried to, which was always a mistake.

We were just coming up to our ten-year wedding anniversary. I wanted to plan something special but had genuinely been too busy, so I thought I'd just ask Jackie what she fancied doing.

"Oh, that's easy." She replied.

"Go on." I encouraged her, pleased that I could stop trying to think of something.

"I want a baby." She replied.

I've got to be honest; I really should have seen that one coming.

"Don't look so horrified." She admonished me.

"Oh, I'm not worried about having a family." I replied, honestly.

"Well, you could try telling your face."

"No, you've got me wrong. I really am happy to start a family, my face looks so pissed off, because I've still got to come up with something, you know, 'a big surprise', for our anniversary."

Jackie threw a pillow at me that very nearly knocked my glass of wine, all over our nice new beige carpet, the irresponsible child!

We sat up until two; it didn't matter because we were both on late turn, the following day. By the time we went to bed, we'd done the whole bottle of wine and serious damage to a second. We were making our way upstairs when I heard my mobile's message alert activate. Assuming it was work, I went back to the kitchen to find my phone but realised, the message must have been on Jackie's, as my screen was blank. I retrieved hers from her handbag and went to take the phone upstairs, in case the message was important, but as I did so, I must have touched the green button because the message came up, which I had not intended; the message read, 'Please think about it, no strings attached'.

I frowned, who was that? I checked the caller ID, but the name wasn't in the contacts, because only the number came up, so the text was obviously meant for someone else.

When I climbed into bed, Jackie snuggled up, and we set about making our family.

**Chapter 14**

I was late turn, so I didn't have to be in until two. I set off early, because I wanted to pay a quick trip to the grave of an old colleague, who was buried in St John's churchyard, in Buckhurst Hill. Back in 1983, an I.R.A. bomb had exploded near Dawn Matthews and me; she'd been killed almost instantly and had, in fact, died in my arms. Although I was standing immediately next to her, I escaped with only superficial injuries.

The grave was on my way to work, so it wouldn't take me long, and I picked a few of the best flowers, mainly roses, from our garden. Jackie was the gardener and always teased me, saying that I was too mean to buy them, but that wasn't the truth, I thought the fact that the flowers had been grown in my garden, made them special and much more personal.

Although I only went once every month or two, when I did, I preferred going in the late morning because it meant, I probably wouldn't bump into Mrs. M, Dawn's mum. That sounds dreadful, but it wasn't. I loved Mrs. M, I really did, but if we met at the grave, I would feel obligated to stay at least an hour and I just didn't have that sort of spare time in my day. Equally, Mrs. M had become really obsessed with the fact that her daughter's murderers had gone unpunished and, with the signing of the Good Friday Agreement, even if they were caught, they would only serve a maximum of two years. I understood Mrs. M's view, of course and unreservedly, but I had to get on with my life and dwelling on the events of fifteen years ago, and letting injustice and hatred get the better of me, would not help.

I spent ten minutes at the grave, which was so well kept, it still looked like it had only just been erected. I placed my flowers and a small card which simply read, 'Brilliant old bill but a better friend'. I had a little chat and told her about the case, yesterday. I found the process quite cathartic, but I didn't for one moment think that she could hear me, or that she was somewhere, in an afterlife. The thing was, if I had died that day, I think it would have been nice if, all these years later, someone still remembered me. I think that's why I did it.

Sometimes I just sat there, and pictured Dawn's face. I'd see her, as clearly as if, she was right in front of me. And I'd think about some of her mannerisms and recall the way she used to talk to me. It was surreal but, in a really nice way, and these were the times, when I missed her the most and when I felt a pain in my heart that you can only feel, when you've lost a loved one.

I had another close mate who hadn't made it all the way, Andy. Andy was a black PC who befriended me, when I was a struggling sprog at Stoke Newington. He was a diamond, but he died from AIDS in 1988 and was buried over in North Chingford. I did visit, but not as often, as I came to see Dawn, quite simply because, Dawn's grave was on my way to work.

There was the usual array of blossom sitting in the main vase, which I knew Mrs. M filled, every couple of days, but there was a small, but brand-new bunch of flowers, and a note lay, at the foot of the grave, which seemed curiously out of place. I examined the accompanying card, on which was written, just one word, 'Dad'. Dawn and her dad had been estranged and were about to reconcile when she was killed. Seeing the card made me feel sad. I left a few moments later.

I was in early for late turn, as I was determined to make sure I met the new DI, my old adversary Kitty Young, before my tour of duty began. To be honest, I really didn't know how to play this situation. Should I be conciliatory? Or perhaps, make it clear, I was going to stand my ground? Was it best to mention the civil court case or to pretend the whole thing hadn't happened?

I even considered first speaking to the DCI but decided that wasn't appropriate because it would be putting him in a difficult position. Besides, I didn't believe in arching your line manager, certainly not without giving them a chance, first. The DCI was a nice fella, but he was weak and scared of his own shadow. He only had a few months left, until he retired, and just wanted an easy life, so whatever happened, I certainly couldn't rely on his support, no matter how right I might be.

It did cross my mind that Kitty might be equally perplexed by the thought of meeting me again, let alone, the prospect of supervising me. Having checked that she was in, I went to the canteen and brought two coffees, which I hoped would be a small, but nice, gesture.

When I entered her office, I loitered briefly in the doorway as I could hear she was on the phone; fortunately, before I had to decide whether to stay or walk away, she terminated the call and shouted out, in a friendly voice:

"Come in, Chris."

"Good afternoon, Ma'am." I replied, in my friendliest voice.

"Come in, come in; please sit down."

"I brought you a coffee." I replied, placing the polystyrene cups on her desk.

"Thank you, Chris. I'm afraid I don't, but I appreciate the thought."

It was ten years since I'd last seen Kitty Young, but her appearance didn't seem to have changed, at all. She was, as she had been, slightly overweight, with very short, black hair and small, pointy features. Her skin tone was very light black, which in colouring, was more Mediterranean than Caribbean; her voice was crisp and deliberate. She was wearing a very masculine, pinstriped, dark blue, trouser suit and an off-white, blouse. The only difference from the Kitty I remembered, was that she now wore small, circular glasses.

"Well done, yesterday. I checked the CRIS report; you charged him last night, excellent." The DI said.

"We did. Then I went over to tell the victim, in person. I did try and call you." I said.

"I know, I got your voicemail. Just try and be a bit more communicative, please, in future." She said.

Was that a bollocking?

"Of course, fortunately we don't get stranger rapes very often, so it shouldn't be a problem, again." I replied.

This was a slightly risky reply because, of course, I was telling her, if the same thing happened tomorrow, I would act in the same way.

Our eyes met properly, for the first time, and we held one another's gaze. This was an important moment and we both knew it. Was my new DI strong enough to challenge me? When she hesitated, I pushed home my advantage.

"Boss, you showed my team off duty, while we were still dealing. I hope you don't mind if I show us off at the correct time?" I asked.

"There is an overtime budget, Chris, and all overtime needs to be authorised by a DI." She replied.

"Well, the budget's delegated to the DSs and I authorised it. That's what the last DI did. I appreciate that you may want to change that, but I didn't know, and besides, we couldn't just stop dealing with the prisoner." I said, not unreasonably.

The DI chewed her bottom lip, like a chess player considering their next move.

I sipped my coffee.

"Tell me about your team." She said, reaching for a piece of paper, which I immediately recognised, as the C.I.D. staffing list.

Just for a second, the question caught me off guard.

"Um; I've got DCs Harte and Clark and a TDC Dorothy McDonald."

"What about DC Patel?" The DI asked, with her right forefinger pointed to the name of the staffing list.

"Rik's off sick with stress; I don't think he's going to be back, any day soon." I replied.

Rik was one of my oldest friends; in fact, we'd first met when we were interviewed for the Job back in '82.

"What's the story?" The DI asked.

"His dad died of cancer, last year, and his mum's got really bad heart problems. His marriage is on the rocks, and his wife's taken his boy back to Pakistan; it's a real mess. I keep in touch with him."

I was just about to add the fact that we were good friends, when something inside, told me not to. What I wasn't going to tell my new DI was, one of the main reasons Rik was off sick with stress was because he was needed to run the family's video rental shop, in Walthamstow. I mean, he was stressed, I wasn't lying, but he and his parents had tied all their money up in the business and he needed to manage that side of things, until he sorted something more permanent out. Of course, Rik shouldn't really have been working in the shop, particularly as they rented out lots of videos, he referred to as, 'under the counter', which were a combination of pirate material and illegally imported pornography, and sometimes, both at the same time.

"So, none of the stress is job related then?" The DI asked.

I shook my head.

"Tell me about DC Harte, he's the Judo champion, isn't he?"

"Akido, boss. Colin's a lovely guy; good to have next to you in a fight." I said.

"I was hoping for a more meaningful analysis, Chris." The DI said, and I felt more than a little put down.

"Colin's a recently made-up DC, who knows the ground inside out, having grown up, here. He's good with prisoners, very good with witnesses, but his knowledge of P.A.C.E. and the law can, at times, be found wanting. He's not academic and just scrapped through his DCs exam …"

I actually knew for a fact that he failed the exam but the marker, an old friend, had at my request, altered one of his answers to make sure he passed.

"… but I'd work with him anywhere and anytime."

"That's a nice thing to say." The DI said.

"I mean it. He's natural old bill, it's like, it's in his blood."

"Do you think we should be thinking about putting him forward as high potential?" She asked.

Had she not heard me? I'd said he wasn't academically bright.

"I'm not sure about that." I replied, cautiously.

"Have a think about it, Chris. We need to identify and promote more visibly ethnic minorities into the higher echelons of the service."

I wanted to reply 'why?' but I kept quiet.

"What about DC Clark?" The DI asked, once again consulting her list.

"Bob's a first-class police officer. Methodical, bright, meticulous, excellent paperwork, conscientious." I replied.

"Praise; indeed; any weaknesses?" The DI asked.

"Don't expect him to turn a prisoner." I replied.

"What do you mean?" The DI replied.

The question surprised me; did Kitty Young not know, what that expression meant?

"I mean, he's not the kind of police officer who's going to recruit many informants, boss. His strength's not so much in the dealing with people side of the job, but he's a fantastic police officer. If you combined Colin and Bob, you'd have the perfect C.I.D. officer." I replied, quite honestly.

"I don't believe in informants." The DI stated.

"They do exist, honestly." I replied as if she'd just denied the existence of god.

"What?" She asked, my reply clearly going way over her head.

"What do you mean, 'you don't believe in informants'?" I asked.

"I think they're more trouble, than they're worth. Traditionally, most corruption's been linked to relationships with informants. I think the job would be better without them, period. I mean, how can we trust someone who will inform on their own family?" The DI said.

I couldn't have agreed less but I wasn't prepared to argue, and replied simply:

"Fair enough."

"Did you know DC Clark was on a Central Board?" The DI asked.

"I know nothing about that, boss. That must have been years ago; he's never mentioned it." I replied, quite honestly.

"It was in '93. He lost his temper with a black prisoner; struck him half a dozen times with his truncheon, about the head. The poor victim had horrendous injuries to his arms, where he was trying to protect his head. I saw the photographs. The victim failed to appear at the Central Board, so they had to drop the disciplinary charges."

"Was he criminally charged?"

"No, it was dealt with internally; abuse of authority." She replied.

"Can't have been much evidence then, otherwise; the CPS would have taken him to court." I said.

"     Keep an eye on him, Chris. Clearly, DC Clarke has got severe anger management problems and some deep routed racist behaviours. I won't tolerate such behaviour."

Now she mentioned it, I did remember the case, but it was before I knew Bob, so it didn't mean much to me. The C.P.S. decided there was insufficient evidence and the Police Complaints Authority agreed but the A.E.M.O. made a huge fuss about it. As a sort of compromise, the P.C.A. backed down and reinstated the disciplinary charges. The Police Federation was furious because they could never wield such influence.

I wanted to stick up for the man who saved my life, but I decided to keep my own counsel because I wasn't going to win this argument and, even if I did, what exactly was I going to achieve?

"And DC McDonald?" The DI asked.

"Dot's passed her DC's exam but she's still doing her accreditation. She's good, sound as a pound, all round. Good with prisoners, knows her legislation, paperwork's improving with every submission ..."

"Weaknesses?" The DI asked before I finished talking.

I shrugged my shoulders.

"None really; needs to talk less during interviews and let the suspect get a word in edgeways, but that's a common mistake and we have discussed it." I replied.

"And you DS Pritchard, tell me about your strengths and weaknesses?"

## Chapter 15

The meeting with my new DI was interesting but I didn't know quite what to make of it. Neither of us mentioned our previous interactions, although it was clear from our initial few words, we'd met and worked together before.

It wasn't unusual for her to want to know more detail about the people for whom she was now responsible, most new DIs would, but I thought her focus on the negatives, the weaknesses, quite unnecessary.

She wasn't the intellectual fool that I'd originally pegged her for, all those years ago; she was much brighter and more articulate, than I'd remembered.

Nor was she a 'detective', in the sense that other detectives use the word. I wondered just how many major crimes she'd dealt with and, wouldn't be surprised, if there weren't many, if any, at all. That was becoming quite common with the new breed of DIs, many of whom had a uniform background.

If she'd made a mistake during our exchange, it was when she asked me about my own abilities, that was naïve. My reply was:

"I don't suffer fools gladly, am scrupulously honest and extremely tenacious. I've been a detective for over ten years. I've worked some of the biggest police corruption cases. I'm very good at paperwork and prisoners; oh, and I'm something of an expert on CRIS, but then, so are most of the DSs here."

"Wow; I am very fortunate to have such an experienced DS." She replied.

I knew she was being sarcastic, but to her credit, there wasn't the slightest hint of hidden intonation in her voice. I sort of respected her for that.

"Any weaknesses?" She asked.

"Of course …" I replied, almost enthusiastically.

"… it's just that none immediately spring to mind!"

I said this with a wry smile and hoped it was being obvious that I wasn't being serious.

The DI raised her eyebrows but didn't say anything.

"Of course, I have some weaknesses…" I said, quickly and before she could say anything.

"… I am very loyal to my friends and a horrible person, if you make me an enemy."

"Is that a threat?" She asked.

"No, of course not. I want us to be friends, boss."

"Good." She replied.

I was pleased with the exchange because, for a change, it had come across just how I would have wished. And then, just when I thought the conversation had drawn to a natural close, the DI asked:

"How's your issue with drug addiction?"

How the fuck did she know about that? Had she drawn all our personnel files? Was that allowed?

"I don't have one." I replied, coldly.

I was probably being oversensitive, but I was annoyed that she'd had the brazenness to ask me, and I tried to communicate my angst in the intonation of my voice.

"Good." She replied.

The meeting had ended, shortly afterwards. I wandered back into the main office where a DS from the early turn C.I.D. team was typing into CRIS. His name was Jim Beam, as in the American whisky; he was a white guy, in his early fifties. Jim prided himself on being, 'old school' which was fine, but I thought he used this stance as a cover because he'd never learnt to do anything the modern way. Jim smoked heavily and often drank before and during work, which meant his breath invariably reeked of alcohol. I didn't have a great deal of time for him, particularly as he considered himself Tottenham's most senior DS, a position I thought I deserved.

By the way, CRIS was the computer database on which details of all reported crime was recorded.

"Hello, Nostrils; what's happening, dude?" Jim said.

"Just met our new DI." I replied.

"Different, isn't she?"

I didn't reply, her office was only ten yards down the corridor, and I wasn't even certain that I'd closed the door as I'd left.

"Need to pick your brains." Jim said.

"Go on."

"You know I'm dealing with these attacks in Lordship Park."

"Remind me."

"We've had five now, always between ten pm and midnight. Young female victims attacked from the rear by a white male, who tries to strike up a conversation with them, and then grabs their breasts and touches them up. It's all very unpleasant and very frightening for the victims. He seems to be getting increasingly confident and it's not going to be long before the assaults go beyond touching."

I was vaguely aware of the issue, but as none of the offences had happened on my watch, so to speak, I hadn't paid particular attention.

"I don't know a lot about it, Jim." I said.

"I just wondered whether that geezer you charged yesterday with rape could be responsible for these?" Jim asked.

"When did they start?" I asked.

"The first attack was in April, the last week, I think, the second, was the following night."

"Well, that excludes my man; he was still in prison then. He'd only been out a few days when he committed our offence."

"Oh well, that settles that, then. It's just, he was a good suspect from the description; white, male, late-thirties, 5'6" tall." Jim replied.

"Anything else of note?" I asked.

"Yeah, he told one of his victim's that his name was Mike, and your guy was Mitch, pretty close, eh?" Jim said.

"After the April attacks, when were the others?" I asked.

"On back-to-back nights in early June, and then one, last Saturday."

That was interesting but it couldn't possibly be Mitchell Manson as he was locked up at the time of the first four offences.

"Have you got a plan?" I asked.

"I'd like to put a decoy out, but can you imagine the paperwork? And besides, we'd have to be very lucky. I mean, Saturday night is the obvious time, but he does only attack our victims, once every five weeks. Anyway, who could we get to volunteer?" Jim said.

"How about our new DI?" I suggested, mischievously.

I had only been joking but Jim took me quite seriously.

"What an excellent idea, I'll have a word." He replied.

*****

Having made sure that Jim didn't tell the DI that it was my idea to use her as the bait to capture a sex offender, I sat down to log on.

The process would take ten minutes, so I leafed through the latest copy of The Job, a monthly newspaper, produced by the Metropolitan Police, which included various articles, classified ads, and sports news. The main headline was about the rise in knife related offences, but it was all boring stuff. The older of us, who could remember the Soviet Union, referred to the publication as Pravda, in deference to its partisan, uncontroversial style.

The early turn station reception officer walked in, looking anxious. His appearance in the C.I.D. office could only mean one thing; there was someone at the counter who wanted to report something serious. As it was only twenty past one, technically, Jim should have dealt with the matter, but from the look on his face, I knew he would appreciate me stepping forward.

"What you got, mate?" I asked.

"How did you guess?" He replied, with a wry smile.

"Just a wild stab in the dark." I replied.

"There's a bloke at the front counter who wants to report a burglary."

"And you can't just create a CRIS report because?" I asked, in the friendliest and least challenging manner I could.

"Because I'm pretty certain the victim is Colonel Charles Beaulieu." He declared.

"I'll be right down." I replied.

## Chapter 16

Colonel Charles Beaulieu was public enemy number one. Several years previously, he'd allegedly had an affair with a married Royal princess, while serving as her Equerry. At the time, the papers were full of scandalous reports of clandestine liaisons and romps in stables, which were reminiscent of a British farce. I hadn't paid a great deal of attention because it wasn't the sort of story that would hold my attention. The whole unsavory affair had died a death and then, only a few months ago, for reasons which were unclear, the princess did a TV interview during which she admitted the relationship, made a public apology to her husband, and asked the country for forgiveness.

I immediately recognised the gentleman who met me in the interview room by the front counter. He was a black man, standing well over six foot, with rugged, but handsome, features. In fact, he'd have made a very credible James Bond.

He was immaculately dressed in a tweed three-piece suit and wore a matching cap; the bottom button of his waistcoat was undone, and a yellow handkerchief burst forth from his chest pocket. He stood up, as I entered, and shook my hand with confidence.

"Officer, thank you for seeing me, so quickly. I really appreciate your time." He said, his voice was immaculate, his accent solid upper class and his mannerisms perfect.

"I understand you're here to report a burglary?" I said, indicating that we should both sit down.

"I am, Officer. I live in Stamford Hill and, last night, intruders broke into my house and then into my safe. They stole something very important. Would you be so very kind and accompany me back to the scene of the crime?" He asked.

"Of course, Sir; but let me just ask a few questions, first. I am right in recognizing you to be Colonel Charles Beaulieu?"

"Yes, Officer; please call me Charles; and your name is?"

"Detective Sergeant Christopher Pritchard." I replied.

A spark of recognition lit up Colonel Beaulieu's face and he pointed the forefinger of his right hand directly at me.

"You're the young officer who was blown up by the I.R.A. bomb in Stoke Newington. Your colleague Dawn Matthews was killed." He said.

"That's nice that you remember." I replied, quite taken aback.

"You've still got the scar. Well, Detective Sergeant Christopher Pritchard, it is my privilege to meet you."

And then I remembered something about Colonel Beaulieu, which I thought I had long forgotten.

"You were captured by the I.R.A. While serving in Northern Ireland, you were captured and tortured by the I.R.A."

I pointed my finger at him in a way, which mirrored what he had done to me.

When it came out that he had been having a relationship with the princess, there were calls to have the medal, which he'd been awarded, in relationship to this incident, rescinded. Quite rightly, it hadn't, but the whole furor had highlighted the terrible time he had endured during his short time in the I.R.A.'s captivity.

"I was but it was nothing really. The media just made a huge fuss over nothing, like they always do." He replied, very modestly.

"Um …" I said, in a manner suggesting I knew him to be lying.

"Anyway, on with the business at hand ..." I said.

"Please." Colonel Beaulieu replied.

He smiled with such warmth that it was even difficult for me, even as a heterosexual male, not to be touched and impressed. There was, indeed, something very charismatic about this man.

"How did the burglars enter your house?"

"Through the front door, I assume." He replied, as if that was the most obvious answer ever.

"You assume. Did they not break it down?" I asked.

"No." He replied.

"Then how did they get in?" I asked.

"I assume they used keys, Detective Sergeant Pritchard." He replied.

"And this occurred, exactly when?" I asked.

"Well, I went to the Guards Club in Piccadilly for dinner, last night. I didn't return until two o'clock, this morning; you know how it is, drinks with a few friends in the garden, went on much later than any of us planned. When I got in, I went straight to bed. Got up this morning, went to the safe, and realised I'd been burgled."

"So, there are no obvious signs of entry." I asked.

"I don't think so." He replied.

"And what has been stolen?" I asked.

"The manuscript to my book." He replied.

"You're writing a book?" I replied.

"I have written a book, officer. It's complete and I was due to be taking it to my publishers this morning, which is why I went to my safe to retrieve it." He replied.

"When did you last see it, there?" I asked.

"Yesterday, about five o'clock, in the afternoon." He replied.

"Was anything else taken?" I asked.

"No."

"So, no signs of forced entry and only the manuscript taken?" I asked, in confirmation.

"Precisely." He replied.

"I must ask, why didn't you just call this in? You know, dial nine nine nine." I asked.

Colonel Beaulieu frowned.

"You think your telephone is being intercepted?" I asked.

"I don't think, I know it is, Officer. And not necessarily by the Service." He replied.

"What do you mean?" I asked.

"Well certain stories have reached the papers, especially recently, which could only have come from information discovered by listening to my phone calls." He replied.

"Have you reported it?" I asked.

"Is there any point?" He asked, in return.

"Could be." I replied.

"I suspect, Officer, that some of the less scrupulous newspapers have employed private investigators to intercept my calls." Colonel Beaulieu explained.

"Okay, it's not impossible; but it's almost impossible to formally get authority to intercept a call, so how could a private investigator do it?" I asked.

Colonel Beaulieu shrugged his shoulders.

I arranged to meet him in an hour, at his home address, and set off to let the DI know what was going on. Colonel Beaulieu's allegation had all the makings of what, the Met now called, a critical incident.

I tracked the DI down; she was in the Superintendent's office and the door was closed.

The Superintendent was a white female in her late forties called Jill Long, who had a reputation for always asking difficult questions; personally, though, I'd always found her as good as gold.

I could see them through a small square window in the door, they looked deep in conversation and appeared to be discussing a piece of paper, which sat on the desk, immediately between them. Just as I was focusing hard to make out exactly what the piece of paper was, the Superintendent looked up and caught my eye, so I was forced to knock to prove that I had been there for a legitimate reason and hadn't just been spying on them.

As I entered, I saw the Superintendent deliberately cover up the piece of paper with another docket. DI Young looked momentarily irritated by my interruption, but quickly regained her composure, when the Superintendent greeted me, warmly.

"Sorry to bother you but we have had an allegation of burglary from Colonel Charles Beaulieu, who is saying the manuscript for his upcoming book, has been stolen from the safe in his house in Stamford Hill. I thought you should know; I'm just on my way up to the scene."

" Stamford Hill's Stoke Newington's ground, isn't it?" The Superintendent asked.

"Most of it is but he lives in the first road on our ground, Little Orchard Lane." I replied.

"Do we know anything else?" The Superintendent asked.

"Apparently there are no signs of forced entry, so he's suggesting the suspect has used a key. Oh, and he didn't call it in, because he thinks the press are tapping his phone." I explained.

"He reported it at the front counter?" The Superintendent asked.

I nodded.

"Kitty, can you go with DS Pritchard? Come and see me, when you get back." The Superintendent directed.

"Yes, of course." DI Young replied.

"I bet it's nice to be working together again. Weren't you two PCs together at Stokey?" The Superintendent asked.

I couldn't help it, but I laughed out loud; it was such an innocent but inappropriate comment.

## Chapter 17

London never ceased to amaze me because, even in the most ordinary areas of the city, you could come across roads containing the most amazing houses. Little Orchard Lane was such a location. Stamford Hill was built between the wars and mainly consisted of larger than average, terraced and semi-detached houses. It wasn't a bad area of London, but it was squeezed between Tottenham and Stoke Newington, two of London's higher crime rate areas, and it was close to some pretty run-down council estates. The area housed a large community of Orthodox Jews, a law-abiding community, who kept themselves to themselves.

Our destination, number twelve, was a large, detached house that had been significantly extended over the years. Colonel Beaulieu's house was very impressive, a five or six-bedroom mansion, hidden behind high wrought iron gates. Entry was via an intercom system, and I immediately noticed several CCTV cameras, strategically placed, about the building.

We were buzzed through the outer defenses and met at the front door by the Colonel, who had changed out of his three-piece suit, into more informal attire. I introduced my Detective Inspector, and he shook her hand, with such elegance and grace, you could have mistaken her for a famous and very glamorous film star. And how did my Detective Inspector react? Like a smitten schoolgirl, she was all giggles and childish glee. The woman was a gibbering wreck!

As the more junior officer, I would normally have stepped back and let the DI lead the conversation, but under these circumstances, I had no choice but to step forward and take control of the situation.

"Colonel …"

"Charles, please call me Charles." He interrupted me.

"Charles, can you show us the safe, please?"

As we walked through the entrance hall, I immediately noticed numerous paintings and photographs, of both the Colonel, in his uniform, and of the Princess. There were other photographs, presumably of family members, and a few of young children but my attention was drawn to those of the Princess.

He led us into an enormous dining room, at the rear, and with his foot, moved a rug that sat on the floor, between a large walnut table and the patio windows. Beneath were a series of innocuous looking floorboards. Colonel Beaulieu bent down and, with the palm of his right hand, slid one board along about three inches; this action exposed a small circular brass catch, which he lifted, with a curled finger, to open up a hinged section of flooring to expose a medium sized floor safe, embedded in concrete.

The suspect would have had to know it was there; there was no way that the safe's discovery had been by chance.

I was a little surprised at the safe's location because, as we'd entered the dining room, I noticed that, above the fireplace, was a large square patch of wallpaper, which was quite obviously a darker shade than the surrounding area and, therefore I assumed a picture had recently been removed from the wall. I had, unconsciously, come to the conclusion the safe was therefore hidden in that wall.

Colonel Beaulieu opened the safe, by entering a six-digit combination on a small keypad, stepped back, and invited us to examine the scene of the theft. I held back to let DI Young go first, which she did, kneeling to get a closer look.

"Who else knows the combination?" I asked.

The question seemed to take Colonel Beaulieu by surprise, which was a surprise, in itself.

"I err, well, just me, really." He replied, hesitantly.

"When did you last change the number?" I asked.

"I never have." He replied.

"Is the number significant?" I asked.

"It's the first six digits of my service number." He replied.

"Now we know that, please change it when we leave." I said.

He nodded.

"So, the manuscript was in here?" The DI asked.

"It was." Colonel Beaulieu replied.

"These other items in the safe, what are they?" She asked.

From where I was, I couldn't see to what the DI was referring.

"The black wash bag contains family gold, mainly seven-ounce bars, and the carrier bag contains fifty thousand dollars."

I waited for the DI to ask the obvious question but when she didn't, I did.

"Were the gold and the dollars in the safe when the manuscript was stolen?" I asked.

"Yes, officer." He replied.

"Was anything else in there? Or just the three things?" I asked.

"Just the three, now two." Colonel Beaulieu replied.

The DI went to reach into the safe and remove the wash bag – I was aghast.

"Kitty don't touch anything." I said, instinctively.

I was just in time; she retracted her hand and stood up.

"We'll need to get everything fingerprinted." I explained, quickly, both to Colonel Beaulieu and my DI.

"Of course." He replied.

I tried hard to ignore it, but I could smell the DI's anger at my action.

"Can you tell me exactly what the manuscript was contained in?" I asked.

"A carrier bag, just like the dollars, a Sainsbury's carrier bag." He replied.

"And what was your book about, Charles?" The DI asked.

"Well, my dear, my life really." He replied.

"It's an autobiography?" She asked.

He nodded.

"And does it contain intimate details of your relationship with the Princess?" She asked.

"I don't think that's especially relevant, do you?" The Colonel replied, and there was a distinct air of command in his voice.

The DI hesitated, momentarily, but her question had been both valid and appropriate.

"I think it's extremely relevant." I replied, firmly.

Our eyes met and, in that moment, the DI's presence was strangely irrelevant.

"Yes" He replied, eventually answering the DI's question.

"And does it contain information about your relationship with the Princess which has not previously been published?" The DI asked.

I mentally congratulated her on both, an excellent question, and not giving up, in the face of the Colonel's obstinacy.

"It does." He replied.

The atmosphere hung heavily with awkwardness because we all knew what the next question was going to be.

"And what exactly does the manuscript contain that is both new and, so interesting, it merits stealing?" The DI asked, again I was pleased that she'd found just the right question.

Colonel Beaulieu hesitated.

"You don't have to tell us, if you don't want to." The DI said.

'Noooooooooooo', I thought! For a start, she should have let the question hang a little longer, and she'd have probably got an answer, and she'd just, completely unnecessarily, given him the way out.

"Then I won't, if you don't mind; terribly embarrassing, and all that." Colonel Beaulieu replied, the relief palatable both in his voice and body language.

I had to let the matter go. If I hadn't just made the DI look stupid by telling her not to touch the wash bag, I might have risked contradicting her, but I just couldn't be that disrespectful.

"I noticed on our way in that you have CCTV." I commented.

"Well, I do, Officer, but it doesn't work. The system's been down for weeks." He replied.

"I bet you'd wished, you had it fixed now." I observed.

It was an irrelevant observation, but I was interested to see his reaction. There was something very wrong about this alleged burglary. None of it made any sense and I was trying to work out whether the Colonel could have made this all up.

"I had the company out two weeks ago, it worked for about twenty-four hours and then, broke again. Yes, of course I wish I'd paid more attention."

His answer seemed sensible.

"And if the suspects did enter through the front door using keys, what keys would they have required?" I asked.

"My front door keys, two, a normal Chubb turnkey and a separate one for the deadlock." He replied.

"And who else has your front door keys?" I asked.

"My parents, but they're in Scotland, and my girlfriend." He replied.

"Have you checked with your girlfriend that her keys haven't been stolen?" I asked.

"Yes and no, they haven't. She's in South Africa on a shoot and the keys are with her." He replied.

"Do you mind if I have a look round to see if there is any other way the suspect could have got in?" I asked.

Colonel Beaulieu hesitated and, just for a second, I thought he was going to say no, but he didn't, instead, he nodded and said:

"Be my guest."

The DI and I inspected the downstairs, thoroughly, both from inside and out.

There was absolutely no sign of forced entry. As we did so, Colonel Beaulieu put the kettle on and made us tea.

When we were outside and out of his earshot, I asked the DI what she thought.

"I think it's the press, obviously. Who else would steal a book and leave a load of cash and gold?" She replied.

"Do you think he could have made the whole thing up?" I whispered.

"Why would he?" She replied.

"I don't know." I replied.

"Seems quite straight-forward to me." She said.

We sat at an island in the kitchen, sipped tea and chatted. There were times, since we'd arrived, when Colonel Beaulieu had acted really stressed but now, his confidence and charm had returned, and his conversation was easy and interesting. We didn't speak about the burglary but about our own lives, which he probed with nicely balanced questions, treading the line, with a perfect balance between interest and intrusion.

As we went to leave, I explained that the Scenes of Crime Officer would be calling later that day, and then I asked to have a quick look around upstairs, 'just in case' entry had, in fact, been made via the first floor.

"I'm sorry Officer, that's not possible." He replied, as I took my first steps towards the stairs.

"Why?" I asked, with deliberate indignation.

"I have no intention of letting you snoop around, any more than you have." He replied, firmly.

"I don't understand, we're not snooping around, we're investigating a burglary, a serious criminal offence." I replied, stopping with my right foot on the first stair.

He shook his head, decisively.

I could sense my DI was about to speak, and I had a jolly good idea that she wouldn't be saying anything to support me.

"Do me a big favour; please go and check for us. You go upstairs, we'll stay here. Just check the windows carefully and make sure there's nothing untoward. Will you do that, please?"

I removed my foot from the stair in a gesture of conciliation.

"Of course, Officer." He replied.

As soon as he was out of sight, I darted back into the dining room. I had seen something earlier, which I needed to check before we left. I just hoped the DI kept her mouth shut.

Next to the dining room table, and along one wall, was a side cabinet, which sat a couple of inches away from the wall. Behind the cabinet, you could just make out the frame of a picture or painting which I now slid out, as I suspected, before our arrival, it had been above the fireplace. It was a painting of a full length, naked woman with her back to the viewer, her head was turned very slightly, so that you could clearly identify her, as the princess. She was standing on a balcony with a coastal view, which, from the blueness of the sea, suggested a Mediterranean setting.

It was discretely done and very professionally painted and, when we weren't there, I felt certain it took pride of place in the room. I wondered whether there were similar paintings upstairs, which would account for his reluctance to let us see them.

As we exited through the iron gates, I turned left and away from our car.

"Where are you going? I need to get back to the nick." The DI asked.

"House to house." I replied, incredulously.

The DI checked her watch impatiently and huffed.

I opened my hands in a clear indication there was, really, no other option.

"Don't take any statements." She ordered.

"Sorry? We're not going to take any statements?" I said, emphasising the word, 'we're, to indicate that she should be doing this with me.

"Open the car, I need to make some phone calls; you can get on with the house to house but don't be long."

I didn't say a word but did as I was told. I was only going to do the two houses on either side, and the three opposite; but I was going to take as long as I could, just to piss her off.

## Chapter 18

The house to house took an hour and a half. My DI was absolutely steaming with anger, when I got back in the car. It was perfect.

"Where the hell have you been?" She asked.

"I've been investigating." I replied, curtly.

"It's taken you ages."

"Could have taken me half the time, if you'd helped. If you're going to come out on enquiries, Ma'am, you gotta be prepared to roll your sleeves up and muck in. Otherwise, you're just getting in the way." I replied.

I started the engine and maneuvered to pull out. I knew this was a pivotal moment in our new relationship. I really hadn't planned for things to come to a head so quickly, but sometimes, circumstances conspire.

"Don't speak to me like that." She barked.

"Like what? I haven't sworn or shouted, I'm not stroppy or annoyed, I haven't said anything that isn't fundamentally true. I used the correct term to address you, Ma'am." I said, deliberately repeating her formal address.

"You're being extremely rude and quite aggressive."

"I am being neither. I am certainly not aggressive. I am simply saying something that you don't want to hear because you know it's the truth. I did have to do house to house, in fact, I got an index for the suspect's car – now you can't criticize me for that, or can you?" I asked, sarcastically.

"You've got a registration number? How? What is it? Have you done a check?"

"I have, and no, I haven't as yet had a chance to do a check, 'cos I've been too busy, doing house to house." I replied.

"Well, what's the story?" She asked.

"I spoke to the occupiers, on either side, both Orthodox Jewish families, both were out yesterday evening and saw nothing. One knew the occupier was the infamous Colonel Beaulieu, the other didn't, but that's largely immaterial, as neither of them saw anything.

But the occupier at thirty-two, an elderly guy, in his seventies, he saw four men go through the gates and towards the front door, at ten o'clock, yesterday evening. He says, he didn't think too much about it, but when he was walking his dog about half an hour later, he saw all four men getting into two vehicles which were parked up in Meadow Road. The first vehicle was a black Jaguar, that's the registration mark he took, and the second vehicle was a white Ford transit. He said that, for a reason which he can't quite explain, it was suddenly like watching a Crimewatch reconstruction, so he clocked the index number and wrote it down, when he got home. Then, this morning he saw Colonel Beaulieu, thought everything must be okay, and threw the number away. We had to retrieve it from his kitchen bin. He says, he was suspicious because, why would someone, who was legitimately visiting an address in Little Orchard Lane, park their vehicles half a mile away, in Meadow Road? And he said, the way they were dressed was unusual, in that they all wore practically the same clothes, black pullovers, blue jeans and black boots. Oh yeah, they all wore gloves. No wonder the guy was a bit suspicious. They were all white, clean-shaven with short dark hair. Two of them carried large black holdalls, which looked like they contained tools, and other equipment. It was the two males carrying the bags that got into the van, the other two got into the Jag." I explained.

"       This is no ordinary burglary." The DI commented.

"       I agree." I replied.

"I reckon we'll discover it's the press. Let's wait and see how long it is before extracts from the manuscript start appearing in the newspapers, shall we?"

"I reckon the suspects will be private investigators, employed by the press, rather than hacks themselves. I wouldn't be surprised if they were ex-Old Bill. You know S.O. eleven two." I replied.

"S.O. eleven two?" The DI asked.

"The technical guys, the ones that break into houses and place probes. They're all part of the job's surveillance team." I replied.

"Oh" the DI responded but I wasn't entirely convinced she knew what I was talking about.

"In fact, maybe it was them?" I said, rhetorically.

But when I thought about it, that was highly unlikely. What reason would the Met have to read Colonel Beaulieu's autobiography?

We had pulled up in the back yard and I was about to get out when the DI said:

"Hang on, Chris. We need to talk."

I undid my seat belt and turned towards her, but I didn't say a word.

"We've got to find a way of working together; I know we've got history. We are both very suspicious of each other, but we must find a way through this or one of us, and I'm saying one of us because this isn't a threat, just a matter of fact, will have to move, elsewhere. Now, I don't want that, I really don't, I know you're good at your job. I know I need good Detective Sergeants to run my teams, so how are we going to make this work?"

I must admit, I was impressed. DI Young had opted for the brave but sensible approach, and she was right, either we had to make this work or one of us, probably me, would have to transfer to another nick.

"Kitty, I'm really fucked here. You're my DI, my immediate line manager, and you're bound to be set against me because of what happened at Stoke Newington. Cards on the table?" I asked.

She nodded.

"You tried to fit me up back then, in the Employment Tribunal, how I am going to trust you?" I asked.

She smiled but not unpleasantly.

"      I need a DI who's going to back me up, even when I'm wrong, you know, when I've made an innocent mistake or made the wrong call. How can I trust you to do that? You hate me, you think I'm ..."

"Please don't tell me what I think ..." She interrupted me.

"Fair enough ..." I said, conceding her point.

"So, let's agree, this is difficult for both of us. Let's try to work together and not undermine one another." I said.

"      Okay, Chris, deal. We'll meet again in a month and see how it's going. What do you say?"

The DI held out her hand and we shook.

If I am being entirely honest, I wasn't quite sure how I felt but I'd give it a go for a month.

# Chapter 19

Normally, at a weekend and, if it was quiet, the C.I.D. officers would only do four hours each and then fuck off, but with the DI in, that wasn't going to happen. So, instead of making a move at six, I stayed on until the DI had gone, at eight. I didn't go out again, but did correspondence, and generally caught up on some paperwork, mainly relating to the Mitchell Manson rape.

My team were all in, so we had a bit of a natter and caught up on the gossip. Dot was telling us all about a couple of abandoned puppies which she was looking after for the R.S.P.C.A. and how she was trying to persuade her husband that they should permanently adopt them.

Colin was recounting stories from his internet exploits, with several women. He was the only one with the internet at home and, he explained, you could speak, in real time, to other people in what he called, 'chat rooms'. It was, he said, the best way to arrange to meet women, as you didn't have to leave your couch, to get a date. He reckoned that, in ten years, traditional dating would be consigned to the history books.

I noticed Bob was quieter than usual and was just wondering whether anything was wrong when he asked if he could have a quick word in private.

I was a little taken aback, because Bob was one of those self-contained, sensible individuals, who you'd never imagine would need anyone's advice. Even Dot and Colin looked surprised by the unusual request and, as we walked off, I saw them pulling facing at each other, as if to say, 'what the fuck's going on?'.

We found an empty room in the Criminal Justice Unit and took our positions across a single desk.

"How can I help you?" I asked.

"I've got an emerging situation and I'd appreciate your advice." Bob said.

I laughed but not unkindly.

"Christ Bob, an 'emerging situation'. What's the problem?"

"I was door stepped this morning." He replied.

"Sorry, door stepped. By whom?" I asked.

"Some reporter." He replied.

"A reporter? What in god's name is that about?" I asked.

"He wanted a comment from me about a relationship." He replied.

"Go on …"

"A relationship they suggest I'm having with Katie Sumers." He replied.

"A Katie Sumers or *the* Katie Sumers?" I asked.

"The" He replied.

Katie Sumers was a former British gymnastics champion who'd represented G.B. in several Olympic games. She'd retired about ten years ago and was now a sports reporter and, really well-known, TV personality.

"And how do you know Katie?" I asked.

"We go to the same gym; we met about a year ago." Bob replied.

"Which gym?" I asked.

"One in Chigwell, the David Lloyd, do you know it?"

I nodded.

"And are you having a relationship with her?" I asked.

Bob nodded.

"And why is that especially news worthy? I mean, you're single, right?" I asked, realising, as I did, that I knew very little about Katie Sumers.

"Because she's married with three children. I don't know if you remember but last year, their youngest got leukemia, it was in the news..."

Now he mentioned it, I did, vaguely.

"... they set up this big charity fund thing to pay for research into childhood leukemia. They got, like, millions in donations. Now, she's going to look like a real bitch, isn't she? You know, what the media's like in this country, they'll bloody well destroy her."

Bob had a point; the press seemed to like nothing more than to build someone up so they could knock them back down. To compound matters, the contemporary image of Katie Sumers was of one clean-cut, highly popular, perfect wife and mother, so her fall from grace would indeed be newsworthy.

Bob shrugged his shoulders.

"Do you know where the reporter was from?" I asked.

"No, I was too shocked. He did thrust some form of ID in my face, but I just ignored him and went to my car." Bob replied.

"What exactly did he ask you? It might be important."

"Did I have any comments in response to the suggestion, I was having a relationship with Katie Sumers'. I ignored him. I didn't say a word. Then he followed me down the street and asked, 'How long have you been having an affair with Katie Sumers?' He asked that question twice, but I just got in the car and drove off."

"How have you been found out?" I asked.

"No idea." Bob replied.

"Have you told anyone? Anyone at all?" I asked.

"Yeah, you." He replied.

"Have you spoken to Katie about what happened this morning?" I asked.

"No, I can't get hold of her. It's a Sunday and she's not working today, so she's at home with the family, it's not like I can just call." He replied.

"When are you next due to meet? You have to warn her, as soon as possible." I said.

"Monday evening, tomorrow, at the gym, as usual." He replied.

"Do you think her old man has got wind of it and told the press?" I asked.

"I don't think so. He's a volatile character; not afraid to use his hands to make a point, if you know what I mean. And he's on the gear, which makes him unpredictable. If he'd have got any inclination, from what Katie has told me, he wouldn't have been able to keep it to himself." He replied.

"That seems fairly conclusive; it must be someone at the gym." I suggested.

"Possibly, I suppose."

"     And let's assume it's someone at the gym, a receptionist or maybe another customer, how much could they possibly, actually know, for a fact?" I asked.

"Not much and nothing for definite." He replied.

"And if it is an employee at the gym, that's how they'd know where you live, because of your membership records and all that." I suggested.

"That makes sense." He replied.

"Listen, you want my advice? Don't contact Katie and stay away from the gym for a while ..."

"But she needs to know what's happened, they might door step her, too." Bob interrupted.

"I know. I'll go to your gym, tomorrow, and speak to her.  I'll let her know what's happened and I'll get her take on it. How's that?"

To be honest, I'd never really had the chance to make amends for Bob's actions when he saved my life, and this seemed like the perfect opportunity.

"Cheers, Nostrils. I mean, if this were to get into the papers ..."

Bob shook his head from side to side slowly, as he considered the consequences.

" … I gotta think about my mum, she's eighty. She'll have a coronary if this hits the headlines. And Katie's old man will go mad."

Something about Bob's comment about Katie Sumers's old man, jogged a memory.

"Her old man, wasn't he in the papers about something quite recently?" I asked.

"He got an O.B.E. last year for services to the community.  He fronts up a lot of stuff about drug rehabilitation, but the irony is, he's on the gear himself. That's what you're probably thinking of. Katie reckons it's because the powers that be, needed the knighthoods and all that bollocks to better reflect the population, so they went out of their way to identify recipients, who didn't reflect the white, Church of England, middle and upper class population. Her old man's a Londoner, through and through, a bit rough round the edges, and all that, so he was the right sort of person, in the right place, drug rehabilitation, at the right time."

"Do you and Katie see a future together?" I asked.

"I don't know. We were quite happy having an affair. We'd never talked about anything more serious. The relationship's fairly intense, though; you know, we'd told each other we loved each other, stuff like that. Now, I don't know what's going to happen."

It never ceased to amaze me, how people can shock you. Of all the guys I knew, both in the job and on civvie street, I would never have thought that Bob Clark would have got himself into a situation like this, because he was just so dependable and, well, not to put too fine a point on it, a bit boring. Although, I'd never previously thought about it, if I had, I would have probably thought Bob was gay.

"Did you say anything to the reporter?" I asked.

"Nothing, not a word. Look, I'm really worried, Nostrils, this really isn't the sort of thing I want to have to deal with. Any advice, I know you've been in a few scrapes in your time?"

"Have you thought about ending the relationship? I mean, it would be a step towards resolution, and it would give you a stronger position to take with the media."

Bob shook his head.

"No can do, Nostrils. I love Katie, too much." He replied.

# Chapter 20

My team were early turn on Monday and there were three prisoners in the bin from night duty. Two were in for the same assault, on an eighteen-year-old, who'd been GBH'd; and a third, had been stopped and searched and found to be in possession of a laptop, stolen during a burglary at Dixons, a few days ago.

Dot and Colin took the assault and Bob the handling. They all seemed pretty run of the mill.

I had been at Tottenham police station for the last three years. It was an interesting place to work, busy, without being stupidly so, but the place was best known for a council estate called 'Plymouth Rock'.

On a quiet Sunday evening in 1986, a PC had been murdered by a gang of black youths on the Plymouth Rock estate and, like half of the Met, I'd spent many hours, over the months following his death, patrolling that concrete jungle. I was at Stoke Newington at the time, which is only a couple of miles to the south,

Since those days, the Rock had attracted millions of pounds of government investment and, as a result, the place had changed, almost beyond recognition, from the dour estate, I'd patrolled, some twelve years ago. In the old days, the ground level had effectively been a large car park, containing mainly wrecks and burnt-out, stolen vehicles. Life existed on the first level, where concrete walkways linked one area to another. These walkways had become notoriously dangerous for ordinary residents to use, with robberies, at an epidemic level, and drug related anti-social behaviour, everywhere. Burglaries were also out of control, as the criminal element targeted the old and the vulnerable.

Now, the walkways had gone, as had, the burnt-out cars. The place had an excellent children's play area, manicured gardens and, perhaps most impressively of all, a complete absence of graffiti.

In fact, crime was so low that the dedicated police unit, the Plymouth Rock Estate Unit, had been disbanded in 1996 and, I'd been recently told, the place was technically one of the most crime free parts of the whole of London. It was a staggering transformation and someone, somewhere deserved a lot of credit.

The world did inherit one thing from the Plymouth Rock Estate that in my humble view, it could really have done without, Councilor Anna Abolla. Anna had been the Chair of the Plymouth Rock Youth Association, at the time of the PC's murder, and had earned notoriety or fame, depending on your point of view, when she declared that the 'PC had bloody well got what he deserved'. She claimed, the police abuse of their stop and search powers had caused such resentment among the local community, it was only right and understandable, the 'people had risen up against the racist oppression of the Metropolitan Police'.

Anna was only young, at the time, in her late teens, but political figures from the Labour party had fallen at her feet to ingratiate themselves and, a decade later, she was now a leading light in the Labour controlled Haringey

Council. In this role, she did everything she could to make the police's job as difficult, as possible. Indeed, a few years ago she withheld funding until police stop and search figures in the Borough, 'truly reflected the ethnic mix of the population'.

But Anna now had a problem. She'd recently been caught up in a scam involving the issue of British passports to illegal immigrants. The original allegation involved her sister, who was accused of providing counter-signatory services for people she'd never met, in return for cash. When the sister was arrested and interviewed, she immediately implicated Anna in a complicated conspiracy, with another relative, who worked in Immigration at Lunar House in Croydon. When I dug further, I discovered that, over the last eight years, her sister had counter-signed some eighty passport applications. Anna, herself, had done, at least a dozen, right at the inception of the scam. Okay, she'd done these some eight years ago, but it did support her sister's story that the whole thing had been Anna's idea, in the first place. The corrupt Immigration Officer had also pointed the finger at Anna but when he'd been released on bail he'd disappeared, probably out of the country, so there was little chance of seeing him again.

I'd interviewed Anna under caution. She was with her brief and no commented, but she did produce a written statement in which she claimed to have no knowledge of the fraud and said that her sister had forged her signatures on the applications.

Then I'd discovered several payments going into her bank account from the Immigration Officer and I thought the case was made, but the C.P.S. had other views, and wanted me to get some handwriting analysis undertaken. I'd used handwriting analysts before and wasn't terribly keen to go down that route again, simply because, in my experience, they never sufficiently committed. They would use terms like 'probably' and 'likely' and 'strikingly similar', but they would never commit to a definite identification, and in cross examination, any decent defence barrister could get a witness to turn a 'probably' into a 'possibly', and bang goes your case.

I got the distinct feeling that the C.P.S. weren't all that keen on prosecuting a black activist and rising star of the left but I would do my best to convince them otherwise, after all, I'd taken an oath that said I would discharge the law 'without fear or favour', and I intended to do just that.

I was reviewing the file when the Station Reception guy from Early Turn walked into the C.I.D. office.

"What you got?" I enquired, politely.

"There's a woman downstairs who says she wants to report a rape; I haven't asked her any questions. I've put her in the interview room." He replied

"Sounds like a case for the C.I.D. Let me go to the loo, grab a pen and paper; I'll be down in two minutes." I replied.

**Chapter 21**

Sitting in the interview room was a very ordinary, white lady, in her late twenties, wearing jeans and a blue T-shirt; her dark hair was tied up in a bun. Very noticeably, she had a large notebook open on the table, in front of her, and was holding a pen, in her right hand, as if she was about to start writing notes, at any second.

I introduced myself and she wrote my name down, at the top of the page, underneath where she had already recorded the date, time and location.

These were not the actions of your average rape victim, and immediately, I was on my guard.

"I understand that you would like to report a serious offence." I said, choosing my words, carefully.

"I would like to report a rape." She replied, in a very matter of fact way.

"Please tell me everything you can. If you don't mind, I'll make notes as you talk, so please don't be offended, if I am not always maintaining eye contact." I replied.

It was my stock phrase for these situations.

"Yesterday, my sister was raped, and the suspect is a police officer who works at this police station."

My alarm bell went off; only another police officer would use the term 'suspect'.

"Do you know his name?" I replied.

"He said his name was Tristan." She replied.

"Are you in the job?" I asked.

"I am. I'm a DS at the Crime Academy." She replied.

"Can I ask your name?" I said, tentatively because, for some reason, I sensed the question, despite its validity, might annoy her.

"I am Karen Blubecker." She replied.

"Is that your sister's surname, too?" I asked.

"No, she's Costa, Marianne Costa."

"Where's Marianne, now?" I asked.

"She doesn't want to pursue this, but I do, so I am making a third-party report of rape." She replied.

The concept of the third-party reporting of alleged sexual offences had only recently been introduced and this was my first experience of it.

"Would you feel more comfortable talking to a female officer?" I asked, aware that I would have to ask some intimate questions.

"No, you'll do." She replied, disingenuously.

"Karen, can you tell me the story, from the beginning?"

"Story? Are you suggesting my sister has made this up?" She responded, angrily.

"Not at all; I apologise, if I used the wrong word. Please just talk me through what happened?" I replied.

Karen took a deep, impatient breath and frowned, as if she was considering whether or not she was going to accept my apology.

"Marianne was in the Anne Boleyn, yesterday lunchtime, with an old school friend. They were sitting in the garden, when they got chatted up by two blokes, who said they were police officers. She was like, 'my sister's a police officer, do you know her?', and anyway, they got on really well and then they decided to go to a hotel, you know, for some, you know. Anyway, while they were there, she was raped."

It wasn't the most convincing 'story' I'd ever heard; nor the most detailed. I needed to try to put some meat on the bones.

"Do we know Tristan's surname?"

"No"

"Do we know the other guy's name, the one in the pub?"

"No" Karen replied but there was an intonation in her voice that I couldn't quite interpret.

"Which hotel did they go to?" I asked.

"The Traveller's Lodge in Wood Green." She replied.

"Did your sister see a warrant card, or did anything else happen, to confirm they were actually police officers?" I asked.

Karen shook her head.

"What happened to Karen's friend?" I asked.

"She went home on her own, before it all happened." Karen replied.

The questions were going to get awkward and difficult, but they had to be asked, no matter how painful.
"Did your sister go, willingly, to the hotel?"

Karen nodded.

"At what point did she withdraw her consent?" I asked, pleased that I'd probably selected the appropriate question.

Karen shuffled in her seat but didn't respond, immediately. I waited. I knew better than to fill the silence.

"She withdrew her consent, at the hotel." Karen stated, curtly.

"At what point?" I asked, my voice, as gentle and unchallenging, as I could make it.

"When the bastard, without asking, put his penis in her anus." She replied.

"And when she withdrew her consent, how did she communicate that to this Tristan?" I asked.

Karen looked really, really, uneasy – she clearly had something to tell me which was not going to cover the family name in pride. I had already guessed, but eventually, she came clean.

"My sister was …"

She paused.

"Karen, whatever you're going to say, I won't be shocked or judgmental, I promise."

"… thank you …" She said, almost resentfully.

"… my sister was having sex with both men but, while she was in a compromising position, the Tristan guy took advantage and forced his penis into her anus. At first, she didn't know what was going on and thought she was having a poo. When she realised, she told him to remove it."

"And did he?" I asked.

Karen nodded.

"Immediately?" I asked.

The question was potentially key to whether an offence had taken place and Karen would have known this.

"I don't know; you'll have to ask her." She replied.

"Will she talk to us? Does she know that you're here?"

"No" She replied.

I didn't know to which of my two questions Karen's, 'no', related but it was immaterial. Besides, it was my own fault for asking such a poor question, after all the interview training, I'd completed, I really should have known better.

"Do we know the room number at the hotel?" I asked.

"I'm thinking crime scene." I added, unnecessarily.

Karen shook her head.

"Look, please don't overreact, but I have to ask ..."

I paused, waiting for her permission to go ahead with my question; she nodded.

"... how much had your sister had to drink?"

"They had two bottles of white wine, between them." She replied.

"How did they travel to the hotel? It's too far to walk?" I asked.

"I don't know." She replied.

That was probably a lie, I suspected that her sister had driven them, something which Karen wouldn't want to admit, having just told me she drunk at least a bottle of wine.

"I'll go to the hotel and try to speak to whoever was on." I suggested.

Karen nodded.

"Have you got any descriptions of the men?" I asked.

Karen, again, shook her head.

"I'll check the pub for CCTV. Did Tristan say where he worked?" I asked.

"Here, at Tottenham." She replied.

"In uniform? Do we know any more details to help identify him?" I asked.

Karen flicked through a few pages of her notebook.

"I've checked Aware; there is one Tristan at Tottenham, a Tristan Jones, who's on a Home Beat; but this male told Marianne, he was on the Robbery Squad. Do you have a Robbery Squad?" She replied.

"We do, but it's based at St Anne's Road. I thought I knew most of them, but I don't know a Tristan. Perhaps the CCTV will help. If Tristan Jones is the Home Beat officer, Taffy Jones, then I very much doubt he's our man, Karen. Taffy is in his mid-fifties, completely bald, and he walks with a limp because, the last thing I heard, he's waiting for a hip replacement. In fact, I haven't seen him in weeks, so he may have gone off sick, to have the operation."

"Look, sorry what was your name?" Karen asked, her voice now more conciliatory.

"You seem a decent enough guy. I know, without a victim, you've got very little you can do, and I'm not entirely sure they were actual police officers, but I want this recorded. You do that, and I'll speak to Marianne and get her to substantiate, I promise." Karen said.

"I'll create a CRIS report. I'll go straight to the Anne Boleyn to make sure I secure any CCTV; shall we exchange mobile numbers?"

"What do you do at the Crime Academy?" I asked, as Karen stood up to leave.

"I'm an instructor on the Sexual Offences Investigation Techniques Course." She replied.

## Chapter 22

I tried to find the DI, but she was out at some local council event, so I decided to make the initial enquiries to secure any evidence that might otherwise be lost.

I would normally have taken one of my team with me, but they were all dealing with prisoners.

Although there were numerous CCTV cameras, scattered about the inside and the outside of the Anne Boleyn public house, the landlord informed me, the system had been inoperative for months. A quick glance around the surrounding residential streets, drew a blank, too. Nor did the landlord remember two men and two women sitting together, but he did point out, he probably wouldn't have noticed them because he rarely ventured into the garden. His staff did the glasses collections, as it allowed them to have a quick cigarette. The staff that might have seen them, weren't on today, but I took a note of when they were next on, so I could come back and speak to them.

I had more luck at the hotel. The manager confirmed, yesterday afternoon, a person purporting to be a police officer had blagged a room, on the pretense, he and his colleagues needed to conduct some observations on an address opposite. There were four of them, three men and a woman, and he gave a good description of the guy, who did most of the talking.

"Did he show you a warrant card?" I asked.

"He flashed something at me, it looked official, but I don't think I've ever seen a warrant card before, so how would I know?" The manager replied.

I pulled out my own and opened up the small black leather wallet.

"Was it like this?" I asked.

He nodded but I wasn't awfully convinced. Then I realised, I'd almost missed something.

"How many of them were there?" I asked.

"Four. There was an attractive woman, late twenties, and three other blokes. They all looked like police officers to me, although I did notice that they smelled of alcohol and had clearly been drinking." He said.

Of course, I now knew that the victim had willingly gone back to the hotel room with three other men and suspected, she probably wouldn't be terrible keen to tell her account to a court.

I asked the manager, a thick-set Londoner, in his forties, to show me the room they used, and he did, but the bedding had been changed, several hours ago, and had already been collected by the dry-cleaning service. The room was spotless, and I doubted we'd recover any forensic evidence, but we had to go through the motions. I thought it possible we'd get a print or two, from somewhere.

"What's this about then, mate?" The manager asked, as I stood there glancing around the room.

"A female has made an allegation that she was assaulted in this hotel, by several men, one of whom, said he was a police officer." I replied.

"What? The woman who was with them?" He asked.

I nodded.

"What was their demeanour like?" I asked.

"What do you mean?"

"If they told you they were police officers, did you think they were working? Or were they, like, all mucking around and laughing?"

It was a leading question, and I knew it wasn't the best that I'd ever asked but the reply should help me to assess the situation.

The manager shrugged his shoulders and replied:

"The one that spoke to me, that guy, he seemed sensible and quite serious. He said they needed to use a room that overlooked the main road, so they could see the front door of a house, on the opposite side. The woman kept laughing, giggling nervously, and one of the other guys kept making stupid comments and like, winking at her. If I had thought about it, I'd have thought they were flirting but I really didn't pay much attention, mate. I was just thinking whether they'd be in the room for very long 'cos we were fully booked, so I'd have to do some juggling around."

"And how long were they in here?" I asked.

Again, the manager shrugged his shoulders. It seemed his automatic response, when asked any question.

"An hour, no more." He replied.

" Did you see them leave?" I asked.

"Vaguely aware, I was booking in another customer. The guy called out, 'thanks' and they fucked off. I was just pleased to have the room back. As it turned out, I didn't need it because we had four no shows, yesterday."

"Do you reckon they were genuine old bill?" I asked.

"When I think about it, yes.." He replied.

"How can you be so sure?" I asked.

"Because they didn't pay, and they didn't bung me a few quid. Only old bill would behave like that." He replied.

He did have a point.

The manager left me in the room, when his pager went off, to indicate that there was a customer at reception. I had a thorough but careful look around the room to see whether I could find anything relevant, I couldn't.

I called the DI, she answered, almost immediately.

"Boss, it's Chris Pritchard. You really need to come down to the Traveller's Lodge, on the High Street. We've had an allegation of rape and the suspects might be police officers." I said.

"From where?" She asked.

"I don't know yet, but this is the scene and one of the suspects blagged a room, yesterday, by pulling out a warrant card and claiming to need it for obs."

"Obs?" The DI replied.

"Obs, observations, surveillance." I replied.

"For what job?" She asked.

I thought the DI was not grasping the situation but tried not to let my frustration show in my voice.

"I don't know, I don't think there was a job. I think they wanted to get access to a hotel room so they could have sex." I replied.

"Did they pay for the room?"

"No" I replied, with growing frustration.

"So, we've got an obtaining services by deception, a section three, seventy-eight." She replied.

It was obvious that the DI was struggling to grasp what I was trying to explain. I also thought she was completely missing the important point, that potentially, we had a serious indecent assault committed by serving police officers.

"Boss, we have a third-party allegation, made by a serving police officer, that her sister was raped in this hotel room, where I'm standing, yesterday afternoon, by three serving police officers." I replied.

I didn't think I could put the issue, any clearer.

"Chris, you're going to have to deal, I'm about to go into a meeting with the Deputy Leader of the local council."

"I'm going to call C.I.B., boss. This should be referred to them. I shouldn't be dealing with it, anymore." I replied.

There was the slightest of delays while, I assumed, the DI considered my proposal.

"You will not contact C.I.B., yet. Continue with your enquiries and I'll call you when I'm free. I should be about an hour." The DI said and then she hung up the phone.

I was a bit flummoxed. That was most definitely not the right call, but I needed to get back to the nick and type up the DETS to show me informing the DI and her decision not to inform C.I.B. Then, whatever subsequently happened, I'd be covered.

I told the manager not to let anyone else use the room until we had conducted a thorough forensic examination, thanked him for his cooperation, and headed back to the nick, where I checked in on Colin, Bob and Dot. The two for the assault were just being bailed and Bob had charged the other prisoner with handling and was just doing the fingerprints and antecedents.

I got hold of S.O.C.O. and asked them to do a thorough examination of the hotel room and I made sure the CRIS report recorded the fact that I had informed the DI and that it was her decision not to inform C.I.B., I rather generously added the words 'at this stage' to soften the tone of the entry.

As it transpired, the DI never did call me back, nor did she return to the office, well not before I left, at five o'clock. I had to be away on time because I had a favour to do for Bob. I had to meet his famous girlfriend and explain what had happened to her boyfriend, on Sunday morning.

## Chapter 23

I must confess, if I hadn't known she was going to be there, I would never have recognised her as the famous TV personality. For one, she was much shorter than I'd imagined, and secondly, she was wearing large, square-rimmed, designer sunglasses that covered up much of her face.

"I'm sorry. I don't do autographs when I'm not working." Katie Sumers replied, impatiently.

"No, I don't want your autograph but five minutes of your time?"

Apparently, mistaking me for a stalker, a look of concern flashed across Katie's face, and she looked around, nervously, presumably, to see whether there was anyone else around, to whom she could call for help. I stepped back and away from her, to indicate that I wasn't a threat, while simultaneously reaching for my warrant card, which I pulled out, from my back pocket.

"Please, don't be afraid, I'm a police officer." I said to reassure her.

"Is it one of the children? Oh my god, what's happened?"

The assumption that it must be bad news, when a police officer knocks at your door, or otherwise, approaches you, is very common and, one of the reasons, why most officers learn to start every conversation, with members of the public, with the introduction, 'it's nothing to worry about ...'

"No, it's nothing to do with your children; it's to do with Bob." I said.

"Bob who?" Katie replied, with such conviction, I thought for a moment, perhaps, my Detective Constable had made the whole relationship up.

"Bob Clark, my colleague and my friend." I replied, gently.

Katie eyed me up and down suspiciously but didn't utter a word.

"Bob has asked me to meet you." I said.

Still, Katie held firm.

"Look Katie; we can have this conversation here, in public, standing outside a busy entrance to the gym, or we can have it in private. I know which I'd prefer."

"Let's take a seat in the café." She suggested.

"That's not a good idea, I think we should speak in private. Look, I'm a friend of Bob's. He was meant to meet you today, here, now, but can't, and he asked me to come, instead, to explain what's happened. I am not a threat to you, just come and sit in my car for five minutes and everything will become clear."

I could almost hear Katie's mind turning my words over.

"No, you come and sit in mine." She replied cautiously and, turning on her heel, walked briskly over to a large, brand new, silver, four-wheel drive Lexus.

Katie got in the driver's seat and indicated that I should sit in the passenger seat, but she left her door open, and told me to do the same. I understood her actions, which were very sensible under the circumstances. She raised her sunglasses and eyed me up and down.

"Show me your warrant card, again." She ordered, before my bottom had even touched the seat.

I handed it over and, as she carefully examined it, I took the opportunity to take a closer look at the famous Olympic gymnast. Katie was in her mid-thirties, blonde and attractive, but she had very potholed skin and had obviously suffered from severe acne, as a teenager, which had left several scars on her cheeks and chin. But, of course, I was seeing Katie on the way to the gym, not on her way to a night out on the town, or just before she was about to appear on TV. She also had noticeably large shoulders and, if I'd not known her former occupation, I would have guessed, she'd been a swimmer. She was wearing black leggings, a black T-shirt, and white trainers.

Katie started to remove some of the miscellaneous bit and pieces, old receipts, a Tesco's loyalty card and a photograph of my wife, from the additional pouch in the warrant card cover.

"Do you mind?" I asked, with mock indignation.

"A friend told me that, if you want to know if a warrant card was genuine, you should check for junk. He said, all police officers carry personal stuff in their warrant cards and that, if there isn't any, you should be very suspicious."

Katie was right.

"Bob's absolutely right. " I replied.

Katie returned my warrant card.

"Okay, so I believe you're a real police officer. If you know this Bob, as you claim, tell me something about him." She asked.

"Um, he lives alone in a police flat, in Wanstead." I replied.

"Which floor is the flat on?" She asked.

"No idea, I've never been there. I think it's a place called Buxton House, I mean, I've been to Buxton House but never to Bob's flat. They're two-story buildings, two separate blocks, with garages round the rear."

"What else do you know about him?" She asked.

"He runs and he's a keen photographer; in fact, he won the Met's photographic competition last year, with a picture of a Kingfisher. He used to be a really good boxer, when he was younger. Listen, Katie, he's a DC on my team, I'm his DS, my name's Chris Pritchard, as you can see from my warrant card. Perhaps, he's mentioned me to you? We work at Tottenham together in the C.I.D., we work with Colin and Dot."

Katie shook her head as if the information I was imparting meant nothing to her.

"You're fucking kidding me! He's never mentioned us, not once. Now I'm really insulted." I said, with just a little, genuine indignation.

Katie's face burst into the loveliest of smiles.

"Of course, he's mentioned you. Now, why did he send you to talk to me? What's happened? He's not dumping me, is he?"

"No, he's not. But yesterday morning there was a journalist outside his home address asking him questions about his relationship with you?"

Katie grimaced and pulled her door closed. I mirrored the gesture.

"Shit." She said.

"He didn't say a word and he's not sure where the guy was from."

"Shit."

"It's just possible it's someone at the gym trying to make a few quid by selling the story to the papers. That's why he thought it was better not to come today. That's why he asked me to speak to you."

"Shit."

"Have you had any indications that your relationship might be compromised?" I asked.

Katie shook her head and appeared deep in thought. We sat there in silence for a good minute.

"Is Bob going to finish with me? Is that why you're here?" She asked.

"You just asked me that, no."

"Good, because he's really important to me, but I'm going to need time to think."

"Has your husband got any idea?" I asked.

"I don't think so. Well, I bloody well hope not."

"What does your husband do?" I asked.

"He stays at home and looks after the kids. Well, it's the sensible thing because I can earn much more money than he can."

"Wasn't he your coach?" I asked, pulling the question from a distant memory.

Katie nodded.

"He's a lot older than me."

"Would I have heard of him? Is he famous like you? I'm just wondering, how I knew he was your coach" I said.

"No, not at all; he did get an O.B.E. last year and there was some publicity, perhaps you saw that? There were a couple of articles in some magazines. *Hello* did a piece on both of us and the kids, he was in the Mail on Sunday Magazine, which published a long interview with him. It's made him a bit of a cult figure, or that's what he thinks, anyway."

"So how will your husband react, if he were to find out?" I asked.

Katie shook her head.

"Like any husband would, I suppose." She replied.

Katie took her sunglasses off and threw them on the back seat; then, she rubbed her face with her hands as if she was trying to clear her head.

"Steve will go insane. He'll do everything he can to destroy me. Despite his public persona to the contrary, he's not a nice man, Chris, and I don't want to be with him, another minute. But he'll want the kids and I can't let that happen. The thing is, the papers love him, but they don't know anything. They don't know what he's really like. They don't see the bruising or find the traces of white powder in the bathroom."

"Is he a good dad?" I asked.

"Not really; he's very short tempered and …"

Katie hesitated.

"Go on …" I said.

"… he's dealing with serious substance misuse issues." She replied.

"Which substances?" I asked.

"Cocaine, a bit of grass, that's what I know of, anyway. Recently, I've found needles. He blames me, he says it's all my fault, that I've driven him to it because I make his life shit." She replied.

"He's well connected, too." Katie said.

"To whom?" I asked.

"Bob calls them, 'C11 villains'." She replied.

I smiled because the term 'C11 villain' was such a typically police expression, it was amusing to hear it coming from the lips of a well-known TV personality.

"What do you want me to say to Bob?" I asked.

"Tell him that I need some time to think things through. I've got some pretty big decisions to make."

"Do you think you should speak to Bob before you do that? Can't you talk this through on the phone?" I asked.

"I don't trust phones and I know he doesn't. A few of my colleagues are absolutely convinced their phones are being tapped by the press, as stories keep appearing, where the information could only have come from a private telephone call."

That was almost identical to the claim made by Colonel Beaulieu, and I wondered whether there was something to these allegations.

"When you say colleagues, do you mean other famous celebrities?" I asked

She nodded.

We sat there in silence. Katie was deep in thought. I didn't really know what to say.

"Look, I've got to go, now." I said, as much out of a need to break the silence, rather than my requirement to attend a pressing engagement.

"Wait, hang on, please." Katie said, almost desperately.

"Can you act as a bit of a conduit? As a 'go between', between me and Bob. Just for a few days, until everything calms down a bit? I'd really appreciate it."

How could I say no? And besides, it was another chance to repay Bob.

We exchanged mobile numbers and Katie agreed to send texts to and from Bob, via me, and to use the name Tabitha instead of Bob, just in case anyone was monitoring her phone.

"Tabitha?" I asked.

"She's my sister. If someone read a message with her name in it, they would just assume we were talking about my sister." She explained.

"Gosh, very covert. Have you done this sort of thing before?" I asked, as a joke.

But Katie took me seriously.

"Of course. When you've been in the public limelight as long as I have, you get used to sneaking around." She replied.

"I think I'd hate being famous." I replied.

"People might like it at first, but in the end, everyone hates it. For me it's a by-product of the job I do. I can't make a living without everyone knowing who I am. But the last thing I need right now, is my relationship with Bob coming out. I'm just about to sign a contract with ITV and they want me to do a new celebrity sports quiz to rival BBC's Question of Sport. Shit, what the hell am I going to do?"

While it was clear that Katie was worried about her husband finding out, I thought it was interesting that she appeared, almost equally concerned, about the impact upon her career.

"Why don't you and Bob just call it off for a few months?" I asked.

Katie didn't reply but the expression on her face suggested that she didn't want to.

"It would be the sensible thing. I mean, just for a few months until it all dies down."

"Is that what Bob wants?" Katie asked.

"No, in all fairness he doesn't. Although, as his friend, I did suggest it to him." I replied.

"Listen …"

Katie was struggling to remember my name, so I reminded her.

"Chris"

"Thanks, yes, listen Chris. I need Bob in my life, I really don't know what I'd do without him. He's really, really important to me. Without him, I think I'd go mad."

"What? The Bob that works with me?" I said, with mock incredulity.

"Yes, the Bob that works with you." Katie replied, and a smile appeared on her lips, in response to my gentle teasing.

"Fuck this is a mess." Katie said, her face dropping the smile and assuming a deep frown.

A mobile rang and Katie reached into a pocket underneath the steering wheel and retrieved one of the latest Nokia phones. She glanced at the screen and pressed a button to divert or cancel the call.

"Is that Bob?" I asked.

"No, my sister. I'm seeing her later, whatever she wanted, it can wait."

The expression on Katie's face changed and I didn't know quite what to make of it.

"Are you married, Chris?" She asked.

I was quite taken aback by the unexpected question.

"Happily" I replied.

She nodded, knowingly.

"Shall we see what we can do about that?" She said.

I was taken aback by the sudden change in the conversation and completely lost as to how to respond; Katie laughed.

"Your face is a picture."

"Mrs. Sumers, are you trying to seduce me." I asked, quite pleased, I'd suddenly thought of a more appropriate response, than my previous gormless expression.

"No, not at all, Chris. But you'd be perfect for my sister."

"The aforementioned, Tabitha?" I replied.

"The very same."

Katie leaned towards me, and I reacted by defensively arching backwards away.

"Steady, tiger; I'm going for the contents of the glove compartment not your pants."

"Thank god for that." I replied.

"None taken." She responded.

She opened the glove compartment and took out a folder, which I immediately recognised as, the sort you get when you pick up your film, when it's been developed. She opened it up and flicked through a few photographs, before selecting one, and handing it to me. It was a picture of Katie and her sister, standing together on a beach; both were wearing nothing but straw hats and swimsuits. By a process of elimination, I worked out that Tabitha was on the right and Katie's sister was, indeed, attractive, but she was obviously older than her famous younger sister and was, perhaps, a good six years older than I was.

"She's very attractive. How much younger than you is she?" I asked.

Katie pouted.

"Bastard" She said.

"But seriously, she's single, well, divorced, two teenage kids and her ex pays her enough maintenance to feed and clothe a small African republic. He's something high up in the City, and left her for his twenty-three-year-old P.A."

"Katie, I'm happily married. I don't need a pile of shit in my life. So, thank you, but no, thank you."

"Like the pile of shit, I'm in?"

I realised I'd been a little indiscreet, but then it was her own fault, for pushing her sister on me.

"Well, sort of." I replied, honestly.

"Fair enough, Chris; I suppose I asked for that. Listen, thank you for doing this today, I mean coming to see me, I really appreciate it."

"That's all right; Bob's a good friend. I am loyal to my friends and like to help them out, where I can."

"Well thanks, anyway." Katie said.

She leaned across and kissed me; well, that is to say, our cheeks almost touched. Being an English man, I found the gesture quite uncomfortable, as I'd only just met the woman, but I suspected these showbiz types did it all the time.

We parted a few moments later. I liked Katie Sumers and could see why Bob could fall for her. She was certainly attractive and had a sense of humour, but more importantly, there was just something about her.

I agreed to act as a conduit, had absolutely no interest in going out with her sister, but, as I left, I had the strangest feeling that Katie and I hadn't seen the last of each other.

## Chapter 24

The following day, we were late turn and when I sat at my desk, I immediately saw that someone had left a handwritten statement for me to read; attached to which, was a yellow post-it-note, which read, 'I haven't updated the CRIS', which was signed by Peter, one of the DCs, on early turn. It was short statement signed by a Marianne Costa, in which she, 'refused to substantiate the allegation of indecent assault which, she understood, her sister, Karen Blubecker, had made, yesterday'. The statement concluded by saying that Marianne would not attend court and would refuse to give evidence. Well, that was the end of that!

I logged onto CRIS to update the crime report, but when I opened it, was surprised to see the last entry on the DETS page wasn't the one I'd made yesterday, but a line from my DI, saying that I had misheard her and that she had, in fact, instructed me to contact C.I.B. Reserve, to report the offence. I was staggered. That was a complete and utter lie, but I was fucked here, because, ultimately, it was my word against hers and, if it came down to it, the Job would have to believe her because she was the senior officer. I was furious but knew that was a battle I couldn't win. I resolved to try to forget the matter.

I took Bob for a coffee in the canteen, explained what had happened the previous evening with Katie, and that they could communicate through me. He seemed really on edge but that was hardly surprising.

"Any idea what she's going to decide to do?" He asked.

"No, mate. Sorry. But she didn't give any indication that she was going to end the relationship. In fact, when I suggested you two should take a short break until it all dies down, she didn't like the idea." I replied.

"Her old man's a right nasty piece of work. He's a drug addict; she earns it, he puts it up his nose or shoots it up his arm. And he's not against giving Katie the odd slap or two."

"So, Katie was saying. Can I give you some advice?"

Bob nodded.

"Don't get involved in any shit with her old man. You don't want to lose your girlfriend and your job."

"I won't, but fucking hell, Nostrils, he fucking deserves it and it's long overdue."

"Be careful, mate, and really clever, and, if you're going to do something, don't get fucking caught."

It was the best advice I could give him.

"There's only one crime, hey, Nostrils. Isn't that what you boys at Stokey used to say?"

"That's right, mate, only one crime, getting caught." I replied, but I was still holding his stare.

"Listen Nostrils, if I wasn't in this job, I'd be tempted, but I am so I'm not. It's hard to listen to some of the stories Katie tells me. She says, he always punches her in the stomach, so that it's more difficult to detect the bruises. And he's heavy handed with the kids; it's disgusting. How she ended up with him, I don't know. I mean, for fucks sake, he's got everything and it's because of her. He drives a huge, top of the range BMW, they go on the most fantastic holidays, and they've got so much money. Fuck me, it's his job to look after the kids, that's all he does, but they still have a live in au pair. And everyone loves him, he's opened a load of local drug centres, gets his face in all the local newspapers, gives interviews on the radio. And he's a violent, good for nothing, drug addict. Oh, sorry, Chris, no insult intended."

"None taken." I replied.

Most people who knew me, knew that I'd struggled with some drug abuse issues.

I'd never heard Bob so animated because he just wasn't like that. I could tell that he was really stressed.

"But don't worry because I ain't going to do nothing. I need this job too much, what with the dire financial situation I'm in."

"A wise call, mate. You know it makes sense. Did you say her husband's name was Steve Oswald?" I asked.

"That's his name, Katie uses her maiden name, Sumers, but her married name is Oswald."

"Oh, by the way, Katie tried to set me up with her sister." I said.

"Which one?" Bob asked.

"There's more than one? Tabitha, the one whose name she's going to use when she texts me."

"Tabitha's her older sister, she got one that's a few years younger, but I've never met either of them." Bob replied.

"Well, what's this Tabitha like?"

"She's really nice, apparently. She's divorced and, well, how shall I put it, desperate for some male company. Apparently, according to Katie, she hasn't had sex in like three years. What did you say? Are you going to meet up with her?"

"No, I'm happily married. I can honestly say that, unlike any other policeman I've ever known, I have never been unfaithful to my wife, and I never will. It just seems like too much aggravation, to me." I replied.

"Fair enough; Chris, fair enough. Do you think she'll end our relationship?" he asked.

I'd already answered this question but realised Bob wanted more assurance.

"I doubt it. When I introduced myself and said you'd asked me to meet her, she seemed genuinely worried that you'd asked me to see her to end the affair. But I don't know mate, I've only met the woman once, and that was only for a few minutes."

"Good, 'cos I'm really quite smitten with her." Bob said.

"Yeah, I can see why. She's quite a character, isn't she?" I said, perhaps a little too honestly.

Bob smiled and replied with just two words:

"She's captivating."

It wasn't quite the expression I'd have chosen but I could see why he felt that way.

***

My mobile phone had rang several times during our chat but I'd pushed the button to divert the call to voicemail. When we stood up to leave the canteen, I picked up the message, which was from the DI.

"Chris, call me."

I called her back, assuming it was going to be about the C.I.B. referral issue but I was wrong.

"Chris, there's been a serious assault outside Seven Sisters tube. A male has been stabbed several times and is on his way to hospital. Uniform think he's likely to die, they've gone with him for continuity."

"Ok boss …" I replied.

" … I'll go straight to the scene; please can you get hold of the uniform officer and tell him to get pre-transfusion blood."

"What do you mean?" She replied.

"We need pre-transfusion blood." I replied.

I didn't know how to state my request any clearer. What's more, I was gob-smacked that she didn't immediately understand my request, or indeed, tell me that she'd already given that instruction. I wondered whether she had any C.I.D. experience, at all.

"Where are my team, I mean, I'm with Bob but have you seen Dot or Colin?" I asked.

"Don't you know?" She replied, incredulously

I knew her response wasn't entirely unreasonable because yes, as the team DS, I should know what my team where doing.

"I've been dealing with the allegation of rape, the one from yesterday. The victim's withdrawn; we've got a statement."

I omitted to mention that it wasn't me who'd taken the statement, but it was a convenient excuse, as to why I didn't know where half my team were.

"So do you want me to refer this to C.I.B. or not?" I asked.

"Can we deal with that, later, Chris. We've just had a murder, well probably, we need to focus on that."

I detected a hint of panic in my DI's voice. Two serious crimes in two days, was hardly unusual for Tottenham, but I suspected she'd never known anything like it, in Canterbury or Rochester, or wherever the fuck it was, she'd last worked.

"I'll tell you what, boss; why don't you take the serious assault and I'll top and tail the rape and type you up a full briefing." I suggested.

My voice was friendly, and I delivered my proposal with my best, 'this is the greatest idea I've ever had' voice but I knew I was being cheeky, because DIs and DCIs on borough, didn't deal with offences.

The DI paused for too long and I knew I'd just shafted her. I suspected that, because she was new to the Met and new to the rank, she didn't yet know exactly what was, and wasn't, expected of her. More significantly, if as I suspected, she had little or no tangible C.I.D. experience, then she simply wouldn't be capable of picking up such a serious crime. Should I rescue her? If I did, would she appreciate the gesture? I decided to be nice.

"Listen, boss; I'm nearly at the scene so I'll pick this up, can you just make sure that one of my team goes to the hospital and the other two come down to the scene to meet me; I don't care who does what, no hang on, make sure Colin comes to the scene."

"That's what I was going to suggest, Chris. I'll get hold of A.M.I.T. for you."

A.M.I.T. was the Area Major Investigation Team, in other words the Murder Squad.

"I don't think they'll pick it up until he's dead but it's a good idea to let them know." I replied.

"Let me know if you need anything else." The DI said.

Gosh, that was exactly what she was meant to say. I felt almost, but not quite, elated.

***

Outside Seven Sisters tube several vendors operated. There was a flower seller, a traditional greengrocer's stall, and a good old-fashioned cobbler's stand with advertising signs, which must have been eighty years old. All three had been cordoned off with blue and white 'crime scene – do not enter' tape, as had the nearest tube exit. A couple of uniform officers were preventing anyone crossing the cordon.

By the cobbler's stand was an enormous quantity of fresh blood and I understood why the uniform officers were predicting the victim's imminent death.

A crowd of onlookers had gathered to gawp.

I went across to speak to the nearest PC, a young lad, no older than twenty-two, whom I recognised, though I couldn't recall his name.

"Hello, mate. What ya' got?" I asked, in the time honored greeting of a C.I.D. officer, arriving at the scene.

"Hello Sergeant; the victim is the cobbler, a guy called, Chris Crowthorne."

"He's been here years, hasn't he?" I asked, as even I knew him by sight.

"The sign above the stool says, since 1968, but apparently, his dad had it before him but over in East Street market. I was chatting to the guy that sells the papers. Apparently, the suspect is a white male, called Frank Tatler, who hangs out here, most days. In fact, it was the paper seller who intervened, by shouting to Frank that the police were coming. Frank had it off on his toes, ran down Seven Sisters Road and then up Greenfield Road. The guy over there, who's talking to Pete, chased him for a few hundred yards."

I assumed Pete was the other uniform officer and he was chatting to a white male, in his early sixties, who was wearing a green apron.

"Do we know what it was about?"

The PC shook his head.

"Apparently, everyone knew Frank. He was a pain in the arse but fairly harmless. He's got a few previous, but all related to domestic violence, and hadn't been in trouble, for years. He lives in Broxborne with his mum and dad."

"How old is he?" I asked.

"Forty-five, I think." The PC replied.

"Weapon?"

"A knife, that's all we know. Attacked the victim from the rear, without warning." The PC replied.

The lady from the paper stand, the one who said the police were coming, has gone out with four-five to drive round to try to do a street ID; she knows the suspect, really well.

Four-five was one of the small patrol cars, the type that used to be called Pandas.

As we'd been talking, Pete and the man in the apron, whom I assumed to be the greengrocer, came over. I introduced myself to both.

"Sarge, our witness here, Dave, chased the suspect down Greenfield Road. Before he gave up, but he saw something which may be significant." Pete said.

"Let's walk the route then, and Dave, if you can tell us exactly what you saw, and where, that'll be great."

We did just that, during which Dave explained, he wasn't trying to catch Frank but just to see where he went. He said, he'd known Frank for some ten years and had always given him a wide birth, because he'd, and I quote, 'always reckoned he was a fucking nutter'.

"Was he at the station every day? He lives in Broxborne?" I asked.

"Every fucking day. He didn't have anything else to do and used to just hang out around the station making a right fucking nuisance of himself. I think he grew up in Tottenham, which is way he is always here. He's unemployed, always sponging a couple of quid here and there, he drove us all nuts. He'd offer to help set up the stall, you know, unpack the van, things like that, but I didn't need his help and, if you let him help, he wanted a few quid. He was a real pain in the arse."

We turned right into Greenfield Road. Two long rows of residential houses stretched out, in straight lines.

"What was his beef with the victim? Was it Chris?" I asked.

"I don't know. They had words last night when we were packing up. Chris told him to 'fuck off', but that wasn't unusual, and I didn't think any more about it."

"Tell Sarge, exactly what you saw." Pete said to the greengrocer.

"I was about here …"

We were twenty yards along the road from the junction, which was behind us.

"… Frank had been running down this side of the pavement and he was about, where that white van is …"

The white van was about a hundred yards ahead.

"… he stopped, all of a sudden, and looked to the house, on his right. I stopped, too, nervous that he might realise I was watching him. He walked into the middle of the road, passing behind the other side of the van but always looking back at that house. It was as if he was trying to see whether anyone was in, he seemed to be paying particular attention to the upper windows. In order to see him properly, I had to go into the road myself but I didn't want him to see me, so I crawled between these two cars like this …"

He repeated his actions from a short while ago.

" … and looked to my right, but by the time I looked down the street, Frank was running away again, and he turned left at the next junction, and out of sight. And that's it, gents, that's exactly what I saw."

"Did he ever mention that he knew anyone here?" I asked.

"If he had, mate, I wouldn't have taken any notice; he talked constant bollocks, no one ever listened."

We walked down to the white van and studied the house, which, apparently, the suspect had paid so much attention to. It was unspectacular and I assumed he must have known someone living there, which is why he ran away in this direction.

No one was in and enquiries with the neighbours identified, until recently, the house had been occupied by a family from Spain, who rented it from a landlord, who lived in Scotland, and the house was currently between rents. That didn't seem to support the theory that the suspect and the occupier knew one another, so why had he stopped here? It didn't seem to make any sense.

## Chapter 25

We went back to the scene, where Colin and Dot had already arrived and were taking details from everyone in the vicinity, asking them whether anyone had witnessed what had happened. They were good, really good, and a pleasure to work with.

I took a call from Bob Clark. He'd been at the hospital interviewing a witness to an unrelated crime when he got the call from the DI to go to Accident & Emergency. He was, he said, pleased to report, he'd managed to get pre-transfusion blood and, the even better news, that the victim was almost certainly going to survive. He had been stabbed eleven times; three to the upper back and shoulders, but the remainder were defence wounds, to the hands and arms. He said the next of kin, a wife, and several teenage kids, were there, too.

"I'm just curious, Bob, and it's not really important, but when you spoke to the DI, did she mention the pre-transfusion blood?"

I could hear him laughing before he spoke.

"No, but she did say something about Transvision Vamp, you know, the pop group. I did wonder, what the heck she was talking about. I thought, she was trying to tell me that the victim was a member of the group or something."

That made me laugh out loud.

At that precise moment, an area car came to an emergency stop, by the scene; it's blue lights and siren, still operating. As it did so, a T.S.G. carrier went racing by, also on blues and twos.

I walked over, quickly; something significant was obviously happening.

The operator in the front passenger seat unwound the window.

"    They've located your suspect, he's in the McDonalds, in the High Street and he's eating and alone. Jump in."

I looked around but the others were, either out of my direct line of sight, or otherwise engaged, so I jumped in the back and desperately tried to put the seat belt on, which was quite impossible, because the catch was buried deep into the gap between the back seat and upright.

You either get a thrill out of being driven in a police car on blues and twos, through the maze, that is London traffic, or you don't. I don't. I found the whole experience nothing short of petrifying and spent, all the time, looking out of the side window because I really didn't want to see what was coming up ahead of us.

The operator had been on the radio, and he turned to ask me a question:

"Sarge, have they recovered the weapon?"

"No, it's a knife and we must assume, it's still in the possession of the suspect." I shouted back; a normal level of conversation would have been utterly useless, in this environment.

I heard the operator communicate this information to the T.S.G. unit and assumed this would mean that they would only effect the arrest, once they had donned full protective clothing, otherwise called riot gear.

"How have they found him?" I asked, tapping the operator on his shoulder, to attract his attention.

"The witness in four-five spotted him. They've parked up around the corner and the carrier has just arrived. They'll be ready to enter in four." He replied.

"How long will we be?" I asked.

"One minute, Sarge."

"Can you kill the blues and twos; let's not frighten him off?" I suggested.

The operator flicked a few buttons and a welcome silence descended.

The carrier and the panda were parked in a side street, but they had a view of the McDonald's front door which abutted the side road and the High Street.

When we arrived, the T.S.G. officers had almost donned their gear and I asked them to wait a few seconds, while I spoke to the witness. The lady paper seller told me, that although she'd only had the quickest of glances, she was pretty certain Frank was sitting by the window, on the right, as you entered. He was easy to identify because he was a white man, in his forties, and completely bald, as in, not a single hair on his head. What's more, she said, he was wearing a white shirt and blue jeans.

I had a quick chat with the T.S.G. Sergeant and being the only officer in plain clothes, I agreed to take a quick recce into the restaurant, make sure the suspect was still there and sitting were they'd last seen him, and just to confirm, he fitted the description. I also, politely. reminded him, it would be forensically really good for me, if there wasn't any more blood, on the suspect's white T-shirt.

"When you go in and get a definite ID, please leave, gives us a clear thumb up, and then return inside the McDonalds. When we enter, please be pointing out the suspect to us, clearly and unambiguously, so there is no confusion, as to whom we are taking out." The T.S.G. Sergeant proposed.

I thought I'd stand out like a sore thumb, as I was wearing a suit, in a McDonalds, but I was wrong because I don't think I'd ever seen a more eclectic mix of customers.

I opened the door, but didn't need to take another step inside, because the suspect was sitting two tables in, to the right and by the window. He was halfway through a big Mac and was casually glancing through a tabloid newspaper. He fitted the description, white, mid-forties, no hair and white T- shirt. He looked remarkably calm, for someone who, less than an hour ago, had stabbed another human being eleven times. He looked up and caught me staring at him, at that precise second, I had been looking at his top, to see whether there were any obvious blood stains. I looked away, quickly, but wondered whether I'd given the game away.

I stepped outside and looked to my right. A few of the T.S.G. officers were pulling on the last of their gear, although most seemed, all set to go. On the corner opposite the McDonald's entrance, several pedestrians had gathered, having correctly guessed that something was going to happen. I gave the thumbs up signal, to indicate the suspect was still there, and returned into the restaurant but, to my dismay, in the ten seconds I'd gone, the suspect had disappeared.

I knew he couldn't have walked out, as I'd been at the door, all the time. My eyes raced around the place, had he moved seats? Had he gone back to the counter, to order something else? Had he just got up to get a napkin or more sauce? I looked across at his table, the tray was there but most of the food had been consumed. And at that precise moment, eight T.S.G. officers in full riot gear, came charging into McDonalds, quite literally, knocking me to the floor, in their haste to enter and effect the arrest.

As I fell, I caught the back of my head against something hard, perhaps a tabletop, with a real thud. I don't think I lost consciousness but how does one ever, actually, know that?

## Chapter 26

When I came to, I found myself sitting in the back of the police carrier with a T.S.G. officer holding a bag of frozen McNuggets to the back of my head, which had been kindly donated, by one of the staff. When I slipped my hand underneath the improvised ice pack, I felt an impressive bump, something I'd always been taught, was a good sign, after a knock on the head.

"How're you feeling, now, Sarge?" The young officer said.

I blinked several times, and my vision came into focus.

"All right I think, where's the prisoner?" I asked.

"It wasn't him." The officer replied.

"What?"

"It wasn't him. We cuffed him and got the witness to ID but she said, although he looked very similar, it wasn't Frank, that was his name wasn't it?"

I nodded.

"Where was he?" I asked.

"He was upstairs in the toilet. Fortunately, our skipper spotted him coming back down the stairs." He replied.

"Was he pissed off? Being jumped on by you lot?" I asked.

"No, he was fine; the skipper apologised and explained everything to him."

"Where is everyone?" I asked, suddenly aware that with the exception of ourselves, the carrier was empty.

"They're all having a maccy dees. I was left as officer in charge of the crocked DS." He replied.

"Thank you." I replied, sheepishly.

"The skipper says, when they're finished, we'll run you up to Accident & Emergency, you know, get you checked up." He said.

"I'll be fine, just drop me off back at the nick, please. I'll see the Divisional Surgeon, there." I replied.

"Who?" He asked.

"The police doctor, son." I replied, suddenly feeling quite old.

My mobile was ringing, along with my head.

"Are you all right, Chris? I got a call saying you'd been injured by the prisoner."

It was the new DI; I was impressed.

"Yes, boss. I'm fine. It was the wrong guy, anyway. I got knocked over in the kerfuffle and banged my head. I've got a bit of a bump, but I'll be okay. I'll be back at the nick, shortly. I'll pop up and see you." I replied.

As soon as I terminated the call, I received another - it was the Control Room.

"DS Pritchard?"

"Yes"

"We have a call from a solicitor in Stamford Hill. He says that a man, who has just walked in, claims to have murdered a man outside Seven Sisters Underground station. The man's name is Frank Tatler, and the solicitor is Harry Cohen. Mr. Cohen says he's taking instructions and will bring his client to Tottenham police station at four o'clock this afternoon."

I took the address of the solicitors and asked the young T.S.G. officer to get his skipper.

Ten minutes later, the T.S.G. and I were on our way to Stamford Hill to make another attempt to nick the suspect.

I had a right ding-dong with the solicitor, who was less than happy about having ten police officers, clad from head to foot in riot gear, trampling through his offices and arresting his client. He was really aggrieved because he had made an agreement with the person with whom he has spoken, to bring the suspect down to the Station, later in the afternoon. He alleged I had broken that agreement. I tried to explain that I had a duty to arrest the suspect, as soon as possible, in order, both to protect the public, and secure any forensic evidence, but we weren't going to agree, so I told him to speak to the Duty Officer at the nick, if he wanted to make a formal complaint.

The suspect was strange.

The good news was that this time, we arrested the right person and my goodness, he did look incredibly similar to the poor, innocent guy, in McDonalds.

The suspect confirmed his name was Frank Tatler and, when cautioned, admitted to having had a 'bit of a disagreement with Chris, the shoe repair man about British Caledonian Lou'. Exactly what he meant, I hoped to find out, during interview.

The arrest was technically the T.S.G.'s, which was great because it gave me some time to catch up with my team and to brief the DI on the third-party rape allegation.

The first person I met was Bob. He was just back from the hospital, with a pile of blood-stained clothing and other exhibits.

"How's our victim?" I asked.

"He's going to live, but he's a right mess. Fortunately, none of the eleven stab wounds were critical but his arms are cut to ribbons and they're operating, as we speak. His wife is there, she's really nice. Poor, bastard." Bob replied.

"Did you get to speak to the victim?"

"No, but I spent thirty minutes with Mrs. Samuels. She also works on the stall, so she knows the suspect. She says he's always hanging around the station and making a nuisance of himself."

"Does she know what this was all about?" I asked.

"No, she's no idea, but she said her the victim was one of the few people who wasn't scared of him, and she wondered whether, he'd just told Frank to fuck off. She doesn't think it'll be any more complicated than that. Chris, can I have a word? It's nothing to do with this, I just need some advice." Bob said.

I had a regroup of the team, getting everyone together in the canteen to find out exactly where we were with the attempted murder. I was also conscious that I had to do the CRIS report for the third-party rape. Then I'd track down the new DI and update her about both major crimes.

I was in the canteen a few minutes before the others, so I leafed through a nearby copy of Police Review, the national monthly police magazine, copies of which could be found in every police station and building in the country. There was a double page article, on the rise in domestic violence and the headline read, 'One in ten women are the victim of Domestic Violence'. I really didn't give the article more than the most cursory of reads, it wasn't really a subject that interested me, but someone had made a witty comment in the margins.

Over dinner, we discussed our outstanding actions for the attempted murder case. Bob had dealt with everything at the hospital and had even managed to take a short statement from the victim's wife, which, although all hearsay, would be really useful, when we came to talk to the Custody Officer about charging the suspect. Dot had taken statements from two witnesses who could positively identify the suspect, whom they had both known for years. But Colin saved the best until last. Just when our discussions had drawn to a close, he placed an exhibits cardboard box on the table and removed the lid. Secure inside was a twelve-inch silver bread knife. The serrated edge was covered in blood and from the shiny metal surface, the trace of silver fingerprint dust could clearly be seen. I summed my surprise up in just three words:

"You're shitting me?" I said.

Colin's face lit up with the broadest of smiles and we all laughed.

"Where did you find that?" Dot asked.

"In the back garden of the house, the suspect stopped in front of, in Greenfield Road. I was chatting to the greengrocer ..."

"I spoke to him, too." I added, quite unnecessarily.

"... I got him to walk the suspect's escape routes, like you did, and when he showed me the house that he'd stopped in front of, I knocked on a few doors to see if anyone there, actually, knew him."

"Had he been nicked then?" I asked.

"No, it was just after I'd heard you'd nicked the wrong bloke in McDonalds."

Colin was the only person I knew who was either brave or stupid enough, on his own no less, to go trying to arrest an armed and dangerous suspect. What's more, I bet he didn't have any of his officer safety equipment on him.

"Anyway, the occupier was an old bloke who knew nothing about our man, but he did say that he wanted to report a strange event that had occurred, that afternoon. At about one-thirty, he'd been sitting in his rear garden, enjoying the lovely weather, and reading, when, out of a clear blue sky and right into the middle of his recently mowed lawn, landed a sliver bread knife. This silver bread knife."

"You're kidding?" Said Dot and Bob, almost simultaneously.

"I'm not. I think our suspect thought he was going to land the knife on the roof but was probably pretty pumped up, with the adrenalin of the whole thing, and just threw too hard. The knife went clean over the roof and landed in the only garden, for perhaps half a mile, where anyone was actually sitting there to see it land. Well, he didn't see, he heard it fall and when he looked up, saw a big silver bird miles away. Well, you know, with all the stuff that's been in the papers in the last few weeks about things dropping from jets, all that blue ice stuff, the old guy assumed, that's where it had come from." Colin explained.

"But that's a bread knife." Dot replied, incredulously.

"Well what else would you expect?" Bob asked, sarcastically.

"I mean, I know that's got to be it, but a bread knife? It's hardly a weapon of attack, is it?" I added.

Colin shrugged his shoulders.

"We've got a full set of prints off it, too. And there's blood, as you can see, everywhere, which will no doubt be our victims." Colin said.

"Well done, mate; I am genuinely impressed, Colin; good police work." I said.

Bob and Dot nodded, in agreement.

There were already four signatures on the exhibit label; the witness, Colin's, the S.O.C.O.'s, Colin's (again) and I added a fifth, my own. I was taking possession of the exhibit, so I could put it to the suspect during interview.

"We've very lucky not be dealing with a murder." Bob said.

"How close was it?" I asked.

"According to the A&E doctor, the most serious threat was the amount of blood he lost, and according to his first pulse rate and blood pressure reading in the ambulance, he really should have died, before he got to the hospital. He clearly didn't want to go, today. It's a good attempted murder." Bob replied.

I had noticed throughout our conversation, that unusually, but quite understandably, Bob kept checking his phone. He was clearly worried that his private life was on the verge of becoming very public.

"You alright?" I asked, discretely, as we all got up from the table to get on with the day.

He pulled a face that constituted an unambiguous no.

As the others went ahead, I pulled Bob gently by the arm and took him to one side.

"Listen mate, whatever happens, I'll be there for you. You don't have to do any of this alone, do you understand?"

We sealed the deal with a meeting of eyes, like only two Englishmen could do.

\*\*\*

"At about one o'clock today, outside the entrance to Seven Sisters underground station, a forty-year-old white male, called Christopher Crowthorne, the man who has a shoe repair stall, was stabbed eleven times by a man called Frank Tatler. Was it you who attacked Christopher?"

We'd waited for over three hours of private consultation, to ask this question.

A private consultation is the process by which a person under arrest takes legal advice. They do so in private, and anything they say to one another is legally privileged. Quite frankly, the only thing that frustrated me was, that the time these took, came out of the overall time we were allowed to detain a suspect without charge. I always thought that was a basic unfairness but then the legislation which set out the rules P.A.C.E., the Police and Criminal Evidence Act, was written by lawyers for the benefit of lawyers, so I shouldn't have expected anything else.

"Yes" Frank replied.

His response really took me by surprise because, to get an immediate admission, especially after three hours of private consultation, was unheard of. I almost lost my thread.

"Why?" I asked.

"Because he's had an affair with my wife, British Caledonian Lou." He replied, in a very matter of fact way.

"So, you stabbed him, eleven times?" I asked.

"Yes, what man wouldn't? It's an honour thing, isn't it?" He replied.
The bluntness of Frank's replies was unsettling my stride.

"Are you married?" I asked.

"I was." He replied.

"To a lady named Lou?" I asked.

"Yes" He replied.

This was going to be a painfully slow interview unless I could somehow get Frank to be a little more expansive with his answers.

"Frank, tell us exactly what happened, tell us all about Lou, explain how you found out about what Christopher was doing."

"We had words this morning; he's always rude and disrespectful to me. I put it to him; I said, 'why are you treating me like a cunt?' I asked him straight up, man to man, 'have you been fucking my wife, British Caledonian Lou?' and he said, 'yeah that's right, you twat, I've been fucking her brains out, left her in bed only this morning, dripping in my spunk, she was'. Well, a man's got to do what a man's got to do. I went home, got a kitchen knife and came back to sort it out." He explained.

"I am told by the doctor that the first four knife wounds to Christopher left injuries in his upper back. Did you attack him from behind?" I asked.

"I did." He replied.

"That's not very manly, is it? I thought you wanted to settle your disagreement, 'man to man'? You were just a coward." I said, my words were delivered passively and quietly.

I was deliberately testing his reaction, to see how he would respond to a proper challenge.

Frank frowned, as he turned my question over in his mind. Then he shrugged his shoulders in a 'I don't give a fuck' sort of way.

"Is he dead?" He asked.

"Nope." I replied.

"Did you want to kill him?" I asked.

This was a pivotal point because an admission would assist with a charge of attempted murder, as opposed to a section 18, grievous bodily harm. My eyes flicked over to his solicitor because I was interested to see if he would try to influence his client's response. The solicitor didn't move a muscle.

"I did." Frank replied.

This was quite simply the easiest interview I'd ever conducted but the best was yet to come.

I looked across to Bob, an indication that he was invited to ask any questions.

"Tell me a bit more about 'British Caledonian Lou', what's her full name, where does she live, are you still married?" Bob asked.

"We were married in 1983. We're separated, now." He replied.

"What's her full name and address?" Bob asked.

"Louise Tatler; I don't know where she lives now." He replied.

"When did you last see her?" Bob asked.

Frank shrugged his shoulders.

"Guess?"

"Ten years ago."

"So, you tried to murder a man because you think he's having an affair with a woman, who you haven't seen for, at least, ten years?" Bob asked.

"It's a thing of honour, man to man." He replied, almost defiantly.

"Where's the knife?" Bob asked.

Frank laughed, slightly.

"You'll never, ever find the weapon. Not in a million years, you can search high and low, you can tear apart every house in Tottenham and you will never find the murder weapon."

As he was completing his sentence, Bob discreetly reached into the black rucksack by his side and, at exactly the right moment, he produced the knife, which was strapped into the cardboard evidence box. Keeping the exhibit out of the suspect's arms' reach, he held it up and asked:

"Is this it?"

"Yes, that's the one." Frank replied, without the slightest hint of conciliation, or trace of embarrassment.

**Chapter 27**

During the interview, I had felt my mobile phone vibrating several times and when I looked, I had several messages from Katie's mobile. She apologised for the short notice but invited, 'you and your mate', to a charity awards ceremony at Chigwell Police Club where, she was, she explained, the guest of honour. 'Your mate' was obviously Bob. I guessed that the event would perhaps give her and Bob an opportunity to talk things through.

I texted a reply saying that I would get hold of 'my mate' and get back to her, and then I forwarded her texts, to Bob. No sooner had I looked up from my phone, than I felt a hand on my shoulder. I turned around to see Colin looking shocked.

"I need a word, Nostrils." He said, and walked into the interview room, which I'd vacated only a minute or two before.

"You all right, mate?" I asked, with genuine concern.

"Not really."

Colin sat down opposite me and laid a piece of A4 paper on the table between us. I recognised it straight away. It contained several newspaper cuttings, which had been glued to a sheet of paper, to make a short offensive sentence, and the word, N I G G E R, had been constructed from individual letters. On the bottom half of the page was glued a picture of an orangutan, eating a monkey nut.

I wasn't shocked, but only because I'd seen a similar work of art only a few days previously. Colin looked absolutely devastated.

"You all right, mate?" I said the same words I had just uttered, but this time, from my intonation and the gravitas in my voice, it was a completely different question.

"Not really, Nostrils, I feel like I've been repeatedly kicked in the stomach."

I went to speak but after the shortest of pauses, Colin continued.

"... is there really someone, who I work with, that thinks like this? And thinks this of me? I've been in this job nearly eighteen years and I've never felt so offended or upset. Nostrils, I'm gutted. I feel sick."

I was really taken aback by his reaction. Colin was the toughest, hardest and, well, coolest, police officer I'd ever worked with, and I didn't anticipate, for one moment, something as ridiculous and stupid as this piece of paper, could hurt him so much.

"Where did you find it?" I asked.

"It was in a dispatch envelope in my tray." He replied.

"Where's the envelope?" I asked.

"On my desk." He replied, absentmindedly.

"Was there anything else with it?" I asked.

Colin shook his head.

"Fucking hell, mate. It's just a load of bollocks; don't take it, seriously. But you do need to report it."

"But who would do that to me? I work hard, treat everyone fairly, you know, I'm a decent human being. No one deserves to be treated like this, no one."

"I agree, mate. I really do. We need to report this, now. We need to preserve the letter and the envelope for forensics, we need to go and see the DI, right now."

Colin shook his head.

"You can't do, nothing, mate." I said.

"I don't want to do anything, mate. You really don't understand how difficult it is for ethnic minority officers, in the post Achachi era. Everyone thinks we're always playing the race card and I don't want anyone to think that about me."

Well bugger me. I was taken aback by his statement. I had never considered, for the tiniest second, that the Achachi affair would have an adverse impact upon anyone, except white officers. But then I suppose I had never looked at it, from anyone else's perspective.

"Listen, Colin. No one will think that of you, I promise. You are not like that. You have to report this, and what's more, now you've showed me, I have to report it. Doing nothing is not an option. And besides, I doubt this will be personal to you."

Colin face suddenly changed expression.

"Do you reckon?" He asked.

"Of course, I bet this has been sent to loads of people."

I did have the advantage of knowing more about this, than I was letting on. I was also starting to have doubts, as to whether I'd taken the right action, when I found the material planted on my desk. Then I had a minor panic, I'd been so busy over the last couple of days, I hadn't got round to doing another sweep of my desk, to see if anything else had been planted.

Then I had another thought, was this whole shabby affair being done to fit me up, as I originally suspected, or was there actually a racist at work, who'd just been shrewd enough to keep his material somewhere that couldn't be attributed to himself. If the latter was the case, then I was, almost inadvertently, caught up in this?

When I saw the new DI looking through my desk, was she looking for this material or was she looking for something else? But if so, what?

"Who do we tell?" Colin asked, obviously resigned to the fact that doing nothing wasn't an option.

"We tell the DI." I replied.

"I heard you and her have history." Colin said.

I hadn't said a word to anyone at Tottenham about it.

"Joanne Cunningham told me; her skipper, Debbie, told her."

"Any advice?" I asked.

"Not really, mate. I'd never heard of her."

"Let's go and see her now; put the letter in an evidence bag, put the dispatch envelope in another."

"Thanks, Nostrils, I appreciate your support, I really do."

## Chapter 28

The DI wasn't in her office, which was good news, as it gave me a chance to have another look through my desk. Fortunately, I didn't find any more incriminating evidence.

Bob had a quick word and we agreed to pop into Katie's charity event at the police club. I texted Jackie to say I'd be late, and she replied, telling me she was going out with an old school friend, anyway, and that, if I ever listened to her, I would already know that.

When Colin and I eventually tracked the DI down, we discovered that she was already aware of the situation as three other ethnic minority officers, based at Tottenham, had also received them. It appeared, they'd all been sent out, at once. DI Young had already notified Complaints and they were on their way to the nick.

Colin seemed really pleased that he hadn't been individually targeted, but some of the DI's comments, really pissed me off. She said she was dismayed that such a level of racism still existed in the Metropolitan Police. She claimed, she would never have come back to the force, if she knew she'd be the subject of such racist hatred. Her most annoying utterance, however, was reserved for an exchange with Colin, who had the audacity to challenge her, by pointing out that he thought the problem was overstated, to which DI Young replied, in that case, he must have been walking around with his head up his arse. I thought it was an appalling thing to say, completely inappropriate, totally unwarranted, and quite nasty.

As we were about to leave the DI's office, she asked me to stay behind. I was immediately on my guard, but a little less so, when she handed me a copy of Police Review. I frowned.

"Have a look through it." The DI said.

I did. I thought there was going to be some article on racism, which she was going to use to make her point, but I quickly realised that it was the same issue I had glanced through, several days ago; in the canteen, because underneath the headline 'One in ten women are the victim of Domestic Violence' someone had written, in black biro, 'But one in five deserve to be!'. It had made me smile when I'd first read it, but now I realised the DI wouldn't appreciate the comment, so I pretended it was the first time I'd seen it and frowned.

"Gosh" I said, with as much seriousness as I could muster.

"That's awful. It was in the canteen. We sometimes use the canteen for victims of domestic violence, what if one of them had seen it?"

I shrugged my shoulders and replied:

"Well, we shouldn't be putting any members of the public in a police canteen, but I do see your point."

"We need to find out who wrote it, when I do, I'll throw the book at him." She declared.

"If it is, a he'?" I replied.

"Of course, it's a he. I thought you were meant to be a good detective. Next, you'll be telling me, the person who sent out the racist letters to Colin and the others, might be black!"

I decided that, although I was right, I wasn't going to win this argument, so I let the matter drop.

"What do you want me to do?" I asked.

"You tell me." She replied, curtly.

"Well, I've touched it, you've touched it, and goodness knows how many other people, as it was in the canteen, so I don't think a fingerprint analysis will help. I mean, who found it?" I asked.

"I did." The DI replied.

"When?" I asked.

"This morning."

"And exactly where in the canteen?" I asked.

"On the table by the Space Invader's machine. We should get the handwriting examined."

"I wouldn't bother. You never get a definite, besides, there's only a few words to examine."

I looked more closely at the writing to demonstrate that I was taking the matter seriously. As I did so, I recognised the author.

"Make some enquiries, look through the duty states, see if you can identify the handwriting."

"Okay …" I replied, tentatively.

"… but let's say I do find out who it is, don't take this the wrong way, but what are you going to do with that information?"

DI Young bit her bottom lip.

"If you want to do something officially, then you need to do this properly. Inform Complaints, forensically preserve the Police Review, although I think it's a bit late for that now, as that really should have been done immediately. Formally, seize some of the duty states, although this could have been done by a uniform officer, or even a civvie, so you'll need handwriting samples from the whole nick. And bear in mind that the nick's already got a load of shit, with the racist letters, the Chief Superintendent probably won't be too appreciative of even more trouble, arriving at his police station. Look, boss; I know it's a really daft thing for someone to write, I really do. But it was probably done as a stupid joke by someone sitting in the canteen, who was a bit bored and thought he'd have a bit of a laugh. If you take my advice, let it go. Shred the magazine, to make sure no one else sees it, and forget about it. If you're not happy with that approach, you must deal with the thing, formally, and that means Complaints, and everything that goes with it."

DI Young nodded as I was talking, so I suspected my point was pressing home.

"We'll do it your way."

"Who else knows about this?" I asked.

DI Young shook her head.

"I'll shred it. We'll say no more; deal?"

"Deal" She replied.

Which was just the answer I wanted, because the handwriting on the Police Review article, was Colin's.

## Chapter 29

That evening's charity event was black tie, something which I hadn't known, when I agreed to go. I did have a dinner suit, but it meant that I had to go home and then out again, rather than just popping into the police club on the way home, which is what I had envisaged.

This unforeseen circumstance meant that, at about ten to eight, I was driving down Palmerston Road in Buckhurst Hill, where there was a long traffic jam caused by temporary traffic lights. I chucked a right, which took me into the bottom end of Queens Road. This twist of fate meant that I saw my wife entering a restaurant, on the arm of a handsome young man, whom I recognised as being, one of the doctors from the hospital, where she worked.

I only saw them for the briefest of moments and immediately started to doubt my own eyes, but when I drove past her car, a little and very distinctive yellow Fiat Cinquecento, I knew for certain, it was Jackie.

I desperately tried to remember exactly what she had told me she was doing but I couldn't recall anything. I knew for certain, the handsome young doctor was not an old school friend, as she had claimed. Was she being unfaithful? It seemed like it but then I hadn't noticed any issues between us, recently, apart from the fact, she wanted to start a family. What didn't make much sense, was that she would go out for a meal with a bloke, in Buckhurst Hill. I mean, it was literally three miles down the road from where we lived. If she wanted to hide the relationship, that was a ridiculous thing to do. Although, I was really unsettled, I decided, I'd see what she said when she got home, later. I had learnt, over the years, that quick decisions were rarely good ones.

Ridiculous as it may sound, the thing that really did hurt me, was what she was wearing. She had on a short blue dress, which I thought made her look fantastic, and which I always wanted her to wear, whenever we went out anywhere nice. Jackie always refused to, on the grounds that it was too short and made her look slutty. It had become something of a standing joke between us. Why, oh why, had she decided to wear that dress tonight? The obvious answer was, she wanted to look slutty for her date. And why would she want to look slutty? Because she wanted him to fancy her.

I drove slowly over to the police club, trying to make sense of it all, but failing, rather abysmally.

The charity event, which was already underway, was in fact, an awards ceremony with a buffet and free drinks. I was on the guest list and shown as a representative of the Metropolitan Police and, as I entered, was handed a programme, by a woman, who then ticked my name off a list. I noticed that Bob's name had already been marked off, and a few moments later, met him, in the bar overlooking the bowling green. We had a couple of pints and generally kept out of the way. From the hall next door, we heard sporadic rounds of applause, as recipients collected their prizes, and we saw intermittent camera flashes, as a photographer captured the moment, they shook hands with the famous Katie Sumers.

The programme showed there was an interval at nine, for half an hour, and although they were running a little behind schedule, I decided to leave, when the second half resumed. I liked Bob, I really did, but this was a school night, and I didn't want to be getting home late. Besides, I was distracted by Jackie's shenanigans and wanted to get to the bottom of it.

I had just got up to use the toilet when a woman approached me, whom I immediately recognised from Katie's photograph, as Tabitha, Katie's sister. She smiled at Bob, shook my hand very formally, and introduced herself. I offered to buy some more drinks and Tabitha sat down in the chair that I had just vacated. As I glanced back, it appeared that her and Bob had launched straight into a deep and meaningful conversation, which I assumed to be about recent developments.

The bar was suddenly rammed, as everyone emerged from the hall and tried to buy a drink. The two barmaids were quickly overwhelmed. I found myself standing next to a striking female, several years younger than I, who was almost as tall as me, with dark olive skin and an abundance of long, curly, black hair. She had pointy features and was attractive, without being stunningly beautiful.

I deliberately leaned ever so slightly towards her, and our shoulders touched.

"If you do that again, I'll have to call a policeman." She said.

"You'll be lucky, where do you think you are, a police club?"

I leaned into her again and smirked, cheekily.

"Two pints, a gin and tonic, and whatever my new best friend here, wants." I said, surprised that I had managed to catch the barmaid's eye.

"Three cokes, please, lots of ice and straws too." The stranger beside me, chipped in.

I       turned towards her but, as I did so, a hand pinched my bottom with such force, I actually, jumped and let out a little squeal. Instinctively, I turned round and saw the hand belonged to Katie Sumers.

"Bloody hell, Katie, that hurt." I said, rather pathetically.

"Oh dear, would you like me to rub it better?" She said, through big pouting lips and fluttering her baby blue eyes.

"Katie, can I introduce my wife?" I said, indicating the stranger to my right.

"Oh, I'm terribly sorry." Katie said, with what I thought, was a look of genuine concern on her face.

"If you touch my husband's perfectly chiseled arse again …"

She paused and moved her mouth a few inches from Katie's ear.

"…I'll kill you." The stranger said, her face as grave as thunder.

Katie Sumers wasn't fazed, not for a second. She feigned a look of anguish and started panting, heavily.

"But I don't know if I can resist, and besides, it might just be worth it."

Katie touched her fore finger and thumb together in a mock pinching action and moved her hand towards my backside.

I pushed her hand away.

"Sod off." I said, laughing out loud.

"Well, are you going to introduce me to you overprotective other half?" Katie said, extending her hand for a handshake, with the stranger, next to me.

"Of course, Katie Sumers, this is the famous underwear model Lucy Lingerie; Lucy, this is Katie Sumers, who of course, requires no introduction."

They shook hands, very formally.

"Ignore him …" The stranger said, with a smile.

"… hi Katie, I am Wendy. I am a WPC and am here with Sonia Kostas, my niece. She was the little girl with cerebral palsy who you gave an award to for her magnificent fundraising efforts."

The stranger, whom I now knew to be Wendy, said.

"And you are?"

"Chris, Chris Pritchard. I'm in the job, too, over at Tottenham. I'm here at the personal invitation of one of my oldest and certainly closest friends, Katie."

I was of course being sarcastic, as I'd only met Katie once, and for about twenty minutes.

Wendy and I shook hands, by which time the lady behind the bar had arrived with our drinks. We were then consumed with the business of making sure everyone had what they wanted. A few moments later, when Wendy walked off, I felt ever so slightly disappointed. I thought about Jackie and her young doctor and a tiny bit of me wanted to get my own back, by doing something I shouldn't.

I decided to leave Katie, Tabitha, and Bob alone to discuss their problems, so I strolled into the more sedate atmosphere of the adjacent lounge bar. While I was very happy to help Bob, I didn't want to be any part of their decision-making process, because whatever they did, wasn't going to have any consequences for me. I sat at the bar and supped my drink, happy to be away from the mayhem next door.

Ten minutes later, I had finished my pint and was just about to check on Bob, when Wendy stuck her head around the door.

"I was looking for you; I owe you a drink." She said.

"Oh, don't worry I'm fine, really." I replied.

Wendy walked in and sat on the stool next to me.

"My sister has taken my niece home, she was getting very tired, so I thought I'd have one last drink before making tracks myself. Are you going to join me?"

"Of course." I replied, what else could I say?

\*\*\*

I didn't have one more drink; I had three.

I had spent the two hours with an utterly enchanting woman of Anglo- Mediterranean descent, whose father was a Church of England vicar, and whose mother was a former Miss Greece. Wendy was a WPC at Barking and on relief. She told me, she had recently got out of a long-term relationship with a Sergeant called John, that she'd just bought her own house in Leyton and had just started to study for the Sergeant's exam. We got on really well, chatted like we had known each other for years and, I have to confess, I thought she was really attractive, even though her appearance, she was tall and very dark, was exactly opposite to what I usually liked.

When we eventually went our own ways, I was more than a little disappointed that she hadn't asked for my mobile number. I assumed Wendy hadn't enjoyed our time together, quite as much, as I had.

I drove home carefully because I'd had way too much to drink and, also, because I was in a melancholy mood. Did I really think Jackie was being unfaithful? Should I do anything that might jeopardise our relationship?

The way I saw it, I'd been happily married for ten years, and I'd seen too many of my friends and colleagues playing the divorce game, and quite frankly, it didn't seem all that much fun. Besides, I loved Jackie, I really did, and we got on well. The marriage wasn't perfect, we hardly ever had enough time together, and we were rarely in the mood for sex at the same time, but when we were, the physical side was great.

I thought I'd soon get to the bottom of why she was walking into a swanky Buckhurst Hill restaurant, arm in arm, with a handsome young doctor. Nothing I'd ever known about my wife would suggest she was capable of being unfaithful to me.

When I woke up for work a few, too few, hours later, I was less confident about my wife's fidelity because I discovered she hadn't come home. She wasn't in the spare room and her car was nowhere to be seen. I sent her a text message, asking her to give me a call, 'just so I know you're all right, hon', and got on with my morning ablutions.

## Chapter 30

The C.I.D. shift pattern meant that, just occasionally, a C.I.P.P. team had a day when they were neither responsible for dealing with prisoners or investigating reported crimes and this Wednesday, was just one such day. I had a plan. I had done a P.N.C. check on the vehicle in the Colonel Beaulieu case and obtained a name and address for the registered keeper. I intended to trace the keeper and, if there were sufficient grounds, arrest him.

I took Dot with me, and we set off for Court Oak House, in a place called Finchampstead Ridges in Berkshire. The journey should take about two hours. I didn't know the area, at all, but Dot said, she thought it wasn't far from Broadmoor mental hospital and explained, a few years ago, she'd spent several days interviewing one of the inmates about some outstanding murders.

It was nearly eleven by the time Jackie texted me back.

"Sorry, darling. Should have let you know. Spent the night at Julie's, you know, the old friend who I met for dinner. Had a bit too much red wine, so decided not to risk driving home. I am off today; shall we go out for dinner?"

Of course, I was a little suspicious, but I decided not to overreact. Besides, now, Jackie didn't know that I'd seen her, so I didn't want to give that advantage away, until I had a clearer account of events. Sometimes, you just can't stop being a police officer.

It was great to have a couple of hours with Dot and catch up on her life. One of the best things about my job, was that you spent so much time sitting in a car with people, you really got to know them. You were forced to chat, or sit there in silence, and I couldn't do the 'sit there in silence' thing, ever.

On route, I got a call from Bob and asked Dot to pull over, so I could take it in private.

"What the fuck happened to you last night, Nostrils?"

"I was in the other bar, with a girl called Wendy. I thought I should give you time alone to talk things through. So how did it go?" I asked.

"It's difficult, isn't it? She thinks the press will have a field day, that her career will be over. She's worried about everything. She has two kids at private school, so she's saying, 'how am I going to pay, if ITV terminate my contract?'. Also, she thinks her old man will go after custody, so she'll have all that shit to deal with."

"But they always side with the mother, don't they? She'll be fine." I said, trying to sound positive.

"She's worried, mate." Bob replied.

"And when she went to the gym this morning, there was a photographer, taking pictures of her. She didn't see him but one of the staff tipped her off. Apparently, he was sitting in a car, with a long-lensed camera. I mean, it didn't matter, she was there alone but it's unsettled her, even more."

"Bob, why don't you two knock your relationship on the head, just for a few months. Let Katie divorce her old man, on grounds of domestic violence..."

"But the cats out of the bag, isn't it? Someone in the press knows about her and me. So, stopping it now's not going to help, is it?" Bob interjected.

He was right, of course.

"I think she's more worried about what her old man will do, than she's letting on."

"Let me know if there's anything I can do." I said.

"Have you heard about these racist letters?" Bob asked, changing the subject.

"Yeah, Colin got one, yesterday." I replied.

"Area Complaints have picked it up, they've been at the nick, all morning."

"Not C.I.B.?" I replied, surprised.

"No, a uniformed Chief Inspector. He's spent most of his time with the new DI."

"Keep me posted on that." I asked and we said our goodbyes.

As soon as I got back in the car, Dot pounced.

"What's going on?" She asked.

"What do you mean?" I asked, innocently.

"Chris, we've got no secrets; why did you have to take a call in private?"

Dot made me smile, she really did. No one else I worked with, would be so direct. But she wasn't rude, and I kind of appreciated her straightforward, no nonsense, approach to life, the universe and everything in it.

"Dot, darling, you're right we have no secrets, but this is somebody else's secret, so it is not mine to share."

"Very well answered, Sarge." Dot replied.

Finchampstead Ridges was one impressive road. The detached houses were, in fact, mansions, with eight or more bedrooms. They were well set back from the road, deep in a pine forest. To add to the grandeur, along either side of the road, ran a line of California Redwood trees, which were enormous. None of the houses had numbers, just names, and off the main road, were several unnamed private roads, containing even more impressive residences.

We were looking for Court Oak House and were left with no other option than to start calling, door to door, to see if anyone knew where it might be. Two hours later, we'd knocked at every house without success, but we had a change of fortune when we saw the postman.

"The post code is right, but I've worked this round for thirty years and I've never delivered a letter to Court Oak House." He replied, definitively.

At this point, we decided to give up our search and headed back to the smoke.

"So, the owner gave the D.V.L.A. a false address." Dot remarked on route.

"Apparently but I think there's more to it, than that." I replied.

"Go on."

"Well, it took us hours to realise that it wasn't a correct address, didn't it? And besides, I think, whoever registered the car, went to great lengths to make sure the address was feasible. I mean, although it was impossible to find, it was also almost impossible to establish that it was, in fact, false."

"But I don't get it. If you give a made-up address, you'll never get the logbook, or any other correspondence related to the vehicle. Insuring your car is going to be a nightmare, I mean, you'll never get hold of the certificate, will you?" Dot said.

"Unless, of course, you submit a 'divert all mail order' to the Post Office, like you do when you move. Then any letters that are sent to Court Oak House get diverted to your real address."

"But why?" Dot asked.

"I don't know." I replied.

"Does it mean the van was stolen? Have we discovered some sophisticated car ringing operation?" Dot asked.

"Perhaps." I replied.

"Next stop the D.V.L.A., then? A trip down the M4 should help unravel this mystery." I said.

"But the whole burglary was a bit strange, wasn't it? I mean, when you asked me to come with you today, I had a look at the CRIS …"

"I thought I restricted it." I said, interrupting her.

"... it's not restricted, I read it this morning. I mean, who steals a manuscript but leaves thousands of pounds worth of gold and foreign currency? And the alarm's iffy, isn't it? Broken, repaired and then breaks down again, within twenty-four hours."

"Go on, what's your theory?" I asked.

"It's the press. I'll bet you, before you know it, extracts from the book will start to appear in the tabloids." Dot replied.

"I agree. I can't believe that isn't restricted, I know I restricted it." I replied.

"Well, if you did, someone overruled you."

## Chapter 31

As usual, I was late leaving work, so I arranged to meet Jackie in the Volunteer, a pub in High Beech, specialising in oriental food. I think the landlord had married an Asian woman and she did all the cooking. We often went there when Jackie couldn't be bothered to cook.

I confess to being a little bit nervous because this was the first time in ten years that I'd caught my wife lying to me. I was more than a little unsettled. Years ago, I'd been going out with a girl called Carol who, completely out of the blue, left me for her sister's husband. I really didn't want to go through all that heartache again. Besides, I thought Jackie and I had something quite special.

I decided to play the whole thing as coolly, as possible; to give Jackie no indication I suspected she was lying to me by saying absolutely nothing about what I had seen.

I was annoyed when I saw her, I couldn't help it, and I know it was irrational. The thing was, she was wearing jeans and a T-shirt, and I kept thinking how gorgeous she looked the previous evening, when she went out with him! Clearly, she wasn't bothered about whether I fancied her or not. But I was cool and didn't show how I felt.

With that said, we had a great evening and, once I'd relaxed a bit, we chatted easily about our various jobs and what was going on with our friends at work and their lives. As usual, Jackie did most of the talking and I paid particular attention to see if she mentioned any of her male doctor colleagues, but she didn't. I told her about Colonel Beaulieu, and the stolen manuscript, and even to her it seemed obvious, some unscrupulous reporters had stolen it with a view to publishing the most titillating extracts.

Not once did either of us mention the previous evening until we were just about to leave when, almost out of the blue, Jackie leaned into me and whispered in my ear:

"I have a small confession to make."

She spoke nervously and, in an instant, the atmosphere between us changed.

"Go on." I urged her.

"I didn't meet Julie, last night; well, not for dinner, I went out with a guy from work."

"Okay." I replied, cautiously.

"I feel awful. I'm so sorry."

"Did you spend the night with him?" I asked.

I        could feel my stomach churning over.

"God, no. I really didn't." She replied, convincingly.

I breathed in, hard. It was just the answer I was hoping for, but should I believe her?

"Why didn't you come home, then?" I asked.

"I spent the night at Julie's. I had way too much wine and couldn't drive."

I looked at Jackie's face and deep into her beautiful blue eyes, if she was lying to me, she would never have been able to hold my stare, but she did.

"Where does Julie live?" I asked.

"Princes Road, Buckhurst Hill, runs parallel with Queens Road. Sorry, I'm babbling, that was where I had dinner, Queens Road."

Jackie took hold of my hand and squeezed.

"I'm so sorry I lied to you."

I had a hundred questions but decided to say nothing.

"I went out for dinner with a guy called Nipun; he's a doctor from work."

"Okay" I replied, slowly.

"Look, I shouldn't have gone, halfway through the meal I thought, 'what am I doing, I love Chris', and I left. I didn't even finish my main course. I went to Julie's. I was in tears. I poured my heart out, told her how stupid I'd been. We drunk nearly three bottles of wine to drown my tears and I fell asleep on her settee.

"Okay." I replied.

"I had to tell you, I mean, I didn't have to, but I did. I feel terrible, Chris. I don't know why I did it. I was being stupid."

While she spoke, Jackie clung to my hand like she would never let go.

"Why did you? What's going on between you? Does he know you're married?" I asked.

"Nothing, yes, no, oh god I'm an idiot. No, there is nothing going on between us."

"Have you kissed him?"

Jackie looked down and immediately, I knew that she had.

"Look darling, I'm not going to get annoyed or lose my temper. Just tell me what's happened, from the beginning. Tell me the truth, please don't let me find out later, you've lied to me, here today."

Jackie nodded.

"Deal?" I asked.

She nodded again.

"Right, Nipun's a really nice guy …"

I resisted the temptation to immediately interrupt her with a sarcastic comment.

"… and when he arrived late last year, all the younger nurses were completely smitten. He's suave and sophisticated; he had a first from Oxford and a masters from Harvard. He was, well, everything a young nurse looks for in a potential husband, but he took a shine to me, and I was flattered. I'm sorry, it felt absolutely fantastic, and everyone was like, 'he's got a real soft spot for you', and, 'he told me that he can't keep his eyes off you,'. was really, really flattered. Chris, it was completely innocent, I didn't do anything about it, but I did enjoy it and then …"

Jackie paused, so I figured we were getting to the difficult part. I wasn't sure how I felt; I was upset, more than annoyed and hurt, more than angry.

"... then he asked me out, just for a drink and I said, no. Then he asked me out again and I said no, I'm happily married, and he didn't ask me out again, for ages and ..."

Jackie again paused her narrative, but she looked up from the table and straight at me. I anticipated she was doing so, to judge my reaction.

"... and then it happened, in the car park. We'd left work together and we were, like, you know, fooling around, and you know, he flicked an elastic band at me, which hit me in the face, and I pretended it really hurt and made a huge fuss, and, well, you know, we ..."

"Go on." I said, quietly.

"Ended up, you know ..."

"Jackie, I really don't? Did you drop to your knees and suck him off?"

"Nooooo. We kissed, just once."

"A proper kiss?"

Jackie nodded.

"When did this happen? I asked.

"A few weeks ago, and then he asked me out and I said yes, and I'm really, really sorry, darling. I don't know what was wrong with me."

"And that was last night?" I asked.

She nodded.

"But I felt so guilty; I couldn't eat, I felt sick, so I garbled an apology for mucking him around and walked out, just after the waiter delivered the main course. In fact, I left so quickly, my jacket is still there."

"     What did you think was going to happen when you agreed to go out with him? Were you going on to a hotel or back to his place, or something?" I asked.

"Darling, you've got to believe me, but I didn't think, I just didn't. I was excited ..."

The word, 'excited', wounded me.

"... really excited ..."

The words 'really excited', really wounded me.

"... it was just like our first date. I was nervous and a bit scared but in a nice way. But more than anything, it made me feel really flattered. All week, I felt great about myself. You remember how upset I was a few years ago when I was thirty, how down and depressed I was, to be leaving my youth and my looks behind? Well, it was like Nipun had turned the clocks back and I was, once again, young."

"Fuck me, Jackie, you're only thirty- four. You make it sound like you're fifty."

"You don't understand. Everyone fancied Nipun, and he chose me. That blew my mind, and made me go a bit mad, for a few months; but I've never stopped loving you, or wanting to spend the rest of my life with you. Chris, I'm sorry, I really am. I've told you the truth. I kissed the guy once, in the car park at work, I agreed to and went out for dinner but left after the starters because I felt so guilty. That is the extent of my guilt here, do you think you can forgive me?"

I smiled because, although I was hurt, I really could understand. I wasn't a hypocrite and hadn't forgotten that I'd spent two hours last night absolutely enchanted by another woman, but we hadn't agreed to meet again, and hadn't even exchanged phone numbers, a fact which allowed me to maintain the high moral ground.

What's more, Jackie didn't know that I'd seen her and so her confession was unnecessary and, therefore, her account of events much more credible than they would have been, if I'd challenged her, unexpectedly.

"Of course, I can forgive you." I replied.

I thought the conversation had concluded and went to stand up, but Jackie pulled my arm, gently, and I resumed my seat.

"Have you ever been unfaithful to me?" She asked, her voice barely more than a whisper.

"I need to know, Chris. For some reason which I can't explain, I need to know."

"I have never slept with another woman, had any form of sexual relationship, Christ, I haven't even kissed another woman, since the day we met." I replied, both decisively and honestly.

"Then I know I did the right thing by walking out the restaurant. I don't deserve you, Chris Pritchard, but I'm bloody glad I've got you. I love you so much."
"Let's go home and make love." I said, suddenly feeling very romantic.

"No" Jackie replied, firmly.

I frowned.

"I don't want to go home and make love. I want to go home and have my brains fucked out, by the love of my life." She said.

"Where the fuck am I going to find a stethoscope, at this time of night?" I asked.

## Chapter 32

As I'd worked the weekend, today was my last day at work in a run of ten. I was tired and needed the long weekend to recover, and unusually, Jackie was off too, so we could arrange to do something, which would be nice.

The first thing I did when I logged on, was to update the CRIS report for the Colonel Beaulieu burglary, detailing our trip down to Berkshire. I then set out my intention to make further enquiries with the D.V.L.A. I also noticed that S.O.C.O. had updated their page and recorded that they'd recovered no forensic evidence from the scene and that, in fact, from the analysis of several traces, she believed, the suspects had been wearing rubber gloves of the sort used by forensic examiners.

What was curious, was that the CRIS report was restricted, which didn't make a lot of sense, as Dot said she'd managed to access and read the report the day before. I called the CRIS helpdesk and discussed the matter. The woman, who dealt with me, was equally perplexed. She said, from the transaction log, she could see that someone had unrestricted the report, yesterday, but that they'd re-restricted it, about twenty minutes, later. By sheer coincidence, it was during this short window that Dot had accessed it. The woman from the helpdesk was very efficient and said that the access code of the person, who had briefly derestricted the report, didn't look like one she'd ever seen before. She agreed to make some enquiries and call me back.

What troubled me, was that twenty minutes would be about how long you'd need to access the report, print off all the pages, and then re-restrict it. Someone had clearly had a good nosy about and then got out, hoping their visit would go unnoticed, but it hadn't.

From the outset, there was something strange about the Colonel's burglary and, as the investigation progressed, the matter got weirder. I decided to discuss it with the DI, although I didn't expect any useful advice, I thought I'd better keep her in the loop, especially, as she'd originally come to the victim's address.

"Any thoughts?" I asked, after I'd told her the whole story.

"How do you restrict a CRIS?"

"I'll get someone to show you, later. Unless you have any objection, I'll take a day out of the office, next week, and pay a visit to the police liaison officer down at the D.V.L.A. I want to get a copy of the original documentation for the van and see if we can trace the real owner. Do you want to come?"

"Good god, no. I need to deal with a much more serious matter, the racist letters.

I need a discreet word, Chris. I don't know if you're aware, but Area Complaints have picked the job up. They're going to do a spin during the night. Every single desk and locker will be opened, by force if necessary, and searched."

"Everyone? There must be hundreds." I replied.

"That's where I need your help. Can you have a wander round the male locker room and count how many lockers there are down there? The Chief Inspector from Area Complaints wants the details, as soon as possible. I would do it, but I don't know the nick well enough and besides, I can't go into the male locker room."

"So, you'll do the WPC's locker room, then?" I asked.

"Do you think that's necessary? I think it's highly unlikely that the sender of these disgusting letters is going to be a woman, don't you?"

I shrugged my shoulders; sometimes the double standards exhibited by some, made me die.

"Oh, and just make sure there's nothing in your desk that shouldn't be there, you know, Valentine cards from the girlfriend, flick knife, bag of cannabis." She added.

I wasn't quite sure whether she was joking but was really surprised that the DI had imparted this information to me. I was pleased though, because it meant, one, that she didn't suspect me, and secondly, and more importantly, it hadn't been her that had fitted me up. Strange though it may sound, I also felt guilty that I had ever thought it was, perhaps I had been wrong about her all along?

I was also very pleased that, only yesterday, I'd studiously re-checked my desk, just in case, any more incriminating evidence had appeared.

I had to smile though, I mean, we had just had a nasty stranger rape, an attempted murder, had a serial sex attacker on the loose and the details of Colonel Beaulieu's sex life, with a royal princess, stolen out of his safe and what was the main concern and focus of the Metropolitan Police? A few childish, stupid, letters sent to serving police officers who, quite frankly, shouldn't be so fucking sensitive, anyway.

I thanked the DI for letting me know about the searches, agreed to assist, and turned to leave her office when she asked:

"Oh Chris, are you dealing with that passport fraud case?"

"Yeah, I know what you're going to say, that I haven't done the pile of C.P.S. actions in their latest memo but, as you know, boss, I have been busy. If I'm being honest, I think they're superfluous, as there's plenty of evidence to charge both the main suspect and her sister. I'll get on with the case next week, I promise."

"No, it's not a criticism; the powers that be want me to review it. That's why I was in with the Superintendent, the other day. Can you get me the papers and let me read through?"

I nodded.

"Of course, boss. I'm sure you'll agree we have ample evidence, already. Are the powers that be getting nervous that we're about to charge such a high-profile figure?"

"I think so, get me the papers and, if I agree with your assessment, I'll give you the green light to go ahead with the prosecution."

"No problem, give me two minutes and everything will be on your desk." I offered, helpfully.

"Thank you." My DI said and I detected, for the first time, that the atmosphere between us might just be warming, a little.

"Oh, I had a chat with Colin, yesterday." She said.

"He's a nice fella, isn't he?" I commented.

"Yes, he is. I wanted to find out how he was coping."

"Coping with what?" I asked.

No sooner had the words left my mouth, than I realised the DI had switched the conversation back to the subject of the racist letters. I also realised that my question was more than a little tactless.

"Are you serious, Chris? The racist letters, he received one. I wanted to find out how upset he was and whether there was anything I could do to alleviate his distress."

I resisted the, almost overwhelming, urge to say, 'what fucking distress?' and to point out that the DI had never asked me about how the victim of the stranger rape, last week. was dealing with her 'distress' – but I replied, with outstanding self-control.

"And how is he doing?"

"He's hurting, Chris, really hurting. He can't believe that someone he works with, could hold such offensive views."

For a moment I panicked, what if Colin had told DI Kitty about my comment regarding 'black man's meat'?

I heard myself empathising, but I thought the whole thing was complete bollocks.

"Yes, it must have been very distressing." I said.

"Can you keep an eye on him, Chris? I've given him my home phone number, in case he needs to talk to someone; someone who will understand, someone whose been the victim of racial discrimination in this job."

What a load of crap!

"That's very kind of you." I said, through gritted teeth.

## Chapter 33

"Chris, wake up. That's your job mobile going. It's charging downstairs in the kitchen." Jackie said.

It was seven o'clock on Saturday morning and it was the start of my long weekend off, what the fuck was going on? I assumed that the Control Room must, erroneously, have me down as the weekend DS and were calling to alert me about some incident. I sat up.

"It's going, again; Chris. That's the third time in five minutes, go downstairs and answer it, or at least turn the damn thing off."

By the time I got downstairs, the phone was ringing for the fourth time, so I answered it but before I could say a word a female voice said:

"Chris, it's Jill, Jill Long the Superintendent. Can you get yourself into the nick and into my office, as soon as possible, please?"

"Yes, boss, but you know this is my long weekend; Jim Beam's on this weekend."

"I know that. Listen, just get in, Chris. How long will you be?"

"About an hour." I replied.

"Make it forty minutes." My Superintendent said and she terminated the call.

I turned round to see Jackie standing in the kitchen doorway, she was wearing my old grey dressing gown and her arms were crossed, defiantly.

"Please tell me you're not going to work?" She said.

"Sorry, darling; I've got to." I replied.

"Chris, this is our first weekend off together for ages and I had plans. And I'm ovulating." Jackie protested.

"Sorry, darling."

Jackie stepped aside to allow me out of the kitchen, but she followed me upstairs, remonstrating with every step.

"Chris, just tell them, no." She said, several times.

"Darling, I can't." I replied.

"Why?"

"Because I must go in. That was my Superintendent, she gave me a direct order; put quite simply, I don't have a choice. The matter is not up for debate, I wasn't 'asked' to go to work, I was told to do so. That's a lawful order, not a request. I thought you'd understand by now. You do a similar job." I said.

I was starting to clean my teeth so continued debate was impossible. Jackie was really annoyed, and I understood that, I really did, but what could I do? I think unless you've worked in a discipline service, you just don't appreciate the difference that one word, discipline, makes.

Ten minutes later I was in my old Golf heading down the A11 to Tottenham police station and my lovely wife was back in bed, annoyed and frustrated with her police officer husband.

\*\*\*

As I walked into the back yard of the nick, the first thing I noticed was the Chief Superintendent's private car. Whatever had happened was very serious, if it required the attendance of the nick's two most senior officers on a weekend. The last time I'd known such an occurrence was, well quite honestly, I couldn't remember. With that said, the place was eerily quiet, there were no T.S.G. vans, no India 99, not even a dog unit. I was genuinely perplexed as to what could be going on. Whatever it was, it merited my attendance and that fact, started to make me nervous. I suddenly realised that whatever the emergency was, it appeared to be personal, rather than force wide. I hoped I didn't have to wait long to find out.

The Superintendent's office was on the top floor and the door was open, so I went straight in. Sitting around the coffee table were the Chief Superintendent, called Dave Stock, and the Superintendent Jill Long. On the table was a phone and a small red light indicated the device was on speaker mode. As it was obvious, they were in the middle of a conversation, I didn't say anything but gestured a greeting and sat down in a vacant chair.

Dave Stock was a white guy in his sixties who had been a Royal Navy Captain and commanded a destroyer or something during the Falklands War. Everyone said he was a nice guy and the local community loved him but personally I'd hardly said more than two words to him, in the three years I'd been at Tottenham. He sported a full beard, which was peppered with grey, and just about everyone referred to him affectionately as CBE, which stood for Captain Bird's Eye.

They both nodded acknowledgement of my presence and then a male voice on the speakerphone said.

"There's an empty bottle of vodka in the car. That information's just come in from the unit at the scene. We only have the one unit there, everyone else is tied up with a pre-planned operation to evict eighty-odd squatters from some derelict properties in Brighton. I have sent an additional unit from Worthing, but their running time is forty minutes.

We're also checking with traffic because we've just installed a speed camera southbound on the A23. It went live this week but apparently, the film doesn't last very long and may already need replacing.

The unit that's on scene is going to make their way down to the cliff edge but we've got a real issue with radio signal at that location, so their likely to be out of contact for a while, which of course, isn't ideal.

We've requested the R.N.L.I. put out their inshore rigid inflatable. The Coastguard is contacting the R.A.F. to see if they can launch a Search and Rescue helicopter, they should have a response, shortly. Is there anything else at this stage?"

The Chief Superintendent and the Superintendent looked at one another and shook their heads. Jill spoke:

"No and thank you, again. Can we leave this line open, on mute, so we can communicate without the hassle of going through a switchboard?"

"Yes, yes; putting you on mute but leaving the line open." The voice replied.

"Likewise" Jill responded, and she pushed the mute button on the phone.

They both looked terribly serious, and we sat there in silence, for a few moments. As I'd made my way to the office, I thought I'd open the conversation by saying something like, 'this better be serious guys because my wife's going mad', but now I realised that would be an inappropriate thing to say.

"Thanks for coming in, so quickly, Chris …" Jill said.

"… as you will have gathered, we've got a bit of a situation going."

I nodded but didn't say a word.

"The thing is …" Jill hesitated,   and I realised she was thinking how to say what she was about to say.

"What the fuck's happened?" I said, completely spontaneously.

"How well do you know Bob Clark?"

"Not particularly well, boss. Nobody knows Bob particularly well. He's quite a private sort of guy, keeps his personal life to himself. Why? Is this about him?"

The Chief Superintendent nodded but Jill kept speaking.

"Is he married?"

"No, single."

"Children?"

I shook my head.

"Next of kin?"

"I know his mother is still alive but she's elderly. I think she must have had him in her late forties or something like that. His dad died last year. His mum's contact details will be in the Book 1, surely?"

"There's nothing in next of kin." Jill replied.

"How's Bob been, lately?" The Chief Superintendent asked.

"Fine." I replied.

I realised that circumstances appeared to be conspiring to put me in a difficult situation because of Bob's affair with Katie Sumers.

"Do you know any reason why Bob would want to harm himself?" The Chief Superintendent asked.

I didn't think for one second that Bob would do anything stupid; he just wasn't that sort of person.

"No, I don't. Please tell me what this is all about?" I replied.

"Bob Clark appears to have committed suicide." Jill responded.

## Chapter 34

Jill filled me in on what had been happening.

"Apparently, Bob's car was found parked up and locked in a car park, about half a mile from Beachy Head, in Sussex. As you probably know, Beachy Head is tall cliff on the south coast, not far from Eastbourne. The Sussex Inspector, who we were just speaking to, reckons they have about twenty people a year committing suicide, there. Because of this, night duty often patrol the car park, to see if there are any potential suicides, and they try to intercede, before they do the deed. Anyway, at five o'clock this morning, the PC found an old Ford Capri, did a P.N.C. check and it came back registered to Bob."

I knew Bob had an old brown Capri; it was his pride and joy, and he kept the vehicle in mint condition.

"They did a 'please allow' to his home address but got no reply; do you know if he lives alone?" Jill asked me.

"I think so, but I've never asked him. What about his phone? Have you called him?"

"It's switched on and rings out to voicemail, which, in itself, isn't right." Jill replied.

"Is there any chance the car has been stolen overnight? I mean, jumping off a high cliff, just doesn't sound like something Bob would do." I responded.

"There's no sign of forced entry and the ignition barrels intact. The officer spotted some volumes of Blackstone on the back seat and guessed the occupant must be a police officer. They contacted their own HQ first, and then the Yard.  It didn't take IR long to ascertain the registered keeper was in the Job and where he was posted, that's when they alerted us."

Blackstone was the name of the police study books, which contained the information you needed to take the promotion exams. There would be no reason a person who wasn't a police officer would have these in their car. IR was Information Room, a department at the Yard, that is to say, New Scotland Yard.

"I didn't even realise Bob had been studying." I commented.

"Apparently, the whole scenario is quite a well-trodden path ..." The Chief Superintendent said.

"... they find an abandoned vehicle in the car park, a few hours or days later, the owner is reported missing and, usually, their body is found, a short while later, washed up on a local beach."

"Chris, is there any reason why Bob would want to do anything like this?" Jill asked me.

I felt really conflicted. Of course, I knew the personal problems Bob was experiencing but I was told those in confidence. I had no right to blurt them out to the Chief Superintendent and the Superintendent, or did I? This was very serious and maybe it didn't matter, anyway, if he was already dead. In the second I had to consider my next move, I chose a compromise.

"I think he might have had a few domestic issues, lately. Like I said though, he was a private person; really kept himself to himself." I replied.

"I always thought Bob Clark was gay. Has he split up from his partner?" Jill asked.

She used the first two fingers of each hand to put visually the word 'partner' in speech marks.

"Ah." The Chief Superintendent replied, as if that explained everything and he nodded, knowingly.

"Pretty sure he's not gay." I said.

"What domestics?" Jill pushed.

"I don't know the details." I lied.

"Well, what do you know?" Jill pushed.

"He was seeing a married lady, but it was all about to come on top. Honestly, I don't think the problem was serious enough to cause him to do anything as drastic as jumping off Beachy Head, no way. I mean, are you sure his car's not been nicked? I know you've done a please allow but this is our long weekend, he could have gone away for a few days, got a train, seen some mates, gone to visit his mum, I don't know. And then his car gets nicked, I mean, it's old, and those old Fords are easy to nick, aren't they, a Slim Jim down the driver's door, flip the bonnet, hotwire the coil and bob's your uncle."

They sat nodding but I don't think I'd convinced them.

"What about the bottle of vodka?" The Chief Superintendent asked.

"Was it actually in the car?" I asked.

"Apparently." He replied.

I didn't have an answer. As far as I knew, Bob wasn't a great drinker.

"The car was locked, right?" I asked.

They nodded.

"Well, who the fuck locks their car up before they totter off and jump off a cliff?"

"Force of habit?" The Chief Superintendent suggested.

At that moment the telephone, which was still open but on mute, crackled to life.

"Chief Superintendent Stock? It's Inspector Puddephatt. The PC at the scene can't find any trace of your man; he's forced entry to the Capri and turned it over. I am sorry to tell you this, but he's found, what looks like, three small wraps of white powder, down the back of the back seat. The PC says it looks like cocaine, but it could be speed."

"What the fuck?" I said, quite loudly.

It wasn't a very professional response but a completely natural one.

"That's bollocks." I said, to both my colleagues.

Jill put her finger to her lips to indicate that I should be quiet.

"So, it looks like there's more to this suicide, than meets the eye. Apart from the white powder, the PC commented that the inside of the car was immaculate, like it had just been driven out of the showroom. He's seized the drugs and is going to take them back to the nick and get them logged."

"We need to get the drugs and the car forensicated. They should have been left in situ and photographed." I said, ignoring Jill's clear instruction that I should remain quiet.

"I'm sorry, can you say that again? I missed that." Inspector Puddephatt said.

"Can you hang on one moment, please?" The Chief Superintendent said and then he pushed the mute button.

I thought he was going to admonish me, so I started to speak, before he had a chance.

"That's bollocks, Governor. There's no way Bob Clark would have anything to do with drugs. We need to get the drugs and the car fingerprinted to see if his prints are on the drugs or whether anyone else's prints are on, or around, the car."

"But we don't do that if we nick someone in the street with drugs in his car, do we? Surely, we should treat this in just the same way. Otherwise, this could look like we're trying to cover up. Besides, this is a Sussex matter, I can't be telling them how to deal."

With that, he unmuted the call.

"Inspector Puddephatt, please proceed as you would, normally. If there's anything we can do, then let us know."

"Yes of course, thank you. There's not a lot more the PC at the scene can do, and he's night duty, so I've told him to get off home, after he's booked in the drugs. The early turn PC is from Worthing, he should be there in about twenty minutes, he'll pick things up. Quite frankly, I don't suspect there'll be a lot more to do, apart from recover the vehicle, then, wait and see what happens. The inshore lifeboat has still not set out and that's coming from Newhaven, so it'll be a good while yet. Of course, if you're man does turn up, he'll have to be nicked for possession of class A."

Chief Superintendent Stock thanked him for his assistance, and they left the line open, in case of developments.

There was one obvious line of enquiry, to speak to Katie Sumers, to see if she had any idea where Bob was, but I couldn't do that, while I was sat with the Chief Superintendent. I needed a reason to excuse myself and then fortune, or rather Superintendent Jill Long, gave me one.

"Chris, can you go to Bob's home address, I'll get someone from early turn C.I.D. to get a warrant. Get into the place and see if there's anything to assist us, like a suicide note or …"

She hesitated, unable to think of anything else.

"…or a map of Beachy Head." I suggested, a little sarcastically.

"Or perhaps some more drugs." The Chief Superintendent added.

"Bob Clark is not a drug addict." I replied.

"Then what were they doing hidden in his car?" The Chief Superintendent asked.

"I don't know." I replied, somewhat meekly.

I was grateful for the chance to leave and thereby call Katie. I stood up.

"I don't think we'll need a warrant; we have a common law power to enter to preserve life. I think we probably have sufficient grounds, under the circumstances. I mean, if we genuinely believe he might have taken his own life, or to be in the process of doing so. Besides, if Bob's already dead, it won't matter and, if he's alive, he's hardly likely to complain, is he?"

The Superintendent agreed and the Chief Superintendent nodded.

"Where exactly does he live?" I asked, pointing at the file to which Jill had kept referring.

"In a police flat in Wanstead. An old friend of mine lives in the same block." Jill replied.

I scribbled the address down on the back of my hand and set off for the address.

## Chapter 35

The first call I made was to Jackie. She had the right hump, until I explained that one the DC's on my team was missing and that it was suspected he'd killed himself.

"Oh my god, who?" She asked.

"Bob, Bob Clark, the guy who was going to come to our BBQ, last summer, but then didn't? You felt sorry for him because he said he was too embarrassed to come, because he didn't have anyone to bring, remember?"

"Oh, the gay guy?" She responded.

"No, he's not gay but yes, that's the bloke I mean. His car's been found at a car park in Sussex where lots of people go to jump off the cliff and kill themselves."

"Beachy Head?"

"Yeah, how do you know that?" I asked.

"I've just heard of it." She replied.

I filled her in and promised I'd do everything I could to get home, as soon as possible. She said not to worry and that she completely understood.

I pulled over to make the next call because I anticipated it might be more difficult.

It rang about seven times, and I started to compose a message to leave on Katie's voicemail, which would be able to stand up to her husband's scrutiny should he listen to it. I cleared my throat and then, suddenly, I heard a child's voice.

"Hello?"

"Hello?" I replied, thinking for a moment that I might have dialed the wrong number.

"Mummy's in the shower." The child said.

"Where's Daddy?" I asked.

I was prepared simply to hang up if her old man came on the line. I thought it wouldn't look too suspicious, as the child would say the caller asked for Daddy, which is hardly the action of an illicit partner.

"Daddy's out; oh, mummy's here now."

"Hello?" Katie said.

"Katie, it's Chris Pritchard, the bloke who's liaising between you and Bob. Are you okay to talk?" I asked.

"Hang on … yes, my parents are downstairs but I'm in the bedroom. Is everything okay?"

"Do you know where Bob is?" I asked.

"No, haven't seen him since the awards thing at Chigwell. Why?"

I was reticent to advise her the full circumstances because it might worry the life out of her.

"He's, well, he's gone missing." I replied.

"But he's not meant to be at work, today; he's off, all weekend. What do you mean, 'gone missing'? Where was he meant to be that he's missing from?" She asked.

This was turning out to be an awkward conversation, especially as I'd decided to be economical with the truth.

"Have you any idea whether he had any plans for this weekend?" I asked, but Katie slightly misunderstood my question, because she replied.

" We didn't have any plans for the weekend, we'd agreed to avoid each other for a few weeks, remember? I thought that was your idea?"

"No, did Bob have any plans; you know, on his own? Was he going to see his mum or something?" I asked.

"Uh, no." She replied.

"You don't sound terribly sure?" I asked, hopefully.

"Fuck, Chris, he did say he was going to do something but, Jesus, I can't remember what it was, for the life of me." Katie replied.

"Was he going to visit someone?"

"Nope." Katie replied, but very uncertainly.

"Was he going to the Gym, the David Lloyd centre?"

"No, he was going to avoid the gym for a few weeks, remember? You told me that." She replied, more confidently.

"Listen, I've got to go, Steve's back and he's coming upstairs …"

I could hear an angry male voice in the background repeatedly calling out Katie's name.

With that the call terminated.

My phone rang immediately.

"Chris Pritchard." I answered.

"Chris, it's Jill Long. Bob's car has disappeared."

"I beg your pardon?" I asked, incredulously.

"Bob's Capri, it's disappeared. When the early turn PC from Worthing got to the car park, the car was gone."

"So, Bob's alive? He's made his way back to his car and now he's driving home. Perhaps he changed his mind about jumping?" I suggested.

"It may not be that simple. The PC on the scene thinks the Capri might have been stolen." Jill explained.

"What?" I asked.

"Well, when they arrived there were two caravans parked up in the car park, travellers. They reckon that they've had the Capri off which, of course, was insecure because of the broken passenger window.

"Were the travellers there, all the time? The Sussex Inspector never mentioned them?" I remarked.

"Yeah, he did but it must have been during the conversation we were having with him, prior to your arrival, this morning. The night duty PC did knock at the caravans to ascertain whether they'd seen the driver of the Capri, but they didn't get an answer, which is hardly surprising, as it was five in the morning. The theory is that one or more of the travellers woke up this morning, saw the Capri, apparently abandoned, with a broken passenger window, and has taken it for a ride." Jill said.

"They probably thought it had already been stolen." I added.

"Exactly." Jill said.

"For fuck's sake, boss. Now we've lost the opportunity of fingerprinting the car!"

"Um." Jill replied.

"Boss, with the greatest respect, I don't give a flying fuck what you think, I am telling you beyond any doubt, Bob Clark has absolutely nothing to do with the gear in his car. He's being set up."

In my fifteen years' service, I'd never spoken in that way to a senior officer. With every urge in my body, I wanted to apologise but didn't, I held my ground and swallowed hard.

"Did you hear me, Jill?"

I deliberately used her first name, which was a huge thing, in itself.

"Yes"

Again, I wanted to apologise but I fought the desire.

"I appreciate your loyalty, DS Pritchard." She said, after perhaps a good five seconds.

I breathed a sigh of relief.

"Thank you, Ma'am." I replied, using the formal address to indicate that I wasn't challenging her but simply making a point.

"Let me know what you find at his home address, Chris. And thank you, you're a good friend to your colleague."

Jill hung up. I had always got on with her, but I now felt a new, and increased, respect for my Superintendent. She was old school and wouldn't have appreciated being spoken to like that by a junior officer, but she hadn't overreacted and had demonstrated a decent dose of patience and understanding.

# Chapter 36

When I arrived at Buxton House and found Bob's flat, I had to smile as I realised, I'd been here years before. When I first went to Stoke Newington from Training School, I briefly worked with a PC called Dean and this was his old flat. I had dinner there one night and had popped around a few times over the following months.

About a year after I worked with him, Dean was arrested for failing to stop at the scene of an accident and drink drive. He was banned from driving for two years and the Job sacked him. I gave character evidence at his Central Board but to no avail. Dean was always a real handful and, quite frankly, the Metropolitan Police was a better place without him. With that said, he never did me any harm and I was glad I could, at least, be there for him in his hour of need. I thought that it said quite a lot when I was the only person who stepped up to help him.

And then years later, I was out with Jackie at Lakeside Shopping Centre in Thurrock, when I saw a couple acting very suspicious, in the lingerie section of Marks & Spencer's. Jackie asked me what the matter was, and I told her, I thought the couple 'over there' were shoplifting. She asked what I was going to do about it. Then the bloke turned round and, for the first time, I could see his face, and yes, you've guessed it, it was Dean and his wife Jessica.

Dean looked up and caught my eye.

"Nostrils, you old cunt." He called out, way too loudly, and across ten meters of knickers and bras.

We met and embraced like long lost brothers, introduced our partners, and chatted for a few minutes about times past and happy, and not so happy, memories. At some point in the conversation, I asked what he was doing? I meant in life, generally, but he took me literally and replied, with candor:

"Oh, just a bit of freetail therapy."

*** 

I knocked several times at Bob's flat but, as I expected, there was no reply. I looked through the letterbox; the hall seemed like any other hall in the world, and provided no additional clue, as to where the occupant might be. I called at the addresses either side, but no one answered.

I was just vying up my options, which seemed to include just one, putting the door in, when a male, in his late forties, emerged onto the communal landing from the stairwell. He was sweating heavily and from this and his attire, I deduced he'd been for a run.

He nodded to acknowledge my presence and then leant against a wall to stretch out his leg muscles. It took about ten seconds to notice the smell of sweat seeping from his every pore.

I was unsure quite what to do so I knocked again at Bob's door.

"He's not in, mate." The jogger said.

"Are you, his neighbour?" I asked.

He nodded as he switched legs.

"Are you the press?" He replied.

"My name's Chris Pritchard, I'm Bob's DS; do you know where he is?" I asked.

The jogger stopped stretching and turned to give me his full attention.

"He went out really early this morning; well, I heard his door slam at about three-thirty. I was just getting a glass of water from the kitchen, and I remember thinking, he must be on an early spin."

"Listen, have you got five minutes? We're a bit worried about him." I asked.

"Of course, mate. Come in, I'll put the kettle on and, while it's boiling, I'll jump in the shower."

The jogger reached down and rolled back the corner of his doormat to reveal a house key, which he took out and used in the door lock.

Twenty minutes later, I was sitting in his lounge with a nice cup of tea and a selection of biscuits. The jogger had introduced himself as Peter Bromfield, a DCI from the Flying

Squad at Tower Bridge. I knew the name, and for a few minutes, we did that thing all police officers do when they first meet, which is try to find common connections. In the end, we identified half a dozen detectives who we'd both worked with.

"So how well do you know Bob?" I asked.

"Yeah, quite well. We've been neighbours for two years. We're both single guys, so he comes in occasionally to watch the odd game of rugby or an important football game, like England. He's a nice bloke, not your typical policeman, you know, he's quite a serious individual. Mind you, haven't seen much of him of late, just the odd, 'hello', as we pass on the stairs, that sort of thing. Come on tell me, what's happened? You said you worked with him, right?"

"I do. We're on a C.I.P.P. team at Tottenham, this morning his car's been found in a car park in Sussex, not far from Beachy Head, and everyone's thinks he's killed himself." I replied, candidly.

"Poor cunt ..."

"I'm not convinced myself." I interjected.

" ... is that why the press were here, this morning?" Peter asked.

"Oh, you mentioned the press, earlier. Where they here, this morning?" I replied.

"A bloke was loitering at the bottom of the stars. I challenged him, well politely, and he showed me his press pass. I told him to fuck off, that this was private property. How did they find out so quickly about the suicide?"

I hesitated. Of course, I knew the reason the press was here was nothing to do with Bob's possible suicide, but I didn't want to give anything away.

"I'd actually assumed they were here because of the Katie Sumers thing." Peter went on to say.

I eyed him, cautiously.

"What Katie Sumers thing?" I asked.

"Okay ..." Peter replied, apparently regretting that he might have said too much.

I decided, to move things along, we both had to be honest.

"I know something about the Katie Sumers thing, but I don't want to impart information to you that I've been told, in confidence. But, clearly, you know something about the matter."

"Look, all I know is that, on a half a dozen occasions, I've seen a woman who, while heavily disguised with a headscarf and sunglasses, is clearly the sports presenter, Katie Sumers, coming to and from Bob's flat. She drives a big Lexus four by four and when she visits, Bob moves his own Capri out of his garage at the rear of the flats and leaves it open for her to drive straight in."

Peter stood up and pulled the net curtain back on his lounge window.

"That's his garage there, the one with the padlocks on."

I stood up and my gaze followed his pointed finger. I saw, the otherwise indeterminate garage, amongst a row of about fifteen.

"Gosh, you keeping a log?" I asked.

Peter smiled.

"No, the first time I just noticed by chance and then I observed the ritual several times, over the last few months. As you probably noticed when we came in, these doors slam closed unless you try, very hard, to resist the spring. I like Bob, I really do, and he's a great neighbour to live next to, you know no loud music or late-night parties, but he always lets the door slam, when he leaves. Well, if I hear the door slam quite late in the evening, and then I look out the window at his garage, Bob will open it, to let her drive straight in."

"Have you spoken to him about the relationship?"

Peter shook his head.

"I think you're right. I think the reporters were here for the Katie Sumers thing. He told me that they door stepped him last week."

"Do you need to get in?" He asked.

"That's what I'm doing here. The Chief Superintendent at Tottenham ...

"Is Jill Long still there? The Superintendent?"

"Yeah"

"She's a lovely woman." Peter added.

I nodded.

"She wants me to get in to see if there's anything which will help us work out what's happened."

"Like a suicide note?"

"Exactly."

"So, you heard him leave at three-thirty then?"

"Yeah, definitely."

"Was he in last night?"

"As far as I know, but I wasn't paying any attention, to be fair."

"If you're not going to work, where do you go at three-thirty in the morning?" I asked.

"The airport." Peter replied.

"That's true. But he's scheduled to be back at work on Monday, we're lates. I suppose, he could have gone to the airport, but then, what the fuck is his car doing in a car park in deepest Sussex?

"Stolen at Gatwick Airport, within minutes of him parking it." Peter suggested.

"Maybe he left the keys in the ignition by mistake when he parked up?" I countered.

It suddenly seemed that we had a viable supposition.

My phone rang; it was the Superintendent Jill Long.

"Hello, boss."

"Hi Chris, have you secured entry?" She asked.

"Not yet, I'm making some enquiries with the neighbours. I'm currently with a DCI from the Flying Squad, Peter Bromfield, who lives immediately next door. Peter heard Bob leave at three-thirty this morning, we were thinking that perhaps …

" … Chris, we've got two lifeboats and a search and rescue helicopter deployed. Sussex have set up checkpoints on several roads out of Eastbourne to try to locate the stolen Capri. We've advised the Commissioner's Office and Press Bureau. I need you to get into Bob's flat now. Do I make myself clear?"

"Yes, boss. I was just checking to see if any of the neighbours had a spare set of keys. I'll get in straightaway; I'll call you back the moment I find anything relevant." I replied.

"And you do realise, don't you?"

"Sorry, boss?" I replied, for a moment at a loss as to what she was driving at.

"If he does turn up, and let's pray he does, you'll have to bring him in for possession."

"Yes, boss." I replied, quietly.

I ended the call and turned to Peter, who had already stood up.

"As you may have gathered, I'm getting some grief for not effecting entry, yet. The powers that be are convinced he's jumped off Beachy Head."

"I'd offer to help but I'm already late for an appointment. I do however have a sledgehammer in the garage, if that'll help."

I laughed.

"Or I could just give you his key? We keep a copy of each other's in case we lock ourselves out."

***

It was strange being back in Dean's old flat. Superficially, nothing had changed. I mean, it was the same layout with the old kitchen and bathroom, but the place had been redecorated and now had wooden flooring, throughout. The flat was immaculate, a bit like Bob's desk at work.

Being in Bob's flat felt awkward. I have never wanted to undertake a search, less than I did that day, but I had a job to do.

A cursory glance in the two bedrooms located nothing untoward but, in the kitchen, the lack of just about any food, whatsoever, was disconcerting. The fridge was empty, save for a bottle of sour milk, and there was no evidence my colleague had consumed anything, for a long time, because there was no washing up and the bin was empty of any food waste. Curiously, I could find no alcohol in the house, either.

But I did solve the mystery of Bob's continually ringing mobile phone, because the device was in the kitchen, on charge, and was showing twenty-seven missed calls. Was it significant that he'd left without it? With that said, would someone, who was going to end their life, put their phone on charge?

Next to the phone was a pile of correspondence, which I leafed through. Bob sure had a frightening amount of debt. He had a MasterCard that was nearly at its five grand limit and a store card, on which he owed a little over three thousand. There was also an agreement to get a consolidation loan for fifteen grand with a company called HFC and the repayments were £520 per month, over ten years, with an annual interest rate of a staggering eighteen percent. Finally, there was a letter from a care home in Essex, saying that the outstanding balance had been cleared.

That was a worrying financial position, as it meant he must have been using over half his salary just to make loan repayments. With that said, I knew a lot of old bill that were in the same situation, so it wasn't that unusual. Was it enough for Bob to want to go and top himself?

I found a set of keys and searched Bob's garage but with no meaningful outcome. I did have to smile because, hanging from the garage roof was a tennis ball, on a piece of string, carefully placed, so that Bob would know when to stop the car, as he was pulling in. What's more, he'd pinned a large piece of carpet to the wall of the garage so that, when he opened his car door, it wouldn't strike the rough surface of the breezeblock.

Upon my return, I sat down in the lounge and noticed, on a coffee table next to the settee, a small book entitled 'Tide Tables 1998'. It was face down but opened on the page for Beachy Head and on today's date. Clearly, Bob wanted to know the state of the tide, before he set off in the early hours. When I found the book, my heart sank. I had rather liked the idea that his car had been stolen at Gatwick and driven to the south coast by the thief, but this was clear evidence that Bob himself had gone there.

I tried to work things out. Although it was now obvious, Bob had, indeed, gone to Beachy Head that morning, there was, I thought, nothing in his flat to suggest he had taken his life. What's more, I just couldn't come to the conclusion that the pressure he was under, in respect of Katie Sumers, was sufficient to merit such drastic action – even, if you chucked into the mix, his high level of debt. With that said, of course I didn't know whether there was other stuff going on in his life that might cause him to do it. Had he, for example, just been diagnosed with a terrible and terminal illness?

My phone rang; it was the Superintendent, Jill Long.

"Chris?" She asked.

"Yes boss, I'm in Bob's flat, I've found some evidence that Bob went to Beachy Head but there's nothing ..."

But I didn't get to complete my sentence.

"They've found a body." Was all my Superintendent said.

I was in utter shock and think, for the first and only time in my life, couldn't physically speak, for at least ten seconds; although, with my Superintendent repeatedly saying, 'Chris', down the line, it felt much longer.

"Is it definitely him?" I asked, eventually.

"They don't know, yet. It's been washed up on the shore, in somewhere called Pevensey Bay, I gather that's not far away, five miles east or something."

"Five miles? That seems a long way ..."

I looked at my watch, it was just after ten o'clock.

"... mind you, I suppose it's been five hours now, that's only one mile an hour."

"Sorry, Chris. I really am. Let's wait until we get confirmation and then I'll go and see his next of kin, his mother. Please come with me."

"Of course." I said, meekly.

"There's nothing else to be done here, I'll make my way back to the nick, then." I said.

"Is there anything there? You know, to bring in?" Jill asked.

"Just one thing but it's not particularly important." I replied.

We both hung up.

I picked the Tide Tables book up and examined today's readings. It had been high tide at five o'clock, that morning, and there were marine charts showing the flow of the water, every hour before and after high tide. Something didn't make sense. If Bob had jumped into the water from Beachy Head at high tide, then five hours later, his body should have gone west not east. I was sure Jill had said his body had been found five miles east.

I heard someone at the front door call out, 'hello', and assumed Peter had come back.

"Come in, come in." I called out, still staring at the tidal chart, and scratching my head.

"What the hell are you doing here?" Bob asked.

## Chapter 37

"Where the fuck have you been? We thought you'd killed yourself?" I asked, with an equal mixture of amazement and delight.

"What?" He asked, with astonishment.

"Your car was abandoned in a car park at Beachy Head, a Sussex PC found it. Fuck me, Bob, half the world's out searching for you, helicopters, search and rescue, lifeboats. They've even found your body."

"Chris, what the fuck are you talking about?"

"Where's your car?" I asked.

"In my garage." He replied, speaking slowly, as if I was a simpleton.

"What? Out the back?"

"Yes. I'm not having a good day. I've just had it broken into; some wanker broke into my car down in Sussex. I reckon it was some gypsies that were parked up, nearby. They're a fucking walking crime wave."

"In Beachy Head?" I asked.

"Yes."

"That was the PC, the PC that found your car. He broke in to search it. It's the same reason I'm here. Everyone's convinced you've jumped off Beachy Head."

"Why the fuck would they think that?" He asked.

"Apparently, loads of people do it, every year. And they usually abandon their cars in the car park where you parked up. What were you doing? They did try calling you but ..."

"I know, I forgot my phone, this morning. I left it on charge in the kitchen. I remembered just after I'd set off, but I didn't really need it, so it wasn't a big deal."

"And apparently, there was an empty bottle of Vodka in your car?"

"This one?" He said.

He held up an empty bottle of Smirnoff, which he'd been holding in his right hand, all the time, but which I'd completely missed.

"Yes." I said.

"But it's not mine. When I went to get out of the car, I trod on it and thought, I'd drop it in the foot well, take it home and get rid of it, later. I just hate the fact that some thoughtless twat is quite happy to drop a glass bottle at such a beautiful spot. I was just tidying up."

"What the fuck have you been doing?" I asked.

"I was taking photographs of the sunrise over the sea and set against the cliffs. The tide was perfect, the weather just right. Look, I was going to add it to my collection, and, if I was happy with the finished article, I was going to enter it in this year's Metropolitan Police Photography competition."

As he spoke, Bob walked over to a series of five pictures that were lined up, across the lounge wall. I stood up and took a closer look. They were of various and well-known UK locations, each entitled, 'Good Morning'. The first in the series was, 'Good Morning, Grimsby' and the photograph was of the sun rising over a busy harbor scene of fishermen and their trawlers; the second was 'Good Morning, Anglesey' and recorded a deserted beach, apparently in the aftermath of a heavy storm because there was jetsam and flotsam sprawled everywhere.

"Oh, fucking hell, mate. Fuck me, I hope this morning's photographs were worth it." I said.

"I doubt it, I didn't take any. The clouds came out, just as the sun was rising. I waited to see if the sky would clear but gave up, in the end." He replied.

"How come you're involved?" He asked.

"I got a call this morning, first thing, from Jill Long and the Chief Super. The shit really has hit the fan." I replied.

"Did you tell them about Katie?" He asked.

"No" I replied.

He breathed a long sigh of relief.

"Thanks, mate." He replied.

"I did say you'd told me you'd had a few domestic issues, but I didn't mention any details and certainly didn't say anything about your friend."

"Thanks." He replied.

"The press have been round, again." I said.

"What, while you were here?" He said.

"No, they came before me. Peter, the guy next door, told me."

"Oh" Bob said.

"He knows about Katie; in fact, he told me. He's seen her sneaking in and out. I think your secret's safe with him." I said.

Bob nodded.

"I thought we'd been very inconspicuous." He said, ruefully.

"Not discreet enough, apparently." I replied.

"I can't imagine it was Peter that ratted me out to the press, he's a nice geezer. He's a DCI at Tower Bridge."

"I know." I agreed.

"Well, hadn't you better tell everyone I'm alive and well?" Bob said, pointing to the mobile phone that was in my hand.

"Fucking hell, Bob, it's not as simple as that. Technically, I've gotta nick you?"

"What for?" He asked.

"Possession of a class 'A' drug." I replied.

### Chapter 38

I really should have arrested Bob, or at the very least, made sure that he came with me back to the nick, but I didn't. He wanted, he explained, a few hours to sort everything out. He was worried the newspaper would run with the story tomorrow morning and needed to drive up to Bishops Stortford to see his mum and tell her what was going on. He also wanted to try to find somewhere else to stay, albeit temporarily, so he could avoid the press. I had offered him a bed at my place, but he declined saying, he didn't want to get me involved.

Bob had no explanation for the drugs down the back seat of his car. I believed him.

Since he'd left his flat, only a few hours previously, his car had been broken into, his flat searched and, worst of all, he was looking at being arrested for a serious criminal offence. The latter would mean he'd be suspended from work and then, potentially, lose his job. He'd also lose his home because he lived in police accommodation. And I whole-heartedly believed, all Bob had done that day was to indulge his harmless hobby and driven to the coast to take a few photographs.

Bob assured me, he'd get up to his mum's place, find somewhere to live and be back to sort out the mess, before the end of the day. We agreed an account, in which he would say, he'd arrived back, thirty minutes later than he had, and therefore, the two of us would have missed each other.

I couldn't nick him, but it wasn't a straightforward decision. If I was caught lying, I was likely to be in serious trouble.

My phone rang; it was Jill Long. I took the call standing opposite Bob and with my finger to my lips, to indicate he should be quiet.

"It's not Bob's body." She said, before I'd even said a word.

" Thank god, for that. Well, he hasn't come home, so goodness knows where he is." I said.

"We'll just have to wait and see if his body turns up." She said.

"I still don't buy the suicide theory." I replied, determined to make it appear that I had no idea where he was.

"But if he hadn't jumped off the cliff, and if it was him who got back in his Capri, then where is he? Surely, he'd have turned up by now?" Jill suggested, quite logically.

I felt awkward, I didn't like lying, I really didn't, especially to someone who I liked and respected.

"What was it you found at his flat?" Jill asked.

"Only a book giving the dates and times of tides. it was open on the page for the south coast of Sussex, so Bob had been doing some research, before he went." I replied.

"Oh, that sounds ominous." Jill commented.

I decided to be partially honest, Jill, I thought, at least, deserved that.

"Listen boss, there are lots of his own photographs, up on the walls in his flat, so he's obviously a keen photographer. And I do know he won the Met's best photograph competition, last year. Do you think it was possible, he'd just gone to the coast this morning at sunrise to take some pictures?"

Bob was listening to every word. He gave me the thumbs up sign when I mentioned the photographs on the wall.

"That makes sense but where's his car?" Jill asked.

"Perhaps he came back to the car park, got in it and drove off, not realising all the fuss that was going on. I mean, it was unattended for at least twenty minutes." I replied.

"    So, where is he?"

"Maybe he's gone to see his mum, or he's with a girlfriend, or he's gone somewhere else to take some pictures, you know, like further along the coast? Maybe he's getting his car window fixed, as we speak."

I was being helpful now and I hoped Jill took the bait.

"I hope you're right, Chris. I really do. Then all we'll have to deal with is the drugs issue. Did you find any more at the flat?"

"No …" I said, dismissively.

"… there is no way, on god's Earth, that Bob Clark is a drug addict." I replied.

"You'd be surprised, Chris. The Met's got a real problem with young officers being on the gear. The thing is, they're already on it when they join. It's a generation thing."

"Boss, Bob is my age; he's hardly young, and besides, I've worked with him for two years, I would know. I'm more experienced than most in that area of deviancy."

"Perhaps." Jill replied.

Then, after a brief pause, she asked the only sensible question left.

"If he's not on the gear, then what was it doing in his car?"

"I've no idea. I can only assume someone planted it." I replied.

"Why?" She asked.

Of course, the only reason I could think of, was to do with Katie Sumers' old man, and even that, was far-fetched.

"I don't know." I replied.

"Occam's razor." Jill said.

"Sorry?"

"     Occam's razor. It's the principle that when trying to work something out, the most obvious solution is probably the correct one. If drugs were found in someone's car, the most obvious solution is, they belong to him." Jill explained.

I couldn't argue but every bone in my body told me that Bob Clark was not a drug addict.

"Are you going to stay at the flat?" Jill asked.

"No, boss, I've got to get home. My wife was furious that I had to come to work this morning and I need to get home to explain." I said, trying to move the conversation on.

"Do you want me to call her? I'm very happy to do so." Jill offered.

"No, but thanks for the offer. I had a quick call with her earlier and told her what was going on. She's fine, and does understand, but she's a nurse and this is our first and only weekend off together, in months, so I think, she has plans."

"Have you got children?" Jill asked.

"No, we are trying, if you know what I mean, and I think those were the plans my wife had made, if you know..."

My sentence petered out because halfway through, I realised, I was probably sharing too much.

Jill laughed but not unkindly.

"Well best you crack on, then." She said, through a chuckle.

I was just about to hang up when I realised that it might be useful to know what their plans were.

"So, what's the next move?" I asked, as matter of fact, as possible.

"We're just getting cell site on his phone; we've submitted an urgent application."

"What you're tracking his phone?" I asked.

"That's the idea." She replied.

"I wouldn't bother, boss. His phones in his flat with more missed calls than an Indian call centre."

***

After the call with Jill, I had a quick chat with Bob to make sure we got our stories straight. We agreed that the safest thing for him to do was to leave his phone at the flat. We actually decided that he would say he hadn't been home at all, and that he'd claim to have driven straight to his mum's from Sussex. He said he'd give me ten minutes to get clear and then he'd slip out as quietly as he could.

"See you late turn on Monday?" I said.

"If they let me out." He replied.

If I am being honest, I thought they'd probably suspend him for the drugs.

"Can you give Katie a call?" He said.

"About what? I can hardly tell her the truth, can I?"

His mobile went off, but we ignored it.

"Okay, probably safest not to." He replied, despondently.

"Look Bob, this will get sorted, I promise you. Just make sure you come back in a few hours and pick up as if nothing's happened. Play it dumb when they mention the drugs. Tell the whole truth, well apart from the bit where you came home, forget that detail."

"I will Nostrils, I will. Thanks mate. I do appreciate you not forcing me to come in."

"No problem, dude." I said.

We shook hands and I left, closing the door very quietly behind me. I checked my watch, it was still the morning, well just, and so I had the rest of the day to relax.

As I walked to my car I noticed a BMW parked up and the driver, a male in his forties, was obviously watching the communal entrance. He actually looked like a surveillance officer but I guessed he was another press guy. As I got near him he jumped out of his car and started to come towards me.

"Can I help you?" I asked.

"Bob Clark?" He asked.

"No mate; my name's Chris Pritchard."

"Do you live here?"

I shook my head.

"Just visiting."

"Do you know where Bob Clark is?"

"Never heard of him, mate." I lied.

I knew it was a futile attempt to put him off the scene, but I thought I'd give it a try.

"He drives an old Ford Capri. Lives in these flats somewhere?" He said.

"Honestly mate, no one like that lives here, as for a Ford Capri, I haven't seen one of those for years."

"Thanks, anyway." He said.

"No problem, mate."

I did think about sending a text warning Bob or even calling him but of course I couldn't without compromising us both.

I set off home.

## Chapter 39

I went home, feeling emotionally knackered.

Jackie was out but as her car was in the drive and her trainers missing, I calculated, she'd gone for a run and wouldn't be long. She'd started running last year and built up from a miserly 200 yards to an impressive 10K, in just a little over twelve months, which was fantastic. Although, she'd not lost any weight, her body shape had significantly changed and she looked good for a woman in her mid-thirties; perhaps a little, too good, if she was going to attract the attention of younger, handsome doctors.

These thoughts and my own insecurity drew me to her mobile phone, which was on the bedside table. I picked it up and then put it down again; but a few moments later, it was back in my hand, and I was flicking through her messages, until I found the name Nipun.

My heart started to beat faster. I knew I shouldn't be reading the messages between them, but it was irresistible, like gawping at the scene of a terrible car crash.

The last message was from Nipun to my wife; it was just five words long and read:

'If you ever change your mind...'.

I scrolled up to the preceding message:

'My darling, Nipun. I am so very sorry about what happened, last night. I have never wanted anyone, as much as I wanted you, you know that. I can honestly say, my heart misses a beat, whenever I see you. But I am married to a lovely man, a faithful man, and an honest man, and I just couldn't bear the guilt. I was so impressed by your self-control, not many men would have been able to do what you did. It makes me want you even more, which is really crap. I think we would have made a lovely couple, just at another time and in another place. Love xxxx"

I was just reading the message for a second time, when I heard Jackie's footsteps coming to a halt, outside the house and noticed her heavy breathing.

I flicked back to the main screen and put the phone down, hoping that it would go blank before she entered the room.

I walked to the bathroom and locked myself in. I needed a few minutes to get my head round, what I'd just read.

I was in shock. Did Jackie love this Nipun? Had more happened than she'd said? What did she mean by, 'self-control'? What self-control was needed, if she just walked out the restaurant, as she'd said?

"Hi darling." Jackie called, up the stairs.

"      Hi" I shouted back, as if everything in my life was just perfect when all I really wanted to do, was scream.

*  *  *

When Jackie queried why I'd been in the toilet for such a long time, I said I'd got an upset stomach.

I was at a complete loss, as to what to do. Should I confront her? Admit that I'd looked through her messages and that there was obviously a lot more going on, than she'd told me? The biggest thing was that I felt so fucking stupid. I'd genuinely believed everything she told me; I'd not questioned her or challenged her. Instead, I'd swallowed the whole story.

I suppose there was a string of truth to what she'd said, she clearly hadn't gone through with whatever was planned, she did feel really guilty, and she had told him that their relationship was over. At least, the message I read confirmed those bits.

In the end, I decided to say nothing and, although I did my best to hide how I was really feeling, several times during the evening, she asked me whether there was anything wrong and I just said I was worried about work.

When we went to bed, Jackie wanted to have sex, but I really wasn't in the mood. In fact, I didn't even want to touch her. I rolled over and turned my back on her. I couldn't sleep, and lay there for, what seemed like, ages. Suddenly, I felt Jackie move. I stayed still, pretending I was asleep. I heard her pick her phone up and the light from her screen illuminated her side of the room. Was she texting him?

A few seconds later, her bedside light came on.

"Chris?"

I ignored her.

"Chris, I know you're not asleep."

"How?" I replied, grumpily.

"Because you're not snoring." She said.

"What do you want?"

My voice was aggressive and angry; I could feel my emotions boiling up.

"I think your phone's going off, downstairs. I can hear it vibrating."

This was the last thing I suspected she'd say. I thought she was going to ask me what was wrong, or whether I'd looked through her phone, or just about anything, except 'your phone's going off'.

I got up, put my dressing gown on, and went downstairs. My phone wasn't ringing but Jackie had been right, as I got into the kitchen, it started again.

I had expected it to be Bob or Katie, but I didn't recognise the number.

"Hello?" I said.

I spent the next hour on the phone to a very distressed and extremely drunk, Clare Maddison. She was insistent that she wanted to drop the charges; she couldn't, she said, face going to court. She felt sorry for Mitch because he'd had such a terrible childhood. I explained, she probably wouldn't have to go to court and that, if she withdrew the charges, Mitch would be out and about and free to attack someone else, or indeed, come back to see her. What I was saying wasn't entirely true because, as his parole licence had been withdrawn, Mitch would have to complete his current sentence, before being released, but I didn't mention that. Then I told her how brave she'd been, and how well she'd done, and that, however hard, she had to do the right thing and continue with the prosecution.

I felt sorry for Clare, of course I did, but it was a difficult conversation because it kept going round and round. She was so drunk, and just when I thought we'd got there, she'd say, 'I'm not going to court', and the whole dialogue would reset to the beginning.

This was one of the downsides to giving your phone number to victims, but generally, it was a price worth paying.

I was also conscious I'd have to make a note of our conversation because it was disclosable the defence at the trial would have a right to know about it. I thought I'd keep the record very brief, so as not to give them any ammunition to undermine our case.

During the conversation, Jackie got up and made a coffee. Then she sat up with me in the lounge, listening to the conversation. I appreciated the gesture, but her presence meant my mind kept wandering from my conversation with Clare, not that I needed to pay much attention.

Eventually and with much relief, I hung up. It was two-thirty in the morning.
Jackie was on her second cup of coffee.

"That sounded like a difficult conversation." She commented, as I took a massive exhale of breath.

"She was drunk." I replied.

"We need to have one of those." She said, staring into her coffee, as if she was reading a script, etched onto the surface.

"What a drink?" I asked.

"No, a difficult conversation." She replied.

### Chapter 40

We sat up talking until it was getting light.

During our deep and meaningful, I admitted that I'd read the messages on her phone between her and Nipun.

Jackie, in turn, admitted that she'd been economical with the truth, when she told me about what had happened, on her date. She had got second thoughts, but not during the meal in the restaurant in Buckhurst Hill, but back at the hotel in Chigwell. To be precise, he'd put his penis inside her and they'd started to have intercourse, when, suddenly, she said that she'd changed her mind. According to Jackie, at that precise moment, Nipun stopped and withdrew. She said, she went into a meltdown of guilt, got dressed, and went to her friends, as she'd previously said. Though her explanation did fit with the text she'd sent him, I did of course realise, it meant that technically, she'd been, in every sense of the expression, unfaithful to me. But that wasn't what hurt, I mean, sex is just sex. I was devastated by the ease with which she'd lied to me, and I think, if I am being honest with myself, equally upset that I'd been so gullible to believe her. And where did this leave us? I realised, of course, I could never trust her again, not ever. But then, could anyone ever trust anyone, under any circumstances? The answer, apparently, is no.

I genuinely wanted to know, what I'd done wrong. And I wasn't just being clever, and trying to make Jackie feel awkward, I wanted to know, both, so I could try to assess my liability and so that, in another relationship, I wouldn't make the same mistake, again.

At first, Jackie was reluctant to put any of the blame on me, but that didn't last too long. She said that I worked too much and quoted yesterday, as the perfect example. I had, she said, ruined our long weekend off, together. When I argued, the circumstances yesterday, with one of my DC's missing and possibly dead, were exceptional, she replied that I always said that.

She also said that she didn't trust me and suspected on some of the occasions when I said I was working, I was out shagging. This really surprised me for several reasons, not least of which was that I had never been unfaithful to her since our first date over ten years ago. When I told her this, she just burst into tears.

Finally, she said that she desperately wanted to have a family but that I had not seemed particularly bothered. She explained that she put my attitude down to the fact that I was too wrapped up in work and other women to want to commit further to our relationship by having a family. I told her I was happy to have a family but that I didn't think blokes felt the absolute necessity to have children in the same way that some women did.

When I asked her how any of her criticisms of me, whether justified or not, meant that it was all right for her to have sex with another man, she just sat staring at an empty coffee cup.

When we went to bed, we made love. We usually did after we'd had an argument but this time it was different and not in a good way. Jackie was just so upset and didn't stop crying. At first, I was reluctant because her obvious distress didn't exactly get me in the mood, but she seemed to really need sex. It was weird. It was as if the act of intercourse would reaffirm our commitment to one another. When we uncoupled, Jackie cuddled up to me and hugged me tighter and more passionately than I had ever known. When I woke up, it was mid-morning, the sun was high and streaming through a small gap between the curtains and my wife was still completely wrapped around me.

I threw a few clothes on and wandered down to the High Street to buy some eggs, bacon, and bread for breakfast. It was a truly glorious summer's day, and the temperature must have already been nearly eighty degrees.

I felt curiously happy, considering the events of the previous night. I knew, Jackie and I would work through our problem. I did love her, I really did, and I wanted our marriage to work. Okay, she made a mistake, but I couldn't help feel, she'd been principally driven by her physical desire for Nipun, rather than anything else and strangely, that didn't bother me, as much as it might have upset someone else.

In town, I bumped into a PC from Tottenham. He was an area car driver on B relief, but I couldn't remember his name, for the life of me. Although, he was well into his forties, he had a young child, a boy of no more than four, with him.

"Is this your lad?" I asked.

"Yes, this is young Darren. I've got two older ones, too, but they're with their mum. Max is twenty-one and Molly eighteen."

This was such a typical scenario. I didn't know any of the facts, but I'd wager that he'd met his first wife before he joined the job, and their marriage had lasted really well until, probably when he was about forty, and just thinking his heyday was over, a young attractive WPC joined his relief. That young WPC was now his wife and the mother of young Darren. If he was lucky, his older children would still be talking to him; if he wasn't, they'd never forgive him for what he had done to their mum.

"Have you heard what's happened?" He asked me, as we stood next to one another in the checkout queue.

I wondered how he'd already heard about Bob Clark.

"What?" I asked.

"Complaints spun the nick last night. They searched every desk in the C.I.D. office."

This was the search that DI Kitty Young had warned me about. It was Area Complaints and they were looking for evidence relating to the racist material.

"Did they find anything?" I asked.

"Apparently they found snide Rolex's and duty free cigarettes in a DC's desk."

"Sounds about right. And no prizes for guessing whose desk that was." I replied.

"Yeah, it was Dippo's. He's been nicked, apparently."

"Fuck me, oh sorry ..." I said, realising that such a remark was completely inappropriate, in front of a small child.

The guy laughed.

"You haven't got any kids have you, Nostrils?"

"We're trying." I replied.

I suddenly realised what I'd said and how terribly grown up it sounded.

"Dippo's only a few months from his thirty, isn't he?" I asked.

The guy nodded.

Dippo was on Jim Beam's team, and he was a right Del Boy character, always doing booze cruises and bringing back stuff, which he sold around the nick. A few years back, I'd bought a fake Rolex from him for fifteen quid, but the thing fell apart, a week later.

The queue moved forward, and we said our goodbyes.

I'd been out of the house for no more than forty minutes and, upon my return, was surprised to find the front door slightly open.

"I'm back." I called out, as I pushed the door open with my shoulder.

I walked into the kitchen to deposit the shopping but there was no sign of Jackie. I stopped moving and listened, to see if I could hear the shower, nothing.

"Hello." I shouted.

I walked back to the front door and glanced outside. Her car was gone. Then, I noticed a small handwritten note on the table, I picked it up.

'You cheating bastard. We are history. Not because you did it, that's bad enough, but because you let me go through all that shit, last night. I will never forgive you!!!!'

## Chapter 41

I don't think I'd ever been more confused in my life.

I dialled Jackie's mobile, but the call went straight to voicemail, she'd obviously switched the thing off. I left a message saying I had no idea what had happened, or what she thought I had done, and asking her to ring me to explain what was going on, and why.

I'd suddenly lost my appetite and put the groceries away. I scratched my head a lot and kept looking at my phone.

There was a knock at the door, and I opened it to see my elderly neighbour, Ted, standing there. We had the best neighbours in the world, Ted and Gladys, a couple in their late eighties, who were absolutely lovely. We'd sort of adopted them as surrogate grandparents. Ted was dressed in a suit and tie, as he always was, and he wore a flat cap, as he always did, whenever he left the house.

"Come in, Ted, come in." I said, politely.

I didn't really want to see him, particularly as I was expecting Jackie to call, at any moment, but I just couldn't be rude to him.

"How are you doing, son?" He asked, kindly.

At that moment I knew something was wrong, I just didn't know what.

"I'm ok." I replied, slowly.

"Is there any reason, I shouldn't be?"

Ted produced a newspaper from under his arm, which he handed to me, it was the News of the World.

I opened it out and read the headline:

'TV star gets her head down'

And the sub-headline read:

'Katie Sumers's lewd sex act with senior Met Detective'

My eyes darted about the page but stopped when I saw the two photographs that accompanied the article. They were taken, a few seconds apart, during my meeting with Katie, in the car park, of the David Lloyd centre. The first, showed Katie and me getting into her Lexus; the second, showed her leaning across me, her head above my groin. It looked like she was about to give me oral sex. I realised that the second photograph had been taken when she leaned across to retrieve the photograph of her sister, from the glove box, but it looked incredibly damning.

I scanned the article and noticed that the story, 'continued on page 4'. I flicked the pages; there were more photographs of Katie, close shots of her wearing her sunglass, probably taken just before we'd first met.

Finally, when Katie and I had parted that day, she'd leant across and kissed me on the cheek. It was absolutely nothing, and I'd actually thought at the time, quite a friendly gesture. There was a photograph, which had captured this innocent moment, but from the camera angle, the peck on the cheek looked like a full-on snog.

What was really clever, or perhaps devious, would be a better word, was the way the photographs were set out. The pictures told the story, and the reader didn't really need to acquaint themselves with the written article.

When I looked up, Ted had gone.

I sat down and read the whole piece.

'Famous TV personality and 38-year-old, mother of three, Katie Sumers, has been caught cheating on her husband, and former coach, Steve Oswald, with a mystery man, who she met at the local gym.

Last year, Katie's youngest daughter, three-year-old Megan Oswald, was diagnosed with a rare form of leukemia and Katie led a worldwide campaign, raising more than £3 million for research into the disease. These latest revelations, however, are set to tarnish the whiter-than-white image of this former international gymnast and popular TV presenter.

Sources have revealed to the News of the World that the affair started last year, when Katie's daughter was still having treatment.

Last Tuesday, the News of the World caught Katie and her 'special friend' having more than a casual conversation, in the car park of the David Lloyd Leisure Club, in Loughton, Essex. One passer-by who witnessed the sordid sex act, said she was disgusted that the couple could behave in such a way, in a public place, frequented by families and children.

To make matters worse, the mystery man is believed to be a senior Met police officer, married with several young children.

In this year's Queen's birthday honours' list, Steve Sumers received an O.B.E. for services to the community, in recognition for the extensive contribution he has made to the establishment of drug rehabilitation centres, in several of London's most deprived communities. Sources close to the popular local hero described him as being completely devastated by the shocking revelations.

Katie Sumers and her husband were yesterday unavailable to comment but the News of the World can confirm, the alleged sex act has been referred to Scotland Yard's Complaints Investigation Bureau, who will conduct a full investigation to ascertain whether any criminal offences have been committed.'

I read the article three times. There were four fundamental flaws; first, they'd got Bob and me mixed up; secondly, no lewd sex act took place; thirdly, whether it was Bob or me, neither of us were senior Met police officers, and lastly, I didn't have any children.

No wonder Jackie had disappeared.

## Chapter 42

I didn't know what to do next.

I needed to speak to Jackie, Bob, Katie, someone from the Complaints Investigation Bureau and someone from the nick, probably DI Kitty Young, although, I'd feel happier talking to the Superintendent Jill Long.

I really hadn't done anything wrong, well not much, anyway. My only transgression was not arresting Bob when he returned to his flat. Actually, that was wrong, my biggest sin was not reporting his return and letting everyone keep searching for him, when I knew he was safe and well. If Bob didn't drop me in it, I'd be all right, but I wasn't sure that, with everything coming on top for him, I could be certain Bob would say the right thing.

I therefore decided, I needed to speak to Bob first, but his phone went to voicemail and an automated message informed me that the voicemail was full. I tried Jackie again, but with a similar result, and then called Katie, mainly to find out, if she knew where Bob was – she didn't answer, which I suppose, shouldn't, by then, have surprised me.

I sat down, feeling in a bit of a daze. Then, I had a thought, what exactly had Jackie taken? A quick search revealed that our medium sized suitcase was missing, along with a surprising amount of clothes, underwear, and toiletries. For someone who packed in a rush, Jackie had sure taken a lot of stuff. Jackie was due back to work on Monday for night duty, so I didn't think she'd have gone that far. I assumed she would be staying with a friend until things died down.

I got a text from Colin; it suggested we meet at my partner's resting place, which was a bit cryptic, but I knew he meant St John's Church graveyard in Buckhurst Hill. I guessed he'd seen the News of the World and was concerned about meeting anywhere too public. I texted back one word 'twenty' and set off.

I drove quickly down that part of the A11 which cuts through Epping Forest, just to the north of Chingford, making sure that I wasn't being followed. I switched the radio on and caught the end of the 11 o'clock news, on one of London's numerous local radio stations:

"Police are becoming increasingly concerned for the safety of one of their own officers, who disappeared, in the vicinity of Beachy Head, on Saturday morning. Robert Clark, a detective constable at Tottenham police station, is a white male, thirty-five years old and of slim build. Police are also seeking information about his brown Ford Capri, registration mark DST 123Y, believed to have been stolen, from a car park in Sussex, between eight and nine, yesterday morning. Anyone with information about the missing officer or the stolen car, should contact their local police station."

I briefly wondered how my life had suddenly become so complicated. Of all my problems, the News of the World article was the least because, it simply, wasn't true and the immediate consequences, that is to say the Complaints investigation and Jackie's reaction, were easily manageable, once I explained to them exactly what had happened. My biggest concern was poor Bob. The fact that he hadn't given himself up was disconcerting and didn't make much sense. When I'd let him go, he'd promised to hand himself in, by the end of the day.

As I pulled into park by the pond, opposite the church, my mobile went. I was so desperate to see if it was Jackie calling, I dropped the bloody thing down the side of the driver's seat. The phone rang out before I could extract it. I cursed myself. The screen informed me what I already knew, but not what I wanted to know, because it read, 'One missed call, unknown caller.'

I waited to see if a voicemail would come through. I did; I listened.

"Hi Chris, it's Jill Long here. I don't know whether you're aware yet, but there's an article about you in this morning's News of the World. Can you please give me a call? I'm at home, so you can get me on my mobile."

She then reeled off her number, but I already had it saved in my phone. I decided to call her back, after I'd met Colin.

The graveyard was much busier than usual but then it was a Sunday, and several people were visiting their departed loved ones, arranging flowers, and generally tidying up.

I made my way over to Dawn's grave and I'd only been there a minute, when Colin arrived. He sat next to me on a near-by bench.

"Hello, mate." I said.

"Nostrils." He replied, with a wide grin.

"Is this about the News of the World thing?" I asked.

"Nope."

"Have you seen that?" I asked, surprised.

"Not myself but Dot just told me. She called, when I was on my way."

"Do you know where Bob is? You know he's missing, don't you?" I asked.

"Dot told me that, as well. She thinks the two things are connected. She thinks it might be Bob that's having the affair with that Katie woman and not you."

"She's right." I replied.

"Then how come they've got pictures of you?" He asked, not unreasonably.

"It's a long story but I was meeting her to deliver a message from Bob. And there was no blow job."

"Oh, I'm genuinely sorry about." He said, still wearing a wide grin.

"So, if it's not about Katie Sumers, and it's not about Bob, why do you want to see me? Not that it's not great to meet a mate." I said.

"I think there's something underhand going on, mate." He said, turning his body so he was facing me.

"Just what I need, another problem ..." I said, sarcastically.

"... 'cos life's a real breeze at the moment."

"Listen, Nostrils. I've been seeing a girl called Randy."

"Randy? Are you shitting me? Is that her real name?"

"Shut the fuck up and listen. Randy works with Anna Abolla."

"Okay." I replied, somewhat taken aback.

"Anna Abolla, as in the Labour councilor." He added.

"Did you know, Anna Abolla and our new DI are best mates?"

"Really?" I replied.

"And that Anna's trying to get our new DI to NFA your passport visa investigation. The one against her sister." Colin explained.

"It's not just against her sister. Anna's involved in it, too." I said.

Few people knew that piece of information because the original allegation only involved Anna's sister. It was only when my enquiries dug deeper, I realiseD Anna herself was involved.

"Ah, I didn't know that ..." Colin said.

"... apparently, Anna's told her sister, she has a very good friend working at Tottenham and can get the whole thing put to sleep. Because Randy knew that I worked there, she paid particular attention, and then reported back."

"That's very interesting because, only the other day, Kitty asked to review the file. Well, I tell you, mate, I won't let her NFA it, there's too much fucking evidence. Even if they NFA the case against Anna, which I don't agree with, but which I could live with, there's massive evidence against her sister."

"My mate reckons it's all going to be dropped."

"Who is this Randy, girl? You've never mentioned her before." I asked.

"I'm happy to tell you, Nostrils, but you can't say anything to anyone, not yet anyway. I met her on the internet, and we've been seeing each other about six weeks. It's not serious, we're just friends who fuck, really."

I nodded.

"She's Anna Abolla's P.A. She can listen in on her office phone, but she's also overheard several other conversations."

"But there's more to it. Randy's an undercover reporter. Apparently, the press have been after Anna Abolla for like, ever."

Colin was right. Over the years, Anna Abolla had been the subject of numerous negative stories, in the right-wing press, who hated her with a passion, since her comments after the Plymouth Rock riots.

"Who's she working for?" I asked.

"Some independent company that makes programmes for Panorama. She was actually recruited as a P.A., but then this producer chap approached her. They offered her a small fortune and fitted her out with all the equipment. She says she's disgusted by what's been going on and that she's really happy to be the one to uncover it. Oh, and of course, they're able to listen to Anna Abolla's voicemails."

"What, how?" I asked.

"Apparently, when you set up your voicemail the default PIN number is 1234. If you're lazy and don't change it, anyone can dial in and pick up your messages, by putting in that code. Anna's never changed hers, so, every so often, they dial in and make a note of anything interesting."

"That's about the third time I've heard someone say about their mobile phones being tapped." I commented.

"Well, they're not being taped. I mean, they can't listen to real time conversations, just to messages that are left." Colin replied.

"Why is Randy telling you this?" I asked.

"Because the BBC have refused to run with the Panorama story. You know, they're all left wing lovies. Well, the powers that be, don't want to attack one of their own, do they? Randy is furious. It also means that the last six months of her life have been a complete waste of time."

"Has the DI actually agreed to drop the passport case?" I asked.

Colin shrugged his shoulders.

"So, she hasn't done anything wrong, not at this stage, has she. I mean, she might well look at the file and tell Anna that there's nothing she can do." I pointed out.

"I suppose not." He replied.

"Oh, hang on. I saw the DI looking through my desk the other day, she must have been looking for the file. It's all starting to make sense now. How's this going to play out? I mean, why shouldn't I go straight to C.I.B.2? You know, once Kitty drops the case." I asked.

"You could do, I suppose. You know Complaints turned the nick over, Saturday night? Looking for anything connected with the racist letters?" Colin replied.

"Yeah, I bumped into a PC in Loughton this morning, he told me." I said.

"I might be wrong but is it just possible, the DI thought they'd find something when they spun your desk the other night? You might have something in there that at least justifies your move to another less operational role. Then you'd be out of the way, and she could quietly NFA the passport case." He said.

"But this doesn't make any sense." I said.

"Why? Looks pretty clear to me. Complaints find some old corres that you should have dealt with, ages ago. You know what I mean. You're placed on a desk job and, meanwhile, Kitty drops the case against her mate Abolla and her sister. Job done, mission accomplished, Bob's your uncle, Fanny's your aunt, and their two kids Steve and Mary."

"I get the picture but what you don't know …"

"Go on." Colin encouraged me.

"… is that only the other day, Kitty tipped me off about Complaints coming in to search the nick. In fact, she solicited my help to count the lockers in the male changing room, in the basement. Now, why in god's name would she do that, if she intended me to get into any trouble?" I explained.

"Well, have sex with my aged Wellingtons." Colin exclaimed.

## Chapter 43

I appreciated the heads up from Colin, I really did, but I couldn't work out why, if what he told me was right, Kitty had tipped me off about the search. It didn't make any sense.

I returned the Superintendent's call. I told her that I was not having a relationship with Katie Sumers, that I'd only met her a couple of times, and the first time was when I sat in her car, last week. I also said that she did not, at any stage, perform any indecent act on me. She asked me why I was meeting her, I said I was running an errand for a friend but that I couldn't say any more about that, without betraying a confidence. I explained that the papers had obviously got me confused with someone else. I thought she'd put two and two together, but she didn't.

Rather sensibly, Jill suggested I contact the Police Federation, first thing tomorrow and get them on the case. She said I might be able to sue the newspaper but that it would only be worth it, if I had suffered harm, as a direct result of the article. I explained that my wife had left me and asked whether that counted as a detriment or a benefit. She laughed and must have thought I was joking.

Jill suggested, it might be a good time to take a week's leave. I told her I was going to the D.V.L.A. in Swansea, tomorrow, to make some enquiries, in connection with the Colonel's burglary and that I could make it an overnight stay, if she didn't mind. If I did so, I explained, I'd be out the office for a couple of days, at least. She agreed on the basis that I didn't claim any overtime, which seemed fair.

I felt very guilty about not telling her about Bob, but I was in an awkward position. As I felt the conversation coming to a natural close, I had to ask whether there'd been any developments.

"No, his phone's switched off, so cell site doesn't work. There's no trace of either his body or his car. We put an appeal out on the news, but nothings come in. The Chief Superintendent went to see his mum, but she's not seen or heard from him for a week. Sussex nicked the travellers for theft of his car, but they denied any knowledge and have been released without charge." She explained.

And then I cracked. I had to tell her at least a little, of what I knew.

"It was Bob who was having the affair with Katie Sumers, not me." I said.

Jill didn't say anything for a few seconds.

"Did you hear me boss?" I asked.

"So, yesterday, when you said he was having a few domestics, is that what you meant?"

"     Yes" I replied.

"Did he know that it was all coming on top with the press?" She asked.

"Yes" I replied.

"Does he take cocaine, or any other controlled drug?" She asked.

"No, definitely not." I replied, emphatically.

"Are you two best mates, out of work?"

"God no. I don't know a great deal about him. Last week, he came to me with this problem, the Katie Sumers thing, he'd been door stepped by a journalist. Prior to that, we were, well you know, friends but not lifelong buddies." I explained.

"But he saved your life, Chris. I thought you might be close."

"I know and, of course, I shall be forever in his debt, but Bob's quite private. He's not like your usual police officer, he's a bit quieter and he's actually a bit more sophisticated. I like Bob, he's a great DC to have on the team, but we'd never be best mates."

"Fair enough, Chris. I understand." She replied.

I felt better after I'd told Jill most of what was going on, but I didn't tell her that I knew he was alive and well, that was one bit of honesty, too far.

When we ended our call, I checked my watch. It was midday and the temperature must have been in the high eighties.

Without Jackie I was really at a loss, as to what to do, with myself. I hoped that, if I went home, she'd be there but I knew, in my heart, she wouldn't.

I     called Bob and Katie, both phones diverted straight to voicemail – what the fuck was happening?

I left the car where it was, and took a ten-minute walk to visit the oldest friend I had. Fifteen minutes later, I was sitting in Mrs. M's kitchen, drinking tea, and telling her my story of woe.

Mrs. M, or to be more accurate Mrs. Jenny Matthews, was Dawn's mother. Mrs. M and I had been friends for years and she was the closest thing I'd had to family, since my mother died, when I was eighteen.

She lived in a lovely house right next to Epping Forest and I'd stayed with her and Dawn for a few months, back in '83. When I look back, those were the happiest months of my life, but they hadn't lasted long enough, and I always felt a little robbed.

Mrs. M was the best listener in the world, and I told her all about Bob, Katie Sumers, the newspaper article, Jackie's disappearance, her fling with the doctor, Kitty Young and the racist letters. She interrupted, occasionally, with an appropriate question to clarify the facts and make sure she had a comprehensive understanding, as to what was going on. Then she hit me with a question that absolutely blew me away.

"Christopher, darling, are you more worried about losing your wife or your job?

## Chapter 44

I was off on Monday and got up late because I'd lain awake worrying about everything until it was getting light.

The first thing I did was check my phone – nothing, not a single missed call or message! I slumped back down on the bed, in frustration.

I dialled the same three people for what felt like the hundredth time. I wasn't expecting anything except a cut to voicemail, when Jackie's phone rang, but it wasn't the normal ring but an elongated tone, then the phone cut to voicemail. I realised that my wife was abroad.

I phoned the Police Federation and spoke to a lovely lady, called Susan. I explained everything to her about the newspaper article and how it wasn't me but a colleague that was having the affair. She asked me a curious question about whether I wanted to sue the paper for money or have the story retracted.

"Are they mutually exclusive?" I asked.

"Look Chris, if you want money, let the story run uncorrected, for as long as possible; that way, financially, you're in a stronger position. If we challenge them and they realise their mistake and publish an immediate apology, the damages you could potentially get would be very limited."

I asked Susan to give me twenty-four hours to consider my option and told her I'd get back to her.

I slumped back on my bed feeling really pissed off. I lay there for thirty minutes, turning everything over in my mind. Then suddenly, and for no reason I could easily articulate, I sprung to life and, with a completely unnecessary urgency, went to the box under the bed where we kept our passports. Jackie's was missing.

What was Jackie doing abroad if she was due back at work that evening? Perhaps she'd gone for the day, to Calais or Boulogne, like people do for the day to buy cheap booze and fags? But that wasn't anything she'd ever done, or contemplated, before.

I don't know why but I decided to turn the house over. I really didn't know what I was looking for, or what I expected to find, but there wasn't a drawer, cupboard, or potential hiding place that, over the next hour, I didn't search. I even got the stepladder out and looked through the loft.

I found several interesting items and a couple that made me feel like shit.

At the back of several of the bedroom drawers were chocolate bars, which was a genuine surprise, as we never had any sweets in the house, I didn't think we were particularly bothered about them but clearly, I was wrong. Obviously, my wife was a bit of a secret eater, which might explain her failure to lose any weight, despite her regular and varied attempts at dieting.

I found half a dozen books of the adult variety. I suppose this was no big deal, but what was curious, was the subject matter of the literature, which was heavily focused on two subjects, female submissiveness, and lesbian relationships. When I was younger, one of the books called, 'The Story of O', had been the subject of much schoolboy joking and innuendo; although, at the time, I don't think either my mates or I had any idea what it was about.

Hidden under the lining in Jackie's bra drawer, I found two cards. The first was an unsigned Valentine's Day card, with some soppy message about the sender being a secret admirer; but the second, was a birthday card, signed by Nipun, and the handwritten message read, 'I want to hold you in my arms and wrap you so tightly, our naked bodies merge as one and our friendship becomes complete.'

For a few minutes, I thought through the beating I would give him for daring to send a card to my wife containing such an intimate message. But deep down, I knew I wouldn't do such a thing, after all, that would cost me my job and, as I'd discovered during my deep and meaningful with Mrs. M, that meant more to me than anything.

The discovery that hurt me the most, I found under the stairs in a small gym bag. My wife had a small collection of sexy underwear which included, a black basque, stockings and lacy knickers, none of which I had ever seen before. So many times, over the years, I had begged Jackie to wear sexy underwear for me. I'd given up asking. She always said that she thought it was degrading. Now I discovered, she had obviously bought some to wear for someone else. I felt dreadful. When I emptied the bag out, I found that several items still had their price tags and, at the bottom of the bag, was the receipt. The clothes had been purchased two weeks ago, so it didn't take much to realise, she'd brought them for her night of passion with Nipun.

I felt like I didn't know my wife of ten years, at all.

*** 

I knew it was a stupid idea, but I did it anyway.

At half seven that Monday evening, I parked up at St Margaret's Hospital, waiting for Jackie to arrive at work. I knew it was unlikely, but I think deep down, I wanted to meet this Nipun chap. At quarter passed eight I knew my wife wasn't going to work that day.

I walked into Accident & Emergency, not quite sure what to do or say, when I saw a colleague of Jackie's, called Angela, standing and studying a hand-held clipboard. Angela was a pretty young thing, probably about twenty-four, but she had one of those eyes that slants at a slight angle, so it feels as if she is looking to the side of you.

We'd met once at a Christmas party. I approached her, confidently, determined to front it out, if I could. On the way home that night, I remember Jackie telling me a curious story about an occasion when Angela got very drunk and started complaining that her husband had the most enormous penis. It was, she claimed, so big that she couldn't take it all inside her. Since I heard that piece of information, whenever Angela's name came up in one of Jackie's work-related stories, all I could think was about the size of her old man's, old man.

"Hi Angela, is Jackie about?" I said, as if it was the most natural thing in the world to ask.

Angela looked up, frowned, and opened her mouth but the absence of words indicated she knew I shouldn't really be asking that question about my own wife. She flicked her head towards a nearby door, on which the sign said 'Triage'.

I followed her into the small room, closed the door behind me, and we sat down facing each other, across a small table. I decided to let Angela speak first.

"Chris, Jackie's not working tonight." She said.

I said nothing, hoping she'd keep imparting further information, but she didn't, so eventually, and after an unnatural silence, I asked:

"Do you know where she is?"

My voice was quiet, unthreatening.

"She's reported sick. I don't know where she is, I really don't." She replied.

I nodded.

I was really tempted to ask whether Nipun was on duty but decided not to place Angela in such a difficult position.

"Thanks, Angela. I appreciate you talking to me." I said.

I stood up to leave.

"Sit down Chris, if you've got two minutes? I'll have to be quick. I've got loads to do."

"Go on." I said, politely.

"You can't honestly expect Jackie to show her face at work when everyone here knows what you've done to her? She has some pride, you know."

"I haven't done anything. The News of the Screws got it all wrong."

Angela smirked, sarcastically.

"I hardly know Katie Sumers. The bloke she's shagging is one of my colleagues, not me. I have done absolutely nothing wrong. But, and please don't take this the wrong way, you're not the one I should be having this conversation with. I should be explaining to my wife, but she's fucked off in a huff and isn't answering her phone, so I can't tell her, can I?"

The smirk had left Angela's face.

"     If that's the truth, I am truly sorry for you." She said.

"Do you know where she is?" I asked.

I guessed that Angela did know but she shook her head slowly from side to side to indicate that she couldn't tell me.

"Changing the subject, completely, how's that charming young doctor?"

"Sorry?" Angela asked.

"Nipun, that's his name. I know that because he sent my wife a lovely birthday card, last month. Such an intimate message, too. I was really touched." I said.

"     Are you talking about Doctor Silva?" She asked.

She appeared genuinely surprised by my question and I realised that I could have messed up, here. Well, I thought, might as well be hung for a sheep as a lamb.

"I don't know his surname. All I know is that he's having an affair with my wife." I replied.

Angela smiled, but not unkindly.

"You do know who you're talking about, don't you?" She asked.

"No, Angela, I've never met him. All I know is that a doctor called Nipun and Jackie have been having an affair."

"Chris, I'm really glad you told me." Angela replied.

"Don't tell me he's shagging you, too?" I asked.

"Yes and no, Chris. Dr. Nipun Silva is my husband!"

## Chapter 45

Angela and Nipun had met while they were both at university and been married for three years. I learnt that Nipun had now finished his time in Accident & Emergency and since over to do six months in geriatrics, as part of some rotation policy for newly qualified doctors.

Angela told me that their marriage was over and that they largely went their own ways. They didn't have any children and they'd discussed initiating divorce proceedings but neither of them had got around to it, yet.

When I asked whether she had any idea about Jackie, she replied, with painful honesty, that while she knew Nipun liked Jackie and got on very well with her, she thought she was way too old for him. He usually, she said, went for much younger women. She then told me a story about her catching Nipun chatting up a young Philippine chambermaid, on their honeymoon.

She was really cross that Nipun had decided to date someone at work, but she actually seemed more distressed, by his choice of partner than the fact that he was being unfaithful to her.

"Do you know where they are?" I asked, assuming that they were together but not knowing for certain.

"Nipun got a phone call, yesterday morning. He said, someone he knew had to pull out of a conference and was asking him to go in his place. He said it was for five days and that if he could get hold of his Registrar and get her approval, he'd be mad not to go, as it wasn't going to cost the Health Authority a penny, as it was already paid for. If I'm being honest, Chris, I was very happy for him to go, as it would mean, I'd have the house to myself for the week, and all we've been doing lately, is bicker."

"There's no fucking conference." I said.

"No, I think there is because he spoke about it, a while ago. Oh, and I saw brochures. It's a conference on the latest development in geriatric medicine."

"Maybe, I've got this wrong? Perhaps, they're not together and it's all been a bit of a coincidence. Can you tell me, what time Nipun received the call yesterday morning?" I asked.

I quickly calculated that Jackie couldn't have heard about the article in the newspaper, until, at least, ten thirty. It followed, therefore, that if he'd had the call at nine, it wasn't from my wife.

"About half ten, maybe quarter to eleven." She replied.

That wasn't what I wanted to hear.

"And did you believe him, did it all seem credible?" I asked, clutching at straws.

Angela shrugged.

"We've only been married a few years, but I can honestly say, a third of everything Nipun told me, was a lie. Chris, he even made a pass at my sister! He's an absolute nightmare. The only thing I can say in his defence, is that I really don't think he knows, he's doing it, half the time, and even when he does, he can't stop himself.

"Really? That's very generous of you." I said.

Angela sighed.

"Listen Chris, Nipun is probably the nicest, most charming man, you could ever meet. He's super clever, witty, and has oodles of charm. When he focusses on you, fucking hell, it's like, 'wow', you really don't know what's hit you. You don't stand a chance, but as soon as you've fallen head over heels in love, he turns the tap off and moves on to the next one. I was only twenty when I married him. I was so young, I didn't see it, well, not until the honeymoon. I made such a scene, we had to change hotels. If he's turned his attention on Jackie Pritchard and given it to her full blast, well, she's older, been married for years, it's hardly surprising, is it? But it'll pass, as soon as he's climbed the mountain, he'll move on to the next."

"Are you calling my wife a mountain?" I asked, half-jokingly.

I didn't think the situation was amusing, not for a minute, but I didn't want to let Angela see, just how much her words were hurting me.

"No, of course not. Jackie's lovely. All the younger nurses, here, really look up to her; she's like the mother hen. And do know what, Chris?"

I shook my head.

"She loves you to bits. She's always talking about you, how proud she is of you, how brave you are, how hard working. I can honestly say, in the couple of years I've worked with Jackie, I've never heard her say a bad thing about you."

I smiled but inside I was dying.

"Hang on, where is the conference?" I asked, bearing in mind that I knew Jackie had been abroad and her passport was missing.

"Paris." Angela replied.

\*\*\*

I sat in the car, in the hospital car park, for a good hour; just thinking things through. I realised that, with all probability, my wife was just about to spend her second night in a Paris hotel room, with a twentieth century version of fucking Casanova. I also realised, in reality, there was absolutely nothing I could do about it. At some point during my reflection, I remembered the story I'd heard about the extraordinary size of Nipun's penis and felt even worse.

I knew life was unfair, I really did. Good people got terminal illnesses, young children died of cancer and lovely families were wiped out in car accidents with drunken drivers, who walked away without a scratch. I knew all these things, but I still couldn't help feeling sorry for myself. I had never been unfaithful to my wife; I'd never even contemplated it. And yet, because of a stupid and inaccurate newspaper story, and because, just before that was published, some good-looking geezer from work had turned my wife's head, my marriage was now over. I was about to become that most common of creatures, a divorced policeman; the only difference being, I wasn't leaving my wife for some stunning young WPC. In every way, therefore, this was a pile of shit.

When it was after ten, I set off for Tottenham nick.

I had agreed with the Superintendent to avoid the nick for a couple of days but I needed to pick up some paperwork, so I could make my enquiries with the D.V.L.A. in Swansea, where I had an appointment, the following day.

My plan was simple. I would wait until night duty were on and then slip in and out without anyone, hopefully, taking any notice of me. I only needed to go to my desk and pick up one folder. If I saw anyone from night duty C.I.D., I'd say a quick hello, avoid getting drawn into any conversation, and fuck off, quickly.

When I got to the nick, however, something was wrong. There were twenty or so police officers, and Derrick and Matt from night duty C.I.D., standing on the pavement, opposite the nick. The side road, to the north, was cordoned off, with a blue 'do not cross' tape and the station itself, was cordoned off with red tape. The place had been evacuated. I parked down the High Street and wandered casually up to have a quick chat with my C.I.D. colleagues.

Matt saw me approach and nodded a greeting. I sidled up beside him.

"What's happening?" I asked.

" Gas leak, again." He responded.

"Didn't they have a gas leak last week and have to evacuate?"

"Yep. Apparently, whatever they did, didn't work." He replied.

"I've got to get some corres. Anyone got any idea how long it's going to be?"

"Apparently, it shouldn't take long ..."

With that several of the PC's radios crackled to life and declared 'all clear'.

"You were right." I replied.

I joined the general melee of returning staff and made my way up to my desk, on the first floor. As I entered the office, I immediately noticed that some of the desk drawers had been forced open, obviously during the search for the racist material. I glanced upwards, at the ceiling tile, which concealed my find, but it appeared undisturbed. My desk was undamaged because, like all experienced C.I.D. officers, I never locked it. That way, I could easily deny the contents, should I ever need to do so. It was an old trick, I picked up in my early Stoke Newington days, when I first went on the Crime Squad.

I took a quick look through my trays. They'd obviously been searched, thoroughly because everything was in the wrong order and, I guessed, the contents had been removed, searched, and then just dumped back, without any thought, as to where they'd each come from. It therefore took me several minutes to find the file marked, 'Colonel Beaulieu Burglary'. I opened it, quickly, to check it contained all the documents I required for the D.V.L.A. visit, when I noticed a white envelope, with my name written on the front. It looked like a birthday card, so I sat down and opened it. The envelope contained a formal invitation, written in stylish gold writing, with a traditional fountain pen and, at first, I assumed it was a wedding invitation, but I was wrong.

'Dear Christopher Pritchard,

You are cordially invited to The Green Man, Toot Hill, Essex at 8pm on 12th July 1998 to share a romantic meal for two.

Dress required is smart casual for the first part of the evening but entirely optional, thereafter.

Xxx'

I turned the card over but there was nothing on the back and, a sweep with my finger inside the envelope, revealed no other clues, as to the sender. I popped the card in my back pocket and thought no more about it.

Derrick offered me a tea, but I said I wasn't staying. I half suspected that he wanted to mention the Katie Sumers episode, but I was grateful when he didn't.

"What do you reckon then? It's discrimination, isn't it?" Derrick said, as I stood up and got set to leave.

"What's that, mate?" I asked, without conviction.

"They force open and search every desk in this office ..."

"Shouldn't lock your desks, should you..." I interjected.

"... see, I taught my team well, they didn't have to banjo any of theirs."

"It's not that, Nostrils, Complaints only did our desks. Didn't do uniforms' lockers, just assumed the letters must originate here. It's fucking outrageous." Derrick said

I paused.

"Are you seriously telling me that none of the PC's lockers were opened and searched?"

"That's right. They didn't even do the Community Support, or the Crime Desk, just us in this office. It's just discrimination, and they didn't search the black officer's desk." He replied.

I walked over to Colin's desk and, from the order and general tidiness, thought their assumption was probably correct.

"Well, they'd hardly search Colin's desk, would they?" I asked.

"Why not?" Matt asked.

It suddenly occurred to me that it might not be common knowledge that he'd received one of the letters, so I ignored Matt's question.

"Guys, got to go. Don't take it, personally, I mean, they may have had specific intelligence that the letters came from one of us in this office. I'll catch up with you later."

I was pleased to cut the conversation short. I had to be so careful what I said, especially as Kitty had tipped me off about the search, and that I'd already nearly let it slip about Colin getting one of the letters.

As I drove home, I decided to conduct a thought experiment. I did these, when I was trying to work out a case, or a similar problem, and it always helped, although sometimes, more than others. The thought experiment was to be about Kitty Young and went something like this.

I think it was safe to assume Kitty didn't really like me; the feeling was mutual. Yet since her arrival, we'd had a number of interactions and, I had to admit, to being slightly impressed by her attitude. She hadn't shied away from the issues between us, she'd agreed to give the situation a trial period, and then reassess how we were getting on. Most impressively of all, she'd warned me about the impending search. That she chose to do so, must mean, she didn't think I was up to no good. Why else would she demonstrate such a level of trust in me?

Work wise, I thought she was struggling. She, clearly, had never been a detective and was, to all intents and purposes, a newcomer to the Met, so she'd naturally take a few months to find her feet. On the other hand, she was much brighter than I'd previously thought, and she was also quite articulate.

The information Colin had imparted was interesting but not damning. So, Kitty had a friend who'd asked her to review a case? It wasn't completely ethical for her to do so but it probably wasn't anything I wouldn't do, myself. There would only be a problem, when and if, Kitty decided to NFA the prosecution and she hadn't, yet, done so. Consequently, it followed that she hadn't done anything wrong.

Was Kitty connected in some way to the racist letters? They did all start at about the time she arrived. But what would be the benefit to her? Surely, it wasn't all a huge ruse to get me into trouble. But then, if Kitty didn't plant the material in my desk, who did? And why?

I couldn't come to any conclusion, so I gave up.

My mind turned to Bob. He'd now been gone for forty-eight hours, what the hell was he up to? Why hadn't he surfaced? The longer he was absent without leave, the bigger was my lie to the Superintendent that he hadn't come home. Clearly, the powers that be genuinely believed he'd jumped off the cliff and that his body would eventually wash up, somewhere. Of course, I knew differently but I was starting to wish I'd never got involved with him and Katie. After all, somehow, their problem had now become my problem and I was quite capable of creating enough of those, without anyone else's help.

If Bob hadn't gone to his mum's and he wasn't at home, then where was he holed up? He'd have had to lose the car. And what the fuck were the wraps of cocaine doing, stuffed down the back seat? I was certain that wasn't his scene, and I would know, having been on the gear for three years.

And what was he doing for money? They were bound to have a tracker on his bank account and, if he made a withdrawal or used his card to buy anything, it would ping up. Not using a bank account is easier, if you've had time to plan your escape but not if, as Bob had done, you've suddenly got to disappear.

As I turned into my road, I desperately hoped to see Jackie's distinctive yellow Fiat parked outside the house, and a few lights on within, but there was no trace of her car and the house was in darkness.

I felt really fed up.

**Chapter 46**

I had a restless night. Every hour or two, I woke up and checked my phone, to see whether anyone had called or left a message. They hadn't. I started to feel quite lonely.

Just when I'd dropped off to sleep, Dot rang to ask me whether I was coming into the office. I explained that the Superintendent thought it would be wise for me to stay away for a few days and that I was going to use the opportunity this provided to go down to Swansea and meet with the D.V.L.A. Police Liaison officer.

She moaned that with Bob gone, Rik sick and me in Swansea, that left just her and Colin to deal with seven prisoners. I apologised and suggested she speak to the DI and ask for someone to come across from another team to assist.

At the end of the conversation, which had hitherto been very businesslike, Dot asked me how I was doing. The tone of her voice was strange; there was some kind of hook in it.

"I'm okay." I replied, tentatively.

"You sure?"

"Are you referring to the News of the World article?" I asked.

"Yes and no." She replied, a response that wasn't particularly helpful.

"Dot, are you all right?" I asked.

"It doesn't matter, Chris; forget it." She said, and then she hung up.

I really didn't know what to make of it all.

The drive to Swansea took longer than I thought because of a somewhat ridiculous incident at Membury Services.

I had stopped to use the toilet and grab a cup of coffee. I'd just got back in my car when, a white bloke, overweight, and about fifty years old, tapped at my driver's door window. It was so unexpected that I jumped and spilt some really hot coffee down my nice, clean, white shirt and slightly burning my hand.

I jumped out of the car, flicking the coffee off my hand and cursing.

"Fucking hell, mate." I said, clearly pissed off.

This had better be good, I thought.

"Sorry, governor, sorry." He said, in a thick Irish accent.

"For fuck's sake, mate, look at my fucking shirt." I said.

"Sorry, governor, but you'll be pleased I did."

"What?" I asked, placing the coffee on the ground, and undoing my shirt buttons.

"Want to buy a TV? Flat screen?" He asked, his face full of anticipation.

"What?" I growled.

He pointed to a white van, which was parked a few yards away.

"I've got a van full of stolen flat screen TV's, the latest models, Sony, Panasonic. Take your pick."

I stopped what I was doing and said very quietly, but quite firmly:

"Just do yourself a favour, mate. Go and get in your van and fuck off, now. Don't say another word."

"And who the fuck, do you think you are?" He said, turning to face me properly, for the first time.

"I'm a police officer, now just fuck off and we can all get on with the rest of our day."

I knew I should probably nick him, but I really wasn't in the mood, and besides, I was in the middle of Wiltshire, without a police radio and I'd noticed that, sitting in the driver's seat of the bloke's white van, was a second, younger, white man, and the last thing I wanted, was a rough and tumble, in a service station car park.

"You ain't a fucking police officer; you're a fucking tosser. Go fuck yourself, you fat cunt."

Fat cunt? Fat cunt! All right, I was a couple of stone overweight, but this guy was eighteen stone. Suddenly, this had become personal. Besides, I was trying to do this guy a favour, by telling him to get on his way, and how was he repaying me? By calling me a tosser and a fat cunt.

"What did you say?" I asked, my voice aggressive.

"A fat cunt and deaf?" He replied.

I reached into my back pocket, took out my warrant card and said the line.

"You're under arrest for handling. You don't have to say anything, but it may harm your defence if you do not mention when questioned anything you later rely on in court."

"Oh fuck." He replied, a look of complete astonishment on his face.

Within five minutes I was really regretting my hasty decision. I got the bloke to sit in the back of my car and dialled, nine nine nine. The operator took my request for a uniform assistance but told me that I was looking at forty minutes wait, as the nearest available officer was dealing with a burglary in Blunsden, wherever that was. I asked if they could dispatch a traffic unit, but they were all tied up with a fatal accident on the outskirts of Swindon.

The guy I'd nicked was keen to explain that the TVs he was selling, weren't stolen, that he'd bought them legitimately, and he even produced a receipt from a hotel in Marlborough. He told me that the TVs were secondhand crap and only a few of them worked but he told punters they were nicked, so they'd think they were getting a bargain and, when they realised, they weren't, they wouldn't have the balls to complain. So, basically, the whole thing was a scam but not a case of handling. He even opened one of the TV's he was selling. The set was heavily wrapped in clear polystyrene, a bit like they had just started doing to suitcases at airports. The bloke said, that unless the punter had a carpet knife on them, the package was almost impossible to remove, in less than ten minutes, by which time, he and his van would be long gone.

I did say to the bloke that I'd tried very hard not to nick him, and that I had given him an opportunity to walk away. He agreed and seemed genuinely annoyed with his own stupidity. He said that his mouth was always getting him into trouble and that he really should have learnt, by now.

Thirty minutes after we'd met, it was like I was chatting to an old mate. We got on quite well. After an hour, I formally de-arrested him, cancelled the uniform unit, shook hands, and went our separate ways. The whole episode had been somewhat bizarre, but no harm was done.

I was just about to set off when my message alert activated.

'Please call this number, urgent.'

Neither my phone book nor I recognised the number.

## Chapter 47

"Chris?"

"Who's this?"

"Katie?"

" Yes, listen, I'm on my sister's mobile. Are you with Bob?"

Clearly, Katie didn't know Bob was still missing.

"No, why? What's going on?"

"I need to speak to him, urgently. Where is he?" She asked.

I had to be careful because the official line was that Bob had been missing since Beachy Head and, although I knew that wasn't true, if I told Katie, then the secret would be out.

"He's disappeared, Katie. I was hoping you'd know. For fuck's sake, I've been after you for days, did you not get any of my messages?" I asked.

"No, as soon as I knew the story was coming    out, I ditched my mobile, sorry."

"So, when was the last time you heard from him?" I asked.

"Friday evening. I wanted to meet up, but he said he was going to Sussex first thing in the morning and had to be up, at like, three."

"What was he going there for?" I asked.

Of course, I knew the answer, but I wanted to ascertain whether she did, too. I suddenly had the feeling, I was walking through a minefield and, one wrong step, could be disastrous.

"He wanted to do some photography; something about the sunrise and the chalk cliffs. Anyway, when the shit hit the fan, I dumped my phone and thought I'd lie low for a few days but every time I call his phone, it just rings out."

"I have no idea where he is, Katie; he's not at his mum's; he's not at work and, just to confuse things, everyone thinks he's killed himself, by jumping off Beachy Head. They're searching for his body as we speak."

I hadn't thought through what I was saying because Katie went hysterical. Of course, I knew, he hadn't killed himself because I'd seen him at his flat later that morning but Katie heard what I'd said and took it, quite literally. All I could hear was her screaming and sobbing.

Eventually, I managed to get her to listen long enough for me to tell her, I was convinced that he hadn't killed himself and it had all been a big misunderstanding. I stopped short of telling her that I knew that, for a fact.

"So, when did you actually last see him?" I asked, desperate to get the conversation on to a firmer basis.

"I told you. Last week at the awards ceremony, he gave us a lift home. In fact, we were really lucky, we got stopped by the police and he'd had four pints, but he talked his way out of it, by saying he was in the job."

"Oh, fuck me. Where was that?" I replied.

"Abridge, not far from my sister's house."

"What, was it Essex and not the Met?" I asked.

"No idea." She replied.

It was unusual for an Essex officer to let a Met officer off with drink drive. Bob had been very lucky, indeed.

"But where is he, Chris? If, as you say, he's all right and not done anything stupid, then where is he? He hasn't called me or sent a message and it's been three days."

"I don't know, Katie. I really wish I did but I don't."

"What if he had an accident, you know, while he was doing his photography thing, down in Sussex. What if he fell, you know, like off the cliff?"

It wasn't a bad guess, all things considered but, of course, I knew it was wrong.

"Don't be ridiculous." I replied, quite convincingly.

"What's happening at your end? You know, after the newspaper article?"

"My agent's dealing with it. I'm not in any fit state to see anyone, so I'm staying with my sister." She replied.

"What about your old man? Where are the kids?" I asked.

"The kids are with my mum, but Steve's gone berserk. He gave me a really bad hiding and stormed out the house. He says he's going to kill Bob, that's why I've got to speak to him." She replied.

"How real is that threat?" I asked.

"Steve's got some really tasty mates, Essex boys, he calls them."

I suddenly had a rather uncomfortable thought.

"Katie, just so I know; is there any chance Steve thinks you're having an affair with me? I mean, it was my photograph in the paper and not Bob's."

"No, he knows it's a policeman called Bob Clark."

"But the paper didn't give any details of your boyfriend, did it? Other than to say it was a police officer."

Katie didn't say anything, and I got a horrible feeling.

"Katie, did you tell Steve who you were having an affair with?"

"I had to, Chris. Steve was threatening to kill the kids, unless I told him. He said he'd cut their throats, all of them, unless I told him who it was and where I could find him. I tried to hold out, but he took a knife from the kitchen drawer, it was horrendous, Chris. I told him I didn't know where Bob lived because he was married but he didn't believe me. I gave him a false address, but then he said he was going to take one of the children with him and, if I'd lied, he send them to heaven. What was I supposed to do, Chris? He was going crazy. He smashed the house up. He said he'd destroy me, he said he'd kill Bob. He even ..."

Katie stopped in the middle of the sentence, as if she was about to say something, she might later regret.

"He even what?" I said.

Katie didn't reply.

"Katie, what were you going to say?"

"It doesn't matter, Chris." She replied.

"So, you haven't been able to warn Bob?"

"No, I kept calling but his phone just went to voicemail."

"Did you leave a message?"

"Yes, I told him to call me, urgently."

"Did you tell him that he might be in danger from your old man?"

"No but I think that was fairly obvious, don't you?" Katie replied.

"Did you tell the police or your solicitor, or anyone, that Bob might be in danger?"

Katie started to cry.

For the first time, I started to think that something serious might have happened to Bob, after all. But it had happened, after I'd left him on Saturday. That would explain why he'd not returned to sort everything out.

I set off again for Swansea, but I was now concerned that Katie's old man was involved in Bob's disappearance.

## Chapter 48

The meeting at the D.V.L.A. should have been straightforward.

I needed to examine the registration documents and any other paperwork relating to the van that the witness had seen. The fact that I couldn't find the address in Berkshire seemed strange, particularly when the postman suggested the address we had didn't exist. There was obviously some kind of deception going on but I can honestly say, I didn't have a clue as to what guise it took.

I was a bit fed up because I had a ten o'clock appointment and waited until twelve before I was ushered into an impressive office, which must have belonged to a very senior civil servant. I was invited to sit one side of a large wooden table and across from me were three serious looking gentlemen, all perfectly turned out in immaculate and expensive suits.

I had been to the D.V.L.A. at Swansea several years before and on that visit I met the Police Liaison officer, a small smelly guy in his fifties in a small smelly broom cupboard sized office. Something strange was going on.

"Sit down, Detective Sergeant Pritchard. Would you like a drink? Tea, coffee, water?" The man sitting in the middle said, with a crisp Oxbridge accent.

"Tea, white, no sugar." I replied.

The man nodded towards the woman who had seen me in and who had apparently been waiting to receive my drinks request.

"DS Pritchard, can we see your warrant card, please?" The Oxbridge man asked.

I opened the small black wallet out and handed it over.

"Would you please be so kind as to introduce yourselves?" I asked, with accentuated politeness.

"… I assume that none of you is PC Evans, the PLO?"

The Oxbridge man smiled, examined my warrant card but curiously didn't return it.

"We are representatives of Her Majesty's Government, Detective Sergeant Pritchard and we'd like to explain the delicate position which your investigation is placing us in."

"And you are?" I said.

I allowed the tiniest hint of frustration to enter my voice.

The man to my left spoke next; he had a cultured Scottish accent. He was the only one of three to have any documents in front of him and he glanced at these as he spoke.

"Detective Sergeant Pritchard, I understand you are investigating an allegation of burglary at an address in Stamford Hill, the home address of one …"

He glanced down but the gesture was superficial, as no one in the country would need to read the name of the Princess's infamous partner.

"... Colonel Charles Beaulieu."

This was starting to irritate me.

"And you are?" I said, my voice rising.

The lady who had seen me in chose that moment to return with my tea.

We sat patiently and quietly until she departed.

The Oxbridge man spoke as soon as the door had closed.

"Detective Sergeant Pritchard, if I tell you that my name is James Kempton and that I work for the Home Office, will that satisfy your curiosity?"

"Is that your real name?" I asked.

"No, but I can show you identification with that synonym; it is, how shall I put this, the name I use when I am at work." He replied, his face completely deadpan.

"     So, are you Military Intelligence?" I asked.

The Oxbridge man smiled but didn't reply. The Scottish man spoke next.

"We'd like to commend you on your investigation, Detective Sergeant. It was very thorough. To be candid, son ..."

He quickly corrected himself, although his use of the term 'son' hadn't come across as offensive, probably because he was old enough to be my father.

"... my apologies, Detective Sergeant, we didn't anticipate that you would get this far. I mean, you have another fourteen crimes assigned to you."

His observation meant of course that he knew a great deal about me, a point he successfully made.

"Okay, so what has Colonel Beaulieu's burglary got to do with you? Are you worried because his manuscript was stolen, and you're concerned that it may leak to the press and damage national security?"

"Something like that." The Scottish man replied.

And then the penny dropped. They weren't worried about the burglary at all, only my investigation into it.

"Did you have a warrant?" I asked.

I sensed just the smallest ripple of a surprised response, but my question didn't solicit a verbal reply.

"We would very much appreciate it if you could conclude your investigation, as complete, and endorse the crime report with comments to the effect, there are no more meaningful lines of enquiry. In fact, we've drafted a few words for you." The Scottish man said.

He handed me a paragraph of typed script on an otherwise blank piece of A4 paper. I glanced at it.

"What do you want me to tell my DI?" I asked.

The Oxbridge man turned towards the Scottish man who selected another piece of paper, which he handed to him. Having read it, the Oxbridge man handed it back.

"I don't think she'll pay much attention." He said, almost dismissively.

" What about the Colonel. I don't think he's a man who'll be easily fobbed off."

" I'm confident you can handle him, Detective Sergeant." The Oxbridge man said.

"Gentlemen, where's my top cover here? I mean I can do what you say. If you entered the house to seize the manuscript under the power granted by a lawfully obtained warrant, then there's no crime to investigate. But what if it all goes wrong? What if the Colonel gets so obsessed with the perceived treatment, he's received at the hands of the establishment that in a few months' time, he walks into a primary school and shoots dead a classroom of children? Where will you be when the public enquiry commences, and I'm held to count for the failings of my investigation and blamed for the consequences? Where will you be then? I don't even know who you are? Or, what if the Colonel makes a complaint and they look at my investigation and decide it's unsatisfactory and conclude that I didn't do a proper job because the victim was black, like with the Hassan Achachi murder?

I'll be disciplined and perhaps returned to uniform or busted down to Constable. Where will you be then? Happy to give evidence for me at my discipline board? I doubt it! No gentleman, in its current guise, your request leaves me too vulnerable. But I'm open to suggestions."

"Detective Sergeant, we have the authority to order your compliance." The Scottish man said, his voice barely more than a whisper.

"With the greatest of respect, I don't think you do. When I joined the Metropolitan Police, I took an oath to discharge my duty according to the law without fear or favour. I report to her Majesty, not to you."

"And who exactly do you think we work for? If not her Majesty?" The Oxbridge man asked, carefully selecting each word.

"Gentleman, I would like to assist you, I really would but I want some top cover. I want something that assures me that when this all goes tits up, I'm not left vulnerable."

I chose the words 'tits up' quite deliberately to demonstrate to my new friends that I didn't come from the elite corridors of power, from which I suspected, they emanated.

The Oxbridge man asked me to step outside, while they, 'had a little word', and I duly obliged.

I immediately checked my phone, which I'd turned to silent before I went into the meeting. I had several missed calls from Dot and one from the Wiltshire police control room. The latter I ignored as it was bound to be about the TVs in the van guy, and I called Dot.

"Chris, I'll call you back, stay right where you are." Was all she said, before hanging up.

I knew the second she rang; I'd be called back into the room because that's just how life works but I was wrong. As it transpired, I would be kept waiting for over forty minutes.

My phone rang.

"Dot? Is that you? I don't recognise the number."

"Yes, Chris. I've borrowed OJs phone..."

OJ was a civvy analyst in the Borough Intelligence Unit.

"... I have a message from Bob ..."

"Fuck me, you've spoken to him? Thank god he's all right. I was really starting to worry. Where is he? Why's he done a disappearing act? Have you seen him? How did he get in contact with you?" I said, before she had finished her sentence.

Dot ignored my avalanche of questions.

"He's not good, Chris. It sounds like he's having a breakdown. He says he's safe but frightened and he doesn't know what to do. He knows Katie Sumers's husband is trying to kill him, he doesn't want to be nicked for the drugs that you told him were in his car. He says that'll cost him his job and, of course, as he lives in a police flat, his home, too. He's up to his eyeballs in debt but, most important of all, he's worried that he'll lose Katie. He can't see any way out. He says he's sorry about getting you involved and about your picture appearing in the press."

"Where is he?"

Dot ignored my question.

"He needs a way out and he needs our help." She said.

"What does he want us to do?" I asked.

"What do you mean?"

"Well, what's his plan?"

"Chris, his plan is for us to think of a plan."

"Oh, no problem then, it'll be a piece of cake." I replied.

## Chapter 49

I struck a deal with the gentlemen from the Home Office.

They provided me with their calling cards and, even though I knew the names they contained were false, there would be a record of their existence and, if the worst came to the worst, I could always produce them to support my version of events. What's more, my trip to the D.V.L.A. was a matter of record, which would be difficult to expunge. Finally, I was allowed to retain the piece of paper with the proposed wording for the CRIS report. As the Scottish man had handled this without gloves, I knew that it would have his fingerprints on it. I had at least something tangible.

Although they never articulated as much, I worked out that the powers that be needed to see what the Colonel had written about the princess and, probably on the grounds of national security, had obtained and executed a search warrant. That explained why the Colonel's alarm was repeatedly disabled. It also explained how they were able to effect entry, so expertly, to both the house and the safe. I'd be surprised if they hadn't used the opportunity to conceal a few listening devices about the property, whilst they were at it.

Morally, ethically, and legally, I didn't have a problem with what I was being asked to do. My only problem was that the Colonel might play the race card. If he did so, I'd be in trouble. For male white police officers, the situation was so dangerous in the Met, it was almost better to be accused of being a paedophile, than a racist.

*** 

On the way back to London I got a call from Susan at the Federation, asking me whether I wanted her to contact the News of the World. I was in a real dilemma, here. In an ideal world, my answer would have been, 'yes and get them to retract the story and issue an immediate apology'.

That might well save my marriage and make Jackie feel extraordinarily guilty, as well. But if I did so, it might soon come out that Katie Sumers' lover was, in fact, Bob Clark, which would drop him even further into the shit. So, it looked like I would just have to suck it up. I asked Susan not to do anything, a decision which she wrongly interpreted as me going for the big payout. I didn't bother to correct her; it wasn't important, in the greater scheme of things.

I    then got a call from Jill Long, the Superintendent. She wanted to know how I was doing, which was sweet, but it made me feel even more guilty about not telling her, I knew Bob was alive and in hiding. I said that I intended coming back to work the following day, if that was all right.

"Of course, Chris. Oh, there's been a bit of a development on the Bob Clark matter."

My heart missed a beat, but I sounded as cool, as I could.

"Oh yeah." I said.

"Sussex have got prints off three of the wraps."

"And?"

"They're unidentified." She replied.

"So, they're not Bob's then. So that clears him, doesn't it?"

"Not really, Chris. They're probably the dealers, the person from whom the drugs were purchased."

"But it helps Bob, doesn't it?" I suggested.

"Well, it's not bad news. And the substance was cocaine, pure, top grade."

I knew Jill was right. The fact Bob's prints weren't on the drugs did help but it didn't exonerate him. The problem for Bob was, he'd owned that old Capri for like ten years, perhaps longer, and he maintained the vehicle in excellent condition, a habit that would have required regular cleaning. It was therefore very difficult for him to claim he knew nothing about the drugs, so where the fuck did they come from?

"Am I right in thinking the drugs were found down the rear of the back seat, boss?" I asked.

"Yeah, I think so." Jill replied.

Somewhere at the back of my mind, something was tugging.

"Has your wife returned, yet?" She asked.

"No, boss. I think she's getting her revenge on me by going to Paris with a young doctor."

I was surprised by my own candor, but I desperately needed to tell someone.

"Oh, I'm sorry, Chris. I'm sure she'll come back. Have you got children? I know I've probably asked you before."

"No, we were trying. Well, I suspect my wife still is." I replied.

I laughed and Jill did too.

"Oh Chris, you poor thing."

The line went quiet for a few moments and when Jill spoke again, the intonation in her voice had changed.

"I need to see you. Come up and see me when you get in, tomorrow."

"Yes, boss ..."

And then I asked.

"... boss, how's DI Young? I haven't heard from her, at all. Are you keeping her in the loop?"

"Come and see me tomorrow, Chris." Jill replied and then she hung up.

I was left feeling that something important was happening, but I had no idea what. Then it dawned on me,

Jill knew about Bob, and I was going to be in big trouble for not saying anything.

## Chapter 50

I went to the hospital that evening to see if Jackie turned up for work, but she didn't, which meant she was probably spending her third night in gay Paris with Doctor Dong.

The house was cold and lonely, so I turned the heating on, and the music up, and drowned my sorrows in seventies rock and a bottle of expensive Saint Emillion.

I fell asleep on the settee and woke up at one thirty, when my phone started to vibrate, on the coffee table. I looked at the screen to see an incoming call from Jackie and immediately sat up. I pressed to accept the call and put the phone to my ear.

"Hello?" I said, meekly.

I could hear the sound of muffled voices and sporadic traffic.

"Hello, Jackie?"

Still nothing.

It appeared that Jackie had called me from her pocket, by accident. While I didn't really want to, I just had to listen. I had the most surreal experience because, only a few minutes later, she went into a building and the traffic noise abated. I then listened, while my wife laughed and joked with what sounded like another man, although I couldn't be entirely sure. What I could be certain about, was that wherever she was, my wife was having a really good time. Her voice was slightly slurred, and she kept hiccupping and, every time she did, she giggled. Eventually, the conversation ceased, and I listened intently for any further activity. When I heard her snoring, I hung up.

I woke up at ten, with a hangover and a message from Colin to meet him, 'at the usual place', at midday, on the way into late turn. I took this to mean the cemetery in Buckhurst Hill, where we'd met last week.

I prepared a full fat fry up and sat there at my tiny dining room table, feeling dehydrated, knackered and emotionally drained. Having cooked a plate full of food, all I ate was one sausage, in a piece of folded up white bread. I just didn't have any appetite and that was unusual.

I called the phone number from which Katie had called me, yesterday, and her sister answered.

"Tabitha? It's Chris Pritchard, the friend of Bob Clark. Your sister rang me from this number yesterday."

"Oh hi, Chris. Katie's not with me now, can I get her to call you, darling?"

"Well, it's actually you I want to speak to. In fact, can you meet, later? It's really important."

"Of course, it's probably safer if we meet, rather than you and Katie."

"Tabitha, don't say anymore, not on the phone, anyway. Listen, do you know the Bald Faced Stag, in Buckhurst Hill?"

"Of course." She replied.

"Can you meet me there; just before closing this evening, say ten-thirty? It might be really good for us to get our heads together. Katie's right to stay low. You can make sure she knows what's going on?"

"Of course, Chris. I'll be there." She replied.

As I was getting changed, my mobile rang again, and I answered, without even looking at the screen. It was Jackie's dad, and he wasn't a happy chap. He berated me for being unfaithful, lectured me on the sanctity of marriage, and told me how I'd brought embarrassment on his family and shame on his daughter. I should, he said, go that morning to a solicitor and initiate divorce proceedings, for the purpose of which, he insisted, I should fully admit my adultery. He emphasised, repeatedly, that he never wanted to see me again and that, if he ever did, he would 'box my ears in'.

I listened patiently and grunted the occasional apology. Of course, I wanted to tell him that I had never been unfaithful to his daughter and that it was her who had been unfaithful to me.

I wanted to emphasize Nipun's race because Jackie's dad was a generational racist; that is to say, he was brought up in a time, when such attitudes were embedded from an early age. I remember her dad telling me once, that he'd never seen a 'coloured person', until he was in his twenties. I also remember Jackie telling me that her first boyfriend had been black and, when she'd taken him home, her father had, quite literally, chucked him out of the house.

But I didn't say a word because the truth would hurt him irrevocably. So, I took the bullet for Jackie, it was the least I could do for the woman I had loved, with all my heart, for the last ten years.

## Chapter 51

I arrived at the cemetery early, but everyone was already there. And when I say everyone, I mean Colin, Dot, Bob and Dawn's mum. They were all standing around the grave chatting, except Bob, who was sitting on a nearby bench, looking absolutely dreadful. There was something very reassuring in the knowledge that everyone had come together, although, of course, Mrs. M's presence there was happenchance.

Mrs. M was the first to speak.

"Chris, my darling. What is going on? We're all being very polite but clearly something has happened. Is it about the article in the paper?"

"Sort of, Mrs. M." I replied, as I gave her a hug and kissed her, gently, on the cheek.

"Well then, all of you back to my house. It's five minutes down the road. I'll make tea and bacon sandwiches and you can talk in complete privacy. I won't interfere. I'll be like the three wise monkeys. I won't see, hear, or say anything."

And that is exactly what happened. In no time at all, we were sitting around Mrs. M's kitchen table, the frying pan sizzling in the background, while we discussed how we were going to extradite Bob, and myself, from the dreadful mess which our lives had suddenly become.

The mood was solemn and quiet; the only light was Mrs. M, who busied herself making sure that she had everybody's order exactly right.

"Was that tea with one sugar or two?"

"Do you like a lot of milk or just a drop?"

"Red sauce or brown, or neither."

"Fat on or off?"

It was only four or five days since I'd last seen Bob, but the Bob that now sat in Mrs. M's house, was almost unrecognizable. He hadn't shaved and had a short, thick dark brown beard. His eyes were bloodshot, his skin tone decidedly grey and he had dark circles around each eye. He looked like he needed sleep and smelt like he desperately needed a shower. He also seemed to be in a state of shock because his mannerisms were dampened and his responses slow and thoughtful.

For a good few minutes, none of us had said a word about the elephant in the room but I was conscious time was getting on and three of us needed to be at work by two, which gave us about forty minutes to make some progress.

"Right, guys ..." I said.

"... let's try to identify the problems. Get them all on the table, before we try to decide what the fuck we're going to do about them."

"I'll go first, there's something I need to know before this goes any further." Bob said, quietly.

"Go on." Dot said and put her arm round him.

"Don't be nice to me, you'll make me cry and besides, I haven't had a wash in four days."

"I don't care." Dot said, pulling him in closer.

"Chris, was Katie giving you a blow job?"

I was quite shocked by the question. It was the last thing in the world I expected him to say. I was, however, determined to stay calm and to remember that he was going through a very difficult time.

"She wasn't. It was the timing of the photograph. Katie was leaning across, from the driver's seat, to remove a photograph of her sister from the glove box." I replied.

"Oh. Why was she doing that?" He replied.

"You do remember that I was meeting her at your request, don't you? I was doing you a favour?"

"I know, I'm sorry. I'm just really screwed up at the moment." He replied.

"Katie was getting out a photograph of her sister to show me. She wanted me to go out with her." I explained, with more patience than Bob deserved.

He took a deep breath, exhaled slowly, and visibly relaxed; clearly my explanation rang true.

"Sorry, mate. I just couldn't get it out of my mind. I'd done so much, risked everything and then I saw that picture in the newspaper and thought everything I'd done, was for nothing."

"Bob, I haven't touched Katie, she wanted me to take her sister out on a date and got a photo out from amongst some holiday snaps that were in her glove compartment. The photo in the paper looks terrible but it's just taken at exactly the precise moment to make it look like she's giving me head. It's so convincing that Jackie's left me." I said.

There were gasps of surprise from the others and Mrs M. went to console me, but I said we needed to move on, and I'd sort the Jackie thing out, in my own time.

"The biggest problem as far as I can see …" I said

"… is that two police forces, the R.N.L.I. and half the Royal Navy have been searching for a missing DC, believed to have committed hari-kari at Beachy Head, and the four of us have lied to everyone. I take full responsibility because, once I'd failed to tell Jill Long that Bob had returned to the flat, and failed to arrest him for the drugs, I set in course a chain of events, which has brought us here. The thing was, I just couldn't bring myself to nick him."

Everyone nodded, including Bob.

"Bob, just tell me one thing. When I left you on Saturday, you said you were going to your mum's to tell her about Katie, and then you'd come back and 'sort things out'. Everything would have been fine, if you'd done that. What happened?" I asked.

He shook his head.

"I can't remember. I just started to panic, I felt like I was losing everything. I knew that the story was going to hit the papers. I knew my mum was going to find out. You said I was going to be arrested for drugs, which I knew nothing about, and certainly couldn't explain. That would mean I'd get sacked and lose my flat. I might even go to prison. Remember last year, a DC from Richmond got done in a nightclub in Croydon with some cocaine? He got twelve months inside, did six and had to come out on a tag. And I'm up to my eyeballs in debt and it's not really my fault. I had to escape. I just went out and kept walking and walking and walking. I got to a phone box and called Katie, but her phone just went dead. The next day I saw the newspaper headline and thought I'd lost her, too."

"She dumped her phone because she kept getting calls from the press about the affair." I interjected.

"Listen, I'm seeing Tabitha later to find out what's going on with Katie. I'll report back."

"Please tell her to get Katie to get in touch." He pleaded, almost desperately.

"I will, I promise." I said, although, as they'd both dumped their mobiles, I wasn't quite sure how that was going to happen.

This was not the Bob Clark I'd grown to like and respect, so much; this was the shell of a man, and it was difficult to understand how quickly and easily the deconstruction process had occurred. Were we all so very fragile, underneath?

I don't know why, perhaps it was something she'd let slip, but I had my suspicions that Dot had been looking after Bob longer than she was letting on.

Colin spoke next:

"Listen mate, we're here for you, I promise. We'll make sure you get through this, fuck knows how, but we'll make sure. Nostrils here, he's been in worse scraps, haven't you mate?"

I laughed.

"I have, actually." I replied, thinking of a Bangkok hotel room.

I was a little concerned that Colin was getting involved when he didn't have to. I mean, I'd lied to Jill Long, and let Bob go, without arresting him, and Dot had been putting him up, but Colin, as yet, hadn't done anything wrong. I decided to keep my peace for the time being, but I would have to mention it, eventually.

Mrs. M was very discreet and didn't say a word until we started to get ready to leave.

"Chris, please let Bob stay here..." She suggested.

"... I'll look after him, he can have your old room. He can have a bath and I'll do some dinner, later. No one will think of looking here for him, will they?"

It was a great idea and very nice of Mrs. M to propose it, but it wouldn't do.

"No Mrs. M. This isn't your problem." I said.

"Now you listen to me, Christopher. I couldn't be there for Dawn, when she needed me, but I can be here for

Bob, now. I want to do this and you're not going to stop me."

I nodded my consent.

"But only on one condition." I said.

"Go on." Mrs. M said.

"He doesn't bath, shower, wash or clean his teeth. It's essential that he looks like he's been sleeping rough for a week."

"Okay." Mrs. M replied.

"I can feed him though?" She asked.

I nodded.

"Listen guys ..." I said, addressing everyone.

"... there is a way out of this, but we're going to need a slice of luck and careful coordination. We have to stick together, all understand?"

I looked at each of them in turn; they all nodded, even Mrs. M.

"Bob, it's really important that you lay low for just another day or two, and whatever you do, as I said, don't wash or clean your teeth, or anything. Your story has to be, you've had some sort of mental breakdown ..."

"Well, that's true." Dot interjected.

"I know, and when lying, you should always stay as close to the truth as possible, right? We'll need some plan to have you found and identified but not until you're exonerated for the drugs, and we can make sure Katie's husband isn't able to blow your brains out. That way, you won't have to be nicked and you can just have a few months off sick with stress; then, come back as right as rain. I've even got an idea how this pile of shit can help pay off some of your debts. What do you say?" I asked, my question directed to him.

He nodded and for the first time that afternoon, I saw, just the tiniest hint of a smile.

"But how are you going to sort the drugs problem out?" Colin asked.

"I've got an idea; just, leave it with me." I replied.

We agreed to meet, at the same time tomorrow, at Mrs. M's, who said, she'd do us lunch, and suggested we skip breakfast.

As we thanked Mrs. M, and Dot and Colin went off to use the bathroom, I guided Bob to one side.

"Where's your car?"

The question seemed to take him by surprise, but I couldn't think why.

"Sorry?" He said, clearly stalling for time.

"When I saw you Saturday, your Capri was in the garage, at the flat. Where is it now? If you went 'walking and walking' as you say, where the fuck is your car? Is it still at the flat?"

"It should be in the garage," He replied.

"I don't think it is. I'm sure, I'd have heard. They did a full POLSA search, at the flat; no doubt, they'd have looked in the garage. If it were there, it would have given away the fact you'd gone back home. So where is it?"

He shrugged his shoulders.

"I haven't seen it since before I spoke to you." He said.

It was a fucking mystery and the detective in me, didn't like it. I knew Bob was lying to me, I just didn't know why.

## Chapter 52

Late turn was quiet, which gave us all a chance to catch up with our case papers. There was no sign of the DI and, when I asked around, it appeared that everyone had assumed she'd either taken the day off or was at court. I thought the latter suggestion, highly unlikely.

I had just updated and closed the Colonel Beaulieu burglary case, when my mobile rang and the Superintendent asked me, when I was going to pop in and see her. She had asked me to report to her when I arrived, but I'd clean forgotten.

"I'm so sorry, boss; I just forgot that you wanted to see me." I said, as soon as I entered her office.

Jill smiled, a lovely reassuring smile.

"How are you?" She said; standing up and walking towards the coffee table area, where there were two comfortable chairs. We sat down.

"I'm all right, thanks, I think. The wife still hasn't come home; she's gone to Paris with a doctor friend."

"A male, doctor friend?" She asked, tentatively.

I nodded.

"Sorry, Chris. I'm sure you'll be able to sort it out."

"Perhaps. But last night she called me from her pocket, and I had the delightful experience of listening to her having a really good time."

Jill grimaced.

"I don't know what he was up to, but Jackie seemed to be doing a great deal of agreeing." I said, jokingly.

I realised that I was suggesting that I'd heard Jackie having sex, which I hadn't, but I didn't think it would do any harm to drum up some sympathy, from my Superintendent.

"Gosh, I am sorry. Did you speak to the Federation about getting the paper to withdraw and apologise?" She asked.

"I can't really, can I? Not without dropping Bob Clark right in it." I replied.

"So, you're taking it for him. Just like he took a knife for you." She said.

I nodded.

"Yeah, I suppose you could say that." I said.

"No news on Bob?" I asked.

I knew I had to tread carefully through this conversation, but not to ask, would have seemed odd.

"No, nothing. It's all very strange." She replied.

"I thought you were convinced he'd committed suicide?"

"But you're not, are you?" She said.

I suddenly felt a rush of blood to my cheeks and hoped I wasn't blushing.

"No, boss. Nothing I ever knew about Bob would suggest to me, he'd take his own life but then, where is he?"

"Um." Jill replied.

"Sussex say that the body normally washes up, within two to five days and, although it's not unheard of for one never to turn up, it's quite rare. Was Bob, perhaps, making it look like a suicide, you know doing a bit of a Lord Lucan? The Financial Investigator says he owes a lot of money. And then there's the car ..."

"What do you mean?" I asked

"It's disappeared. Was it nicked by the travellers? Perhaps. Or did Bob actually get back in it and drive off?"

I had to admit, Superintendent Jill Long was getting closer to the truth.

"But he'd have gone to his home address, wouldn't he?" I asked, innocently.

"Maybe, Chris. And what about the drugs?" She asked.

"They, I agree, are a mystery. I have never known anyone less likely to be a drug addict." I said.

"I'm going to ask you a question, Chris. You can answer, completely without prejudice." Jill said.

"What do you mean?" I asked.

"I want the truth, but I won't tell anyone what you've said. Were the drugs yours?"

I hadn't seen that question coming, something which the expression on my face clearly demonstrated.

"Okay, clearly not. I'm sorry, didn't mean to offend you but I had to ask. I mean, you were on the gear, once. I thought you might have relapsed."

I sighed heavily and paused, before I replied.

"Do you know, boss, I was, but that was years ago and besides, they'd be in my car not his, wouldn't they?"

"So, you're not in any way involved in this?" She asked.

I don't think I'd ever felt more awkward than I did at that precise moment. Of course, I was involved. I was, 'up to my eyeballs', involved but not in the way Jill suspected. I liked and respected Jill Long and the last thing I wanted to do, was to keep deceiving her, but what choice did I have? I felt like shit.

"Not at all." I replied with such sincerity and conviction that, for a few seconds, I even believed it, myself.

"Good. Thank you, Chris. I'm sorry I doubted you, but my antennae were telling me, something wasn't quite right. I'm glad you've put my mind at ease. I just thought, perhaps, you'd got back on the gear, and, you know ..."

Her sentence petered off.

"They're not mine, boss…" I replied.

"… and why would they be in his car?"

"Well, you were with him on Thursday night, weren't you? At the police club? That's only a couple of days, before he disappeared."

"I was but we travelled in different cars. I don't think I've ever been in his Capri. How do you know about us being at Chigwell?" I asked.

"My husband told me. He was there. When I told him what was going on at work, he said he'd seen you at Chigwell."

I'd never met Jill's old man. I was vaguely aware that he was a DS somewhere, perhaps at the Yard, on some squad.

"Does your old man know me?" I asked, as politely, as I could.

"Chris, everyone in the Met knows you, well those of a certain age, anyway. You don't survive being blown up by an I.R.A. bomb without everyone knowing who you are. Your face was in the papers for days, afterwards. And you can still see your scar, it's very noticeable."

"Great …" I said, sarcastically.

"… no UC work for me, then?"

Jill laughed.

"I don't think so, do you? Anyway, listen Chris, it's because I think the Job owes you one, I'm going to go out on a limb and confide in you. I shouldn't, and I could get into a great deal of trouble, if you ever reveal, I've told you this. Do you assure me, you'll treat, what I am about to tell you, in the strictest confidence?"

I raised my right hand, as if I was taking an oath, and replied:

"I do, Ma'am."

"You've just been the subject of an intelligence led integrity test."

I hadn't got a clue what she was talking about. Was this about Bob?

"I assume that I passed. Otherwise, I'd be having this conversation with someone from C.I.B."

"Correct" Jill replied.

When I was at C.I.B., I'd been loosely connected to the new Integrity Testing Unit, when it was in its infancy. I didn't know a lot about them, or how they worked, but I did know two things; one, they only ever targeted someone against whom there was existing information of corruption and secondly, if the subject passed the test, they were never told. The latter had always seemed a bit unfair to me, but Jill seemed to be breaking that rule.

"Go on then, boss; what was it all about?"

"Sworn to secrecy?" She asked, her eyebrows rose.

"I promise." I assured her.

"The Job received an anonymous report that you were manufacturing and sending racist material. Someone had already received an offensive letter and, as you know, several more were received last week."

"I know, Colin on my team got one; he was quite upset, actually. Boss, they're nothing to do with me." I assured her.

Of course, I now had another dilemma. Did I say anything about finding the stuff in my desk? I thought I'd wait and see how this played out. After all, I always believed in the maxim - when you don't know what to do, do nothing.

"What was the test?"

"Last week, they searched your desk ..."

"Yes, I know; they did all of them, in the C.I.D. office." I replied.

"No, before then. They searched your desk and found loads of magazine cuttings and other evidence to suggest you were the sender. But they weren't sure whether the evidence had been planted and, as the desk was unlocked, proving you knew it was there, would be difficult."

"Go on." I encouraged her.
"They set up a hidden camera on your desk and then DI Young told you there was going to be a search. Obviously, if you were guilty, you would remove the material from your desk, but you didn't. You didn't do anything. The only conclusion one can therefore reach, is that you didn't know it was there, in the first place, and it had, in fact, been planted to incriminate you."

My mind was racing. Should I tell her that I had, in fact, found and removed the material? If I did tell her, that meant I hadn't passed the integrity test at all, I'd failed it! And where on earth, did they think the racist material had gone now? They must surely have checked to see whether it was still there. Then, I realised something.

"The gas leaks. They were made up so they could put the camera in and out, weren't they? That's how they got the police station evacuated."

Jill nodded.

I tried desperately hard to think when they'd happened, in relation to my own finding of the racist material.

"So, what's going to happen next?" I asked.

"Tomorrow, Complaints will come to the nick and search your desk, recover the material and then interview you, probably in a few weeks. I don't think they'll be in any hurry. Now, I realised, unless I told you what had been going on, you would probably have a coronary heart attack. I'm telling you this, so you know there's absolutely nothing to worry about. When they interview you, they will, in fact, know that you knew nothing about it being in your desk. So just tell them the truth, and your account will be corroborated by evidence of the hidden camera that shows you did nothing. I had to tell you, Chris. It just wasn't fair to let you go through months of worry and anguish, when I know you've done absolutely nothing wrong. But I'm taking a risk telling you. I hope you don't let me down."

"Hang on a second. Kitty, I mean DI Young, sorry, she told me that there was going to be a search. She asked me to count the number of lockers in the PCs changing room. She wasn't being nice, she was setting me up, hoping that I'd remove the material from my desk and that action would be caught on camera."

"You had to be forewarned, didn't you? It was all part of the test." Jill explained.

"Did she know about the material being found in my desk?"

"I don't think so. She wasn't told much. Just to inform you, in a subtle way, that there would be a search of the station."

"Who else knew?" I asked.

"Just DI Young and me. Well, of course, the DI was already involved. We were the only local officers included. Not even the Chief Superintendent knows."

"Thanks for letting me know, boss. I really appreciate it."

I stood up and turned to leave.

"Be careful, Chris. Someone's trying to drop you in the shit. Keep on your guard and don't give them any ammunition."

'Don't give them any ammunition', Jesus, with the Bob Clark situation about to erupt, I'd loaded an AK 57 with enough bullets to commit mass murder!

As I was about to leave, I had a thought.

"Boss, how long ago did DI Kitty know she'd be posted here, to Yankee Tango?" I asked.

"Oh, a few months now. I met her back in May, why do you ask?"

"It's probably nothing." I replied, while thinking exactly the opposite.

## Chapter 53

I wished I hadn't found the material in my desk. Timing wise, I must have done so between C.I.B. originally, searching my desk and, them putting the camera in. By removing the material, I'd greatly complicated matters.

The situation also exposed my decision, not to report finding the stuff, as a serious error of judgment. The best solution I could think of now, ridiculous as it might sound, was to put the material back in my desk. So, I'd be planting evidence on myself!

I needed time to think but, as soon as I walked back in the C.I.D. office, Dot told me there were four prisoners on their way in for a mobile phone robbery. At that precise moment, twelve hours work, was the very last thing I needed. Besides I had an important meeting with Tabitha, at ten thirty, so I couldn't be late off.

Dot could clearly see the anguish in my face.

"Don't worry, Chris. Me and Colin will deal. You do whatever you've got to do."

"Dot?" I said.

"Yes, Sarge?"

"Did I ever tell you how much I love you and how much I want you to have my babies?" I joked.

"I'd rather put pins in my eyes, Sarge." She replied.

I laughed out loud.

I needed time to think. There was a lovely, old-fashioned pub, near Lordship Park and, ten minutes later, I was sitting in a quiet corner, sipping a pint of real ale, and turning everything over in my mind. I realised, I didn't have long to make a decision because, if I was going to put the material back in my desk, it had to be in the next few hours.

To help me understand what was going on, I jotted down a few bullet points in my daybook.

- X planted RM in my desk
- X sent RM to Colin and others
- X tipped off Complaints that there is RM in my desk
- Complaints searched my desk and found RM, which they left in situ and plan Integrity Test
- So far, X's plan has worked perfectly, but then I found and removed the RM
- The following day I saw the DI searching my desk, she seemed to be looking for something specific, I now reckon, that was the Anna Abolla case papers
- Complaints put a hidden camera on my desk
- Complaints direct DI to inform me of impending official search, to trigger me into action.
- Complaints wait to see if I remove the RM, but I don't, not because I don't know it's there but because I have already found it

I picked up my phone and stepped into the deserted beer garden at the back of the pub.

And then it dawned on me. I'd been looking at the problem from the wrong angle. Who had anything to gain by planting the material on me? Only one person, was the conclusion to which I came.

"Boss, sorry to trouble you."

"That's all right, Chris. What is it?" Jill Long said.

"When you said, 'DI Young was already involved, which is why Complaints were able to include her in the integrity test', what did you mean?"

"I don't think I should have said that. I've been rather indiscreet."

"Boss, I need to know, how was she already involved?"

"Well, she was the first person to receive one of the racist letters, before she'd even arrived at Tottenham. It said something like, 'Monkeys not welcome in the Met', or words to that effect. She reported the matter, straight-away."

"Thanks, boss. I just wondered. Thanks again for giving me the heads up, I won't let you down."

I hung up.

I had all the information I needed.

By the time I'd finished my pint, I had decided, the time for prevaricating was over. It dawned on me that my career had almost no chance of surviving the next few days. There were just too many ways for circumstances to turn against me. With this realisation, was born an uncharacteristic boldness. In poker terms, I had decided to go, all in.

## Chapter 54

Having done what I had to do at the nick, which included putting the racist material back in my desk, I left Dot and Colin up to their necks in paperwork and headed off for my rendezvous with Katie Sumers's older sister.

Tabitha was to one side of the bar, with a large glass of white wine and a book. Seeing that her glass was full, I didn't bother to ask whether she wanted another drink, bought my second pint of the evening, and sat down next to her.

"Hi, darling." She said, putting her book down, still open on the page she was reading.

"Tabitha." I replied, taking a long gulp of Directors.

Tabitha seemed relaxed and in no hurry to initiate the conversation, which kind of surprised me.

I observed her, carefully. She was, perhaps, five years older than her famous sister. She was attractive and expensively dressed in designer jeans, over which were pulled, knee high leather boots. She wore a black and brown leopard print blouse, which opened to expose a significant cleavage and the hint of a black bra. She had shoulder length fair hair, cut in the latest, 'Rachel from Friends' style. You could tell she and Katie were sisters.

"Well, has Bob turned up?" She asked.

"Nope." I replied.

I wasn't going to tell anyone what was really going on.

"Then I suspect Steve has killed him, darling." She declared, with a complete absence of emotion.

"What?" I replied.

"Well, apparently, Steve set off to find him on Saturday, when he got wind that the story was coming out. He gave Katie a hiding and threatened to kill the kids, if she didn't reveal where he lived. Katie said he told her that, by the end of the day, Epping Forest would be home to another rotting corpse."

"What a charming man." I said.

"Listen darling, Steve set out with a boot containing a body bag, a spade and enough lime to decompose an elephant. He wasn't fucking about, Chris. If he found Bob, Bob's dead, I assure you. I know that for a fact."

Perhaps I should have feigned more concern because, if I hadn't seen Bob, Tabitha's news would, most surely, have worried me.

"How's Katie?" I asked.

"She's alright. Two black eyes and a fractured right arm but she'll live. She's got a PR firm on her case."

"Is she going to report the assault?" I asked.

Tabitha shook her head.

"Where is she? Still at your mum's?"

"No, the press started to gather outside, so the PR company has moved her somewhere else. She's worried about Bob, distraught. Like me, she's convinced he's dead. The PR company told her, their contact in the police thinks Bob's killed himself. I'm sure he hasn't killed himself. He went to Beachy Head to take some photographs, not jump off a cliff..."

"... but it is worrying, he's still missing." I added, quickly, but with little conviction.

"Where's Steve?"

Tabitha shrugged her shoulders and took a large sip of her wine.

"I wouldn't know, darling." She added.

"No, I suppose not. Assuming Bob's not dead, what's the future for him and Katie? Is there one?" I asked.

Tabitha frowned.

"That's a strange question, Chris."

"Well, what's the answer?" I said.

"My sister describes Bob as her soul mate. But then, when Steve Oswald is all you've ever known, that's hardly surprising, is it? Steve was Katie's coach when she was fourteen. I know for a fact that he was having sex with her, before her fifteenth birthday. He's sixteen years older than her, so he was thirty then. He's from a very rough family but he briefly escaped into the world of gymnastics, when he was at school. He was going to the Olympics but had a bad motorbike accident and that was the end of his career. I know for a fact that he deals drugs and that he gets the gear off his cousins."

"What exactly?"

"Cocaine, mainly, but heroin, too."

"And you? What's your weapon of choice?" I asked.

I met her stare and held it. She sipped her wine, nervously.

"I don't use any drugs, mate. Not me; you've got it wrong, mate."

The use of the address, 'mate', was completely out of character and told me what I needed to know but I played along.

"Sorry, didn't mean to offend. I just know what you showbiz types are like."

"Me, showbiz? No, you're confusing me with my older sister."

I laughed, and so did Tabitha, but it was mutually false.

The bells sounded for last orders.

"Another wine?" I asked.

"Just a small glass, darling" She replied.

I returned to the bar but slipped Tabitha's old wine glass into my pocket. It protruded ridiculously but no one was looking at me. I returned to the table with our drinks but excused myself, saying I needed to retrieve my mobile phone from the car. It was just an excuse to hide the wine glass, or to be more precise, Tabitha's fingerprints, which would be all over it.

## Chapter 55

I slept better that night than I had done for weeks. It felt good to have resolved at least one problem.

Tabitha had agreed to contact Sussex police, first thing the following day, to admit that the wraps of drugs, in the back of the Capri, belonged to her and Bob knew nothing about them.

When the police had stopped Bob, while he was giving her and her sister a lift back from Chigwell police club,

Tabitha had panicked and pushed the drugs down the back of the seat. Drugs, incidentally, that she admitted getting, every week, from Steve Oswald. She said her sister knew nothing about, 'their little arrangement'. I suspected Tabitha was also sucking her brother-in-law's dick.

Of course, Tabitha had no reason to be aware of the subsequent trouble she had caused. She didn't know that the PC, who searched Bob's car at Beachy Head, had found the drugs and that everyone thought they were his. I told her that I'd been instructed to arrest Bob if he ever reappeared.

I also told her that there were fingerprints on the wraps and that, if she refused to agree to give herself up, I would be able to link her to the drugs, by comparing the prints on them to those I would get off the wine glass. I was cutting a few corners, I mean, I wouldn't do the fingerprinting myself and it was, just as possible, the prints off the wraps would belong to the dealer, in this case Steve, and not her. But I made a good case and she agreed to comply with my request.

She was, she said, disappointed that I had felt compelled to trap her into confessing. She claimed, if I'd just explained the circumstances to her, she'd have come forward, voluntarily. Perhaps she was telling the truth, but I hadn't been prepared to take that risk.

***

We met at Mrs. M's, at twelve o'clock, as arranged. It gave us a little over an hour to have something to eat and to plan our next moves.

Bob looked even worse, and I was pleased to see he'd done what I'd told him and not cleaned himself up, in any way. He did smell a bit but that would all help with the deception.

I talked him through my meeting with Tabitha. She'd texted me that morning to tell me she had an appointment at Eastbourne police station tomorrow, with her solicitor. Bob seemed mightily relieved.

"I can't believe I didn't realise. Of course, I was lucky to talk myself out of a Breathalyzer but, quite frankly, so much has happened since then, I haven't given the incident a second thought. I never knew she was a coke head." Bob said.

"What about Katie?" I asked.

"God, no. She was always complaining about her old man doing line after line, and he did a bit of brown, as well. She thought he was dealing, if only to help fund his own habit. Oh, I wonder?"

"Wonder what, Bob?" I asked.

"I did think there might be something going on between them, you know, Steve and Tabitha. I know it crossed Katie's mind, but this might explain that, too. Well, Katie found some texts between them, and a friend once told her, he'd seen them meeting somewhere or other. I bet they weren't having an affair, I bet he was supplying her. That would make more sense."

Dot intervened.

"That's all very interesting, and it's great that you've solved the drugs in the car issue; but what do we do now? How can we explain Bob's disappearing act? We need to work out our story so that it fits all the circumstances."

"There's something I need to mention, before we do that, because it's very relevant. Katie Sumers's husband, Steve …"

"… Oswald …" Bob interjected.

" … yes, Steve Oswald is, according to Tabitha, determined to kill you."

"       Lots of jilted husbands say that." Colin said.

"From what Tabitha was saying, it was more than just a threat. Apparently, having forced Katie to tell him where you lived, he made a series of phone calls to his contacts and ordered one of them to get hold of a body bag, lime, and a shovel."

"Are you serious?" Dot asked, incredulously.

"       It's what Tabitha said, and she can only have heard that from Katie, can't she? When I spoke to Katie, a couple of days ago, I knew there was something she wasn't telling me. I'm guessing, that was it. Her old man wasn't fucking about when he said he was going to kill you." I replied.

"Then we have to treat that threat very seriously." Colin said.

"I agree... " Dot said.

"... is it even safe for him to reappear, yet? I mean, does he need to go into witness protection or something?" She continued.

"I can't see the Job putting one of their own officers into witness protection because he's shagged a famous TV personality and her old man's got the raving hump, can you? The Daily Mail would have a field day."

"But we do have to do something, surely?" Dot said.

"I'm not worried about Steve Oswald. And Chris is right; we can't expect the Job to protect me. I am responsible for my own actions. I have made my bed and now I must lie in it. Let's take the threat from Steve out of the equation. I need to get this mess sorted out. I've been sleeping in Dot's garage for four nights and I can't impose on Mrs. M for much longer. I'm going to go home, have a shower, sleep for twenty-four hours and then deal with the consequences; in that order. Thank you for everything you've all done, but I can't do this anymore. I've had lots of time to think, and I need to get on with my life."

Dot looked really worried, but it was Colin who said what we were all thinking.

"What are you going to say?" He asked.

"I don't know, I just know, I've had enough. And it's not fair to expect you lot to get even more involved. I mean, I'm imposing on Mrs. M. I fucked up your marriage, and now, your career's hanging by a thread, too. Poor Dot has been hiding me like a fugitive since Sunday..."

"Fuck me, you've been with Dot since Sunday? Dot, does your old man know?" I asked.

"No, Bob's been in the outhouse at the bottom of the garden. Gordon would have gone mad. I've been able to keep you warm and fed, and that's the main thing. I'm sorry I had to mislead you all, but it was best that way. You never know who's listening to your calls and besides, it gave me a chance to find out what was actually going on without compromising anything. But eventually, I knew I had to come clean." Dot said.

"I'll never forget it." Bob replied, quietly.

"And I'll never drop you, or any of you in it, I promise." He added.

"You can go home, Bob, of course that's one option. But it will look much more convincing, if you reappear by chance, so to speak." I suggested.

"How? And then what?" He asked.

"You need to come back but not of your own volition. We need, you need, to make it look like it wasn't intended. Then you claim to have had a mental breakdown, to be able to recall nothing about the last week. I mean you look the part; you really do … "

Everyone nodded.

"     But what's he going to say about where he's been and why he disappeared?" Dot asked.

"Right, although Katie says, you told her you were going to Sussex to do your photography, no one else has, yet, worked that out. Apart from everyone in this room, the last time anyone saw you, or to be more precise, the last time anyone thinks they know where you were, was Beachy Head. So, if we all keep mum, no one will ever know that you made it back to London, right?" I said.

Everyone nodded but Bob hesitated.

"Has anyone else seen you in London? Anyone at all who knows you? Think carefully, Bob, this is crucial."

He shook his head slowly.

"     So, run with the story that you went to Beachy Head to commit suicide. Changed your mind, returned to your car, which had been stolen, and then decided to head for Brighton, where you've been sleeping rough, ever since. You were worried about the Katie thing; you were heavily in debt, and you just couldn't cope. I mean we're not straying too far from the truth here, are we? We're just making sure that we're not asked loads of awkward questions about why we've been looking after you and covering up. Any thoughts?"

"Your phone's been at home, all the time, hasn't it?" Dot said.

Bob nodded.

"So, no cell site to contradict your story; that's really good." Colin said.

"That is good." I commented.

"The car's the problem of course. You drove back from Brighton on Saturday. So where is your car, the Capri?" Colin asked.

It was the same question I'd asked Bob the previous day.

Bob didn't reply and I knew he was hiding something. I sensed he was turning over in his mind whether to tell us the truth or not.

Colin obviously spotted this, too, because he said, bluntly:

"Bob, what the fuck actually happened on Saturday? You haven't told us, have you? I think we've got a right to know. If you'd just been doing a bit of photography, how come you suddenly disappeared?"

"Well, I knew I'd be nicked for the drugs, didn't I? And the press were all over the Katie Sumers story, so I knew that the shit was going to hit the fan, there, too. And guys, I haven't told you this before, but I owe like fifteen thousand pounds on credit cards, I'm up to my neck in it. I just couldn't face it all."

"There's more to this, Bob. What is it that you're not telling us?" Colin asked.

"Well, by Sunday evening, he was sleeping in my outhouse with my tortoises.  We have a missing twenty-four hours." Dot said.

"So, what the fuck went on during those twenty-four hours, mate? And where the fuck is your car?" Colin asked, the volume of his voice rising with every word.

"You don't want to know, you really don't. Yes, we do have a problem with my car, but there's more than one car to worry about." He replied.

## Chapter 56

Bob didn't tell us what had happened or why he'd disappeared, but he did try to persuade us not to get involved. He said, he appreciated everything we'd already done, but that he'd take it from here. When he told us what he had to do, to clear the decks and then reappear, we all knew, he couldn't possibly make it, alone.

If Bob was going to survive, we would have to work as a team, and all take responsibility for a part of the plan. But we'd be taking a big risk. I was concerned that Colin, especially, didn't have to get involved. Dot was already committed, as she'd been putting Bob up, and so was I, because I'd lied to the Superintendent to cover up his return. When I put this to Colin, his reply was blunt.

"Go fuck yourself, Nostrils; you're not writing me out of this one. If we don't stick together, if we're not prepared to take a risk for each other, then what's the point? I didn't join this job for an easy life; I joined this job to be part of a family, and a family that sticks together, when the chips are down. That's when you learn who your friends are, not when the going's easy but when your backs are against the wall. This is it; this is our moment. When that mad woman plunged at you with that carving knife, what did Bob do? I mean it wasn't his life that was about to be cut short. Did he think, 'gosh I'd love to help Nostrils but it's not my problem?' Did he fuck! He dived across the room and risked everything for someone he hardly knew. And why? Because that's what you do ..."

He paused and looked around the room.

"... when you wear the blue."

It was a captivating call to arms, and I felt tears in my eyes. I looked around to see Dot nodding, sagely, and even Mrs. M, muttering, 'well said', over and over, again.

From that moment on, there was no turning back.

Although we didn't know what had happened, we did know what we had to do, to extradite our friend and colleague from this mess.

We had entered Mrs. M's house as a small, close-knit team of police officers, who plied their demanding trade together, in a busy, occasionally dangerous, corner of north London. We left as a band of brothers, who's future careers, even perhaps our future freedom, relied on each other's success in executing our own part of the plan; and thereafter, our ability to stick, unwaveringly when questioned, to a certain version of events, which bore little resemblance to reality. We had to hope no one discovered a loose end and we needed a decent dose of luck.

If we made it through, we would never be able to talk about this, with anyone.

I was jolted out of my thoughts by my mobile ringing. It was Susan from the Federation, who told me, the legal team from the News of the World had contacted her. They'd asked to meet me and my legal representation for a, 'without prejudice' meeting, whatever that meant.

"Did you contact them?" I asked, slightly annoyed, because I knew for a fact, I'd asked her to hold fire, for fear of making matters worse for Bob.

"No, I didn't Chris; you asked me not to. They called me this morning and asked whether I'd seen the story, last Sunday. I said, I had, but played everything close to my chest. The man's name was Butler and he said, he had been instructed, by the Editor, to reach out to you through the

Federation. They've realised their mistake, that they'd included your photograph, instead of that of someone called Bob Clark. You know Bob, right?"

"I do." I replied.

"It's DC Robert Clark and not you, who's having the affair."

"I know, Susan." I replied.

"Well, they are keen to remediate."

"What does that mean?" I asked.

"They want to settle." Susan replied.

"What? As in, pay me some money?" I asked.

"Yes; 'quick remediation', those were their exact words and they're also offering an unreserved published apology, in the next edition, this Sunday." She replied.

"But does that mean they're going to run the correct story, you know, with Bob Clark's name and photograph?" I asked.

"I don't know, I suppose they'd be able to, wouldn't they? But they'd look pretty stupid." Susan replied.

"What's the next step, then?" I asked.

"They want to meet, tomorrow, at a law firm, in Moorgate. I can come with you, and we'll hire a lawyer for you. You'll have to have a lawyer present, otherwise any agreement won't be valid. You'll even be able to agree the wording of the apology, in advance. I really think you should agree, Chris."

"Of course, it's a no brainer. Let me know where and when. Thanks, Susan. Text me the details." I said.

***

The first thing I had to do when I arrived, was to report Colin sick. Of course, he wasn't sick. At that precise moment, he was on the train to Stanstead airport, where he would collect Bob's Capri.

Bob knew he had to maintain the pretense that it had been stolen from the car park in Beachy Head, and the best way to do that, was to make sure no one found it. So that Saturday afternoon, he had driven his Ford Capri, twenty miles along the M11 to London's fourth airport. There, he booked it in for the next month, aware that the best place to hide his car was in plain sight, amongst another six hundred holidaymakers' vehicles. He had provided a false name and address and paid by cash.

We did, briefly, debate whether the car could be left in situ, but I didn't like the fact that, when someone found it, they might notice it was geographically much closer to Bob's address than Beachy Head and, if I was investigating the matter, that would make me suspicious. It was best if the Ford Capri disappeared off the face of the Earth and that was precisely what Colin was going to make happen.

Colin had grown up in Tottenham and knew a lot of people who made their living illegally. One of these was an old mate, who ran a dodgy garage in Finsbury Park. If your car needed an MOT, or an insurance cover note, his mate could, for the right price, provide one. His mate also specialised in ringing - that is to say, putting new identities on stolen cars. For a fee, he would replace the original chassis; engine and registration numbers, with those cloned from a legitimate make and model. This time, however, Colin was going to use another string to his mate's illicit bow. For a thousand pounds in cash, his mate could make a vehicle vanish. Colin said he had a contact with a metal yard in Bow, who would simply crush the car and then sell, what was left, as scrap.

If Colin did his job properly, by the time we finished late turn, Bob's car would no longer exist, a situation that would corroborate the illusion that it had been stolen.

That would just leave one vehicle with which to deal.

## Chapter 57

I'd definitely made a bold play in respect of DI Young, but on my journey to work, I felt a nervous, as to how my decisive move was going to play out.

I thought, if things were going to go badly, they would do so, very soon after my arrival that afternoon, and, as I'd been in a good hour and had still heard nothing, I took this as a good sign.

When the Superintendent told me that Kitty claimed to have received a racist letter, before she'd even started at Tottenham, I knew it was her that was trying to fit me up. It was the only scenario that made any sense. As soon as she knew she was going to be posted to Tottenham, I suspect she made some enquiries and discovered that I worked there. She therefore claimed to have received the letter and, when she arrived, planted the evidence in my desk. She then made the anonymous tip off that the sender of the letters was me.

Kitty was the only one that could gain by fitting me up. First, she would get her own back for the court case, because I made her look pretty stupid; secondly, she would keep the issue of race, right at the top of the Met agenda; thirdly, with me gone, she could quash the Anna Abolla fraud case; fourthly; she could play the victim of racial abuse card, AGAIN, and probably get another sizeable payout in compensation; and lastly, she would get the next rank on the back of it, as the Met wouldn't dare fail her at the next Chief Inspector selection process.

When she'd warned me about the impending search, she wasn't being nice; she was simply setting me up for the integrity test. No doubt she thought I'd have something in my desk that I shouldn't have. I'd be caught on camera looking through my desk and then I'd be captured as I removed the racist material. What she didn't realise was, that by an enormous stroke of luck, I'd already found and removed the material and, actually, I didn't keep anything in my desk that I shouldn't.

I shouldn't have been surprised; she'd tried to plant evidence on me, when we were at Stoke Newington.

Having decided in my own mind that it had to be her that had put the racist material in my desk, the only dilemma I was left with, was how to deal with the matter.

Since the Hassan Achachi enquiry, black officers were, to all intents and purposes, untouchable, let alone a black officer, who was also senior and female. To make her even more difficult to move against, Kitty had already successfully sued the Metropolitan Police for racism, won her case, and received £80,000 in damages and an apology from the Commissioner.

I realised that formally reporting the matter would be very unlikely to bear fruit, unless Kitty had been, caught bang to rights, which she hadn't. All I had was circumstantial evidence and conjecture.

What's more, if I did officially move against my Detective Inspector, I would have to admit that I hadn't properly dealt with the matter, when I'd found the material in my desk. Not only would this expose me to potential disciplinary action, it would also, irrevocably undermine the actual case against Kitty.

I had a horrible feeling that, if I formally reported the matter, the whole episode would end up with Kitty getting another payout and then, quite frankly, I'd have to kill myself.

I had therefore decided to try an innovative approach.

I had removed the racist material from the back of the ceiling tile and placed the contents back in my desk, exactly where I had found them. Then I had written Kitty a letter, which I had sealed in an envelope, and placed on her desk. It read:

'Dear Kitty,

I believe that, once again, you have been trying to fit me up; this time with evidence to suggest that I have been sending racist letters.

I have conducted an investigation, have recovered fingerprints on several of the pieces of paper, and have a witness, who saw you put the cuttings in my desk, and another, who saw you going through my desk, late one evening, several weeks ago. On the second occasion, you were also speaking on your mobile.

I haven't formally reported the matter because I don't want the furor that will follow but will do so, if any more letters are sent, and, if I EVER discover you are trying to fit me up again.

Very happy to discuss the matter; feel free to approach me at any time.

Finally, I don't think you need to review the Anna Abolla case. I understand she is a friend of yours, so I don't believe your intervention would be appropriate, do you?

Kindest regards

Christopher Pritchard'

I knew the move was a gamble and, of course it was a huge bluff, but, if my instincts were right and she had sent the letters, it would be very difficult for her to do anything, at all, without taking the risk that she would expose her own culpability. I was offering her a score draw, when she deserved a heavy defeat, and I calculated she'd be wise to take it.

There was no sign of the DI and, at five, the Superintendent called me into her office to inform me that Kitty had gone sick with work related stress and was unlikely to be back, for several months. She asked me whether I would like to act up as the temporary Detective Inspector and I agreed. Of course, this meant that I had been right, and Kitty had sent the letters and tried to fit me up. I'd like to say I experienced a warm glow of satisfaction, but it would be more accurate to say, I was fucking delighted.

## Chapter 58

A few hours later, I got a text from Tabitha asking me whether I could meet her, urgently. I texted back, saying I was at work at Tottenham and, if she wanted to see me, she could come to the police station. If I am being honest, I didn't really have much more to say to her.

Within the hour, I got a message from the Station Officer that there were two women, waiting in the interview room to see me; he said they'd asked for me, by name.

It was the first time I'd seen Katie, since the awards ceremony at Chigwell, where she'd been dressed up to the nines. The Katie I now met, was barely recognisable, even from the Katie, I'd met at the gym. As I entered the room, she stood up, and took off her sunglasses, to expose two badly swollen black eyes, or, more accurately, two yellow eyes, as the bruising had started to come out. Her lower right arm was in plaster, from hand to elbow, and she looked exhausted. We hugged, superficially, and I asked her how she was doing, which didn't even elicit a reply.

Tabitha was more composed and hadn't got up when I entered the room. We vaguely nodded an acknowledgment, in one another's direction.

We sat down and I offered them tea but they both shook their heads, dismissively.

"Well? Where's Bob?" Katie asked.

"No idea, I thought, or rather, I hoped, you were going to tell me. He hasn't been in contact?"

"He can't, can he? I've got rid of my phone and he's doesn't know where I am. Are you telling me, no one's seen him, since he went to Sussex, on Saturday?"

"As far as I know. Everyone assumes he's committed suicide. Though, I don't think he has." I replied.

"Where's his car?" Katie asked.

I gave her a mental tick for asking a very sensible question. I hoped that, at that very moment, the vintage Ford Capri was being crushed to the size of a compact washing machine.

"Sussex reckon it was stolen by pikies, when he was at Beachy Head. In fact, I think they nicked a couple of them but didn't have enough evidence to charge."

"So, Bob definitely didn't come back from Sussex?" Katie asked.

"Not as far as I know." I replied, lying.

"If he did, my husband killed him, you do know that, don't you?" She asked.

"Is that what's worrying you?"

Tabitha laughed, sarcastically.

"Yes, darling, yes." She said.

"Chris, the last time I saw Steve, he was getting ready to get rid of Bob, once and for all. He wasn't planning on giving him a hiding, or rearranging his teeth, or breaking a few bones..."

Katie held up her plastered arm, as if to demonstrate what she meant.

"... he had every intention of killing him and then disposing of the body."

"And this was before the story appeared in the paper?" I asked.

"Yes, it was on the Saturday. Some reporter contacted him on Saturday morning and asked him, what he thought about his wife's affair and did he have anything to say." She replied.

"That's when he came home and did this ..."

Once again, Katie held up are arm as evidence.

"... and threatened to kill the kids, unless I told him, where he could find Bob. Then he spoke to one of his mates to help him arrange things. Sent him to a garden centre, somewhere. Told him to pay for everything with cash." She continued.

"What time did he leave the house?" I asked.

"I don't know, about twelve, midday? Why? I don't know exactly, why? What does it matter, if Bob didn't come back?" She asked

"I just wondered." I replied, but I realised I'd made a bit of an error, by asking such a loaded question.

"But, none of that matters does it? Not if Bob never came back from Sussex? Then Steve can't have done him any harm. But then, where is Bob, because Steve has definitely done a bunk?"

"What do you mean?" I asked.

"Well, he fucked off on Saturday, which can only mean, he's killed Bob and is now in hiding somewhere. That's why I'm so damned worried. If he'd not been able to find him, 'cos if he's, like you say, missing in Beachy Head, then Steve would have come home. But he hasn't resurfaced since he left on Saturday morning and the only explanation, I can think of, is because he's murdered Bob and gone abroad, to lie low, for a couple of months."

"What you're saying does make sense, but unless there's some evidence, any evidence, to suggest Bob came back from Sussex, then there's nowhere we can go with it." I replied.

Katie sighed.

"I'm sorry and I understand your concern but as far as everyone else is concerned, Bob killed himself down in Sussex, his car was stolen because it was insecure …"

"What do you mean, insecure?" Katie asked.

"When the police found it, they broke in to search it for any evidence, or other information to suggest, where he was, or what he might be doing. They smashed the driver's window, so, when they left it, albeit for less than an hour, someone else nicked it."

Tabitha shuffled uneasily in her chair, and I suddenly realised that she hadn't told her sister about the drugs.

"Is there any other reason why Steve would have disappeared, I mean, assuming he's not murdered Bob? Perhaps to escape the media attention, the embarrassment of his family; he might be feeling ashamed by the revelations about your marriage. He might actually be heart broken, isn't that possible?" I asked.

As I knew for a fact, Steve hadn't killed Bob, I was genuinely keen to identify why he might have disappeared.

"Not that I can think of." She replied.

"Perhaps, he thought you'd go to the police, you know, after he assaulted you like that." I suggested.

"I doubt it, he's never worried, before. But I've never seen him so angry, and he didn't pretend he was doing anything else, except killing Bob. In fact, I think he was enjoyed telling me, what he was going to do. He'd done it before, you know." She said.

"What? He's killed someone else. Who? When?"

"He told me once, when he was pissed. Said it was someone who threatened to expose him …"

Katie stopped midsentence.

"Expose him doing what?" I asked.

She hesitated.

"Don't worry, I won't say anything to anyone." I assured her.

"It was a few years ago. This investigative journalist was going to do an article on him supplying anabolic steroids to his gymnasts; one of them had come forward, like years later, and wanted to sell the story. Steve said he put an axe in his head in the car park of a night club, in Romford."

I immediately knew the murder she was talking about, but it must have taken place about eight years ago. I was at C.I.B. at the time and there was some suggestion of police involvement, because the journalist was working with a private detective, who was ex-old bill. The investigation had died a death.

"Steve's been unfaithful to me, for years. And, yes, Tabitha; don't think I don't know about you two, I've seen the texts …"

Katie said this without turning her head towards her sister and I waited to see Tabitha's response, but she kept very still, and no denial was forthcoming.

"... he had a couple of regular hookers, too; nice high class girls, but whores, still the same. He stayed out a couple of times a week, told me he was at his mates, what a load of crap. No, Steve had no reason to be as annoyed as he was with me, that was all about his ego."

"There was never anything going on between Steve and me." Tabitha said, rather unexpectedly.

"Really?" Katie asked, incredulously.

"Really. The truth is, Katie; Steve supplied me with ..." She hesitated, as if she had suddenly remembered she was sitting in a police station.

"... gear."

"It just gets better and better." Katie said, sarcastically.

"If Steve is abroad, where would he be?" I asked.

"Spain, possibly. That's where they all go, isn't it? Although, he's got a cousin or something, who's set up a few businesses in Riga, to move money through."

"Riga?" I asked.

"It's the capital of Latvia, one of the Baltic States. His cousin's married a local woman and they set up a property business and have invested in a few hotels and things like that. As far as I can gather, dodgy Essex boys invest their drug money there, which he returns to them clean, for fifteen percent, of course."

"So, Spain or this Baltic State, then?" I asked.

"That's where he'll be. But I'm serious, Chris; he's killed Bob and then gone to lie low. You need to take me seriously; I don't think you are." She said.

"Listen, Katie, I hear you. I really do. Leave it with me. I'll give you a call, tomorrow." I said.

I was of course aware that, by tomorrow, Steve would no longer be suspected of murdering her boyfriend.

## Chapter 59

When I got home, I discovered Jackie had returned and cleared out a few more of her clothes and toiletries. She hadn't taken everything, far from it, but the wardrobes were starting to look bare, and the bathroom was positively Spartan. She'd obviously been in the house a while because she'd even made herself a cup of tea and a bacon sandwich. She left evidence to tidy up. I was shocked when I found her week's dirty laundry in the washing basket. What was going on? I certainly wasn't going to wash and iron it for her.

I couldn't believe that, in only seven days, my happy marriage had disintegrated, before my very eyes. It had started when Jackie went out for dinner with the doctor, but that should have been a one off and the fire easily extinguished. The newspaper report was the accelerant, a five litre can of petrol, poured straight over the dying embers and whoosh, there went ten years of contented wedlock. I understood why Jackie reacted as she did, and I knew her well enough to know that my alleged act of unfaithfulness, would be nothing when compared to her perception of my hypocrisy. The fact was, though, I hadn't done anything wrong, absolutely nothing. Even if our marriage was over, I wanted Jackie to know that I wasn't to blame, so that she could remember our years together, without bitterness. That's why I was looking forward to tomorrow's meeting with the News of the World representatives.

The thing was, I'd only had three serious relationships in my life, and each had been terminated by the other person. Back at Stoke Newington, Sarah had left me when she became pregnant and then, a few years, later Carol had dumped me, in favour of her brother-in-law, a famous footballer. Now, Jackie was leaving me for a well-hung doctor. I knew I wasn't the most interesting guy in the world, but it was dawning on me that I was incapable of sustaining a life-term relationship.

But I did have something to cheer me up. I had a dinner date with someone at a restaurant in Toot Hill and I had a good idea who the invitation had come from.

I was just about to get into bed when Colin rang.

"Hello mate, how are you feeling?" I said.

"Much better, thanks; Sarge. Sorry to have to go sick today but I feel much, much better now. I'll be in tomorrow at eight." He said.

"So, everything's okay, then?" I asked.

"Nostrils, everything is as sugary as a Brazil."

"A what?"

"As sweet as nut, mate."

We both simultaneously hung up.

I mentally ticked off another problem, as solved.

We weren't out of the woods yet, but matters were progressing nicely.

### Chapter 60

I met the Federation solicitor in a coffee shop, just opposite the law firm, in Moorgate. He was a slight, white male, wearing small round spectacles. He was roughly the same age as me and very well spoken. His name was Justin Pritchard, but we quickly established, we weren't related. Susan, the Federation lady, had left a message to say, she couldn't make it, but that didn't matter.

"Well Mr. Pritchard this seems clear cut to me. I spoke to your Superintendent, yesterday, Jill Long. She gave me a brief outline of the issue. So, I can make the right representations on your behalf, please answer a few questions."

"Of course." I replied.

"Have you ever had a personal relationship of any kind with Katie Sumers?"

"No" I replied.

"Was Katie Sumers giving you oral sex in the car when the photograph was taken?"

"No." I replied.

"What was she doing?"

"She was leaning across to get something out of the glove box." I replied.

"What?"

"Some photographs, of her sister. If you must know, she was trying to set me up with her." I replied.

"The picture of you kissing, is that accurate?"

"Yes, we touched cheeks, when we said goodbye. Our lips never met, and we certainly didn't kiss kiss - if you know what I mean."

He nodded and made a few notes.

"Why were you meeting her?"

"Because my friend and colleague, who was in a relationship with Katie Sumers, wanted me to warn her that the press had door stepped him and were onto their relationship. I'd never met or spoken to her before that meeting. But can we not disclose all that information? I really don't want to drop my mate, in it."

"Your friend's name is?"

I hesitated.

"I need to know. I won't disclose it unless they already know it. I suspect they do, which is why they're so eager to settle." He added.
"Bob, Robert Clark." I replied.

"If it came to court, would Robert confirm your account, if we need him?"

The accurate answer would have been 'he's in hiding but yes, if the chips were down, he could corroborate my story' but I replied:

"He's missing at the moment; it's possible he's committed suicide. His car was found abandoned, at a car park in Beachy Head, on Saturday morning."

"Of course, Susan mentioned something about that. Right, before we go in, is there anything else I need to know? Please think carefully."

There were of course a great many things I should really have imparted to him.

"Absolutely nothing." I replied, confidently.

We were in the meeting less than an hour. After about twenty minutes, Justin and the News of the World guy disappeared, into a separate room. Ten minutes later, Justin returned.

"I think, we're nearly there, Mr. Pritchard. They're keen to settle, they realise their mistake and, just so you know, they won't be using the photographer who sold them the pictures, again."

"Okay." I said.

"They'll put the following apology on page two of all the editions on Sunday."

He placed a piece of paper on the table between us; it read:

Last Sunday the News of the World published an article which suggested Katie Sumers and an unidentified police officer were having a personal relationship. The article included several photographs of Sumers and a police officer, two of which were taken in a vehicle. Although published in good faith, this newspaper now accepts that a mistake was made in respect of the identity of the officer, and that the male in the photograph, was not, and never has been, in a relationship with Katie Sumers. The paper also withdraws the suggestion that a sexual act took place in the vehicle.

We would like to apologise unreservedly to this officer for the error and any inconvenience caused.

I read the apology, twice.

"Short but to the point, I suppose." I said.

"It seems a bit unfair, the story last week, was on the front page with big headlines; yet the retraction is going to appear on page two, hidden away, where no one's going to see it." I added.

"That's always the way. Have you ever seen an apology on page one of any newspaper?" He asked.

"And Mr. Pritchard, they're offering compensation of five thousand pounds. Oh, and my legal fees, of course."

"Advice?"

"We can push for more but it's in the right ballpark. I can go back and say you want eight?" He replied.

"It's really not about the money, I just need something that my wife will read. Then she'll realise, she's made a mistake."

"What do you mean?" He asked.

"When the story hit the papers, last Sunday, my father-in-law read it, before anyone else, and phoned the missus. I was out and when I came home, my wife had left me."

"Has she come back?"

"Nope; and she won't return my calls. In fact, she buggered off abroad, to Paris, I think."

I didn't mention that she was with another man.

"And when I asked you, when we were in the café, whether there was anything else, you didn't think about mentioning this, because?" He asked, frustration clear in his tone.

The truth was, it didn't even cross my mind because there was so much else going round in my head.

"I forgot." I replied, meekly.

Justin went off again. I sat playing worm on my mobile phone. When he returned he said:

"Twenty-five..."

He paused.

"... if you sign the agreement today."

## Chapter 61

I'd never been to Toot Hill before and had to look it up on a map. I was surprised when I found it was only a few miles east of Epping, as I thought I knew the area well.

I was early; I was always early. On this occasion, this habit did provide me with the opportunity of selecting a small table, in the dark corner of the lounge bar, facing the door, so that I could see my dinner companion, when they walked in.

I was more nervous than I'd expected. The last woman I'd 'dated' was Jackie and that now seemed a very long time ago. Had the dating game changed? Were there any new rules? Would I make a complete idiot of myself? Should I tell her that I'm married? Should I mention that my marriage was a complete disaster? In the end, I decided to stop asking pointless questions of myself and just see how the evening went.

When she walked in, I was absolutely spellbound.

Nearly six feet tall, with long, curly black hair, which was swept around the back of her head, so that it all fell over her right shoulder, Wendy looked gorgeous. She wore skin-tight, black leggings, black high-heeled shoes, and a short, lightweight, black leather jacket, which was open, exposing shapely breasts. As she walked from the door to the bar, every man in the place looked at her, much to the annoyance of several women. Her entrance was a performance, in itself. I wanted to burst into a round of applause. Wendy hadn't seen me and, having placed an order, she swung round and leant backwards against the bar to survey the door, apparently anticipating my imminent arrival. I watched her, completely absorbed by her effortless presence. She looked in my direction and caught my gaze. She smiled the warmest smile and, simultaneously, tilted her head to one side. It was a very natural and endearing gesture. There and then, I fell completely under her spell. That's all it took; we hadn't even spoken a word. I heard the words, 'this woman is going to ruin your life', transverse my thoughts but I wasn't listening to the clear and unambiguous warning, from my subconscious.

We had a wonderful evening and the fact that my wife had just spent four nights in Paris with her new boyfriend, meant that I could enjoy the whole experience, guilt free.

I don't know whether it was because of her Mediterranean roots but Wendy was very tactile and there was barely a moment, when she wasn't stroking my arm, rubbing her shin against my calf or holding my hand. It was really endearing and terribly sweet.

I did everything I could to prolong the evening, I ordered desert, something I never did, then coffee, and finally, a brandy before, rather sulkingly, asking for the bill, just a few minutes before the place was going to close.

As we waited for the bill to arrive, I did briefly consider suggesting we should continue the evening elsewhere, but everything had gone so well, I was worried that a rejection, or indeed any kind of rebuff, no matter how gentle, would taint the experience. So, I decided that I'd play it cool and simply say, I hoped to see her again, really soon.

"I've got an apology to make." Wendy said.

"Oh?" I replied.

"I can't invite you back, sorry. The timing's not great."

Despite having just decided that I was going to play it cool, I was both delighted and deeply disappointed by her statement. Delighted, because it suggested Wendy did want to have sex, but deeply disappointed, because it obviously wasn't going to happen. I assumed by the phrase 'the timing is not great', Wendy was telling me that she was having a period.

"Oh, that's okay, I understand." I replied.

"No, please let me explain. My dad's down for a conference in London, tomorrow. I'd completely forgotten he was coming and, while it's not a problem me going out, I think he'd be really embarrassed if I took a stranger, well, you know, someone he hadn't met before, home. Besides, I couldn't enjoy sex sleeping only few feet from dad, who may I remind you, is a man of the cloth."

Wendy laughed and the waiter placed the bill on the table.

I was almost lost for words.

"Changing the subject, completely; where do you live, again?" She asked, with a cheeky grin.

"Only down the road. Oh, I've had a thought, why don't we go back to my place?"

I smiled.

"Now that's an idea. You live in Loughton, right?"

"Yes." I replied, tentatively.

"How far is that from Leyton?"

"Five, six miles? Why?"

"That should be far enough away from my dad." She replied.

We had barely crossed the threshold and were, quite literally, tearing each other's clothes off. It was fantastic! I hadn't had sex like it, for years. No, I'd never had sex like it. It was the most passionate sexual experience, I'd ever had. The most erotic thing ever, was her teasing. Basically, she seemed to get aroused by taking me to the brink of orgasm and then, not letting me cum. She'd stop whatever she was doing, and I'd moan, she'd giggle, roll over and bring herself off.

I confess, it was the first time I'd ever seen a woman masturbate, well, except on one of Rik's dirty videos.

Eventually, at about three in the morning, she announced that she was shattered, which I took as a signal that I might be allowed to, finally, reach complete satisfaction. Wendy sat on me and began to ride. She was facing the bedroom door, with her back towards me. Her long black hair fell straight down her back, as her stunning arse rode up and down my cock. I knew the image would stay with me a long time. I could feel her gyrations, getting quicker and quicker.

"Come on, then. I want to feel it inside me. Come on, darling, come on."

It would have been great, it would, undoubtedly have been, the best orgasm I had ever had, if only my wife hadn't chosen the first of my vinegar strokes to walk into the bedroom.

## Chapter 62

I never thought, for a second, that Jackie would be coming home, after she'd finished her shift. She'd stormed off and then I spent another hour, while Wendy sorted herself out. I tried to get to sleep for the hour or two that remained of the night, but my mind was racing so much; in the end, I just got up and went into town for a coffee and to buy a paper.

As I drove into work, my phone went – it was Dot.

"Chris, great news; they've found Bob."

Dot was very careful just in case anyone was listening to our conversation. I played along.

"Alive, I assume?"

"Yes, he's had some sort of breakdown and he's been sleeping rough."

"Where?" I asked.

"Brighton. He's all right but they detained him under the Mental Health Act. Apparently, he was about to set fire to himself, but someone called the police."

That piece of information was new to me. We'd discussed various ways he could be found but no one had suggested such a drastic course of action. Mind you, it had obviously worked. The important thing was, the police perceived that they'd found him, as opposed to him giving himself up.

"Is he alright? He's not injured or anything?" I asked.

"No, he's fine. Apparently, he did go to commit suicide on Saturday but, when he came to it, he couldn't do it and when he went back to his car, someone had stolen it. He didn't know what to do, so he made his way towards Brighton, where he's been sleeping rough."

"Where is he now?"

"Still in Brighton, I think. Sussex police want to question him, but he's not well enough, so he's going to be transferred to hospital. We should get down and see him as soon as possible."

"I agree. You on your way in?" I asked.

She was, so we hung up, saying we'd pick the conversation up, in the office. The important thing was, we'd done the bit for the record, so to speak, and, if anyone was listening, they would have heard exactly what they thought we should be saying.

So far, so good. If everyone believed that Bob had never returned to London and had been on the south coast for the last week, then we'd be, almost, out of the woods.

*  *  *

"What am I going to do, now?" DS Jim Beam asked me, as I walked in the office.

"Sorry?" I asked.

"Oh, good news about Bob, mate." He said.

"How do you know? I've only just had a call." I asked.

"It's all over the nick, Nostrils. Everyone's talking about it."

"What have you heard, Jim?" I asked.

"Only that he's been on the streets down in Brighton and that he went to set himself alight. Apparently, the police stopped him, after he'd struck the match. How close was that? Someone was saying, it's because it was him that's been having the affair with that famous TV woman, and she's dumped him. You got the blame for that, didn't you? Someone else was saying, he's up to his neck in debt, owes like fifty grand. But what am I going to do about my rapist?"

I realised he was referring to the allegations of indecent assault which he was investigating; the ones where the suspect had grabbed at the victims.

"What do you mean?"

"Well, our DI had agreed to act as bait, but now, she's gone long term tom and dick, I've got to find someone else. Do you fancy donning a shirt and some heels?"

"Sorry mate, I only do that on Wednesdays, at my exclusive Conservative club, in Mayfair."

"Yes, I can imagine you all dressed up, with an orange in your mouth. But what am I going to do? Do you think Dot would agree?" He asked.

"Probably, she's as good as gold. No more attacks, then?" I asked.

He shook his head.

"We were going to put the DI out, this weekend."

"We're off this weekend, so using Dot's going to cost you a fortune, mate. And it's a bit of a long shot, isn't it? He hasn't done it for weeks, has he?" I replied.

"I looked at your CRIS, you know, for that stranger rape. Your man is a dead ringer for my suspect, but you say he was in prison."

"Yeah, it's quite a convincing alibi, isn't it?"

Then I had a thought, or to be fair, Jim had exactly the same thought, because we both said the same two words, simultaneously.

"Home leave."

"Fucking of course, I'll give my probation contact a call and check." I said.

"Fuck me, I bet that's it; of course, it is. If the prisoner's done a really long sentence, they get Home Leave before they're finally released, to help them adjust back in to the community, don't they?"

I left a voice message for the wonderfully named, 'Dan Dan the Probation man', asking him to check Manson's Home Leave dates. Then I went downstairs to deal with a prisoner that had been brought in, by early turn, for burglary. I read through the arresting officer's IRB. The male occupier of a house, just around the back of the nick, had been in his bathroom shaving, when he heard someone repeatedly ringing his front door bell. He was expecting his mother-in-law to call, really couldn't be bothered to speak to her, so he ignored the door and continued shaving. Then, a few moments later, he heard someone kicking his front door down. He rushed downstairs to discover two young black males, in his hallway. He managed to grab the lad nearest to him but the other one got away. He detained the youth and called the police.

When I first started policing, fifteen years earlier, the criminals were often the children of respectful, law abiding, and often very religious, parents. These days, the criminals were the children of the aforementioned criminals, so there was really no hope, and I could only see things getting worse.

Every time a black youth was arrested, the Met were accused of racism, but it was the black youths that were committing all the crime, so what the fuck were we meant to do? It had got so ridiculous that, on one occasion, when I attended the scene of a burglary, the neighbour, who had called police, asked me why the 999 operator had asked him the colour of the suspect, 'do you come quicker if they're black?' he asked me, accusingly. I didn't bother replying. If he really couldn't work out why we would need a description of the suspect, then I wasn't going to explain.

I'd won my battle with Kitty Young, but she'd be back, probably promoted, and even more dangerous. She was untouchable, and I knew I'd made the right decision not to officially try taking her on, by formally reporting, what she'd done to me. I knew that, had I done so, I would have been the one to suffer, in the long run. Kitty would have probably ended up winning the employment tribunal case and being awarded another load of money.

I was miles away when someone tapped me politely on the shoulder

"Are you dealing with Lester Cunningham? Are you DS Pritchard?" The owner of the finger, asked.

"Yes, and yes." I replied, turning around.

"Oh, how are you?" I said, instantly recognising the duty solicitor.

She was a friendly black lady, a few years older than me.

"Can we have a quick chat?" She asked.

"Of course, how are you?" I asked.

"Yes, I'm fine, thank you. Can you just outline the evidence, so I can advise my client?"

I walked around the custody suite, peering into spy holes, and after several attempts, found an empty room. I pushed the heavy, sound proofed door, open and the duty solicitor and I went inside. I took her through the evidence, which was pretty compelling, and she scribbled, copiously, in her blue A4 notebook. Throughout my diatribe, I kept trying to recall, when we'd last worked together. The lady felt so familiar, I assumed it must have been a protracted case, perhaps with interviews, going over several days. I just couldn't recall which job it was, and decided, rather than put myself through any more self-imposed torment, to just ask her.

"I'm so sorry I can't remember but which case did we work on, recently?"

"I'm sorry, I don't think we've ever met before." She replied.

I was taken aback. One of us was going mad and I was sure it wasn't me.

"We definitely have, I'm sure. When were you last at this station, with a client?" I asked.

"I've never been to this station, before. I only work part-time, and I'm signed up to do Tower Hamlets, but the service asked me, as a favour, because the lady covering this area, this afternoon, went into labour, six weeks early. Detective Sergeant Pritchard, I assure you, we have never met before."

"But …" I went to disagree, but she interrupted me and very patiently explained.

"This happens very often. Some time ago now, I was an actress, and you probably think you recognise me because you saw me on TV."

I felt a bit stupid, but she was being very gracious. To recover a little dignity, I asked:

"Oh, what were you in?" I asked.

She named a popular BBC soap opera, and I remembered her character, straightaway. If I recall, this lady played the mother of the first black family that appeared on the show. There was a husband and two children, and her eldest child, a girl called Ruth, was still on the show, and now, one of the main characters. I didn't watch it myself, but the popularity of the show was so high, storylines often appeared in daily newspapers. What's more, the actress who played Ruth, had just been selected to represent the UK, in the Eurovision Song contest. Keen to continue the interesting conversation, I asked the duty solicitor.

"How's Ruth?"

"She's all right, I think, Detective Sergeant Pritchard. I haven't seen her for perhaps ten years."

"Oh, I am sorry. Have you fallen out?" I asked, before adding, quickly.

"... of course, you don't have to tell me if it's personal."

"Detective Sergeant Pritchard, I don't know quite how to put this ..."

She hesitated and I realised that it must be a sensitive subject for her."

"You do understand, she's not actually my daughter? Don't you?"

She was speaking very slowly, as if she was explaining something to a very young child.

At that moment, I felt more stupid I had ever done in my entire life.

## Chapter 63

The suspect no commented the interview, which was expected. I mean, unless he could come up with an extraordinarily good excuse for kicking somebody else's door down, how could he possibly answer to my questions?

The solicitor asked me to call her back, when we were going to charge him, and she headed off to her next client, who was down the road at Stokey.

I informed the Custody Officer that we had sufficient evidence to charge, and he authorised the taking of the prisoner's fingerprints, DNA and photograph. The Custody Officer, a male Sergeant, no older than twenty-three, informed me that DS Beam had been down looking for me, and had given him a message to deliver.

"Go on." I encouraged him.

The Custody Officer looked down at a piece of paper on his desk, where he had apparently, scribbled a note.

"He said, he's got a fax from Probation and it's a hit. It all matches. Does that make any sense?"

I was delighted. We'd solved at least five nasty, indecent assaults. The SMT will be happy, as the clear up rate for major crime on the Borough, will look really impressive.

I popped the lad I'd just interviewed back into his cell, so I could start getting the forms ready, when the Superintendent appeared.

"Have you got ten, Chris?" She asked.

It wasn't a question and, five minutes later, I was sitting in her office with a cup of black coffee in my hand.

"Has Mrs. Pritchard come home, yet?" She asked.

I shook my head.

"I'm sorry, Chris."

"Shit happens, Ma'am." I replied, pragmatically.

"Did the Federation sort the News of the World out?" She asked.

"Yes; they've agreed to print an apology and pay me some compensation." I replied.

"Good, quite right, too."

"I am surprised at how quick and easy the whole process was, though. I mean, you hear stories of people, like Jeffrey Archer, taking the paper to court, don't you? That must take years, mustn't it? Yet they settled with me, within a week. Now I think about it, that doesn't make sense."

"Big difference is that, with Jeffrey Archer, the paper knew it was right, whereas with you, they knew, within hours of the story being published, they'd got it badly wrong. And they didn't publish your name in the article, did they? Which makes it less damaging, easier to settle. I am afraid to report, the News of the World has tentacles, which reach deeply into the Met. Normally, that's a bad thing but on this occasion, it probably worked for you. I suspect they were told very quickly they'd made a mistake by getting you and Bob Clark mixed up. And they wouldn't want to go to war with the, 'Angel of the Arndale Centre', would they?"

Jill was referring to a headline from the Sun newspaper in the days after the I.R.A. bombing.

I wondered whether Jill was telling me she was the one who had the contacts in the newspaper, but I didn't ask.

"If you don't mind me asking, how much did you get?"

"Twenty-five thousand. Strange really, when, I got blown up in the I.R.A. bombing, I only received fifteen."

"What a Criminal Injuries pay out?"

I nodded.

"Well, when you get your twenty-five don't forget the Convalescent Home, will you? I'm a trustee and we always appreciate a donation, no matter what size."

"You've got a deal. I went there myself, a few years ago. They were brilliant. I will send a cheque but I'm going to split the money with Bob, you know, help him out a bit." I replied.

"That's nice, Chris. I am aware that he's got a few …"

She chose the words, carefully.

"… financial problems. It's actually Bob I'd like to talk to you about."

"How is he?" I asked.

"He's all right, I think. He's in a hospital; well, it's more of a clinic, in a place called Ticehurst …"

She checked her watch.

"… right about now, I've got a couple of officers picking his mother up and taking her down for a visit."

"I'm sure he'll be fine; all he needs is some time. It just goes to show, doesn't it?"

"What do you mean?" She asked.

"I thought Bob was one of the most solid guys I'd ever met, and then this happens. He gets himself in a load of debt, it all comes on top in respect of an affair he's having, and something clicks, and he drives down to Sussex to jump off a cliff. It just goes to show, you never really know someone, do you?"

Our eyes met and, in a nanosecond of non-verbal communication, I knew that Superintendent Jill Long suspected that all was not, as it seemed. I smiled and shrugged my shoulders, casually, but inside I prepared myself for the questions, which I knew were about to come.

*** 

When I pulled up at home that evening, the last thing I expected to see was Jackie's little yellow Fiat outside. I assumed she'd come round to collect more stuff, so I parked up the road to give her a few minutes to get everything sorted. After about fifteen minutes, it dawned on me that that wasn't what she was doing so I steeled myself and went in.

Jackie was sitting on the settee watching television like nothing had happened. I decided to play along.

"Hi honey, I'm home." I called out.

"Hello, darling." She replied, without looking up.

"Tea?"

"Wine, oh my god wine, please. After the last twenty-four hours I've had, wine is the only solution." She replied.

She was wearing pyjamas so I could only conclude that she was settled in for the night.

I opened a bottle of Rioja and poured two big glasses. When I returned to the lounge, the television was off.

"      I'm just going up to get out of my suit, I'll be back down in a mo."

I noticed immediately that Jackie's clothes and toiletries had returned to their rightful places. I stripped down to my pants, lay back on the bed and tried to take it all in.

Only a few hours ago, Jackie had come home from work still dressed in her uniform and walked in to find Wendy and I having sex in her bed. To make matters worse, Wendy had fronted her out, asking her what the hell she thought she was doing walking into a room without knocking. Jackie countered with the convincing argument that it was her bedroom, at which Wendy told her that it probably wouldn't be for very much longer. To cap it all, Wendy told Jackie to fuck off because she wanted to finish what she'd started.

Jackie had obliged and stormed out, slamming each door she passed through so hard that I was certain she must have inflicted structural damage.

Now Jackie was back, and I had to decide how to play this. Did I even want our marriage to continue? I was both annoyed and hurt by the way she'd taken the News of the World article as gospel and didn't even have the common sense to challenge me about it. It seemed to me, it was just the excuse she'd been looking for to guiltlessly fuck off to Paris with her young doctor friend. Should I tell her about the apology to be printed in Sunday's paper? Or should I just let her squirm and suffer when she reads it. Mind you, my position of strength was somewhat weakened by what happened last night. I mean, it hardly portrayed me as the innocent injured party, did it?

The thing was, a little over a week ago Jackie and I had a good marriage, or so I thought. We got on well, had great if occasional sex, there was enough money coming in that we could live a comfortable if unspectacular life and we'd just agreed to start a family. Then everything had fallen in like a house of cards in a hurricane. I wasn't sure how much of that was my fault. I mean, last night was bad but then my wife had just spent four nights in Paris with another man. And before that, she spent a night or at least part of a night in a hotel room with him.

There was one thing I had to consider though. When I'd first met Jackie, I'd been addicted to heroin and Jackie had been so very patient with me and given me last chance after last chance to give up. I must have failed to give up a dozen times and each time she'd stuck by me. Perhaps she deserved another chance too? Or more to the point, perhaps our marriage deserved another chance. I picked myself off the bed, pulled on some slops and went downstairs to discuss our future.

## Chapter 64

With Jackie home, I had a slight problem. I had an important job to do, the last in the long list of matters with which we had to attend to extradite Bob from his hole. To undertake this task, I needed about four hours, maybe more, which meant I had to lie to Jackie about what I was up to. I suspected she would know I was lying and think my unexplained absence was something to do with Wendy, which it most definitely wasn't. Much as I might want to, I couldn't be honest with her.

I told her I was going to spend a few hours with my old friend, Rik, which was partially true. When she looked at me suspiciously, I suggested she buy the News of the World. It was a diversionary tactic, but it worked.

I left the house at eleven o'clock and drove to Walthamstow to meet one of my oldest friends, Rik Patel.

Rik and I had first met at Paddington police station back in '82 when we were interviewed to join the job. Then we'd lived together at Stoke Newington section house for a couple of years. Rik was one of the nicest blokes you could ever meet. Genuine, kind and funny, so very funny, though often it was completely unintentional. When he joined, he was one of very few Asian officers in the job and he, my black mate Andy who died of aids and I were known as the United Nations by everyone. We were a close-knit trio and socialised together all the time. I taught Rik to drink, and he was an excellent pupil. I had so many happy memories of the three of us in the White Hart in Stoke Newington High Street.

Rik was a DC on my team, but he'd been sick with stress for the last year. It was a long story but, basically, he was running his parents video shop in Walthamstow because his dad had died, and his mum was really ill. It wasn't strictly allowed but I wasn't going to be the one to say anything to anyone. Besides he kept sending in the sick notes and I kept passing them to HR.

I met Rik in the shop, and we greeted one another like long lost brothers. He made me a coffee and we chatted about old times and felt nostalgic. We remembered to include our dear departed friend Andy in our reminisces. And all the time customers kept coming in and having clandestine conversations in whispered tones about the quality of the pirated versions of the latest films. One guy was offering to sell, another was returning a DVD and demanding his money back. Rik didn't bat an eyelid to my presence.

Eventually, when the shop was empty of customers Rik asked me what exactly I wanted to use one of his garages for?

"I need to park a car there, mate."

"For how long?" He asked.

"Forever; well, at least the next twenty years." I replied.

"So, when you say 'park' you mean 'hide'? And will you need regular access to it?"

"Oh, fuck no, I never want to see it again. You're right, what I'm actually doing here Rik is disposing of it in the safest way I know." I replied.

"What about Colin's mate in Finsbury Park? He'd be able to do that for you. He uses that scrap metal dealers just off Stoke Newington Church Street to crush them."

"It a good idea but not possible on this occasion, for reasons that it's really best you don't know." I replied.

We couldn't use Colin's contact to get rid of the two cars because it was important Bob's Ford Capri and this BMW 5 series, were never linked.

"Why don't you just drive it into the forest and set light to it?" He asked.

"That'll never work; for a start when you set fire to something you always attract attention and once someone's looking at it, they're bound to find something to identify the original vehicle. If we strip the index plates and the chassis numbers off, you'll still have the engine number somewhere, won't you? We did look at putting it in a container and sending it to Timbuktu, but the shipping company wanted the registration certificate, bills of laden, an export licence and a load of other shit. Then I remembered my old mate Rik and his garages, and I thought ..."

"Look Chris, you can have a garage for as long as you like, really you can. And if I haven't got to keep the space clear in front of it then great 'cos that makes my life a lot easier. But technically the garages belong to my mum, well they did belong to dad but obviously now they're mums. So, I might have to call you one day and say like, can you move it; you know, if she decides to sell them, or if she dies and we have to sort out the estate."

That information was a bit of a worry, but I really didn't have any choice.

"Listen mate, how many garages have you got?"

"Eight, three are rented out and I use two for storage. The other three are full of family crap, you know baby seats, old carpets, a couple of bikes that we haven't used for years but one's cleared out because I was going to rent it, you can have that one. It's the end one."

He opened a drawer and removed a key, which he handed to me.

"Do you know where they are?" He asked.

I had been there once, years ago. They were a few miles away and were in a small service road that ran parallel to Leabridge Road.

"I can't remember, mate. I mean I've got a vague idea. Right from Markhouse Road towards Hackney and then there on the right, aren't they?" I said.

"Yes mate, you've got it, but I'll draw you a map."

"How much do I owe you?" I asked.

"Nothing, mate. Strip the vehicle as best you can. Park it up and forget it. If anyone ever finds it, I'll just say a geezer called Tony gave me five hundred quid to rent the garage for two years and I've never seen him again. How's that? Make sure there's no prints in it and we'll be fine."

It wasn't a bad proposal. I mean, Rik's mum owned the garage so if it was ever found they'd have to link Rik's mum to Rik; then Rik to me; then me to Bob Clark and then Bob to the owner. It was unlikely they'd be able to follow that trail in a few year's time when everything had gone cold.

I nodded slowly but Rik could clearly still detect a trace of concern on my face because he said:

"Listen Chris, you've been a brilliant mate and a great boss. You've not caused me any grief since dad died. I'll make you a promise here and now; I'll make sure those garages aren't sold for at least the next ten years. Does that put your mind at rest? Deal?"

He held out his hand and we shook.

That was great news. Now I just had to relocate an expensive car from one garage to another about five miles away, strip it of as many identifying marks as possible, wipe it clean of fingerprints and get on with the rest of my life. It'll be a piece of cake, I thought, but deep down inside I knew this had the potential to go horribly wrong.

Bob had parked the BMW 5 series in the garage two up from his own at Buxton House. When he first told me, I couldn't believe what he'd done but the more I thought about it the more I understood because he had to hide two cars as fast as possible.

He knew the garage two up was empty and unlocked and had been for years. He had used it himself several times over the years. He also had to get the BMW off the street and out of sight immediately. That seemed the obvious solution although he did realise it was only a temporary one. The garage was also close to the scene of the incident so he could relocate the BMW and then quickly get on with the less dangerous task of relocating his Capri somewhere safe. He did the latter by shooting along the M11 to Stanstead where he could lay it low.

My unenviable task was to take the BMW from the garage next to Bob's and relocate it in Rik's garage in Leabridge Road where it could hopefully rot to dust.

I was worried because there'd almost certainly be an interest report on the car, so I had to avoid at all costs attracting the attention of the old bill. I also needed to avoid being spotted at Buxton House and, believe me, it wasn't every day that a BMW 5 series was seen there.

The person I was most worried about was Bob's neighbour because I knew his flat overlooked the garages, he would recognise me and he'd got previous for keeping a close eye in whatever was happening.

The thing was, I had this horrible feeling that I was going to get caught. I can't articulate why; I just had an ache in my guts. I'd recently read a book by a guy who got caught drug trafficking in Thailand and he described that, on the day he was arrested at the airport, he'd experienced the strongest sense of foreboding. I now felt exactly the same anticipation of impending doom and it manifested itself in tightness in my chest and a feeling of butterflies in my stomach. A few times when panic gripped, I thought I'd forgotten how to breathe. I knew this was stress, but it didn't make it any easier to deal with.

I'd parked my old Golf outside Rik's garage and then got the bus down to Whipps Cross hospital and walked the half a mile to Buxton House. All the way, I felt the weight of capture weighing heavily on my shoulders. When I got to Buxton House I slipped in like a ghost or at least that's what I tried to do. I was quick. In no time at all I had the garage door open and was sitting in the BMW. I took it steadily, the last thing I needed to do was to drive off at speed and have everyone looking out their windows at the flash German car and the wanker driving it.

As soon as I was on the main road, I took the opportunity to glance about the interior – what a fucking mess. Empty cigarette cartons, old coca cola cans, discharged McDonalds and crisp packets were everywhere. The ashtray overflowed with butts, many of which had fallen on the dashboard and carpet. I picked up a discarded roll up and sniffed – it was the end of a used joint.

I drove, oh so, carefully. I didn't care whether anyone cut me up; I wasn't bothered if someone wanted to race me away from the lights. I did my very best impression of an eighty-year-old man taking his driving test. My strategy worked. Fifteen minutes later I pulled into the access road, which led to Rik's garages and pulled in next to my old Golf.

There were a few kids playing football about twenty yards away but otherwise the coast was clear. I wondered why I'd ever been so stressed.

I had brought a roll of black bin liners, which I now retrieved from my own car which I'd parked earlier and started to fill them with everything I could find from the BMW. Four bags later I had completed my task. There were only two items that wouldn't fit in the bin liners, and I put these straight into my boot. I then cleaned the car inside and out with dusters and chamois leathers until I was satisfied that there was absolutely no trace of any previous driver's prints.

I removed the registration plates and the chassis numbers and dropped them into my now full-up boot. Finally, I parked the BMW, reversing into the garage with great care and closed the garage door.

I then got back into the BMW, turned the interior light on and adjusted the driver's seat so that it was almost flat. For the first time in a week I relaxed, I mean truly, genuinely, and completely. We'd made it, Bob had resurfaced in entirely believable circumstances, Bob's Capri was a pile of untraceable scrap metal, and the BMW was brilliantly hidden in the safest of places.

I knew what I was about to do was stupid, but I justified my actions by telling myself I deserved it after the stress I'd recently been through. What's more, it was fate that I'd found it. Besides, I'd only do it the once, of that I was certain.

I tapped the syringe to remove the air bubbles and injected. I had found my old friend in the glove compartment, all set and ready to go, with everything I needed. Fuck me, there was nothing like it!

## Chapter 65

When I woke up, I had no idea where I was. Everything was dark and there was a strange but familiar smell in the air. I felt cold and hot at the same time, which sounds ridiculous, but heroin can do that to you. My mouth was uncomfortably dry, and I coughed several times to clear my throat. I had a frightening flashback to a damp room in Bangkok and I sat up, quickly, to stem the rising panic attack.

I was in a car, in a garage or underground somewhere. My hands circled the steering wheel and my memory started to return. I felt the little light by the driving mirror and threw the switch.

On my lap was the discarded tourniquet. The needle had fallen by the side of the seat, and was pointing upwards, making its removal difficult.

I'd injected into the vein in the crease of my left arm, on the inside of the elbow, and being out of practice, I'd not made a very good job of it because blood had trickled down, in a line, to my wrist and had now dried into a scab. I scratched it off. By the time I had done so, I had remembered everything. I felt absolutely disgusted with myself. I couldn't believe I'd been so stupid. I'd been drug free for years, and now, I'd just risked everything. Why,

why, why? Because it was right there, was the only answer I could think of.

I squinted to see the time on the BMW clock; it was just after six. I'd been out for about three hours. Jackie was going to wonder where I'd gone. And I couldn't call her, because I'd deliberately left my phone at home, that morning. The last thing I wanted to do was leave a trail of my movements, which would take them straight to this car.

When I was happy that my head was once again, clear, I opened the garage door and set about completing my day's work. I removed the BMW's car battery and carefully placed it on the floor behind the driver seat because the boot of my Golf was full. I dug out the syringe and chucked it away, across some wasteland. I gave the BMW one last wipe down, threw several dust blankets over the vehicle and closed and locked the door.

I was tempted to throw the key away, but something told me to keep it, just in case. I'd bury it in my garden when I got home.

Apart from shooting up, the day had gone well. I'd managed to remove the BMW from its temporary hiding place to a much more permanent, and considerably safer, location.

I trusted Rik to let me know if anything happened, in respect of the garages, but I was certain I wouldn't have to worry about it for many years. It was interesting, because Rik hadn't once questioned me, as to why I had to hide a car. Goodness knows what he thought but he would never have guessed the truth. Not that I knew the truth myself, not at that stage anyway, but I had a good idea.

When I got in, Jackie was clearly suspicious, and no doubt thought my elongated absence was Wendy related. She was wrong but when I checked my phone, I read a lovely message from Wendy, saying she hoped I sorted everything out with Jackie and that, despite everything, she'd still be interested in seeing me again.

Jackie and I went out for dinner that evening to a nice Indian in Highams Park.

During the meal, I told Jackie all about Bob. She'd never met him but had often heard me talking about him. Of course, I gave her the official version; that he was heavily in debt, it was all coming on top domestically, and that's why he'd decided to take his own life.

"Hang on, are you talking about Bob Clark, the gay guy on your team?" Jackie asked.

"Yeah, that's right but it turns out he's not gay."

"But you always described him as eminently sensible. Now if you'd told me it was Colin, that would make more sense."

"Yes, it was Bob. Just shows you, doesn't it? You never really know someone." I replied.

Jackie frowned, almost as if she didn't believe me. Of course, she was right. Bob would never try to kill himself. He was a sensible, level headed individual, but this was the account, we'd all agreed to give.

Only yesterday, the Superintendent had given me a really hard time. She suspected something was wrong but couldn't quite articulate what. At the end of my interrogation, and I use that term deliberately because that was what it felt like, she did admit that Sussex were satisfied with Bob's explanation and were going to close the case, which was great news.

The waiter brought over our poppadum and drinks.

"I got the News of the World. I saw the apology. I'm sorry, Chris. I shouldn't have just jumped up and left, I should have had more faith in you."

I said nothing but reached across the table and held her hand.

"So, who was she?" Jackie asked, as she crunched.

"Katie Sumers." I replied.

"No, you idiot; the girl in my bed."

"Her name's Wendy." I replied.

"But who is she?"

"A WPC, I met her when you were away."

"She's gorgeous. If you continue seeing her, it will be the end of our marriage. I can't compete, Chris. How old is she?"

"Six or seven years younger than us, I think. Look Jackie, I didn't think you were coming back. I thought it might make me feel better, you know, considering you were in Paris with Doctor Dong."

"Well, she certainly made you feel better, from what I saw. And what are you talking about, Paris and Doctor Dong, what does that mean?" She asked.

"All right, Nipun, or whatever his name is."

"Chris, I've no idea what you're talking about." She replied.

"You've been abroad since Sunday, haven't you? I called you and your mobile had that foreign ringing tone."

"Yes, Chris; but I haven't been in Paris. Whatever made you think that?"

"Where have you been, then?" I asked, ignoring her question.

"I went to Julie's parents' apartment, in Javea." She replied.

"On your own?" I asked.

"Good god, no, with Julie. She was going away with a couple of other friends, I just tagged along."

"What did you tell work?" I asked.

"I went sick, well, it was partially true because, after I saw the picture in the paper of that TV woman giving you a blow job, I was bloody sick."

"So, you haven't been to Paris?" I asked.

"No" She replied, with a dismissive flick of her head.

"And you haven't been with Nipun, the doctor?"

"No. Why on earth do you think that? I think he was going to some conference, somewhere. Chris, my relationship with him, if that's what it was, is over. I hope, I never see him, again. When my dad told me about the News of the World article, what upset me the most, was not that you were seeing that Katie woman, but that you'd let me suffer so much, when I confessed everything to you about Nipun. I couldn't understand, how you could do that to me. I thought you'd say, like, look Jackie, don't feel too bad, we've both done things we shouldn't, but you didn't, did you? You let me die inside, knowing, all the time, that only a few days before, your cock had been in someone else's mouth. That's what hurt me the most. That's why I threw a few things in a bag, stormed out, brought a ticket at the airport, and had a few days in Spain to get my head together. Of course, now I know that you weren't seeing Katie Sumers, I realise I made a big mistake.

I knew that Jackie was telling me the truth; there was absolutely no question about it. She even seemed slightly bemused by my questions and completely at ease with the conversation. All I had to do, was to compare her attitude now, with how she had been when she first told me about Nipun.

I decided, there and then, never to see Wendy, again.

## Chapter 66

*Friday 18th September 1998 – two months later*

The Police Convalescent Home, Goring on Thames.

It was a lovely, mid-September afternoon and, although the first leaves were starting to fall, the sun still retained sufficient warmth for us to sit outside, in T-shirts and shorts.

The three of us, Colin, Dot and I, were visiting Bob, who was spending a couple of weeks in the Police Convalescent Home. This was a stunning, flint coated mansion, set beside a beautiful South Oxfordshire valley. I'd spent several weeks here myself, back in '88, but there had been a new wing added which effectively doubled the capacity. It was like a five-star hotel but with the added benefit of expert physiotherapy facilities and experienced psychiatric support.

It was the first time any of us had seen or spoken to Bob, since his reappearance because he'd gone into a rehab clinic and then he'd gone to stay with his mum, for a bit.

Under normal circumstances, we'd all have visited him, ages ago, but these weren't normal circumstances and we decided to let everything calm down, before we met up. I was confident the Convalescent Home was the right place to get together. One, because it would seem entirely natural that we would visit him there, and two, I knew the Manager would never allow the deployment of covert listening equipment on his premises.

We'd had a fantastic meal as Bob's guests and were now taking coffee and relaxing on wooden benches on the rear patio, while admiring the outstanding view, across the rolling countryside.

"Everyone here is suffering from one of four things …" Bob explained.

"… it's either neck, back, knee or nut."

"So, it's nut, for you." Colin commented.

I cringed a little because no one likes to hear they've gone mad, do they?

"Except it isn't, is it?" Bob replied, candidly.

In that second, the atmosphere changed and we looked at one another, furtively.

"I wish I was having physiotherapy, some of the young physio's here are just stunning." Bob said, lifting the atmosphere.

I was aware that other people were leaving the main building and coming to sit on nearby tables.

"Shall we go for a walk? There's a lovely spot on the other side of those woods where we can find some privacy." Bob suggested.

We strolled off, away from the old building, past the swimming pool, and onto a track, which led slightly downhill and away. As we did so, we split naturally into two pairs, with Colin and Dot, walking ahead, and Bob and I, behind. I put my arm across Bob to indicate he should drop back a bit, to allow us to talk.

"Have you heard from Katie?" I asked.

"No. It's too dangerous." He replied.

"How are you coping with that?"

"It's got to be like that, hasn't it? When there's no choice, there's no choice. It hurt, at first, but time's a great healer and all that bollocks." He replied.

"Listen, Chris. I'm so sorry for getting you involved in all of this, especially you. I mean, that photograph of you and Katie. What happened with your missus?"

"It's a long story. It caused a bit of a wobble, but when she saw the apology in the newspaper, the following Sunday, she apologised for not giving me the chance to explain before she fucked off."

"Where did she go?"

"She fucked off to Spain with a mate. I wrongly thought she'd gone with this doctor, from work, so I ended up shagging a girl called Wendy and Jackie came back and caught us in bed and, well, I told you it was a long story, didn't I?"

"Oh, for fuck's sake, Chris. Are you and Jackie all right now?"

"Yes mate, better than all right. She's pregnant. I'm not meant to tell anyone until she's had the scan at twelve weeks, so don't say anything."

"Oh, congratulations, mate..." Bob replied, his face breaking into a broad smile.

"... it's about time one of us had some good news."

"Well, I think it's mine. If my original suspicions were right, and Jackie did fuck off with the doctor, I suppose it could be his, the timing would be about right."

"You're kidding, right?" Bob asked me.

"Well, I'll soon know." I replied.

"How? Are you going to ask for a DNA test?"

"I won't need to, mate. If he's the father, Jackie will be having a brown baby." I said.

We both laughed.

"Listen Chris, thank you for the money. You didn't have to, really, but I can't say I'm not eternally grateful."

I had split the twenty-five grand I'd got from the News of the World, with Bob. I mean, it was largely thanks to him that I got it, and I knew, he badly needed it. Besides the gesture supported the story that he was going to commit suicide because of the debt he was in. I also sent a grand to the Convalescent Home, as Jill has suggested.

"Just don't get in that much debt, again." I said.

"I won't. You do know how I got into that much debt, don't you?" He replied.

"Of course not, that's your business." I replied, worried that I'd overstepped the mark with my advice.

"No, no, listen. My dad died last year, remember?"

I nodded, although I only had a vague recollection, he'd taken some compassionate leave.

"My dad was suffering from dementia and had to go into a special home, but the local council were making mum sell the house to pay for his care bills. So, I took care of them. That's the only reason I got into debt. I didn't want mum to have to sell up. The costs nearly killed me, and I ended up living on credit cards."

"They couldn't do that, could they? I mean, force her to sell the house."

Bob laughed.

"It wasn't that straight-forward because, it transpired, mum and dad had never been married. I couldn't believe it when I found out. They just pretended to everyone they were, and of course, mum took dad's surname. So, the house belonged to dad and not to mum. Technically, she had no claim to it, until he died, when he'd left it to her, in his will. We could have fought it, but the legal fees would have cost a fortune and there was no certainty we'd win. It was better for mum that I told her I'd sorted everything out. She didn't know I was, in fact, paying for everything, myself."

Suddenly, it all made sense.

We were walking around a copse, with the valley, to our right.

"Sit on the bench, there." Bob called out to the other two.

He stopped walking, so that we were just out of their hearing, and he spoke in a whispered tone.

"The Wendy girl you just mentioned, the one Jackie found you in bed with, is she the girl from the police club? The one you met that night we went there for the awards thing?"

I nodded.

"She's fucking lovely. I think a mate of mine used to work with her at Limehouse, on relief."

"That's her." I replied.

"You still seeing her?"

I nodded.

He slapped me on the back, and we set off to join the other two. We sat on the bench; Bob stood opposite, facing us. Dot, who was sitting between Colin and I, held our hands like a mother would her two children.

"We're sitting comfortably, ..." She said.

"... so, you may begin."

"As you know, I went to Beachy Head to take some photographs to enter in this year's Met Police photographic competition. I won last year, you know."

"Get on with it." Colin heckled.

"Alright, alright. Well, as I was saying, Beachy Head, photographic competition. When I got back to my car, I was pissed off that someone had broken in. I strongly suspected the do-as-you-likies, who were in their caravans, nearby. But what could I do about it? So, I drove back to London, with the wind in my hair, because of the smashed window. I parked the car round the back in my garage because, obviously, it was insecure, and went home to find donkey bollocks, here ..."

He nodded towards me.

"... in my lounge. Anyway, knowing that the story about me and Katie Sumers was going to hit the papers, imminently, I intended to go to see my mum to explain what was going on and tell her that everything was going to be all right. And I needed to find somewhere else to stay, temporarily, as the press knew where I lived.

When Chris told me about the drugs being found and that his instructions were to arrest me, as you know, we agreed to pretend, he hadn't seen me and I assured him that, after I'd seen my mum, I'd drive straight back and get everything sorted. I mean, I was genuinely worried about the drugs and my first thought was that Sussex old bill had planted them, although, I know that's bollocks now, but I did know, there'd be forensically nothing to link them to me.

After Chris had left, I checked my phone and there was, like, a zillion messages and missed calls. I'd meant to take it with me that morning but just forgot, as I was still half asleep, when I set off, at three in the morning.

If I'd checked my messages and calls there and then, it would probably have changed what was about to happen, but I didn't. I left my phone where it was because of course, the story Chris and I had agreed, was that I'd not been home, so the phone had to stay there, too.

Anyway, I stuffed a load of cash in my pocket because I knew I wouldn't be able to use a cashpoint or a credit card, got back in the old jalopy, and set off for mum's, in Bishop Stortford. I was conscious of who was about, and I noticed a car following me, down the A11. I did a bit of anti, you know, twice round the Robin Hood roundabout, but it was definitely on my tail. I knew it was the press, and I really didn't need them following me all the way to my mum's and potentially getting her involved, so I pulled in to one of the car parks in the forest. There was one guy in the car, and I pulled up and got out, to confront him. I didn't want a fight or any trouble; I just wanted to ask him to stop following me. I thought, maybe if I said a few words, which he could use in the article, then he'd be happy, or that maybe, if I let him take a few photographs, he'd fuck off.

I walked over to his car, but he didn't get out, straightaway, which I thought, meant he was getting his camera ready and was going to start taking my picture. I tapped on his window. I remember thinking that he wasn't the same press bloke that had door stepped me a few days, previously.

I heard and saw the boot ping open and realised the driver must have pulled the release catch, from inside the car. This momentarily distracted me, so I wasn't looking, when the driver's door suddenly flew open, with real force, and I was knocked backwards, several yards. He'd obviously used his legs to push the door and I suddenly found myself sitting on my backside, several yards away. I was like, 'fucking hell, mate, what the fuck did you do that for?'

Seconds later, the man was out of the car and closing on me. He was carrying an axe, a fucking axe, like you'd chop wood with. I hadn't seen this coming and was totally unprepared.

I desperately tried to scramble away, but I backed up against a tree, and then the axe fell. I thought I was dead; it was coming straight for my head, so I just closed my eyes and waited. Instinctively, I shrunk a little further down. Then I heard a deep thud right next to my head. I thought I'd been hit and opened my eyes, expecting to see blood trickling down, but the very top of the axe had struck and caught the tree trunk, and the blade had stopped, literally millimeters, from my head."

Bob held his right hand forward and demonstrated a gap of about an inch, between his forefinger and thumb.

I reacted quickly, as if suddenly stung into motion. The man was standing over me, so I kicked out with my legs and pushed him to the side. He had still been holding the axe handle and I sensed him trying to pull it out of the bark. I kicked again, this time harder, and pushed with both hands against his waist, taking hold of his belt, as I did so. He fell to my left and, importantly, lost his grip on the axe handle. He rolled half a turn away from me. I jumped to my feet and tried to pull the axe out myself, but it was stuck solid. The man was getting to his feet now, and I didn't have any time to think or to assess my options. I pulled frantically at the axe, and it started to come loose. I wiggled it from side to side, while looking at my attacker, who was pulling something from his trouser pocket. I recognised the device, even before he pushed the small silver button to release the blade.

In a sheer panic, I tugged, for one last time, at the handle.

There were only a few feet between us when the axe came free and in one movement, I ripped it from the tree and directed it in the general direction of his head. There wasn't enough time to do anything else. It wasn't even a deliberate strike and I hardly aimed it. at all. It was more like one continuous motion, which started with me desperately pulling at the handle, with all my strength, and ended, when the wrong side of the axe hit the man just behind his ear. And it caught him at an angle, which undoubtedly reduced the impact area. He had just leant forward to plunge the knife into my neck, but I struck him, first and fuck me, did I hit him hard. I even heard a crack, like when you break a leg or an arm. I don't think either of us had expected the axe to come free and he looked as surprised, as I did.

He staggered momentarily, and I twisted the axe around and adjusted the grip, so that the blade was forward. I fully expected to have to hit him again, but he suddenly sat down, almost as if it was an intentional decision. He looked dazed but he still had hold of the knife. I told him to drop if or I'd hit him again, and to my amazement, he did.

This clearly wasn't a member of the press. I thought, it could have been a case of road rage; perhaps, I'd unwittingly cut him up, back in Wanstead? Or was it someone Katie's old man had sent to kill me? But even if Steve had discovered what we were up to, he didn't know where I lived, and Katie would never tell him, not without warning me, surely?

'Who the fuck are you?' I said.

The man lay back, he didn't look well at all. Surely, I couldn't have done him that much damage? I'd only struck him the once, and with the wrong side of the axe head. There wasn't any blood, so what was going on?

'Do you need me to call an ambulance?' I said, police officer mode cutting in.

Suddenly, he started to have a fit, his whole body seemed to go into spasm and although his eyes were open, they rolled back and up. I vaguely remembered something about making sure someone that was having a fit didn't swallow his tongue, but I felt no compunction to go delving around in his mouth. When I was a kid, we had a guy at school who used to suffer from epileptic fits, and this looked just like one of those.

The fit lasted about a minute, but it felt much longer. When it was over, I checked for signs of life. I couldn't get a pulse and he wasn't breathing. He was completely lifeless. I panicked and went to call an ambulance but of course, I didn't have my phone. I ran to his car to try to find his phone, but he didn't have one.

I went back to the body and shook him, I even considered mouth to mouth, but he was dead. I've been a policeman long enough to know when someone's dead. I examined his head. Just behind his right ear was a mark where the back of the axe had struck him, but when I touched the area, I noticed, what I can only describe, as a dent, about the size of a two pence piece. The blow had literally cracked his skull and when I touched it, it moved, as if it had become separated. And the bit that moved was pushed in, you know, lower than the surrounding skull."

With the forefinger of his right hand, Bob was showing us the action he was describing. It looked like he was poking an invisible hole.

"I thought 'fucking hell what have I done? I've killed the fucking guy!' Mind you, he was going to kill me, that was for certain.

I checked his pockets and found a wallet, with credit cards and other shit, in the name of Steve Oswald and, of course, realised he was Katie's old man. So basically, I killed the husband of the woman I was having an affair with, great! I was really fucked, here. I know, he'd attacked me, first. I know my actions were self-defense, but this was one pile of shit.

I had a quick look through the BMW. What did I find? In the boot was a garden spade and a fork, what, I can only describe, as a fucking black body bag, and two bags of lime! There was even a receipt from B&Q for the lime and I saw that he'd purchased all the stuff, that morning. I realised this was planned, that Steve had set off that morning to kill me and dispose of my body.

I had a simple choice, to flag down a passing car on the main road and call an ambulance and the police, or to do to Steve, what he had intended to do to me. I fucked up guys; I chose the latter. I shall regret that decision for as long as I live.

I put him in the body bag and dragged him a long way, into the forest. The bag made it much easier because it had handles. It took me three hours to dig the hole, but I did it deep. I then filled the bag with lime and dropped it in the hole.

Then I had to get rid of two cars, mine and the BMW. I drove the BMW back to Buxton House and stuck it in a garage, which I knew nobody ever used, next to mine. At least, that way it was out of sight, and no one was likely to find it, for a while. This bought some time. Besides, I needed to go back to my flat to pick up some more money. I was so heavily in debt, I was considering declaring myself bankrupt, so I'd been putting aside some cash, for the last few months, and I knew I'd need that now.

By the time I got back to my Capri, it was getting late, so I drove to my mum, spent an hour with her, told her not to tell anyone she'd seen me but, whatever she heard about me, I was alive and well. I then put my car in the long term at Stanstead. And the rest, well, you sort of know. Dot put me up in the shed at the end of the garden and fed me, until Mrs. M took over. Then the rest of you sorted everything else out.

I really fucked up, guys. I put you all in an impossible position, but you stuck by me, can't tell you how much that means. I couldn't have done it without you."

We sat there in silence.

I think I had guessed what had happened, well, parts of the story, anyway. Now, it all made sense. At the time, I just couldn't understand where Bob had disappeared to, after he'd assured me, he'd be back to sort it all out, after he'd seen his mum.

"When you coming back to work?" Colin asked.

"I'm not. I'll probably wait until I go on half pay and start looking for something else. I can't be a police officer, not now. In less than thirty minutes that Saturday afternoon, my life changed, irrevocably. Not only did I discover I was wanted for possession of drugs, but I also then killed someone. Of course, that also terminated my relationship with Katie, the only person I've ever loved. I couldn't end up with her after what had happened. Well, I could but, of course, that would make me suspect number one in her old man's disappearance."

"Are they still investigating that?" Dot asked.

"I was interviewed, ages ago, by a DI from the Special Enquiries team. I didn't get the impression they had any idea I was involved. I actually think, they think, Steve's fucked off to Latvia or somewhere. I played down our relationship, you know, said we were just having sex, that there was really nothing more to it. I suspect Katie's said the same. Of course, no one knows I ever came back from the south coast, so I have the perfect alibi."

"There's been no publicity." Colin added.

"That's because they think he's just fucked off and I suspect Katie has done everything she can to support that theory. And, of course, that's probably what she believes." Dot said.

"Have you had any contact with Katie?" I asked.

I knew I'd already asked the question, but I did so again, so that Bob's answer could be heard by everyone.

"Nothing; that's best, anyway."

"Do you think Katie knows?" Dot asked.

"She knows Steve set out, that day, to kill you. Whether she's told anyone that, I very much doubt. So, there's very little to link you two. And the fact he disappeared just as the News of the World story was published, probably adds weight to the theory that he's just fucked off abroad." I replied.

"I don't think Katie will have any idea what's happened and that's how it's got to remain." Bob said.

"I'm sorry, Bob …" Dot said, as I braced myself for some straight talking.

"… I'm glad we helped you; you know that. But for goodness sake, you should have just dialled 999 and reported it. You didn't half complicate everything, and we've all put our careers on the line for you. You'd done diddly squat wrong. You didn't have to act like you had. You would have survived the subsequent investigation."

It was a fair point and I think we'd all been thinking it.

"Guys, Steve Oswald is black. I never knew that, until I found my attacker's identification and realised it was him."

That was certainly news to me. I didn't realise he was black; I just assumed because he was married to Katie Sumers, he was white.

"Did you not know that when you were shagging Katie?" Colin asked.

"I never did, although in all honesty, I never thought about it." Bob replied.

"You've never seen a picture of him?" Colin asked.

"No, why would I? Hardly going to go out of my way to look at my girlfriend's husband, am I?"

"He'd just been given an O.B.E. for services to the black community." Colin said, incredulously.

"I knew he'd got an O.B.E. for doing stuff in the community, of course, I did, 'cos Katie told me and didn't stop moaning about it. But Katie never told me her hubby was black, why would she? When he attacked me, I can honestly say that it never crossed my mind, it was Steve fucking Oswald. I thought it might be a motorist I'd cut up, without realising it. It did vaguely cross my mind, after he died and before I went through his pockets, that Katie's husband might have sent this guy to get me. But not for a nanosecond did I think it was her husband. When I'd identified who he was, I realised I was completely fucked." Bob explained.

"Why?" Colin asked but I, and I suspect Dot, already knew the answer.

"Guys, I am a white, male, police officer and I have just killed a black man, who's a local community hero. To make matters worse, I've also been shagging his wife. It would have been labelled a racist murder and I wouldn't have stood a chance. The job, the criminal justice system, the press, every fucker, would have hung me out to dry. Whatever happened, I wasn't going to be able to get any justice, was I? Look at the Achachi murder, no one's allowed to say what really happened because it doesn't fit with what the black community and the white middle class Labour voting liberals want you to believe. If I'd done the right thing, if I'd called it in, I would have ended up standing trial. Is anyone going to argue with me?"

No one said a word; no one moved an inch.

Even though there was no one within half a mile, Bob lowered his voice, almost to a whisper.

"None of you know this, but I was the officer who was accused of assaulting a black prisoner, called Winston Fortune. It was years ago now, and despite the fact there was absolutely no evidence against me, the A.E.M.O. insisted I was disciplined. It all became very political. A.E.M.O. said that if I wasn't charged, they would formally advise against members of the ethnic community joining the Metropolitan Police. They were holding the job to ransom.

Anyway, Fortune failed to appear at my Central Board and the case was dropped.

He was an unreliable witness and had changed his account of the incident, like, four times, which is why the C.P.S. wouldn't run with it. What's more, I did draw my truncheon, but I never used it.

When he failed to appear, the Police Federation made an enormous fuss about my malicious persecution and A.E.M.O. backed down, saying they wouldn't again interfere in the disciplinary process.

Can you imagine the field day the A.E.M.O would have if I'd put my hands up to killing Steve Oswald?"

No one contradicted him because there was a lot of truth in what he said. It didn't make what he'd done right but I understood why, in his moment of crises, he'd made the decision he had. It was a very similar situation to the one I'd found myself in with the racist letters, even though I was completely and utterly right, I couldn't possibly go up against Kitty Young and survive. So, I'd made a bad call, just like Bob had. It was just that Bob's bad decision was ten times more serious than mine.

The thing was, as a police force we'd got ourselves in a right state and, as a white officer, you had little credibility when it came to any racial incident.

"When I was sat in Dot's shed, I was repeatedly asking myself, how could my life have changed so much, in just half a day? All I'd done was go out early one morning to take a few photographs."

"Life can be a real female canine." Colin observed, dryly.

We all nodded.

# Epilogue

## BBC news

*17<sup>th</sup> May 2007*

Police who discovered human remains in Epping Forest last week, have confirmed the identity of the body to be that of Steven Oswald, a former gymnastic coach and local hero, who was awarded an O.B.E. for his work for London's black community.

Oswald disappeared in 1998 shortly after revelations emerged that his wife, Katie Sumers, was having an affair with a Metropolitan Police officer, Detective Constable Robert Clark.

Last year, Katie Sumers, the former G.B. Olympian and TV presenter, died from ovarian cancer. She was due to receive a posthumous lifetime achievement award, at this year's BBC Sports Personality of the Year ceremony.

A postmortem examination of Oswald's body has revealed the cause of death to be multiple, severe head injuries, apparently inflicted with an axe. A weapon was also recovered from the burial site and has been submitted for forensic examination. Defense injuries to both lower arms, suggest Mr. Oswald fought bravely for his life.

This evening police and forensic experts are searching an address in Wanstead, East London, where it is understood the former detective, Robert Clark lived, at the time of the murder.

In 1995 Detective Constable Clark was the officer alleged to have assaulted Winston Fortune, a young black youth, in an unprovoked racist attack. At the time, the case received widespread media attention. Although facing disciplinary charges for abuse of authority, Clarke was acquitted and allowed to return to work, when Fortune failed to attend the hearing.

Robert Clark died in 2004 from natural causes.

Sources close to the Association of Ethnic Minority Officers are suggesting this was a racially motivated crime.

A spokesman for Essex Constabulary admitted that there were now few tangible lines of enquiry.

Representatives from Mrs. Sumers' family were unavailable for comment.

An inquest will be opened tomorrow at Epping Coroner's Court.

Printed in Great Britain
by Amazon

23104871R00280